MW00714841

A Hundred Days

by Michael I. Kassner

To Danny

Mike Kasser

Chapter 1

underworld

As I hide here in the shadows, invisible in my silence, the scene through my windshield begins to unfold. My eyes burn red and drip hatred while I watch, while I wait. I can see them now, sitting beside the fire... with friends, with family, wine. Ah, what a perfect sight, a black tie charade right out of the picture books. Food, laughter, spirits. Perfect.

But I'll bet they never expected to see me. Nope, not in a million years, I can guarantee that.

None of the sonsofbitches in that house, on this night, could have had any idea that this was the one party they would never forget. One that was about to be burned into their minds forever.

The hosts are my only prey. I've come here to taint their reality, to splash blood on their precious painting, and render it worthless. I'm the cancer they've been trying to avoid their whole lives - a left winged anarchist they stoned and left for dead deep in the closet of their past.

But alas, I refused to die and finally denounced all that was good as I fled into the darkness. My wounds still reek and ooze infection to this day, but I live. And now as my heart screams in my chest, I realize that I have never felt so alive, or so lustful for destruction. You see, that's where my enemies made their mistake. They underestimated the power of one, and the sweet lure of chaos. That's the beauty of anarchy. It's like a pill, a quick fix. Black salvation without commitment or remorse.

But once you allow it to heal you, the moment you accept it, and let it in, it then murders who you were, and becomes your new God. It allows your life to have meaning again.

Brutal meaning.

And tonight, I was preparing a sacrifice for my God, and nothing was going to stand in my way, or cheat that meaning.

My mind starts to systematically retrieve a flood of images from its depths. Images of countless days spent watching as doting fathers picked up their sons from little league, and the endless sight of fathers playing ball with their sons in the park, and fathers putting their arms around their sons at picnics, and fathers teaching, and fathers guiding, and fathers, and fathers, and fathers, and FATHERS!!! Goddam them.

Goddam them all!

I feel tears start to sting my eyes and slice down my cheek like hot tar, for there in front of me, in that house sits a man. A man whom I have never seen, but have come to despise. This man would not recognize the person I was on the street, yet we share an identity. I can see him. I can see him in there right now, sitting just beyond the expensive flow of the drapes, nestled in comfortably amidst the fine furnishings. Yes, I can definitely see him now. The man I've come for.

It has to be him, relaxing down there with his guests, unaware. Unaware that tonight karma has come full circle, and that tonight, he was about to be found guilty of all his sins. The disease I am fixated on suddenly rises up, walks to the window and peers out it carelessly. A woman comes up from behind him and starts kissing his neck. I feel my veins begin to throb with fury as I vibrate here in the drivers seat, my shirt soaked and my heart racing on as I hold my ground.

As I wait.

Slowly my head starts to turn towards the rear view mirror in the same reluctant way it had done a thousand times before, so that I could once again glare deep into the jaded soul of a Bastard Son. But tonight, with hell as my witness, it would be for the last time. Suddenly I feel my breathing become quicker and my body begins heaving upwards with every gasp. It feels like I am being crushed, suffocated. I drop my head down, but my eyes are forced back upwards moments later by my swiftly expanding diaphragm, and I again focus in on the reflection in the small mirror. But alas, it seems my usual impression has somehow fallen away, and I discover the image in the glass is now that of Satan himself. It is a sight I simply cannot bear to look at any further, for the entombment of the car and my true identity are just too much for me to negotiate and now I am running towards the house in question. Bullishly. Deliberately. Not thinking, not rationalizing. My feet were just moving forward, crashing on mindlessly and destroying all the terrain in their path, ripping up the manicured flowers, smashing through the pretty ornaments as my legs slice their way towards the front door. As I close in on the entrance, I begin to hear the echo of music playing from inside the place. My fists automatically begin to clench, but they are stopped and morphed into a vicious claw. They've become twisted and deformed due to my uncontrollable hyperventilation. I fight hard to release the spasms that have overcome me, but it quickly turns into a losing battle, and I must stop. I have no choice, for my body has now succumbed to an uneven mix of elements in its system, and rudely dropped me to my knees. My mouth is also rigid and puckered from the overabundance of oxygen in my blood, so I hastily pull my shirt overtop my mouth and form a crude seal. Slowly but surely my lungs start to recycle and neutralize the air. After a few minutes, my torso straightens, and my hands and arms follow suit. My shirt eventually slips off my nose and snaps back down around my neckline.

And nothing was going to stand in my way, or cheat that meaning.

The brave sentence I spoke earlier begins to echo on inside my skull. And I knew the blood in those words must be spilt.

Save the rage. Save it boy, you're going to need it soon.

Newly focused, I stagger to my feet and regain my composure. I'm not even twenty feet from the door now. I look over at the window in an attempt to re-establish my target, and I discover that the happy couple has sat back down. My breathing is dead even now. Uncontrolled anger has fallen back into calculated hate. I go over the lines in my head that I will use to get inside. I had to get inside. Then he would pay. They all would.

For this was no dress rehearsal. This was the opening night of a one act tragedy.

The next dozen paces or so are hard, but eventually, I reach the door. I stand there and stare at it for a moment, almost in a state of disbelief as I focus in on the door-bell. Suddenly, a small part of me initiates a plea for peace, but the monster that has roamed inside my veins for every minute of every day for so long will have nothing of it. It would have its revenge. It would have its day.

My finger slowly connects with the button on the door and it rings out loudly over the cheap stereo.

Yessirree. No turning back now! Nope, no way! Justice was about to be served!

With my chest still retaliating, I watch through the thick glass as a slender figure stands up and begins moving towards me. My heart is pounding away so hard now I can feel it through my shirt. Then without warning, the doors handle starts to twist. Showtime!

"Hello," a woman's voice says, breaking me out of my trance.

I feel my head size up the body of a middle-aged lady who is drenched in jewelry and perfume. I go to speak, but nothing comes out.

Speak man! Speak you stupid ass, or you'll ruin everything.

I feel my mind start to panic.

Say something!! Hurry up or you are going to blow it man. You're going to blow the whole fucking th...

"Hi there," I wheezed.

It was a good opener, but my voice is still laced with deceit.

"Listen I was just wondering if I could use your phone," I continue, my demeanor still unsteady.

But then, keeping true to my quest, I begin to focus in on my mission and get back into character, for this particular screenplay is not ad-libbed. It is something I'd been rehearsing it my whole life.

"Who do you need to call?" she asks.

I'm really sorry to bother you ma'am," I say, "but my car is dead about a half mile up the road and I was just wondering if I could use your line to call a tow truck."

It is a flawless speech; I am fully saturated within my role. Nothing is going to stop this little event from happening now. Nothing!

"Oh sure," she tells me. "Come on in."

4

I smile politely and walk through the door that is now, very, very real.

"Don't bother with your boots if they're clean," she says, and proceeds to lead me through the hall across from the living room. "Don't bother with your boots if they're clean," I think, as I repeat the innocent statement over in my head. How ironic that little remark was about to become!

"Who's the hippy?" a voice charges suddenly overtop the chatter.

"Stop that Leonard," the lady says as she turns her head and scolds someone in the adjacent room. "He just wants to use the phone."

My eyes follow her words across the place to the man she speaks to. Leonard.
Leonard Dale Lauder.
It was a name that had persecuted and shaped my whole entire life up to this day. To this moment.
He is my own flesh and blood, this man.
He is my father.
But he is a father who had abandoned his mistake of me a long time ago and run off, like a defector, severing all ties within the first stride of his retreat. I was barely three years old when he made his escape, or so he thought, and it took a long time to track him down but now... now he would pay! He would pay for his murder. That's what it really was you know. It was murder. Plain and simple. He just forgot to hide the body, and that little oversight was about to be his undoing.

I stand there in the hallway for a minute and just look at him with a blank stare. I try hard to stay my course, to laugh it off and keep it light, so as not to spoil the ending. The grand finale.
But the more I stare at him, the harder it gets. He is me, no question. Same eyes, same build. Everything matches up. He is just as I pictured him.
Then, just in the nick of time, I push out a laugh, a big fake wonderful laugh in the direction of the doomed man as he sits there in his overstuffed chair and carries on his shtick. And as I watch him boast away, trying with all his wit, to keep the attention and admiration of his equally pathetic guests, I finally begin to see.
I begin to see it all.
His treachery, his cover-ups. All the years he spent cleverly lying to his wealthy new wife and his fake offspring. All the bullshit he constructed to hide his white trash beginnings and hand to mouth roots.
Oh ya, now I see it all.

"I thought long hair was out this season," he snickers, which in turn, sets the rest of the room off laughing.

"Ya, well it's coming back in style big time," I say loosely, following up my stock rebuttal with a textbook head flip.

"The phone's right over here," the lady offers after a minute.
She too is fighting off a sleazy grin. Keeping up my charade, I walk over to the

desktop phone and dial some random number, then secretly hang up and start to listen to the dull buzz of the dial tone as it plays out its never-ending song. I feel my guts shift and tighten in anger as the open mike session rambles on without end.

If he only knew who his half-assed jokes were directed to. Wonder if he'd be fucking laughing then?

Engulfed in bitterness and fearing another breakdown, I force myself to take another deep breath, and then let the receiver slide back down the length of my body. I have to remain cool; I have to ride this thing out. Now at this point, I can't really hear much of what is going on anymore. I am too far gone. Everything around me is muffled and distant. And the people too, standing in that room. They don't actually seem real anymore either. My world becomes numb. I feel my legs become heavy and tingly. It is like I had just become hypnotized, and am now just waiting there mindlessly for some command.

"Earth to Jesus, Earth to Jesus. Come in, Jesus," chuckles the same man.
Laughs Leonard Dale Lauder.
My cue has finally arrived, and it is that half-assed attempt at humor that finally breaks my body free from its sleep. With deadly speed, my eyes spin around and face the living room. Years upon years of anger and shame are beginning their revengeful decent back into my soul. The painted-on smile I half heartedly brandished earlier quickly disappears from my face, which in turn, extinguishes the smug look on his and melts it down into something more afraid. The air becomes deathly still as I continue on with my visual damnation.
One by one, section by section, I carefully map out my war game and sign off on the imminent torture that would follow.

The mood inside the place is anything but jovial now. The happy-go-lucky look on my face is long gone, and now reeks instead, with destruction. I can feel the adrenaline in my system begin to prime up my muscles and disconnect my conscience. My eyes pan about the room dangerously until they stop dead on a mantelpiece over to the left, full of pictures. Without hesitation, I break protocol and start walking over towards it. Just then, the nervous man in the comfy chair pipes up and says, "Hey fella, I think it's time for you to leave"!

My father's words are mute and do not faze me. I just keep walking towards those pictures.
Once in front of the shelf, I scan over the selection of photographs until my pupils catch the edge of the one I am looking for. I drag it off the thick display and quietly stand there, peering down at it in a massive state of decline.
It is an eight by ten glossy of him and his two illegitimate sons, posing arm in arm amongst a wimpy backdrop of flowers and trees. "Happy Anniversary Dad", read the caption on the finely crafted frame.
I knew the phrase I had just read was inflicting a great amount of damage into me, but I did not flinch.
I just stood there like a statue and let my soul bleed.

"Honey, call the cops!" I hear Leonard holler from somewhere behind me.

Suddenly the thin anesthetic I am under drops quickly away from me, and without mercy. I whip around and stab my line of sight directly into the terrified complexion of the sonofabitch that betrayed me.

Without breaking my stare, I send the picture to the floor and deliberately walk over to him. He is falling apart at the seams as I pull out a badly weathered envelope from my jacket pocket and throw it onto his lap. It is a document that would seal his fate.

In another bold move, I twist to the left and kill the power on the stereo. This latest maneuver instantly sobers up the party and paints a noticeable layer of sweat across the creased foreheads of the stunned guests. I can hear Leonard opening up the envelope behind me, but I do not look back at him. I don't have to, for the deadly virus I had just injected into him is already spreading violently throughout his body.

"What the hell is this," he says with a grunt. "Certificate of Birth?"

There is an unspoken note of confusion in his tone, but I know his ignorance won't last.

When I turn back around, I expect to catch him boiling in the fear of his new discovery, but his head remains bent and ridged as he struggles to click in to the importance of the document.

"This is to certify that Eugene Camille Laud..."

His voice stops.

I hear a glass shatter somewhere within the room, but Leonard does not flinch or alter the path of his vision.

He just sits there in a shell-shocked haze and refuses to make eye contact with me.

Come on you sonofabitch. Look at me! Take a good long look Motherfucker because you've just been caught red-handed! I tracked you down like an animal and now you have nowhere left to run. You are dead in the middle of my crosshairs you piece of shit and my fingers are ready to roll. How do like that huh? So you will look at me, goddam you. You will look at me right now... Daddy!"

The threats to him blaze on inside my skull, and although they are not spoken out loud, I know by the look on his face that they are deafening him beyond comprehension. The stupid grin on his face had fled for its life but he still would not acknowledge me. But you know what, that is OK! That is just fucking fine actually 'cause I am already sick and tired of the sight of him.

Knowing that my opponent is not about to draw his sword, I turn my back on tradition and do it myself.

"Heya, Pops," I holler loudly, "Long time no see!"

The cat is definitely out of the bag now, and you can taste the tension in the air. Just for the fun of it, I look over at his wife to rub it in a bit. She is hunched over in the archway with a look of utter disbelief slapped across her face.

"Leonard," she sputters after a minute, "what's going on here?"

Her voice is laced with denial, but he does not answer her either. He just sits in his fucking chair and glares down bitterly at the iron clad piece of evidence in front of him. His joyride is over.

He is dead in the water and he knows it. All those years of thinking he'd gotten away with the crime, he now realized, were in vain. Now I am seeing the real Leonard Lauder: the weak and pathetic one, in all his defamed glory. And even though I was too young to remember him when he left, I know he is still one of my own. He is older and more pitiful of course, but he is definitely blood.

He isn't so funny now though. And the party he is throwing? Well, let's just say it's over, and out of the corner of my eye I begin to see the dense animation of the guests turning their heads nervously towards the front door. It is obvious they are readying themselves for a speedy exit. The disposition inside the house has plummeted to Hell and a thick layer of uneasiness blankets the place like volcanic ash. No-one makes a sound. It is like I am standing in a museum surrounded by wax figurines.

Leonard continues to deny me a line of sight and that is starting to infuriate me!

"Come on you coward," I vibrated. "Look at me! Come on 'Dad'. Look at my face godammit!"

My patience is growing thinner and thinner and my hands begin to clench.

"Do it," I warn him suddenly. "Tell her the truth. Do it now!!"

My words are lethal but warranted. I feel a lifetime of anger begin damming up inside as I stand there waiting for his answer with the invisible gun I'd been carrying around for years still pressed hard against my shoulder and locked onto its target.

"Come on you sonofabitch" my mind blares! Your answer will mimic your fate.
"YOUR ANSWER WILL MIMIC YOUR FATE"

The ultimatum rumbles away inside my skull until it seems my senses can take no more. Seconds drag on like hours, and my heartbeat races on full speed ahead until Leonard, finally realizing that his dirty little secret could no longer be contained, glares up from the piece of paper he holds and prepares to throw his only stone.

"Tell her what?" he snarls as he crumples up the letter and lets it fall to the floor. "Tell her that I got pissed up one night and spawned out a useless runt of a human being! Should I tell her that?" he growls as he reluctantly draws his eyes into the bloodshot path of mine. "Fuck you trailer park," he says.
"Fuck You"!
And with that he stands up in defeat and unleashes his final blow.

"You're no son of mine... You hear me? No Son! Now get the Hell out of here!"

My trigger fell.

I don't recall too much of what happened after that. Only bits and pieces of it remain. But I do remember a fight. A terrible and vicious fight. And I remember the way his face distorted and gave way to my fist as it connected to its chosen target for the first time. I recall the overturning of furniture, and the breaking of glasses, and I also remember watching about twenty or so of his panic stricken guests crawling frantically over one another in a desperate attempt to get out the front door.

And, Oh ya, there was that look on Leonard's wife's face too as she watched me smash the phone across his head. And the blood.

God, I'll never forget the blood! It was everywhere. Just fucking everywhere. His and mine.

I feel no remorse for what happened. I did what I had to do, and there was absolutely no way that it could have been avoided. Fate is a cruel bitch sometimes, and don't worry, I knew that one day, she too would come looking for me. I always knew that.

And the last thing I remember of course was the site of the large living room window, or more to the point, the way it exploded into an unimaginable amount of pieces as me and my wayward father crashed through it and spilled out onto the ground in front of his house. My body finally came to a rest on its back, with my skin immersed in a sea of broken glass on the front lawn of the posh country dwelling. After a minute, I curled myself up into a ball, in an effort to disperse some of the pain. As I did this I noticed that my opponent too, had fallen onto his back and was writhing about the carnage not even five feet away from me. He was groaning loudly and trying to stand. It was a struggle, but I managed to get up from my piercing grave before him and pin him back down. I kept my bloodied hand wrapped securely around his neck and without a second thought, I rose up my fist and prepared to carve another scar into his face.

But something within me stayed the order and my arm would not fall. No matter how hard I tried, it would not move. My foe winced in agony as I re-clenched my weapon and primed the strike. I wanted so badly to continue on with my history lesson, but no matter how hard I tried, that fist of mine would not fall. I watched Leonard peer carefully out from behind his partially closed eye.

Finish him. Finish the prick off. Finish him Eugene, come on!

The voice behind my eyes continued to root me on, but it was not to happen.

It was over.

This fight was over, and in one awkward motion, I rolled off him, and stood up. Leonard quickly squirmed away from me and covered his face. Labored wheezes began to eat up the stillness of the night as I watched the mass exodus of suits and skirts fall out through the front door. I also can see, and am certain to never forget the last look me and my father exchanged with one an other, moments before I disappeared back down the driveway and sped away.

It was a look that was hard to explain. It was one part sadness, and one part disgust. I knew without question that what had just gone down was a tragedy that was set in stone decades earlier, and it was only a matter of time until that bomb went off. There was no way around it. He deserved what he got. But I also realized as I fled the mayhem that hot summer evening, that I would never again lay eyes upon him, I had made sure of that now.

But Godammit, it had to go down that way! It needed to end for me. It needed it to be over.

His answer had mimicked his fate, and a long sad story had finally come to an end. It was an end that would boast no reprise. That was a fact I had accepted a long time ago. This was a genocide mission. Nothing more.

I drove like a madman as I raced away out of that rural maze. I was hurt for sure. But the pump in my chest was doing an excellent job of masking over the damage and forcing some much needed medicine throughout my frame to heal over the multitude of wounds I had received.

The city was a good two hours away, and it wasn't until long after I had skidded out onto the main highway that led back to the concrete asylum I called home, that I did finally ease off the gas pedal and allow my engine to rest. To tell you the truth, I brought the needle right back down to the speed limit and left it there. Didn't need to get stopped by the cops tonight, no way!

The next hour or so was hard. All the years I'd spent cultivating the mutiny at the farmhouse were now being thrown back in my face. My moral foundations were being relentlessly bombarded with questions.

Questions I could not answer. But once again my long time friend anarchy came to my rescue and congratulated me on my latest victory. It made everything OK again. Like it always did. And as I began to make out the immense halo of the approaching city, I was actually hit with the tiniest sense of peace. This feeling, mind you, was usually short lived, for the metropolis I existed in was not one that generally boasted of peace at all, but more that of unrest.

I felt very little emotion as I backed off my speed and rumbled through the barrier of the city limits. I was tired and all I really wanted to do was go to sleep. But as I finally built up enough courage to look down at my arms, I noticed that my skin was saturated in blood from the countless shards of glass it had bathed in earlier. Sleep was going to have to wait. I needed to get to a bathroom and tend to my wounds first.

After a few minutes, I spotted an all night gas station down an off ramp and flicked on my blinker.

When I reached the place, I swung around and backed my rig over into the far stall. I didn't want anyone to see me, or my car. Had to keep a real low profile, no composite sketch this night, thank you very much.

Easing my mangled body out of the car, I crept up the length of the damp cement wall and tried the door to the men's room. It was unlocked. Yes, that was good! Unlocked was always good. I took one last look around the parking lot, then slipped inside and dead bolted the door behind me.

As soon as I was inside I began fondling the porcelain walls in search of the light switch, eventually locating the nodule and flicking it on, only to be temporarily blinded by the oversized fluorescents that lay above the sink. Once my eyes had adjusted to the stark light, I glanced over in the direction of the mirror and let out a sigh. It was not a pretty sight. Seems my victory had not come without its price. Both my eyes were blackened, and the left one was even beginning to close shut from the swelling. My lips and neck too, were also badly lacerated. But my teeth amazingly enough, were still intact. I couldn't believe it! I gripped them and gave them a yank, just to be sure. Yep, still snug. Boy, that was a miracle; I figured I'd at least lost a couple. OK boy, I thought. Enough fooling around. It was time to get to work.

So without further ado, I reached my hand into my pocket and produced a small brown jackknife. It was quite old. I'd had it a long time, but it was still as sharp as hell. I bent down onto the sink and let the cold water run for a bit. In the same breath, I pulled open the knife and began cutting off thin strips from the linen dispenser, to use as bandages. After rinsing off my arms, I dry-wrapped my wounds and finished up my first aid. I was in and out of that place in less than five minutes. Not bad I figured, you know, considering the amount of damage I had sustained. And I left the place nice and clean too. Spotless actually. You always did in this game. That way it was assured that you'd be able to reap its bounty again down the road. Executing one last spot check, I slid back out into the darkness and ducked into my car.

Shaking hands with the devil once again, I yanked the gearbox into drive and made my way down an all-too- familiar road. I was definitely home again, and with a heavy heart, I eventually pulled up beside a row of beat up cars and backed up in between them. It was very late now, and the city was sedate and quiet. This was nice. Rare, but nice. So I sat there for a little while longer and sifted over the events of the last several hours. It was over I kept telling myself, "Just let it die."

And then a few moments later, I did just that. I pleaded innocent and with a long purging sigh, I kissed the day good night and got ready for bed. In one well rehearsed motion, I reached my hand behind my back and wiggled out a chewed up piece of two by four from the base of my seat. In an instant I was flat on my back and reaching around for my sleeping bag. Once I was covered up, I just lay there for a bit longer and stared up at the moon through the sunroof of my ride.

It was nothing special, my car. Just a beat-up old 1971 Pontiac Firebird, complete with rusted out fenders, bald tires, and a badly faded paint job. Yep, it was ugly all day that's for sure, but it was my pride and joy.
It was also my home.

I woke up the next morning to the sound of rain. I admit it was a song I had heard many times before.
It was tapping out a blues rhythm on my hood. And as my eyes focused in on the day, I could begin to see it too, lightly streaking down the length of my windshield. I went to sit up and pull back my sleeping bag, but alas, the events of the night before had come back to haunt me in a big way and my body was consumed with stiffness and agony. My spine was locked up tight, and my knuckles were swollen up like golf balls.

And my neck! Christ! It felt like Id been hit a thousand times!

I did eventually get up though, and as I adjusted my rearview mirror, I was treated to a pretty horrible sight. My face was in terrible shape. My left eye was closed up completely now, and my lips were fat and oozing pus. Feeling somewhat ashamed, I turned the mirror away, only to be hit with another disturbing scene.

It was the imprint of a gigantic city's murky skyline as it began to grind forward and embrace another day of treachery and sin. I could always hear the desperate sounds of its battered heart moaning away loudly as I woke.

The horns, the sirens, the whine of countless vehicles bullying their way towards the core. Millions of people latched on to the worn out titty of the almighty buck. And all of them teetering on the edge of a heart attack! Bunch of bloody lo...

Oh, Oh wait, hold on a sec here. Jeez, I'm sorry. I forgot to introduce myself. Boy... where are my manners? Um yes, yes, my name is Eugene. Eugene Camille Lauder... Uh, the only. Pleased to make your acquaintance.

I am however, not one of those nine to five heart attack people. Nope, my life is a little different than that.

I do not have a big house or a family. I do not work downtown and have a nice dental plan. No sir, I, well... I am a nobody. Naw, it's OK It's true. Sometimes you gotta call a spade a spade you know.

Actually, this old car is my only possession. At one time, I betcha it was quite a looker though. An early seventies muscle car with a big motor, chrome rims, sleek hood scoop. Total sports car in every way I'll tell ya. These days however, it serves a little different purpose.

Housing mainly.

It still had a lot of power mind you, even though it was running very rough from the lack of a long overdue tune up that unfortunately would always be put on the back burner in lieu of food and gas. It had been my permanent address for awhile. Well, I mean, you know, for a few days now. No wait, maybe it's been a few months. Or um, hold on, maybe... maybe it's been a few years now. Actually no. Nope, there's no way that's possible, uh uh.

No fucking way I've been in this car for five years now. That just can't be true! Or maybe. Maybe it is?

Man now there's something I haven't thought about in a long while! You know, how long I've been in here and all. Hey, know what, I don't want to talk about that right now alright!

Look, it's not like I'm the only one in this situation here! I mean there are lots of other people around in the same boat too! Ya! That's right. Actually, there are thousands upon thousands of people out here just like me. What do you think of that huh? In fact, there are entire cities within the cities of people that exist just like I do now, but guess what? You will never see them, or their world, unless you have had to have been there! To say that we are everywhere is an understatement. And it's so great, because we are usually right underneath your nose and you don't even know it, ha ha! We take things from you that you cannot see and would never miss and it's people like you that end up losing out here, not us!

Fuck, it makes me so mad! You all look at us like were a bunch of freeloaders and vagrants. Transients who have shunned society, but in reality, it is society that has shunned us. Nobody starts out this way! Hell, I didn't start out this way! I'm telling you man, I didn't.

But sometimes the little house with the picket fence dream turns its back on you. Then slowly but surely, bits of your humanity break off and fall away. Piece by piece your aspirations begin to disappear and all the things that seemed important to you at one time become quickly replaced by the needs of the moment.

Months pass on like minutes. Years go by almost without notice, and then the one day comes along when you finally decide enough is enough and you turn around to begin retracing your steps, so you can get back to where you started to see what happened.

To see what went wrong.

But when you look down, you realize that you're not on the yellow brick road at all anymore. It's vanished!

You search and search but just can't seem to find your way back. You're positive you must have had a family once; you must have had a home. I mean, surely you lived in a Goddam house before! But as the years go by, things get forgotten. Ties become severed, relations lost. That's just the way it is goes alright. I realize that. I know that for Christ sake!

One day something's there, and the next day it's not. That's just the fucking way things work down here, nuff said!

Calm down Eugene.

I rustle through the crumpled up papers inside my head and try once more to understand. Not to fix. Not to wallow in pity. Just for once, to understand. I'd been struggling with this problem every day lately. I try not to obsess about the past so much. I try not to think about the chain of events that led me here to this way of life, but somehow, someway, those shortcomings always manage to find their way back in.

Why?

Well probably due to the fact that I was only twenty-two years of age, but I felt more like eighty!!

Or maybe, just maybe, it was the knowledge that I was a disgrace in the eyes of society, and a nobody.

Deep down I knew that's what I really was. Homeless, jobless. Pick your cliché man. Christ, I'd been living like this for so long now, to tell you the truth, I didn't know if I was even alive or dead some days. Sure, it's easy to blame, to point fingers. It's easy to hate. Oh hell ya, it's real easy to hate. And believe me when I say I hate, because I do!

I learned to hate a long time ago. Way before the events of the following evening, and I'll tell you right now, there ain't nothing wrong with it! It's a great defense.

It's an iron clad barrier that will always protect you no matter what. Nope, nothing wrong with hate. Hey, you can trust hate. It's always the same and it never turns its back on you. It's constantly there when you need it and it only gets stronger.

Listen, this game is hard! Most of the time you don't even want to know what's real, and more often than not, you end up lying to yourself most of the time just to get by. You ambush your senses with bullshit until you no longer feel the pain. That's the secret out here friend. No one gets in, no one gets out. It's just safer that way. Tell you what; I'm going to let you in on a little story. It's very ironic really. You see, when I was very young, I once ended up getting lost one evening, and was forced to spend the night curled up in the backseat of an abandoned car. I was discovered early the next morning and everything was fine. But never in my wildest dreams did I once think those few chance hours I spent camped out in that rusty old vehicle so many years ago would end up turning into such a long black song.

But they did

They did, and now, badaboom, badabing, here I am! It's a life I've simply accepted. Christ. My brain's already wore out and I've only been awake for a few minutes! Well fuck it! Time to get a move on I figure, so I reach down and manhandle my right leg (that incidentally, had fallen asleep sometime during the night) and set it onto the gas pedal.

You get used to that sort of thing. Hell, you get used to a lot of things out here after awhile. Things you never thought in a million years you'd ever have to. Except for being alone all of the time, of course. You never get used to that. Ah, but who cares about all that garbage anyway? I got more important things to think about rite now. Like, for instance, driving to the nearest service station and taking a long drawn out piss!! Ya, that task is definitely first on my list.

Now why don't I just hang it out the side of the car door you ask? Well, because I tried that once a couple of years ago and then fell back to sleep that way, that's why! Needless to say I woke up to several curious onlookers. No thanks, I'll hold it until I get to the station. I deal with enough humiliation in one day to go ahead and start creating my own. I drive to a different one just about everyday. Shakes things up that way. You don't want to become too familiar when you live like this. No way, too dangerous.
You see, when you are a nobody, no-one] tends to miss you, get it? And that kind of scenario is exactly what every psychopath on the planet lives for and fantasizes about. Now I ain't the prettiest girl at the ball or nothing, but the thought of being sodomized and strangled by some strung-out pervert is just not my cup of tea. So you have to keep moving around. Always. You keep shuffling your routine up all the time, and pretty soon believe it or not, you begin to build up a good arsenal of places where you either bed down, or wash up. And as long as you use these places sporadically, you are usually alright.

But finding a good sleep spot, now that can sometimes be a real challenge. It's quite involved this feat. Why? Well, because one of the biggest challenges you face when you live in a car is the fact that you generally don't sleep that good. So if you go ahead and pick out a bad sleep spot, you end up being constantly woken up in the middle of the night by either a cop, or a "concerned citizen", or like any one of a hundred other different types of situations. Drunks, traffic, you get the picture. So it's imperative that you pick a good sleep spot, or you will screw up your already fragile sleep pattern. And when you start losing sleep, you get run down, and when you get run down, you get sick. And friend, believe me when I say that sick is the last thing you want to be in this game. Oh and just a little tip. If you are thinking of bedding down in a church parking lot with some stupid inclination that religion will somehow protect you, think again!! I'm telling you, it's the last place you want to be and the first place they will find you! Yessir, when it comes to sleep spots, instinct is everything. If your gut says no, you go somewhere else, end of story.

I can't stress this enough! Out here you learn very quickly to avoid any bumps or detours in your routine, or the impending illness that follows and you pick your damn sleep spots wisely! What about staying in a hotel parking lot you ask? Hah! Been there, done that! OK, here's the way that goes down. You drive to the nearest hotel chain and park your heap out by the far end of the property, because you think that you will be less noticeable at a greater distance. WRONG! Then you shut your car down, pull your sleeping bag over your face and prepare to go nighty-night. About a half an hour passes by and your eyes finally shut. You start snoring away for, oh, two or three minutes, and then BAM!!... It happens! The dreaded rent a cop shows up!

Hotel security at its finest has somehow found you (big shocker!) and now is right beside your door, a mere foot away from your head if you can imagine. You begin to hear the sound of his footsteps walking around your vehicle. Then all of the sudden, you hear a blast from his preschool walkee talkee followed in closely by his all too professional voice as he calls in your license plate. You lay their deathly still underneath your sleeping bag, now wide awake and quickly realize how stupid of an idea this really was.

"Ya Lou, we got ourselves a transient out here. Need a confirm on a nineteen seventies... ish Firebird, license plate number LVR 777 click, click, click."

Well now your heart is your throat and all you can do is lie there like a mummy. You know he is right outside your door, looking straight in at you, but you are helpless. You can even see the beam from his flashlight as it creeps up and down the length of your body. You want to spring up and reef on the key that always sit in the ignition, but you can't! No no, not yet! You have to be patient. You have to wait for that one special moment. Don't panic now, its coming!
The glare of his night stick taunts your eyes as it penetrates through the fabric, and again you feel it's interrogation slither all over you, like a snake winding his way around its prey, feeling for the slightest quiver, the faintest heartbeat.

Then... WHAM! Joe security tries the door, and this move sends your adrenaline through the roof! Your hands begin to sweat and shake with anxiety, and your heart starts to pound so fast it almost blows your eardrums out. And even though you have been through this sort of thing countless times before, it still makes you feel the same way. Like shit. And trust me pal, the last thing you ever want is to spend the remainder of the night locked up in some cop shop answering questions about nothing while all of your shit is emptied out onto the table in front of you. No way man, you never want to go through that!

Now the five minutes that have gone by have felt more like a year as you lie there and squirm in a pool of your own sweat. But then, Ah yes! At long last, it happens, as it always does. That special moment you've been waiting for finally comes along.
Protocol!
And it's that protocol that will this night, buy you your freedom.

"Click, Click, unit 7, this is unit 4 on the south side here. I'm going to immobilize the perpetrators wheels until the city police arrive for investigation, over".

Okay now, that's your cue! It's almost time here so get ready. With the predictability of the sun, you hear him turn and start to move away from your car. But you don't make your move just yet, nope! Just hang on now for a few more seconds. The sound of him removing his keys from the ignition is the first sign. Then you hear him walk around to the rear of his vehicle and open his trunk. (This will make you start to smile.)
You can actually feel the heavy tire lock hit the ground after he takes it out of the container in his trunk.
Alright, get ready!

One, two, three... NOW!

Now fling the covers away from your face and then in one smooth uniform motion, twist the key, hit the gas, and bang you're outta there! All you have to do now is make it off the property and you're out of his jurisdiction, and therefore safe. As you look in the rear view mirror you can't help but laugh for your plan has played itself out perfectly. Dickboy is still struggling to get the cumbersome tire block back into his trunk, but he'll never do it in time.

'Ha ha. Bite me' is the standard comeback I do believe.

After you burn out on the street, you utilize a few dark roads, then make your way towards the freeway and drive your ass into another part of town to become lost all over again. This is the safest way to do it.
An hour later, sometimes more, you'll be back underneath your sleeping bag, hidden away once more from the prying eyes of the world. Your heart will have slowed and your adrenaline will have capped itself off so you close your eyes tight and vow that this type of situation will never happen again.
Even though in reality you know that it will never stop.
The moral of the story. Stay away from the hotels!

The best places to catch some shut eye are the older parts of the city in the areas where it is common to see a bunch of broken down wrecks lined up in a row waiting to be hauled away to the junkyard. These are the best places to choose because you can easily camouflage yourself in between them and no one knows any different. It's perfect! Nobody ever takes a second look at a situation like that. Mind you, it is best to wait until nightfall before you do this, for the darkness acts as an excellent shield.

Flea market parking lots are also great too because most of the venders that end up at those places to flog their wares are generally making their homesteads in their vehicles as well. I hate to say it, but it simply comes down to strength in numbers. And for some reason, there's always an undercurrent of belonging in those spots which is kind of nice. And the cops don't really bother you too much either, probably due to the fact that these things are usually held more on the outskirts of town, far enough away from the urban congestion that the police are paid to protect. Nobody really gives a shit about a bunch of vagrants sleeping in the fields outside the city limits.

Now what about showering, keeping clean, stuff like that you ask?

Well, it's not that difficult, really. Public washrooms are everywhere, which means there is lots of hot water and soap around. But you have to be quick. No quality bathroom time here I'm afraid. Not in this gig.

Get in, wash your nuts, scrub your teeth and get out. The all night gas stations with the johns built around the side are ideal, especially if they don't lock them. With those you can simply pop in, do your stuff and pop out again without anybody noticing. I'm telling you, you've got to keep underneath the radar at all times. That's why you leave the place clean, so you don't draw any attention to yourself. This is also where the speed comes in. I can go in, strip down, and have a full sink shower in approximately seven minutes flat. All you really need is a toothbrush, toothpaste, and a towel. The soap is already on the wall.

As for hair care, well, let's just say I wear a hat a lot. But no matter what, twice a week, I stick my head under the tap and give it a good scrub, using the hand soap already provided. Now, I'm not going to land any hairstyle commercials anytime soon, but hey, it gets the grease out.

Your vehicle should be set up accordingly too. The front seat is always reserved for your plastic bag of food, what little food you have, that is. And those culinary provisions usually consist mainly of bread sticks and condiment packages, like peanut butter and jam, or crackers and cheese spread. They don't fill you up much, but these common freebees are good for a quick sugar fix. There are other ways to "eat cheap" out here too, but for the most part, hunger is a very serious problem. It is forever manipulating your perception and playing tricks on your mind. You know, I used to fantasize about girls a lot. Now I just fantasize about what they have for lunch.

Now the backseat of your rig should consist of clean towels and your sleeping bag. These items are always, I might add, put on the passengers side of your car because the drivers seat has to be put all the way back in order for you to properly lie down, so you must keep that area clear. It's also a good idea to get some cheap window tinting for the back windows. This add on is not illegal in anyway, and it provides you with great cover. Remember, you always sleep in the driver's seat with the keys in the ignition. This is crucial, because no matter how much you try and avoid it, there will always be a night come by when you will be found. Regardless of how careful you are, it does happen. And when it does, you will need to be able to make a speedy exit. It is also a good habit to keep a weapon of some sort in your vehicle, out of plain view of course.

Myself, I've always kept around a good sized hunting knife. I hide it underneath the seat in the daytime, but at night just before bed, I pull it out and slide through a groove in the driver's door, just past the vinyl fascia and into the actual door frame itself. This is a great "easy access" spot for it, and if you play around with the angle of it enough, you can manipulate it to act as a makeshift sharpener. Don't skip this part man. Even with all the stealth you think you may have created, understand that you are still a nobody, and you are still a target. Never let your guard down, or think you have won the battle because you never will.

Now does all this sound scary? You bet it does. But that's OK, for fear is the only thing that keeps you alive sometimes.
I betcha I know what your thinking next.

"So like Eugene... how do you eat real food and afford gas and stuff?"

Well, let's start with food. Gotta have it right! But when you are "unemployable", or so they say, and possess little or no money at any given point in time, it coincides with the fact that you eat little or no food, right? Well, not exactly. I mean hunger is definitely a real danger out here as I have previously mentioned, but when you first enter into this odd and penniless way of life, you tend to become incredibly inventive. And after a few days of starving to fucking death because of your "lack of funds", you quickly begin to see the world in a totally different light. You see, hunger has a funny way of eliminating any sort of second guessing, and when submersed in it, you begin to uncover opportunities all around you that you never even thought were there.

Believe it or not, one of the best ways to chow down for free is at the supermarkets. And I'm not talking about stealing. For the record, I do not steal out of stores. I don't have to, because at any given time of the day in those giant marketplaces, they always have a bunch of friendly retired folk on staff whose sole job is to simply give away... you guessed it... free food samples! It is in an attempt, of course, to promote and/or clear out a lagging product that has been sitting docile on their shelves. Crackers, sandwich spreads, desserts. You name it, they're usually available. And it's not uncommon to find all of the four basic food groups together in the same store either. Yessir, the giant supermarket chains are like five star diners for the shiftless! Fine dining for the financially challenged!

No-no, monsieur! Vould you like to try zee special entrée? It is zee frozen meatloaf, a la "plastic cup."
Aaee... Ah! Magnificent!! Yes! ...Ah fuck! OK, actually it's not that magnificent.
I mean, don't get me wrong here. Free food is free food, and once in awhile, it does even have some taste to it. But for the most part, it's just another necessary evil. Like every bloody thing else. You also get a little tired of hearing those nice old ladies say stuff like, "Back again so soon are we? You must really love the bratwurst."

Oh yes! I'm a big fan of bratwurst,, yum, yum. Kind of reminds me of a bad accident I once saw, ya!

On the bright side though, the sample tables do trump the living shit out of the soup lines, which pop up randomly from time to time. The only problem with them is that they are very sporadic and the majority of them are right downtown which is a psycho-ridden coin toss at the best of times, constituting another deterrent. And although the kind folk that put those events on do indeed have only the best of intentions in mind, the help they usually commandeer are mostly volunteers. And with that little element of surprise, the level of professionalism and cleanliness is, well, shall we say, compromised a bit. The truth be told, anybody with two hands and a pulse can work there. I'm not kidding! Don't matter if they got a chronic nose picking problem, or scabies, or anything! As long as they show up they are put to work.

Alright, screw it. I'm not going to pussyfoot around this subject any more! I HATE the soup kitchens alright!! Can't stand them. Why? Because I found a big greasy pubic hair in my soup one day, that's why! That was the straw that broke the camels back right there! I'm sorry, I know I shouldn't be so hard on those joints, but I just can't' seem to get that curly little vision out of my head. Jeez, I could barf right now just from the thought of it!

Now, I will confess that I do still patronize those grub huts once in a while, I have to occasionally. I mean lets face it, beggars can't be choosers. But I will tell you this much. When I do, I eat my shit really fast, and I never look down. There! I have said my piece and I shall not bitch any further.

Now on a more positive note, speaking of free non-pubic fucking hair food! In the summertime, there are always lots of gardens out there to "sample". And when I say sample, I mean just that. I never destroy anything. I just slip in, take a couple of varieties and leave. I can't help it. I know I said I didn't steal, but the lure of fresh veggies is always a big draw, especially after downing seven full cups of bratwurst! And in my own defense, it's not really stealing, it's more like pruning. The amount I lift from any given patch no-one would ever notice anyway. And besides, the rules of engagement for this rap are usually an ass full of buckshot, so you don't want to push your luck.

OK. That basically covers the food end of things, now how about money?

Well, due to the fact that I'm not your typical settled down Ivy League type, finding a regular nine to five job has proven difficult, if not impossible. And the truth be known, this windfall rarely happens for ''folk'' like me.

Don't get me wrong, I put in application after application, even had a couple of interviews once. But when you have no call back number and no legitimate address, it makes it hard. You get busted on a couple of lies here and there and pretty soon word gets around. Eventually you're hooped and no-one will even give you the time of day, let alone a job. Now it's not that I don't want to work. That's the big misconception amongst our community. I really enjoy working, but the plain fact of the matter is that no employer in their right business mind is going to take a chance and hire a person like me. A 'transient'. That's what they all called me. You get pretty used to that phrase after a while. Rejection is something you eventually accept.

But just because you can't land yourself a regular job, doesn't mean there are not ways to make a buck or two in this city. There are definitely avenues available. Now, I will warn you that these "avenues" are usually morally questionable, and most of the time degrading, but nonetheless legal. I guess the staple for me, (and about a billion other people in this town) was bottles and cans. I always carried around an old duffle bag with me when I was out walking, just in case I spotted any empties. Unfortunately though, in a city this size, there is always a shitload of competition out there when it comes to the recyclable trade, and the chance of finding stray empties just lying around on the sidewalk is pretty rare. The real money in this profession lies in the big green industrial dumpsters that sit in the alleyways. Oh don't worry, I know it's gross. I totally agree. But what are you gonna do? I don't really have too much of a choice in the matter.

Personally, I always wait until the evening comes around before I start my pilgrimage. Less people gawking at you then. But you still have to be fast about it, even during the night, because no matter what the circumstances are, there will always be someone else scoping out the same stash as you. And don't be surprised if you see other street scavengers guarding their finds and standing firm in front of one of those big disposal units either.
If you ever come across this... DO NOT go near that particular person's trash can or he or she will literally eat you a fucking live! I cannot stress this little safety tip enough! And when you fill a bag up you keep it hidden away in your trunk. Never keep your find out in the open. That's just asking for trouble.

Now besides the bottle and can trade, there are a few other ways to get a little extra cash in your jeans. You know, like shoveling snow in the winter time. Raking leaves in the fall, stuff like that. These standbys are great, but the one thing I myself really like to do to line the old pockets up a bit, is a trick I actually stumbled on by accident. Here's how it works.

All over the city, mainly in the malls and major department stores, there are always those dressed-to-the- nines type of people hovering at the entranceways that are forever trying to sign you up for a " super low interest rate" credit card (28%), in return usually, for a small, but free gift. Now, for obvious reasons, I always passed these deals by for I knew that there was just no way in hell anybody was going to give me, a homeless, jobless vagrant with no address, a bloody credit card. But then one day, I was forcefully approached by a professionally-attired senior who was obviously desperate for a sale, especially if she was coming up to me. When I told her, like I had told all the others, that I didn't have a job, she peered deviously off to the side and said with a grin. "Oh don't worry about that, just make something up... They never check"!

So I did.

My name, my address, occupation. The works! I gave myself an engineering job with a huge income. Big house, two cars, you name it, I forged it. And then, for all my sins that day I received a shiny new fry pan set. Now, as a man who lived in a rusty old sports car, I needed a set of frying pans like I needed another set of testicles growing on the balls of my feet! But as I walked out of the department store that day staring curiously down at my prize, I had a sudden revelation! It occurred to me that I had just acquired actual merchandise. New actual merchandise! Hell, I was practically a consumer again! And that's when it hit me.

Merchandise can be sold!!

Holy shit! I couldn't believe I hadn't thought of that before. Wasting no time, I quickly drove to the nearest pawn shop and proceeded to transfer the ownership of my goods to the fat blob behind the counter, walking back out the same door a few minutes later with a crisp clean five dollar bill. Well after that I applied for every damn credit card known to man! You name it, I signed off on it. And all the time using the same untraceable info. It was great. I had finally figured out a way to screw the credit card companies. I was living the dream that most of the other people in the world could only fantasize about! I even set up an actual pawn shop distribution route, and for a while there, it was just business as usual. Everybody won in my clever scheme. The pawn shop, the lady at the department store, and you guessed it, little old me.

As soon as I stumbled on to that chance discovery, I realized that there was a whole entire world out there full of free stuff for the taking. You just had to know where to look for it.

In full honesty, I am anything but materialistic, but when you are like me and are of "no fixed address", money, no matter how miniscule, does make your life a hell of a lot easier. Even if it is only for a short

amount of time. Now, I know I am not the most educated person on the planet, and let's be truthful, being stupid does not generally coincide with financial stability. So you know what, you set your pride off in the corner, and you take the money when it comes, however it comes.

You know, I shouldn't really say that I am "uneducated". I mean I'm not stupid-stupid! I did manage to get my grade ten and all that. But that was it. Personally, it didn't really bother me too much that I was unable to finish my grade twelve because I was never really was that fantastic of a student to begin with.

The only thing that the teachers could ever really agree on was, and I quote, "Well kid, you're probably not going to nail down a job at NASA anytime soon, but you can sure fake it well enough."

And who was I to tell them any different because from as far back as I could remember, the only government I ever pledged a flag to anyway was the echo of an unbiased and sometimes two-faced voice of reason that piped up from time to time in the space between my ears. It helped me out more than anything.

Subsequently, my ability to "fake it well enough", was the only skill that ever really did me any good, and due to my lifestyle, I ended up instead with a standard diploma in basic bistro etiquette. Or, "Coffee Shop 101" as I like to call it!

But that was a good thing because those all-night java shops here in the city are complete and total melting pots of sub-city culture. There's more history in those swill huts than you can shake a stick at. They're the hub of the whole damn movement I tell ya! It's really quite an incredible scene in there sometimes. It's like a giant sociology experiment. And the circus goes on all night, especially when it's cold. The first type of people to walk through the doors after the clock strikes midnight are usually your typical larger than life cokeheads. They prance in like they own the joint with their protruding cheeks and sunken eyes darting about. Their skin too, hangs off their bodies like wet cheesecloth from years of passing up food in lieu of the magic dust. In a chemical haze, they glide from table to table dishing out sediments of their manufactured charisma like cheap wharf scrapings at a roadside buffet. Experts in every topic of course, they resemble a quasi late night talk show host that unfortunately, you cannot turn off.

Then after that, the drunks arrive. They stumble through the doors and start telling everyone around them that they're sorry. You know, sorry for being too loud, sorry for being to quiet. And then finally, admitting in a bowl of tears that they were sorry for being sorry in the first place. Yessir, every single zit on society's ass eventually finds their way into them places at some point during the night. And let's not forget the hookers. They were the last form of humanoids to show up for the party, coming in for a quick buzz before the sun broke over the horizon and cast them back into their flophouse netherworlds. They usually sauntered in at around five a.m. But they didn't look the same way as they did at the beginning of their shift when they were slithering up and down their favorite lamppost.

Nope! They don't look anything like that at the end if the night at all! They're downright scary at the crack of dawn I'm telling you! They sit there, all screwed out and slumped over a lipstick-ridden cup with their cheap nylons all ripped to shit and their makeup running. Yeecchh!! It's not a pretty site!

Mind you, I've heard it's no different than being married a couple of years.

And of course, last but not least, you get your typical white trash car-dwelling chum like me. We are the people who sit quietly out of the way, tucked into some dim corner of the joint as we patiently wait all night long for the sun to show itself once again. Hibernating in a state purgatory as we secretly plan out in detail, each and every step of our return to glory, like convicts fantasizing about their big escape. Sometimes though when you do this, you slip up and you allow your mind to wander too far. You start carelessly over-exaggerating about the glorious apparitions of the real world you had seen earlier on the screens of the giant televisions that line the storefronts of the malls. This process happens innocently enough, for it's way too easy to be swept into the overwhelming mass of color-infested monitors as they sit stacked up in the windows and relentlessly puke out the same distorted message .

And it's then that you make the unconscious mistake of letting yourself be caught up in those colorful passages and suddenly, without even realizing it, you accidentally cross the line and put yourself inside that electronic charade. Now, it is you in that commercial that is prancing around on that new lawnmower as your loving family smiles and cheers you on in the background. And then, for just a second, your clothes are suddenly clean again and your eyes are wide and bright. Yes! You are finally back in the land of the living!

The daytime world.

Your fantasy is playing itself out beautifully, but then your eyes begin to drift and focus in, not on the microwaved submissions imbedded in the tube, but more now to the reflection your profile is making in the curve of the glass. The very same glass you ironically just looked up to for salvation. That's when your little daydream starts to turn its back on you and you now begin to painfully understand that this brief parody was nothing more than a self-inflicted hallucination that gained you nothing. It was nomadic at best. Like walking under a lone awning, on a long rainy street. And as the seductive animations begin to fade off, the real perks of your lifestyle begin to sift back into your nostrils. The alcohol, the fumes, the sweat. They all then proceed to suffocate you, which Godammit, you deserve. The schizophrenic rumble of a thousand footsteps assaults you as your mirage implodes and without warning, your fifteen minutes of fame are over.

Now the brutality of your true life has come back and is punishing you for your treachery and you hate yourself for even flirting with the whole stupid idea in the first place! The pain is always worse when you come down, remember that!

Listen, you can't start hoping for too much down here, alright. No way man! Delusions of grandeur are a big fucking mistake in this game. Christ! That's the thing that will break you! You gotta stay lean, you gotta keep tough! Now, I'm not saying you should mope around all the time and not try to have a better life, but you've got to keep things in check. If you persist in conjuring up a false sense of existence, pretty soon you'll end up falling off the edge of that very desire, and then you won't know what the hell world you're in anymore!

You know, I exist in this hole, day after day, night after night, and try with all my heart not to seem hopeless. I drive from place to place and pretend that I actually have someplace to be, someplace to go, but I don't. None of us out here do, but you keep up the lie anyway to try to make your life seem normal. You run your fingers through your hair when you walk into a place with the illusion that you just came off a long shift, and are only there to grab a quick hit of caffeine to perk you up a bit before you head home and plop yourself in front of your TV, but in the end, it's all a fantasy. You're not going anywhere because you have nowhere to go, nowhere to be, and all the time in Hell to get there! The only thing you really have to do in a day is try to not resemble the thing you are. To not stand out and be pointed at. To blend into the crowd, any crowd. That's all you really have to do.

I believe that if there is one thing in this terrible game that finally pushes you over the edge, it would have to be the complete and utter feeling of emptiness in your heart that relentlessly follows you around throughout every minute of every day.

The pain is endless.

It's not the hunger, it's not the humiliation, it's the straight fact that you did not turn out to be the person you always wanted to be. It's the sudden realization that your whole existence is a low-class, poorly-constructed illusion, and that no-one will ever, ever, come to your rescue. That's what kills you out here. That's what ends you.

You know, I remember once, as I sat waiting for the night to come to a close in a particular coffee shop, of an old man who came into the place where I myself had settled in. At first glance he looked like some sort of professor, you know, a real Einstein type. He had long, wavy gray hair, thick-rimmed glasses, and a grey tweed sports jacket. He was intellectual-looking for sure. His steps were quick and light and his actions were large and loud. Once through the door, he promptly grabbed a small black coffee from the service counter, and then sat down at the corner table adjacent from my own. After a minute, he pulled out a medium-sized novel from his breast pocket and began flipping through the pages. I watched him in secret for a while, I couldn't help it, he seemed interesting to me for some reason. But alas, the more I watched him, the more I saw, and the more and more his well planned façade began to crumble away around him for all to see.

I first noticed that the underarms of his cheap tweed jacket were torn and frayed, exposing a putrid and deeply stained undershirt. Dirt-laden hands tipped with yellow fingernails held up his thrift store literature.
Two different shoes, no socks. The painting was starting to take shape. And like the open book he was struggling to read, his own life now seemed to represent the dime novel he held in his hand.
I became sad.
I couldn't help but wonder who he was, and what had happened in his life?
I mean, did he have a family once, a home maybe? Did he ever feel love?
It bothered me deeply to wonder that if now, in this final stage of his life, anybody so much as even knew his name.
I wondered too, that if some day in the future, my fate would look the same.
I mourned him for a long time as he sat there, feverishly trying with all the props he could muster to represent the status quo and blend into the ordinary world. Even if it was only for a brief moment of time, to a handful of strangers.
I guess all of us out here walked that same thin line in one way or the other. Each of us wishing we had honor. Wishing we held the key to some door. The whole scene weighs you down, but even with the many ongoing tragedies that routinely accompany this dark way of life, their is still an underlying sense of unity amongst us.

Now, I'm not a socialite by any means but I always found it strange that for some reason all of us "types" of people usually ended up congregating in the same places. And it struck me funny too, that I could sit next to the same person night after night, rotting my guts out with stale coffee in an attempt to curb my hunger and keep my eyes open, and yet never actually speak one single word to them, but still on the flip side, be secretly happy that they were there. The brotherhood I speak of is fragile, but very real. And even though it is dared not spoken of, the bond between us is solid and in a way, constitutes the only evidence that we exist.

But there are exceptions to this.

For example, the deep sub cores of the downtown area are quite a bit different. In

those parts, well let's just say," that's where the love ends". There are no boundaries or hard and fast rules of any type in those areas. The homeless population is
considerably more violent and unpredictable down there, usually due to heavy and
unyielding substance abuse. Eternal friendships can be bought for the price of a
cigarette, but then violently lost again in that same moment. It's a brutal existence in
the pit and I try to avoid that scene as much as possible. Someone told me once that
one day, hell will seep up from the cracks in the pavement down there.

I believe that.

And all you need to do is spend five minutes of your time in that headspace and
you will too! But thankfully, that sort of shit doesn't usually go on in the coffee
shops, and for the most part, surviving the nights are mainly based on numbness and
compliance. Now, I shouldn't say that everyone who frequents places like that in the
middle of the night is homeless. Some rags, believe it or not, are actually prim and
proper daytime folk, with 9-5 jobs, and condos, and the whole works. They are an
annoying group of people who are just restless and bored. Men and women with a
wild streak who would never dare to expose their nasty little traits to the upstanding
office drones they work with. No way, that would be too risky. You see, everyone has
an evil twin, especially the suits, and it is a lot safer to let that demon off its leash to
run amuck under the illusion of nightfall. In the darkness you can let your inhibi-
tions run free with little or no consequences. You can carouse to your hearts content,
letting that "not so nice" side of you cause as much havoc as you like. Then, when
you've had your fill of your so called "street life", you just slip back into your quaint
little upscale condo on the other side of town, and no-one knows any different.

These posers can be anybody. They can play out any fantasy they wish, and in the
morning, everything goes back to normal. Those people's dark desires are fully satisfied until the next time. That type of shit goes on a lot actually, and you can always
tell who those "scary risk-takers" are right off the bat. You also see a lot of homeless
wannabees around as well. Dangerous street-crawler types once a week until it's
their bedtime kind of thing. They take great pride in living out the Hollywood-
enhanced, clean and tidy version of the less fortunate and lawless, but they edit out
all the filth and discomfort.

Those assholes are the most annoying of the bunch! They go out and spend $80
on pre-ripped jeans, then purposely cut up good leather jackets to make themselves
look tough and poor. Of course when they go up and pay for their "decaf lattes", it's
always in twenty dollar bills. All you would really have to do is kick their ass once
and they'd scurry home, put back on their polyester knit pants and have their room
cleaned before you could say shit!

I hate those types of people, we all do. And you know what, they do get their asses
kicked from time to time. I've seen it. These pussies will be sitting there trying to
look all rough and scary, and then they make the mistake of staring down someone
who hasn't eaten in a couple of days and well, that's the end of them! They get those
customized leather jackets rammed right up their ass! Ahh, enough of them. Idiots
like that don't deserve recognition. They're nothing but a joke. And you know, it's

funny cause you never see those macho desperadoes out here in the winter, Oh no, that's way too real for them! They are fairweather wannabees!

Shit! Oh shit, I did it! I said the "W" word didn't I?

Godammit, I shouldn't have said it. I broke the code! Winter is a swearword. I hate winter!

That's a bad time for us. We lose a lot of "associates" to the elements during that season. And it's pretty easy to tell which ones are not going to make it by the late fall. This shit's hard enough to do when the weather's mild, let alone when it's minus twenty five! Sleeping in a car during the cold season? Now that's a whole different ball game. You really have to plan ahead if you want to survive.

First of all, you have to get yourself one of those in-car warmer thingies, you know, the plug-in type. How you acquire it is up to you. Now they don't really get that hot, but they will keep you out of the morgue. You can occasionally plug these things into the 110 volt power receptors in the parking lots of the government buildings. It's pretty safe because everyone just assumes you are the night janitor or something, but a lot of times these power poles are on a timer. A real short timer! And it never fails, you get all plugged in and slip quietly underneath your sleeping bag, anticipating a nice toasty evening, and then wham! just like that, the hypnotizing buzz of the electric fan comes to an abrupt stop. Then all you can do after that is lie there and enjoy every last little bit of heat you have left because very soon the cold will start to creep on in. The ice will steadily begin to accumulate on the inside of your windshield becoming thicker and thicker with each passing minute as it slowly transforms you into nothing more than a glorified fish stick! Nope, business frontages are too unpredictable for my liking I'm afraid. What you really need to do is find an unassuming side street where someone has plugged in their own rig and pull up behind them.
*** Important Safety Tip*** Make sure it appears that they are asleep for the night before you attempt this!!!

Then take an extension cord and splice it into theirs and set your watch alarm for 6a.m. You are usually safe until that time of the morning, but there is the odd occasion that you will be Godsmacked out from a dead sleep by a very pissed off human being whom you've just ripped off a night's power from. This trick can work great if you find the right situation, but again, you have to keep mobile and not get to comfy in one particular spot. Now, I will be truthful. Sometimes in the dead of winter, for whatever reason, there will come a night where no matter what you do, you will just simply not be able to find a power source. Every attempt you make will ultimately fail. Now, you can't just drive around all night with the heat on and waste precious gas. At some point you have to get inside. You really haven't much of a choice. It's either shiver away for eight hours in some frozen corner of the city and risk hypothermia and death, or you can head to the coffee shops. All making sense now?

It's your choice man, but I recommend the shops. Trust me, it's worth it. It's nearly impossible to get to sleep in that temperature anyway. You shake too damn much to even close your eyes! Your only chance of getting any shuteye in this equation will not actually be until the next day, when you drive your car down into the heated underground parkades of the malls were it will be safe for you to close your eyes. But just a note of caution; when you do this you have to make sure you are totally covered up and you have to sleep this time in the back seat, not the front. This way you are less visible and unlikely to tip off any "do gooders" who are passing by. And it's also a good idea to park your vehicle off in the corner somewhere. This will save you a lot of grief too.

Again, sometimes this trick will backfire, but no matter what happens, understand that there are always the coffee shops. They are a constant in this lifestyle, and don't worry, the staff on the night shift are usually pretty casual about your predicament..., or they're just plain terrified by the sight of you! But either way, it equates to a pretty low stress evening. And the price is right too! Ninety cents is all it costs to reserve your room for the night. The sum total of one regular cup of coffee. You don't get the good brew though, nope, they save that grind for the daytime crowd with the money and the status. In the middle of the night, all you are going to get is the cheap shit. But don't worry, refills are free and the music is usually pretty decent.

Jesus!, you know I couldn't even begin to tell you how many nights I've spent cocooned up inside those joints, bored out of my skull, waiting endlessly to catch a glimpse of the sun so that I could drag my sorry ass through it's rays once again. Yup, they're OK, the shops, but there is one downside to them.

One disturbing downside.

Don't get me wrong, I'm not complaining here. I mean the baristas do get you in out of the elements and all, but I have to confess, there is always one thing that I dread when I am forced to camp out in those establishments during the cold months. One type of thing actually, and it never ceases to unnerve me.

No, it isn't the bitter coffee, or the drunks or the hookers. Nor is it the fact that you have to occasionally suffer through the odd religious sermon from some holier-than-thou block parent. Nope, it's none of that shit at all. It's, well, it's them.

The "Greebs."

They are definitely the worst.

These urban legends are in any given city, at any given time. Especially one this size. And in the middle of the night in the dead of winter, while most of the upstanding daytime folk are tucked away snugly in their overpriced beds, the witching hour and beyond tends to purge out a distorted form of a mutant being known as "the greeb", from the depths of the inner city's many gaping sores.

Midnight... Yep, that's about the time when they awaken and begin their decent upon civilization. They are also known as the bush people.

They get that nickname because they live deep inside the tightly woven thickets down by the river's edge.

You could see them coming in from all around you, sadistically rising up from their frozen tombs and making their way towards the illumination and the warmth of the flickering neon lights like an army of zombies closing in on the living. They are the people whom society has all but condemned to the dark confinement of the nighttime world. And as they would come in from out of the cold, you could easily hear their labored breaths wheezing and contracting in a constant state of illness due to the unlimited years of malnutrition and exposure they've endured.

Their eyes are dead. Long, long dead. A few could afford the price tag of a small coffee if the bottle trade had been fair that day, but for the most part, the majority of them just sit there all night and mumble to the imaginary devils inside their head, a warm cup of water in a take out cup in front of them instead.

The bush dwellers are dangerous, that's all I'm saying. They are human only by anatomy. Their world is a fantasy where anything goes. They live in a twisted-up land of yes, where they are the almighty rulers and they have free range to do anything they please. That's what makes them so dangerous. And they pose a serious and real threat to any outsiders because of this for their minds have lapsed into a distant place where there are no consequences and no rules.

Their tolerance is non-existent, whittled down to that level from many years of relentless submission from the outside world. Their realm is much like that of the animal kingdom. If you are seen as a threat, you are taken out of the picture by what-ever means of weaponry they have access to, simple as that! No second thoughts, no trial. No mercy. It may sound cruel, but for all intents and purposes, they really are just animals. The only difference that separates the two is the fact that the greebs walk upright. I always overhear people saying, "Jeez, how do people end up that way? How do they get so lost?"

I want to answer their question so badly sometimes. I want to tell them that it's from fighting and losing a never-ending battle with humiliation. I want to tell them that it doesn't just happen overnight. Fuck! People aren't born like that for Christ sakes! They get that way over a long period of time. The downward progression always begins with one single degrading act, whatever that travesty might be. But then, that one heartbreak eventually spawns forth another, and another, and another. One step at a time, one embarrassment at a time, that person's metaphor of reality begins to distort, and his or her ego is systematically deleted. Then, finally, that one day comes along when something happens.

Something devastating. And it takes deadly aim at the last remaining strand of hope that person is struggling to protect.

Suddenly their mind, critically wounded and fearing annihilation, splits in two and creates a guardian in a frantic and last-ditch measure to save itself. This "big brother", so to speak, is a perfect all-knowing and ever strong alter image that begins sticking up for that person twenty-four/seven. It materializes as an invisible body-guard that reassures them that it's OK to eat that apple core out of the trash, and, hey, it's no big deal to occasionally piss your pants in public. It also promises them that one fine day in a grand ceremony of reckoning, all the bad people that had caused them harm in the past will bow down at their feet and beg them for mercy.

That's why you steer clear of these types because your life doesn't mean shit to them! "You" are one of the bad people, get it? So heed this warning and you may just stay alive.

You sometimes see them walking around during the day, rummaging through the

28

trash and swearing to themselves, but for the most part, they are the ones that patrol
and rule the night. They are the people that society likes to pretend doesn't exist.
I've watched them from a distance for a long time. It gets quite disheartening after a
while watching them walk around in such a Disneyland state.
Waiting.
Just patiently waiting for that glorious day to come around when they can finally die.
Maybe they're already dead, but their souls just can't seem to find their way to the
other side yet. It's anybody's guess. But whatever they have become, whoever they
are inside, it is important that you keep your distance. I sure as Christ do, but I still
find it impossible not to wonder just what? What was the last straw that finally broke
that person? What was the one single act that so violently flung them into Hell, and
when will that darkness catch up to me? This is an inevitable fact that no-one out
here takes lightly.

Now don't worry, these "greebs" will not usually harm you in public for they
somehow know that the heat and the sustenance they seek and are given can also be
taken away if they misbehave. Therefore, they tend to be fairly docile in a crowd,
thank God. But if they ever come across you inside their domain watch out! Your ass
will be grass for sure! Make no mistake about this. Don't ever go into the thickets
down by the river. It's just too Goddam risky. They will fuck you up badly, and they
won't so much as break a sweat. Even other greebs are at risk if they dare cross over
into another one's territory. I'm telling you, it all points back to the animal kingdom.
That's the bottom line. I avoid the riverbed like the plague these days, but I will
admit that once about four years back, in the daytime, I did venture into their world.
I don't know why. I know it was stupid of me, but I just couldn't help it. My curiosity
was killing me and I just had to know. I had to see that dimension for myself.

The entrances to their medieval looking lairs are relatively small. Maybe two feet
by two feet max. You basically have to crawl into them on your stomach, and that
in itself is disturbing enough. I remember vividly what I saw when I did get inside
though. Shit like that is hard to forget. The bushes themselves are very dense, so
dense in fact, that they almost act as walls and ceilings. It's a giant maze in there.
Reminded me of an underground army bunker, scattered with endless tunnels and
living pods. A multitude of trinkets litter the ground wherever you look. Basically,
anything they can salvage out of the trash ends up in there as furniture. There are
also a lot of old blankets strewn about, reeking violently of sweat, puke and urine.
The smell is absolutely gut-wrenching. It coats your skin and suffocates your soul,
and after only five minutes of that little field trip I was already looking for the door.
And it wasn't just because of the smell either.
Nope, it was the desperation that murdered me. It was thick like quicksand, and I
could feel it trying to take me over.

And getting back out of there wasn't fun either. You see it is very dark in there,
even in the daytime. And because the passageways jut out in every direction, it
makes it quite difficult to find the exact gopher hole you came in from. However,
when I eventually did find that particular doorway, I immediately dropped to the
ground and wiggled my way the fuck out of there. The second I was back on the
outside, I spit out a stagnant clump of air I had been holding in and happily drew in a

fresh gob of good old big city pollution.

And it never tasted so good! After that I ran full out until I got back onto the main road and I never again ventured back into their world. For any reason! My life is screwy enough as it is without exposing my brain to garbage like that. Yup, it's dog eat dog out here I'm afraid, and it's true that sometimes you get so sick and tired of hanging on that you wish you could just fall and get it over with.

Ahh, you know what, I can analyze the piss out of my situation all I want, but in the end, I am what I am. We all are. Man, I'm tired of thinking. Besides, I can feel my stomach starting to growl. Guess it's time for brunch! Well. Sort of... So with my first chore of the day completed and another unsuspecting service station taken advantage of, I crank my engine over for a second time, and low and behold, my old Pontiac sputters to life once more.

Today, I'm on my way to the supermarket up over the hill. I think it's meatloaf surprise day if I'm not mistaken. It's a little bit of a drive from where I am, but dammit!, I just can't resist processed meatloaf!

Oh ya, and by the way, I wasn't a runaway OK! Everybody always assumes that when they see people like me, but nope, that's not how I ended up here. Hey come on! I never bloody wanted to end up here, you get me! But things happened you know. Things that I couldn't help, Things that I couldn't stop. I mean I tried to stop stuff. Oh fuck! Believe me I tried. I'm telling you man, I really did.

But I just couldn't.

See, I got kicked out of the house, that's why I'm here, 'cause I got kicked out. I don't really remember too many details about it anymore, and you know what, I don't even care! I got way more shit to worry about these day's, trust me! Some of the footage is still intact though. I'll show it to you, OK, but you've got to promise to keep it to yourself. Now it's been a long time so the details may be a little scratchy, but I do know that I wasn't even 17 yet, I do know that! And ya, ya, it was dark too.

The first thing I see is me tumbling down the steps of a house that no longer exists in my world. And I can still hear the crushing sound my shoulder made as it connected with the thick concrete slab in a backyard were I finally came to rest. My face is pressed into the dirt now and I am yelling as the impact of the fall shoots a bullet of pain throughout my body. I looked up at that point and saw my mother. Yes, I can still see her. She is crying. She is crying but I cannot help her.

Godammit!... Goddam you Eugene for not helping her! She is there in the doorway now, calling out to me as she peers out from behind a stranger she long regretted marrying not even a year earlier. A slimy drifter type, whose tyranny infected our household from day one.

He has just unveiled his big plans to" liquidate the assets", and embark us on a never-ending semi-trip ride. A move of course that I protested immediately. I knew as soon as he opened his mouth that all he was really interested in was the money from the sale of our place so he could steal it and use it to buy his Goddam freight-liner. "Assets" Fuck! He didn't have two bloody dimes to rub together when he met my mom and he never would. The never-ending semi trip he bragged of was nothing shy of a one way ticket to Hell and I wasn't going to have any part of it!

It was strange, because all through her single parent life my ma had always kept her dating life pretty casual, most I can remember. But this guy, he managed to slither his way inside somehow. He must have persuaded her with a lie of some sort, and convinced her to let him move in. From that moment on, the controlled baptism of fury he laid forth was unrelenting, and without provocation.

The walls bleed endlessly of wrath. Of Carnage.

That is, until the one day, the same day of which I speak, when the world I knew came crashing down the steps beside me. The words he screamed out as I lay in the dirt were blurry and garbled. I struggled to my feet in a daze and looked over at my car. My usual escape was not to be for the keys to the ignition were still deep inside the house. I was desperate. I could see in my mind no hope. But then I heard something. It was a noise, and it was closing in fast from somewhere behind me. It was the sound of a machine, a very powerful machine speeding it's way closer and closer towards me. Suddenly, a lone car screeched around the side of the townhouse, and fishtailed its mass directly parallel to where I was laying. In an instant, the passenger's door swung open, and without another seconds delay, I ran towards it and dove inside.

The heaven sent vehicle was a 1974 Corvette Stingray. Red. Fast.
It was a car that I knew inside out.

You know, I don't carry too much faith around with me anymore. I guess I've generally lost my compassion for the bulk of mankind, but I do believe that everyone in this world, no matter how destitute, is allotted a true friend. Just one. A person that you know will go to the mat for you. A person who can finish your sentences, and who knows things about you, you don't. A best friend that can see through your wall. For me, that persons name was Steve Rojesco.
We'd known each other since the beginning, since we were about three. We had been through it all, me and that guy. I had phoned him earlier on that night and told him not to come by because there was trouble brewing. Advice he flatly ignored thank God!

"Get me the fuck out of here" I groaned as I pulled the door shut behind me.

It was a phrase he had heard before, but this time, I think he knew it was absolute. Without hesitation, Steve rammed that fireball into gear and hit the juice. I could feel the engine rumble and scream as the tires unleashed their anger on the cement and billowed out thick plumes of white smoke. The G-forces on my body were immense as the rpm's climbed higher and higher, twisting the speedometer out of control and I watched then in bittersweet agony as the terrible scene in my side view mirror slowly disappeared out of site. Neither of us spoke for a while, we just drove on and let the roar of the engine drown out our anger.

Steve eventually did clear the air and said in a plain voice... "The usual place?"

"Ya", I answered quietly.

The "usual place" though, was anything but usual. But it was a destination that we both regarded as sacred.
It was a small run down park hidden away deep in the south end of town, amidst the contours of a forgotten haven called Jackson's Coulee. It was there that we would find our sanctuary as we always did.
The sky was pitch-black by the time we idled through the stone archway of the place and pulled up in front of the old pylon barriers of the dirt parking lot. My friend systematically rolled down the electric windows from the sensors on his side, then cranked up the music. After a minute, we both crawled out of that rocket ship and made our way down an overgrown path towards a murky patch of water. When we reached the edge of our well loved paradise, we sat on a half rotted log and began to skip rocks across the pond.

It was a ceremony that we'd been carrying out religiously since we were young kids. The evening air was filled with the sound of a soft churning creek emptying out into the man-made body of water from somewhere over on the other side. That hymn too, we knew off by heart. The moon was slight, but the stars were out in full force. We still didn't say a lot, we just sat their and gazed up at the sky while the soothing dribble of the stream carried our thoughts toward a more pleasant destination.

"You can stay with me," Steve said finally. "You know you can do that, right?"

I wanted to answer him, but no words came to me.

"We got lots of room," my friend continued, "You're not putting anyone out here."

I dropped my head in shame and began speaking to the ground.

"I left her there, Steve. Mom. I just left her there."

"That's not your fault Eugene," Steve shot back. "Dammit! You know that!"

I could tell he was getting frustrated. He always hated to see me like this but still, I knew the truth was the truth.

"I ran away like a coward," I told him, more careful this time.

"Come on Eugene," Steve eventually reassured me. "You know what happened back there is not your doing. You had absolutely no control over that man, none! It wasn't your fault OK? It wasn't!"

"It doesn't matter," I whispered back. "I should have went in and got her anyway. I should have fucking helped her!" My words grew weak and faded off.

I felt Steve lean over and put his hand on my shoulder." Listen", he said softly. "You and me". I heard my friend let out a long sigh. "We go back a long time, right?"

"Ya... long time," I said.

"Please Eugene," Steve begged as his hand continued its first aid. "Come back with me and stay at the guest house until this all blows over alright?"

"That's just it man," I growled. "It's never going to blow over!! That shit back there will go on forever!"

I stood up with my hands clenched in anger and walked over to the very edge of the pond. Steve followed suit and came up beside me. "I'm confused, man," I said. "I'm just so confused! I could see all this coming, but no matter what I did I couldn't change its course, no matter what!"

We both fell silent for a moment. I'm sure each of us was trying in some way to come up with an answer.
"I'm worried Steve," I said as I turned and faced him for the first time. "What's going to happen to her now?"

"Hey now," I heard my best pal cut in. " Don't you go worrying about your mom. She is one tough lady. She'll be OK... She will pull through all this just fine."

Steve's philosophy was gentle and reassuring.

"Come up to the house for a little while," he concluded. "Let me help you Eugene, that's what friends do.
They help each other". My sole confidante paused for a moment as he picked up a rock from the shore and flung it mindlessly into the shallow water.

"No my friend", I said after a long pause. "I can't."

I followed his lead and retrieved a stone from the weathered bank, firing it as well into the misty haze of the pond. We both watched in silence as my rock bounced across the water and sank into its muddy depths.

"I appreciate your offer Steve, I do. You know that, right?" I said clearly as I looked him in the eye and confirmed our bond. "But I have to do this on my own. I have to," I said boldly, "or I will always be afraid. My whole life I'll be afraid, and I'll never be free. I'm sorry Steve," I said lastly, "but this has to be my fight."

I watched my lifelong companion's head drop down as I finished my sentence. But after a short pause, he looked back up again and gave me a forced, but sincere smile. I could tell that he didn't agree with my rogue decision, but I also knew he respected it. I picked up another stone and whizzed it as hard as I could into the algae-infested puddle, even though it killed my shoulder to do so. Then we both just stood there again, me and my best friend Steve, and watched as the ripples from the impact of the rock slowly smoothed out over the water and bled into the stillness of the night.

We stayed there by the edge of the dugout like that for about another half hour, trying hard to saturate ourselves with as much of Mother Nature's tranquilizer as she would give us. I loved that place. We had been coming there ever since we were coordinated enough to put a worm on a hook and hold a fishing rod. It was an oasis where we could always find redemption, no matter what the crime.

"Well," I said finally as I let loose one last rock into the custody of the pond. "Guess it's time to call it a night, huh?"

"Yup," Steve said after a minute. "Guess it's that time."

My friend knew I had to do what I had to do, and he accepted that decision uncon-ditionally. That's what best friends did. We were both quite mellow now. Mother Nature had once again taken us in and nursed us back to health. So with a hint of peace, me and my number one pal turned around and started to head back up the thin outline of the path that led back to his shiny car. As we rumbled back out of the coulee that night through the dense strain of willow trees and past the montage of rusted-out swing sets, I found that my mood grew somewhat grey again. I guess it was because I knew I still had to go back to the house. I still had to return there and retrieve my vehicle somehow. Steve knew this too, so he drove within a blocks distance of my place, and killed the engine.

"You got the keys?" he asked.
"No," I muttered rubbing my forehead deeply. "They're still in the house. But mom may have snuck out and put them on the seat or something," I said with a twinge of enthusiasm.

With a reluctant start, we slowly climbed out of his ride and began walking up the alley in the direction of my house. Once at the edge of the grass, we crept quietly through the backyard and crouched down by the corner of the cement pad that supported my vehicle. I tiptoed around to the side window and peered inside.
My intuitions were bang on. Just as I had hoped, I saw the metallic outline of the keys dangling from the ignition. And the door too, was slightly ajar.

I glanced over at Steve who was still kneeling over by the edge of the cement and gave him a nod. He returned my gesture with a subtle thumbs-up and started back towards his Corvette. With the steadiness of a surgeon, I eased open the driver's door and slid my body onto the imitation leather bucket. In a nanosecond, I had that baby started and was backing out towards the alley. I pulled out onto the front street a few minutes later and idled my rig to a stop. I kept my foot hard on the brake and did not budge it. With a heavy heart, I sat there with my car rumbling away in the middle of the road and stretched out those final precious moments in front of my house as long as I could. I cataloged a lifetime of memories into the next few seconds; for I knew I would never be able to look at that picture again in real life. Only in my minds eye, would it ever come back into view.

"I'm sorry mom," I whispered." I'm sorry for not being stronger."

When I had finally stuffed the storage unit behind my eyes with as many memories as I possibly could, I very slowly released the pressure of my brake pedal, and felt my old sports car start to chug forward.
And as my eyes abandoned the still frame of my old house that night, I could have sworn I saw my mother in the window waving at me, telling me that she was OK Telling me that everything was fine.
I know I saw her there, I know it!
I must have.

Not even a minute later, I pulled up beside Steve down at the far end of the block and hung my head out the window.

"You gonna be OK?" he asked.

"I'm going to have to be," I said.

"Call me tomorrow," he warned as he half-jokingly pointed his finger at my temple.

"I will," I nodded.

Steve flashed me a heartfelt smile, and then we both drove away into the darkness.
I didn't sleep a second that first night. My brain was in too much of a frenzy trying to scrape together a rough battle plan for the immediate future.
The whole evening I just sat there in the dark. Anchored quietly in the parking lot of a vacant mall as I rummaged through the hastily packed suitcases of my thoughts, searching desperately for anything that was still salvageable.

Now I never planned on staying in my car that long. It's true! I figured I'd just camp out inside it for a couple of weeks or so until I got enough cash together to rent myself an apartment. That was the plan, really. Unfortunately my brilliant scheme never materialized, and I never did get a place of my own.
I was never able to get enough cash together at any given time to cover all of the initial costs of securing a pad. I did attempt to get a steady job and clean myself up a bit, but in the end it was not to be. Three months passed by just like that and I remember thinking one morning. …"God, it wasn't supposed to be this long! It was never supposed to turn out like this."

But I guess it did.

Time comes quickly at you out here. And the more time I spent living out of my Firebird, the more familiar I became with it, and the more it started to feel like home.

It was around then that I came to realize I was not the only one coping with this odd situation. It was starting to become easier and easier to pick out other vehicles that were being used as homesteads as well. And it seemed like they were everywhere I looked now. I found it so strange that I was never able to see those types of colonizations before. And now all of the sudden there was this whole other civilization right in front of my face that I never even thought existed!

...But you will never see them, or their world unless you have had to have been there.

It was as if I had found a pair of magical glasses that allowed me to see into a totally different dimension of life that was invisible to the naked eye.
And I found it even more disturbing of how these "people" were now also starting to be able to recognize me too.

That was a little unsettling at first. Nevertheless, I began ending up in the exact same places as they would, persevering too, with the same types of situations. Maybe I was unconsciously following their loose caravans without even realizing it. I admit I would occasionally spy on them from time to time attempting, I think, to pick up on a few of their little" tricks of the trade" to utilize somewhere down the road in my zany apprenticeship. It was quite intriguing at first. You know, discovering this unseen universe. This "Atlantis."
But my honeymoon was short-lived, and soon I began to feel the formation of a dense lump growing on the lining of my soul. That's when I started to see the other side of the coin. The depression, the illness. The poverty.

I watched in disbelief as whole entire families starved themselves down to nothing right before my eyes. Day after day I witnessed the suffering. The children bothered me the most. They would paste themselves to the side window as you walked by, smiling desperately up at you with their rotten teeth and stringy hair, begging you to help them escape from their nightmare as their palms slid down the wet glass. But even at that point, I still did not consider myself to be one of them. Nope, not really, not back then.

I figured I was still above it all yet. A mere tourist in the game. But I do recall a situation, an incident that happened to me early on in my residency that narrowed the difference. It involved the likes of an old man who was sitting inside an ancient station wagon one day in the parking lot of an idle warehouse complex that I, coincidentally, was scoping out in an effort to satisfy my newly acquired thirst for empties.

I remember glancing over at his car and feeling my feet slow down in an unprecedented state of awe. It was because the whole inside of it was almost completely lined with old newspapers that were taped up to the inside of the windows and laid out recklessly on the floor. The front and backseats as well, were also littered with a festering array of stained jackets and other discarded road digs. Christ! It looked like that poor bastard had been living inside that bloody wreck for about forty years, I am not kidding!! Well I'll tell you what, that little horror movie instantly knocked me off

my imaginary pedestal and sobered me right up! It dug in deep and bit a huge chunk
out of my soul. And I remember as I shuffled by his four-doored coffin, how he turned
his head in my direction and deliberately locked me into a glare.

I'll never forget the terrible look he had on his face that day. It was so lost. So
angry. The tarnished lines of misery etched upon his face were like exact rivers in a
timeline that documented each and every wrong turn in his life, and I knew right then
and there as he stared me down that afternoon that he was suddenly suffering from
an eerie case of déjà vu, a mental re-incarnation of sorts. For I know that what he
saw in me was a perfect replica of the young man he once was in the same situation,
standing at the same delicate crossroad in his youth as he pressed his palms together
and tried to make the right decision, to choose the correct path.
  Then, just like that, his look changed shape and melted down into something even
darker. And at that point he did then draw his sword and issue me a stern and absolute warning as if to say to me, to scream to me, to yell to me to change my course.
To change my ways and take the higher road before it's too late. Before I ended up
behind the same cold trance that had imprisoned him forever now. And even though
that chance meeting lasted only a matter of seconds that cool fall day, I will never
forget his warning, or that stare.
  Even today I cannot shake its memory.

And that folks, is how all this came to be. That's how I got here. Crazy, huh? You
bet your short and curlys it is, and now here I am driving like a madman on a bloody
quest for three measly ounces of processed fucking meat loaf!

"Ya Fricken hoe!"

"Hey Dickweed! Watch where the Hell you're going!"

"Goddam asshole!!"

Oops, sorry. Got cut off there. You know some people should take the damn bus!
Don't need anybody scratchin' my ride now!!... (Truth be known, I could roll this
hunk of shit and nobody would even know the difference!) OK, OK, I know I swear
too much, I admit it. I'm sorry, I apologize. I can't help it sometimes, it's my only
way to vent! You know, I never used to swear at all. Well, not really. Not like I
do now. It's true! I mean I wasn't always this jaded. My life wasn't always about
survival. I do still hoard away the odd happy memory inside my head believe it or
not. I still remember being young and carefree, having fun times, having friends! Oh
Hell ya, I had lots of friends! In fact, you know what? I had the best of friends!

We all used to hang out at a place called Central Park but it was nothing like New
York. There were five of us. Steve of course, this kid named Ian, a guy by the name
of Andy, and another dude by the name of Trevor. Oh ya, and of course, me. We
were all real close, and we were together on a daily basis when we were kids. Man,
we were so cool! Every summer for one month we would all go away to a special

youth camp that was specifically set up for kids who didn't have any brothers or sisters. The organization was called "The Young Frontiers Club", and it was designed as a getaway for only children, a category that, you guessed it, all of us guys fit into. We were all only children and I think that's one of the main reasons us five became so close. Because none of us ever had any other blood to bond with, so we all in a sense became brothers to each other.

And our neighborhood was fantastic too. Everyone was on our side; well everyone except old man Walthorp of course. He was kind of a nasty old fucker. I think he was Russian, but no-one really knew for sure. It was common knowledge though, that you never cut through his yard or he'd be out there in a heartbeat to jam a rake in your ass! But with the exception of him, the hood was a gem. The park I was telling you about resembled a giant island. It was surrounded entirely by a six foot high wall of roughly- manicured bushes. The inside of the place too, was scattered with fir trees that supplied ample amounts of shade, and smack dab in the very center of it all, lay a shallow but versatile wading pond. Adjacent to that of course, was a fair sized playground that came complete with a big set of swings, and a merry-go-round and a whole bunch of other injury- causing apparatus.

We were never really that crazy about the merry-go-round 'cause it always made us barf, but we did use to spend a lot of time horsing around on a big blue whale slide thingy. It was made of solid concrete and had a freaky-looking eye drilled through the top side of it. I used to crawl inside its gaping mouth when we were playing a block-sized game of hide and seek and no-one would ever be able to find me as long as I didn't start laughing. One time though, while I was showing off by sliding down the length of it head first, {I believe there was a cute little brunette girl involved}, I accidentally slipped off that marine widow-maker and cracked my head open! Man, there was blood everywhere. Steve and the rest of the guys had to carry me home to my extremely hysterical mother because I was too dizzy to walk. I remember looking up at Steve's t-shirt moments before he dropped me on the front porch, hit the doorbell, and ran for his life.

It was soaked right through with my blood! I'm sure I must have mentally traumatized the shit out of the poor boy that day, but he never said anything more about it. Except, however, to tell me how much of a peckerhead I was for destroying his favorite top. Yep, we would chill out in that dreamland park all day, and then after we had finished our dinner, we'd usually hook up with another group of kids from the neighborhood and play a game of ball tag until it got dark. It was great!

We were so carefree back then, and everything we did, we did with style. When Saturday morning rolled around, I would head down to Steve's house around 5 am, and I could never understand why no-one else in the house was ever up. It boggled my mind. On the flip side, it did give me first dibbs on the box of breakfast cereal that always sat in the bottom cupboard of his kitchen. And it was the good stuff too, you know the kind that was drenched in sugar and came with all those cool toys. You see, that's why I was forced to break into his pad and annihilate his stash. You understand, don't ya? And when Steve did get up, he would always find me passed out on the couch with the box of cereal on my lap and a stupid grin on my face. Despite all that he never got mad. In hindsight, he probably had a right to. But hey,

we were kids.
We had no idea what hate was back then.

Once we'd had our fill of cartoons we would meet up with the rest of the gang and sometimes go down to where they were building the new subdivisions to construct mock weapons from the contractors' scrap piles, and then spend the rest of the day playing war games, occasionally sneaking inside the unfinished houses to catch a little shade. Yep, we just lived to have fun back then and we played out that fantasy for all it was worth, never thinking for one second that it would ever rain.

But as time went on and we became teenagers, we started to drift apart a little. The whole lot of us got transferred up to a bigger school, a high school, and naturally, things began to change. Andy and Trevor joined the football team and started to hang around with a different crowd. Ian, shockingly enough, turned out to be very smart and was hustled into an advanced education program. I was so proud of him. Hell! we all were, but every time we went over to see him, he was always buried under a mountain of homework and never had time to do anything else. But that was OK Actually, it was probably a good thing we joked, "cause one day we'll all probably need to crash at one of his beach houses when he became a zillionaire."
Yes, it seems that we were all beginning to undergo the ritualistic transformation from boys to men. And even though I began to see less and less of those three guys as time went by, we still remained tight and regarded each other as family. Sometimes our daily interactions materialized as nothing more than a simple wave and a nod from across the gymnasium, but that gesture was always genuine and loyal. And even though I only ever see those guys in my mind nowadays, I assure you, they will forever have a home there.

Steve and I, on the other hand, remained very close. It was strange, our friendship. No-one could ever really figure it out. I mean we were completely opposite in so many ways, but we were still the strongest of friends. He was the captain of the basketball team and stood almost a foot taller than everyone else. He had the looks, the personality, and the biggest house on the block. He was easily one of the most popular guys in school. I, on the other hand, was as skinny as a rake, a foot shorter than everyone else, and was about as popular as a scabies outbreak. Not your typical buddy to buddy match up that's for sure, but that fact never made one bit of difference in our bond.

Every day we would sit in the lunchroom and pollute our minds with heavy metal death rock until the bell rang. You see, deep inside, Steve was just as much of a head banger as I was, but his parents would never allow him to grow his hair long, or wear black concert t-shirts like I did. I guess you could say he was sort of a closet metal freak, but that didn't matter to me. What mattered was that we were the same people, and that we could care less what the rest of the world saw us as. Steve would always stick up for me too. He defended my every fuckup, no matter how much I was in the wrong. It was common knowledge not to mess around with me either, or you would have to answer to all 6 feet of him! You know, it's so odd because Steve could have chosen absolutely anyone on the planet to be his best friend, but in the end, that person turned out to be me? That is something that I know in my whole life, I will never be able to truly understand.

But whatever the case may have been, when we did walk down the halls together, man, it felt like I was ten feet tall and bulletproof. I was so fortunate to have that guy on my side. I'm pretty sure my mediocre stint in high school would have been quite traumatic if it wasn't for him.

Grade nine turned out to be a long year, but grade ten flew by like the wind, thank God. In March, the day Steve turned sixteen, his uncle gave him his old 1969 Chevrolet Impala. It was a massive, four-door, emerald-green sedan - a land yacht by every description. But it was his first set of wheels and he loved that tank! We used to cruise around in that monster every day, until of course, he got it high-centered on a huge stump and seized the engine at a house party a month later. After that though, Steve lucked out and got his dream car.

Yep, you guessed it, a 1974 Corvette Stingray. Red! Fast!

He had wanted a 'vette for as long as I could remember. His parents fronted him half the cash and co-signed a loan for the rest. I'll never forget the day he drove up to my house in that baby for the first time. Man, he was talking so fast I thought he was going to stroke out or something!

"Hey, you wanna go for a burn?" he yelled.

"Hell ya!" I said as I happily jumped into the passenger seat and held on for dear life.

"The motor's got 390 horsepower!" Steve hollered as he shifted gears and rocketed past a blue Dodge Duster.

I didn't acknowledge my pal's latest statement, I was too busy shitting my pants! The first thing we did was head straight up to the public swimming pool on the S. E. hill of our neighborhood. We didn't go swimming or anything crazy like that. Nope, we just pulled up alongside the chain link fence beside it with the windows down and the T-tops off and casually hung out there for the rest of the afternoon, listening to music and scoping chicks! We did that sort of thing quite a bit in the days that followed and with a machine like that, who wouldn't?

I turned sixteen myself a few weeks later and got my driver's license on the second try. And not even ten days after that, I had acquired my prized Firebird. I was free, well... sort of. From then on in, me and my pal cruised the downtown strip side by side almost every night. It was heaven I'll tell ya, and for a while there I didn't have a single care in the world. I was just another brain-dead teenager. That is, until the night I ended up a statistic. But even after that terrible night, Steve continued to stick by me. Unfazed by my grim circumstances, or my uncommon decision to deal with it the way that I did. That was a very difficult week for me, the first one.

I mean, after things fell to shit at my former residence, it seemed like everything else in my life fell over too. I was even picked up by the cops once, not long after I was kicked out. Apparently I was found one morning stumbling around Central Park in a total daze, and I was mumbling to myself. I guess I had fallen down or something because my wrists were all scraped up. I can't honestly say that I remember any of that scene, but I do remember calling Steve from the police station and saying something like, "Hey man? Where the Hell am I?"

You know, that was the only time in my entire life where I was so Goddam out of it that I didn't even know where I was! Bad week man, bad fucking week! But my friend didn't miss a beat. He dropped what he was doing and came down to bail me out. He never let on to the cops what my situation was, he just told them that I was upset about a girl and coaxed them to let me go. Steve never grilled me about what happened, or how I ended up at the park either. He never came down on me, or seemed mad, or anything. Nope, he just came to the ongoing rescue of his skinny confused friend. Like he always did.

It's funny you know, when I look back nowadays and think about those guys and how much they meant to me. I guess when you're younger; it's easy to take things like that for granted. I haven't seen or heard from Steve for many years now. I lost touch with him shortly after he bailed me out of the cop shop. It was my fault, I admit it, and that is something I will always regret. You see, I became overwhelmed with guilt somewhere along the line and felt like I was starting to become too much of a burden on the patience of my friend. So I made the decision to disappear into the woodwork for a little while, just until I got my head screwed back on straight.

But it never happened, and I just kept falling deeper and deeper into a pit of shame. I did however, finally get up the courage to venture back into his neighborhood in the late fall so that I could apologize, so that I could explain, but he was already long gone. The neighbors told me that his dad got transferred out of state and that they had moved away at the end of the summer. The news of his departure crushed me beyond comprehension. I was so mad at myself. I knew I should have gone to see him sooner. I should have called him and let him know I was OK or something. Anything! But I didn't. I didn't do a fucking thing. I will forever be haunted by that mistake. It will always twist the knife that lays buried in my soul. But alas, in my own weak defense, I too was busy adjusting to a new life.

It's strange, but those days past, and all of those moments, they don't even seem real to me anymore. It feels like they were someone else's memories.

Just memories now.

My reminiscent shards of glory begin to quickly dissolve into visions of sustenance as my final destination starts to materialize over the horizon and my trip down memory lane comes to an end. It is an upscale strip mall in a snazzy suburb of the city's west end that gains control of my already-taxed mind. You know, the kind of place where you see a lot of really rich assholes walking around racking up their credit cards to buy a bunch of useless trinkets so they can sell them for nothing a year later at their garage sales. But I'm not going there today for the social status of the whole thing, or the trinkets! It's the grand opening of the big new supermarket where I'll be letting my hair down today!

As I enter the parking lot I back my rig in so I am facing the store, but I stay a good three rows back. It's only about 10:30 in the morning and the gratuitous samples of microwave meatloaf don't start to flow until around noon. Guess I got a little time to kill. Boy, there's a news flash, me having a little time to kill! Well, at least it's turning out to be a pretty nice day anyway. The early morning rain has slowed to a stop and the sun is beginning to burn its way through the ozone. Keeping in sync with a habit I've grown to accept, I shut down my spastic engine and begin to wait. After fifteen minutes of listening to the ongoing babble of the city, I watch a long white van pull into the lot and drop anchor.

Without warning, the side door flings open and a good ten to twelve kids dressed in cash-green, badge- ridden uniforms spill out overtop each other and start bee lining toward the entrance. The site of this brings a grand smile to my face and my heart begins to swell for I am quite familiar as to the origins of those outfits. I wore the same kind once, and I wore them proud. The shirts the young men in front of me wear are none other than those belonging to the kids of the Young Frontiers Club, the very same organization me and Steve belonged to as kids. From their sense of haste I could tell that they were stocking up on tuck supplies before hitting the road en route to their annual summer campout. I knew that drill off by heart even to this day, for I played out that skit many times over as a younger man.

God we had us some fun in that club, me and the rest of the guys. We could hardly wait for the day to arrive when we could all dog pile into that same van and head out to the country, far, far away from the watchful eyes of our parents. I remember we always had the same campout leader every summer by the name of Barry... Barry McDool. He was easily the coolest guy around. All the Girl Guide leaders on the other side of the lake used to call him "Barry McDrool" because they said he was so good-looking. Actually, he *was* good-looking that bastard! Any female that he came in to contact with would usually start to salivate and twitch immediately. They were always whistling at him and waving and shit too. Yep, he was definitely our damn idol! Tall, dark, really muscular. You know, your basic chick magnet! I mean this dude was everything all of us other shmucks wanted to turn out to be like when we got older.

And he was really good to us guys too. He treated us like we were number one. He nicknamed me the Genie because he knew I didn't like my real name, Eugene. And you could tell him absolutely anything too and he would always listen. I remember once of a particular campout we all went to, me and the guys, when Barry entered us into a wood stacking competition and we took first place. After it was all over, he called us over to the side and gave us each our very own pocket knife in recognition of our victory. They were really nice ones too. Sleek, sturdy, and oh ya, sharp as hell!! And we wasted no time testing out our new gifts either. We promptly darted off into the bushes and cut down a whole stack of green shrubbery from the branches of the low-lying trees and proceeded to carve them into custom weenie-roasting sticks which we utilized at the following evening's festivities. Yep, Barry was definitely the best and we always looked forward to seeing him when the summer began to call.

I actually bumped into him on the street one day, shortly after I got the boot now that I think of it. Man, I was so depressed and hungry and he picked up on that right away. The first thing he asked me if I was alright, or if I needed anything. That's just the type of guy he was. So I told him. I laid out the whole dismal story to him right there on the sidewalk. Barry was very sympathetic toward my situation and he told me that I was more than welcome to come up to his place that night for something to eat if I wanted. Well I'll tell ya, that was an offer I couldn't refuse. I accepted his invitation with smiles as he scribbled down his address. It felt so great to have seen him again, you know. Aside from the fact that he had offered me the promise of food, I also found the idea of talking to someone who was totally neutral an equally appetizing draw.

Barry lived in a middle-class neighborhood up on the northwest side of the city that was home to many a young family who had bought up the dreary old turn-of- the- century houses and renovated them back to their original splendor. It was a friendly little suburb, pleasantly overrun with lots of little kids and dogs, which could be easily seen at any given time of the day. When I pulled into his driveway later that evening, we exchanged a quick flurry of hellos, then went directly into the living room and began to talk. It was such a great relief to get everything I had been through recently the hell off my chest, and after I had finally finished spilling my guts, I respectfully diverted the spotlight away from my own personal dilemmas and constructed my conversation more towards what was happening in his life.

I asked him first, if he was still involved with the Young Frontiers Club at all. He told me that he had just resigned from the organization the previous summer, about a year or so after me and the gang had stopped going. He said he had left the club because he needed to put his nose to the grindstone and concentrate on a very important career decision he had made.
"What kind of business plan are you working on now McDool?" I teased. "Are you gonna mass produce a life -sized version of your pecker or something"?
Barry puked out a big laugh to mimic mine and we both proceeded to lean back in our seats and howl on like a couple of drunken apes.

"Hey smart ass!" he said after a minute. "You hungry?"

I could tell Barry had picked up on the fact that I probably hadn't eaten much in the last few days and I was do for a good feed.

"Damn straight I'm hungry," I yelped. "I'm always hungry, you know that?"

At the end of my confession I quickly donned a rogue smile in an attempt to make light of my obviously bleak situation. I didn't want to kill the jovial mood we had just built.

"I got just the thing," he grinned as he sprang up out of his chair and disappeared into the kitchen.
About five minutes later he came back out of the nearby room carrying one of those huge-ass protein milkshake thingys and plopped it down on the coffee table in front of me. I couldn't get over the sheer size of the frothy concoction and he made sure I drank every last bit of it too!

"You're wasting away Genie my friend. You gotta get some nourishment into you," he scolded as he shook his head and tipped the glass up toward my chin.

Now the shake itself actually tasted a lot like dog shit, but I didn't want to say anything that might damage his pride. After all, I was starving to death and the shake was supposedly healthy. I didn't stay too much longer after that, I don't think. I'm afraid I had too much on my brain to want to really socialize. To tell you the truth, that whole first week was a write-off. I had a lot to accept. I had a lot to let go.

Jesus Eugene! That was a long way back there man... what are you doing digging up all those old bones for anyway, you dumb shit!

My internal scoldings were a little harsh, but for the most part true. It was important that I concentrate on the present these days due to the particular way of life I had chosen. Dabbling in that days-gone-by shit only leads to more questions and I knew that I'd been down that dead end street too many times already as it was. Letting out a deliberate sigh, I forced my head out from its stare and twisted my field of vision out in the direction of my side window. It was an effective maneuver, but as I did this, I suddenly caught the reflection of my face transferring out from the tinted window of a passing sedan.

Well, one thing is for sure, you definitely didn't end up turning out like Barry at all, did ya?

A long-haired 126 pound metal freak is a far cry from the ripple-chested model -type that he was. Man, I'll never get over the amount of women that would whistle at that guy in one day! It was almost annoying!
Christ! What am I yapping about? Annoying? Hell I'd give my right nut to get a whistle from a pretty lady!
But let's face it Eugene old chap, no female in her right mind is ever going to hook up with a shiftless loser like you OK, so give it up. It's a lost cause man, a lost cause!

My brain justifies the wisdom, but my heart stares straight ahead and does not acknowledge its arrogant counterpart, for it knows deep down that I am lonely. It knows that I secretly yearn to fill the dark void that exists within its walls. You see, one's heart, I've come to realize, will put up with a lot of abuse. But when all is said and done, it will never accept defeat. And I will admit that lately, there is not a day that goes by where my thoughts do not end up drifting off to that place in the sky that I both fear and long for in the same breath. I've never been in love with a woman. To tell you the truth, I've never had more than the sum of five bloody dates the span of my whole entire life!

Now the fact that I have to make up a totally fictional existence to everyone I meet doesn't help, but the simple truth of the matter comes down to the fact too, that I am not handsome, or muscular. Nope, it's true and I'm alright with that statement. I am what I am and that's my reality. Once though, a girl did say that I had nice eyes at this house party I went to with Steve, but I guess after eight shots of tequila, every-body has nice eyes right? Other than that, nobody has ever really given me a second look. And girls are attracted to guys with good looks, I know this. First impressions are everything these days. That's just the way it is.

I tip my head towards the floor as a multitude of excuses continue to dribble out from my mouth and my conscience presses on with its debate. But then without warning, I feel my heart suddenly take advantage of my minds pre-occupied state, and cleverly sneak away from its own trial. I secretly watch it drift up and hitch a ride on a passing cloud, smiling proudly as it floats away unnoticed to a certain plain that lately, it had been visiting often.

It then shows me a place, a fantasy, where I am walking towards a beautiful woman. She is waving to me as she lies on a nearby blanket in a field. When I reach her, I sit close and we start to talk. My mirage plays itself out for a few more moments, but then is rudely extinguished as my ever-present alter ego catches wind of my softer side's latest out-of-body treachery. It then disciplines me by purposely injecting the memory of a terrible scene into the framework of that little daydream that took place in my life not even four nights earlier. It wasn't even my fault either, that thing that happened. It wasn't my fault at all!

I was just walking down the street minding my own business when I accidentally passed by this restaurant. You know, one of those fancy dancy ones with the big windows all around it. So I'm just walking by right, I mean I didn't intend for anything to happen. I really didn't! I was just walking by.
But then I guess I stopped.
Ya, ya, I did stop. I couldn't help it.
Something forced my feet to slow. Something made me.

It was the outline of a young couple having dinner at a small table that was tucked away in the corner against the glass. But it wasn't their primped-up faces or their fancy attire that caught my focus as I attempted to hurry by. No, no, it was their hands that captured me. That's what it was. And more to the point, it was really just her hand, and the way it looked as it lay in his. I confess, I did become fixated on this sight, the picture of her palm resting in his so innocently. I'm telling you, I just couldn't shake that vision off no matter how hard I tried. Then all of the sudden, everything else around me seemed to fade away and all I could see was the imprint of her palm.

I know I shouldn't have stopped. I should have just kept moving, but the pressure on my soul was just too strong. I tried to break off my stare, but all my attempts were in vain, and my feet just seemed to become heavier and heavier as the seconds dragged on. It was as if my legs were boycotting the motion to engage until I realized... until I saw what my heart was trying to show me. It was then that I felt something way down inside me open it's eyes.

My mental caucus quickly screamed out in protest, issuing warning after warning for my body to turn away.
"Move Eugene you stupid fuck!! Move," it screamed! The harsh deterrents blared on but I'm afraid its persuasions were not to be and my stubborn limbs held their ground. All I could do then is just stand there in an autonomic state of paralysis as

the internal war raged on inside me for I really had no say in my actions anymore. Just the simple portrait of their embrace on that table was consuming my every thought.

And I remember thinking at that moment, that I'd have absolutely given my very life right then and there to have the feeling of a woman's hand laying inside mine. A woman who truly loved me and accepted me for all I was, and all I was not.

To be that guy for just one second. God! Just one bloody second out of my life to feel that sensation, to feel that power, that's all I wanted. Just one second.

I continued to hover in front of that window unfazed, happily sedated and at peace as I watched their every move and stole their every emotion. And as I slept there, I could not help but wonder if I would ever honestly get the chance to experience the beauty of life under that spell - if I would ever get to feel that strong of a connection with anyone. The window of time outside the restaurant seemed to take hours, but in reality, lasted less than a minute.

"Get the hell out of here, you freak!"

It was the next thing I remember hearing. The dapper man's words were barely audible through the thick glass, but the connotations projected in his swollen fists were coming in loud and clear. My feet then, and only then, did finally shift their gait away from their concrete strongholds and stumble away. And before I knew it, the chance interlude I had so selfishly taken from the unknown couple was over. I scurried away from the place with my head down, and with a painful sigh, felt the wonderful feeling I had resurrected inside of me, slowly close its eyes.

Wasn't my fault I'm telling you. I didn't even mean to stop, I didn't mean to do anyth...

"Hey Asshole! You can't park here!"
"YOU CAN'T PARK HERE!!!"

My random hallucination was ended abruptly by the stern command of a parking lot security guard whom I failed to spot when I drove in.

"This ain't a rest stop here," the wannabe cop grunted as he rapped hard on my side window and motioned me back towards the front entrance.

In a nanosecond my engine was fired up and my gas pedal was deep-throating the floorboards.

"Suck Me," I hollered out as I cranked my steering wheel around and screeched away.

Now I was really pissed off, and I was also shit out of luck for a feed. Not a great combination in anybody's books, especially mine. I mean I wasn't a huge fan of frozen meatloaf by any accord, but that wasn't the point. The point was that I was very hungry and I desperately needed to get some bloody food into me pronto! I was starting to get shaky and my eyes too, were beginning to haze over from the low levels of sugar in my blood. I'd been through this sort of thing many times before so it's not like it was anything new.

Hell, there were times in my life when I've been so fucking hungry that I couldn't make out the line between fantasy and reality, so I knew it was very important not to push that envelope if I could at all help it. Life out here exists too close to that border as it is.

I'd like to tell you that I had an alternative plan at this point, but I'm afraid that supermarket, the one that was now quickly disappearing behind me, was the only ace in the hole I had going for me today. But as I drove off en route to nowhere, the little voice inside my skull spewed out a nightmarish phrase and I knew I had no choice but to heed its idea. So I merged out onto the main drag and fast tracked my car in the direction of the downtown core. I hated myself for doing what I was about to do, but I knew it was my only option. I would have to head down to the soup kitchen today and hope to God that they were open.

I had basically no money to speak of, even though I did get lucky the day before and stumble upon a whole whack of beer bottles in an alleyway of my usual route. It was an awesome haul, but my poor car was running on nothing more than fumes so I had no other alternative but to put the main chunk of my windfall towards gas. Hoping for a miracle on the tail feathers of my last thought, I nervously thrust my hand into my jeans pocket and fished around for a much needed surprise, but all my fingers came up with was the density of a lone quarter that was surrounded by lint. With the intensity of watching paint dry, I pulled out the thin coin at a stop light and stared down at it in disbelief.

"Them's the breaks," I muttered in a huff. I guess it's more important for people like me to stay mobile, than fat. I kept true to my course alongside the river until I pulled off into a medium-sized parking lot. I locked my wreck up tight and began making my way across the giant steel bridge that lead towards the center of the city.

You can't take your vehicle down there, no way! That's just plain crazy! It will get stripped to the bone inside of a half an hour. You'll come back to virtually nothing more than a bare frame and a thank you note. It's true man! The deep sub-cores of the inner city are brutal. I only frequent that part of town if I absolutely have to, like today. It's just too horrible of a scene. You can almost hold the bitterness in your hands. It's thick like tar and it invades your body like a disease.

Drugs are the main industry for most of the core creatures, surprise, surprise, and whenever you have drugs, you also have a lot of fighting and death. They go hand in hand and they always will. A lot of people go missing down there too, and no-one ever seems to have witnessed anything. It's hard to digest sometimes, that level of insanity, but I think it's because the people that exist in that realm are just so bloody strung out all the time that they can't acknowledge the idea of being straight anymore? I don't know, it's really disturbing though. It's like a roadside carnival show that you can't find the way out of, but whatever the case is, it always puts me on edge.

I walk onward with my guts growling away and after about twenty-five minutes of watching my feet shuffle on below me, I am finally at the corner that sits adjacent from the soup kitchen. But it seems that my luck today has just gotten a little worse for I see that the place is locked up tighter than a drum!

"Shit... Shit... Shit!

"This is not good Eugene," I mumbled. "Now you are definitely screwed!"
My stomach suddenly lets out a loud bark and pleads with me to investigate the situation further, so out of sheer spite, I cross the street only to look up in disgust at the carelessly tacked note that is fluttering in the breeze on the non-profit eateries door.
"Closed till Tuesday."
I become lost for a moment as I review my dwindling arsenal of options. I know there is a food mart close to here, but it is quite small and I am not sure if they even give out samples of food like the big chains do.
I ponder the idea for a few minutes and come up with the same conclusion. It was at least worth a try, so with my head pointing south once again, I turn my body away from the impotent door and begin making my way back through the crowded streets, my eyes now fixated on the regimented lines in the sidewalk as I push my way through the endless river of bodies.

Then, without provocation, I am overrun with the dismal realization that even amongst all these people, I am still nothing more than a ghost. This nagging truth stays with me, and refuses to soften its blow, so I spot an upcoming bench that no-one has claimed and I take a seat. I need to sit. I've had a rough 24 hours and hobbling around this city starving to death is not helping matters much.
Now I wasn't even planted on that log for two minutes when an older lady, prob-ably in her seventies, with a small boy who I assumed was her grandson, came out of a neighborhood convenience store in front of me carrying a half full paper bag. Before I could even so much as blink, the bottom of the bag she was carrying suddenly ripped open and spilled it's contents onto the ground for all to see. I got up immediately and walked over to her. I was just acting on instinct and without a second thought, I knelt down beside her and picked up a stray can of tobacco that was rolling down the sidewalk.
I felt the smallest twinge of accomplishment fall over me because for the first time in a long while, I actually felt useful.

"Here you go ma'am," I smiled. "Wouldn't want that to get away on you now."

But my kindness it appeared was not acknowledged or returned with the same feeling.

"Get away from me you smelly derelict," spat the old lady. Then, with two boney fingers, she carefully plucked the can out from my grip and tucked it underneath her arm, being careful of course, not to touch the parts of the tin that I had.

"Gramma," the little boy said as he pointed his finger at a stain on my jeans. "Why are his clothes so dirty?' "And why does his face look so funny?" was the tot's next query as he stared back up at his guardian in search of an answer. But the squinting child's questions were cut short by the senior's witch-like voice.

"Come on little one it's time to go. Right now!" growled the lady. And with that comment, she quickly scooped up the rest of her groceries and whisked the child away.

The old hag's words were cruel and biting, but it was actually the young boy's innocent curiosities that were really having the greatest impact on me. I knew my clothes were dirty. I also knew that my face wasn't that alluring of a site either. Even though my one eye had broke open to the point were I could almost see out of it again, my face was still generally puffed up and discolored from the vicious fight I had engaged in the night before. I didn't know what to think. I didn't know what to do. My world went black. And to make matters worse, I now felt the glare of a thousand eyes turning toward me. It was like the whole entire city had heard the old woman's damnation and was now waiting for my reply.

But sadly, I had none to offer. The only reprise I could put forth was that of silence. I was embarrassed and ashamed of who I was.
Of what I was.
It was the first time in my career that I actually felt helpless, and the fact that I was just standing there mute didn't help either. A rash of denial held my senses at bay and it wasn't until someone in the crowd yelled out "Loser", was I able to break free from my public stoning.
Now I was mad! In a rush of anger I began pushing my way back through the vast crop of devils that lined the sidewalks. I needed to put as much distance between me and that fucking scene as I could. I shoved people aside at will, bullying my way through the crowds with bitter intent.

Go ahead. Someone just say something to me. Anything! Just say one fucking word to me boy, I fucking dare them! I'll kick their asses so bad they won't know what hit them!

By the time I had reached the food store, my anger had subsided and I barged down the aisles with a menacing stomp. My eyes were blood- red and my hands were locked in a fist. I searched and searched through the cramped store, almost running down the isles towards the end, but there was nothing. Not a fucking thing! No sample lady, no free testers. No nothing! I felt my walk begin to slow as I crested the last corner that held promise. I tried to keep up the aggressive charade I recently created, but I was exhausted.
My mind and my body were badly weakened from a prolonged lack of nourishment and my vision suddenly became uneven and scattered because of this. So I stopped in the middle of the aisle and took in a long deep breath. Once I had regained my composure, I respectively held my head at half mast and began to walk slowly through the aisles once again, this time in search of a meal that fit my budget, instead of the fantasy that exceeded it.

As I neared the bakery section, I noticed a bright yellow advertisement flyer dangling from the roof.
"SALE"... "Dinner rolls", $2.49 per dozen read the sign. With great caution, I reached down into my pants pocket and pulled out my lone quarter. My mind quickly began to do the math on the equation above.

OK...$2.49 divided by 12, is... um? 2, carry the 1, is 20, is??? Hmm. OK Ya. Ya

Eugene, it will be about 22 cents or so. It's do-able. It's do-able! You should have enough for one bun for sure.

I felt my stomach roar in anticipation as I plucked the biggest fattest one I could see out of the pile and stuffed it into an awaiting bag. Feeling somewhat better, I obediently took my place in the express aisle.

There was quite a lineup ahead of me, but I bit my lip and held my spot with patience.

I could feel people all around me begin to stare at the wounds on my battered face but I didn't really care all too much. I was too fucking hungry.

They can stare all they want. Just as long as I get my food, nobody will get hurt.

All of the sudden, a young punk and his even younger girlfriend pushed their way in behind me and began nattering on to each other about some concert they were planning to see later on that night.

I listened half heartedly to their adolescent ramblings for what seemed to be eternity until finally, finally, it was my turn to pay. With a quivering hand, I set the pastry on the counter and forced out a tiny smile. The checkout girl was around my age and very attractive but I didn't give her so much as a second look. I kept my head low and shaded. I knew how bad I looked and I didn't need any more reminders to that.

"That will be thirty-five cents please," the checkout girl said.

"Huh hu... How much is that again?" I asked in a nervous tone.

"The total is thirty-five cents," she repeated.

"Ahh... Um, aren't these on special?" I said quietly, trying hard not to draw any unnecessary attention to my situation.

"Those were on special yesterday," she explained. " But now they have gone back up to their regular price which is thirty-five cents."

Oh shit. Now I was really in a fuck!

The tension was starting to build up all around me now but I didn't have a clue what to do next. I knew I only had the one quarter to my name, but I also knew that I desperately needed the sugar that lay in that piece of bread too. The next few seconds ticked away painfully. I began to hear the dull murmurs of contempt echo out from all around me as I stood there drowning in shame. I shoved my hands into my pants pocket and pretended to look for some more money that I knew I didn't have just to buy me a little time, but my stall tactic was cut short by the interjection of a command.

"Come on buddy," lashed out a voice from somewhere in the lineup.

I felt the sweat on my hands begin to thicken as I gazed over desperately at the empty penny dish. Once again, the biting voice of the checkout girl smashed through my numb senses.

"I'm sorry sir, but I need ten more cents or I'm afraid that I'll have to take the next person in line".

Her tone was so cold, so arrogant. My face grew hotter and hotter and throbbed openly of embarrassment with each long second that dragged by. Suddenly a lone dime bounced loudly onto the counter from somewhere behind me.

"There you go Rocky! Now maybe I'll be able to get to my concert sometime this year!"

The teenager's voice reeked of sarcasm as it exploded into my back, and it was followed up closely with a smug laugh. I looked up carefully at the checkout girl. She too was holding back a grin. I clenched my fists up in a tight ball, but the emotion that came forth was not that of anger and carnage that I had so confidently boasted of earlier. My retaliation crept forward instead, in the form of disgrace. My eyes unloaded their weapons too and focused themselves back onto the floor as I slid the bun off the counter and moped away.
A cold blanket of devastation surrounded me as I watched my feet slowly make their way out of the building.

I watched them for a long time, my feet, as I stumbled on like a drunkard back through the overcrowded streets towards my car. I barely looked up once for the first few blocks, but as I left a crosswalk and made my way up onto the corner of yet another congested street, I was suddenly accosted by a stern proposition.

"Pray for forgiveness," a man's voice bellowed.

I glanced up from my slumber and saw a street preacher standing atop a small wooden box, lustfully delivering his theatrical sermon across the crowd.

"Pray for forgiveness and all of your sins will be wiped clean," he hollered out into the mist.

His words rang about loudly and begged for recognition, but it was only his breath that reeked of whiskey and nicotine that drew any real attention.

"You son... Yes, Yes! I'm talking to you," he said as he pointed his long boney finger in my direction.
"Pray for forgiveness my friend," he warned. "Pray with me now!"

The preacher's words fell to the ground in front of me and scattered like mice.

"Pray for forgiveness you say. Huh..." I muttered up to him.

But no more dialogue did he offer. I dropped my head and walked away. I don't remember how long it took me to get back to my car. Don't remember one single step of the whole trip after the reverend's jab to tell you the truth. I only remember putting the key in the door, and sliding down into the driver's seat. Didn't budge an inch after that. I just sat there for a long time, squeezing that fucking bun in my fist as hard as I could as I stared blankly out the windshield. It was 5:36pm by the time I finally looked down at my wristwatch. In a flash of anger, I viciously tore the bun in half and cast it to the floor, even though my stomach was still howling away wildly. I couldn't help but to destroy that thing. Just the mere site of it was making me crazy. Engulfed in confusion, I rammed my keys into the ignition and prepared to start my rig, but just as I was about to crank it over, I heard a woman's voice vibrate out from the rear of my vehicle.

"Hey baby, I'm over here," her sweet voice cooed.

Is she talking to me?

Suddenly, my eyes became instantly wide and keen. I spun around in a flutter and caught the silhouette of a slender lady in a long dress walking steadily towards my car.

Could it be someone who knows me?

My mind began to rev up on the tailwind of a vague thought. Maybe she has seen me around and wants to talk or something. A new sense of zeal rushed across my skin and caused my esteem to begin to soar.

With a subtle pivot, I ran my fingers through my scraggly hair and flashed the glass in my rear view a quick smile. It wasn't my best look, but it would have to do.

And with that, I reached eagerly for the door handle and began mentally preparing myself for the meeting. God was I ever excited, but no sooner had I formed a grip on the old latch, when the outline of a small boy running towards me entered my vision. I heard the sound of a school bus begin to pull away in the near distance while I watched in dismay as the young lad held up his lunchbox and yelled out a standard phrase "Mommy!"

The figure from behind me suddenly passed by my door and embraced her son in front of my vehicle.

My hand became limp and fell away from the handle as my neck gave out and I accepted another defeat.

It was just another fantasy, just another daydream.

Once again my world fell grey and a thousand visions of my shattered home life began to torture my every thought. I guess it's true when people say that sooner or later, we all eventually find our way back to the true root of our demons. And I knew it was at that exact moment when I too, found my Hell and carelessly watched the door close behind me. I watched in agony as the toddler leapt into his mother's arms and showered her with affection. The lady then turned and started walking back towards my car with the child clinging snugly to her neck and I could hear him rambling on excitedly as they strolled past my window. The young tot's words were high pitched and almost incomprehensible, but a single phrase did, however, manage to escape the child's lips and drive a long, sharp stake through my soul.

"I love you," he said innocently.

An unprecedented feeling of sorrow began to infect every part of me. The lump in my chest became absolute. In a desperate quest for honor, I gathered up what was left of my strength, and conducted one last search for so much as even a trace of hope in my heart, but I found nothing. No matter how hard I tried, I was unable to account for the presence of one single memory. After a long pause, I raised my head back up and I looked out through my windshield only to discover that it had become glossed over and was running with liquid. I glanced over to the west expecting to see the swollen rain clouds beginning their decent on the city, but the sky was clear, and the sun was shining bright on the horizon.

I was confused by this. Where is the rain coming from, I wondered. But as I tipped my head downward and saw the water from my eyes begin to streak across the length of my forearm, I did then come to the solemn realization that this storm, was from within.

No-one wakes up one day and says, "Today I'm going to commit suicide." No. No, that's not the way it happens. You see, that's the catch with suicide. Everyone's thought about it, sure. That's normal and not dangerous. But it's actually when that precise moment in time rolls around where a person begins to truly understand its purpose. It's when you look at it from a totally logical point of view, like a madman, justifying a horrific act with reason and science. It happens when that person passes through a certain boundary in his or her mind where most others would have stopped and dared not venture any further. It's an imaginary line in the sand that one day they deliberately step over, blatantly ignoring even their own warnings. And it is at that precise moment that their whole life, their very existence from then on in, would be decided now, solely by fate. I do remember getting out of my car, but that's it. I don't recall going anywhere specific at the time, but then before I knew it, there I was, peering down stone-faced over the heavy iron railing smack dab in the middle of the giant bridge that led back in the direction of the city's core. I was just hovering there in a daze, staring down numbly into the water below.

I knew right there that I had officially past the point of no return.

Then something overtook me. It was a euphoric sedation of some sort and suddenly, everything around me became tranquilized and surreal. The great city before me fell deathly quiet and still, like it was holding its breath, like it was waiting. The frenzied whine of the speeding motorcars had disappeared. Just like that, gone! And there were no people on the streets or sidewalks anymore either. No horns honking, no bells ringing... there was just nothing. Nothing at all.

The world had gone to sleep and the only sound that was present now was the smooth churning of the massive river below as it faithfully carried it's weight downstream. That's it. That's all there was. It was as if Father Time had stopped dead in his tracks and looked back to see what was the matter. My mind was devoid of all thought, and my guardian angel lay bloodied and dead at my feet. I watched my troubled spirit suddenly rise up and leave my body.

I was ready.

I began to hear the dense rhythm of the water begin to call out and offer me its peace.

It's time Eugene, it's time to free yourself. It will all be over in a matter of seconds my friend, and then all your pain will be gone.

The harmonic prayer flowed through my senses with ease as I stood there and allowed it to erase my conscience.

The peace and love you long for is only a motion away Eugene; it's yours for the taking, right here, right now my friend. Do this now and all your suffering will end. It will all end.

That was it. I had heard all that I needed to hear, so with a deep and final breath, I gripped the edge of the cold steel railing and watched my foot raise up and rest itself sideways atop the horizontal mesh grate.
Slowly but steadily, I inched my torso upward to match my foot and straddled the narrow fence that would deliver me to the other side. In a final sacrifice, I turned my face towards the water. Now I could really feel the pull of the great river. I could taste it's salvation as the waves slapped up against the sides of the structure's huge cement pillars.

That's it Eugene, just one more push. One more inch and it will all be over.

Then, with my eyes closed tight, I tensed up my muscles and prepared myself for the final act.
But just as I was about to heave my spent frame away from the safety of the railing, I was suddenly hit with a sensation from my past that I had all but forgotten. It was a blast of warm air that had mysteriously brushed through the trees on the other side of the gully and deliberately rushed that bounty up towards my nostrils. In an instant my lungs became inflated with the sweet smell of maple and pine. I guess fate had finally sat forward and threw down her lone card. In the span of a heartbeat, my thoughts became vividly overrun with pictures of sunny days and beautiful mountains including visions of campfires and sunsets, full moons and wheat fields. They all barged their way into my head. Seems that it was Mother Nature who decided to come to my rescue. But the dramatic change in the life or death tide did not come without its repercussions. The strange and uncanny voice from the water became furious and began to scream mutiny as it struggled desperately to drive back the soothing apparitions that were flooding into my brain.
But the more the entity tried to hold me to my contract, the more and more the picturesque scenes kept coming forth, bullying the rogue intruder away. The seed finally took root and I began remembering all the times nature had shined her light on me, all the moments she had run her unbiased hand across my shirt and through my hair. So many memories, so many times she went to bat for me with no money down and this latest sacrifice was no exception.

I felt my cold eyes soften and saw my spirit suddenly halt its exodus and glance

54

back over its shoulder.

No Eugene! No! You cannot do this. You must fulfill the contract! You must jump. We had a fucking deal! YOU MUST JUMP NOW!

The damning accusations ricocheted around inside my skull as the netherworld entrepreneur pleaded frantically with me to alter my decision, offering my soul absolutely anything in a last ditch attempt at victory. But the devil, I'm afraid today, was about to be denied. And with a trembling mind, I slowly reversed the precarious balance of my situation and let my body slide back down the railing, resting it eventually on the safety of the bridge. Bit by bit the loose framework of self-destruction I had erected began to crumble away and disintegrate right before my eyes, along too, with the voice that controlled it.

The river's deceptive smile changed hands and twisted its current into a snarl. The white caps of the waters' rapids now glared up at me like jagged fangs as the battle for my soul raged on.

The river became more rampant with each second that passed; enraged no doubt, that it had just been cheated of its prize. Slowly but surely the false utopia I was willing to pay so much for, began to fade off into oblivion. And recognizing that opportunity, the scattered ramblings of the corrupt city wasted no time in rushing back to wreak their havoc on my eardrums once more. However this time around, they came through ten times louder. It felt like the cars were whizzing by me at a thousand miles an hour. And the sidewalks were jammed solid with people again, not empty anymore. Nope, no way! And all of them talking, talking, talking... screaming at each other as they scurried by, uncaring, unfazed.

My hands finally went limp and released their deadly grip from the thick railing and I suddenly found myself back in the real world. There I was, standing once again, amongst a billion people, faceless and alone. Just another ant on the pile, another speck of sand thrown down somewhere on the beach.

When I found enough courage to step away from the railing, I was hit with a whirlwind of emotions that had been waiting patiently in the shadows to punish me. My face began to squint and distort, and my knees followed suit by buckling out from underneath me, sending the top half of my spent frame toppling backwards. This domino effect slammed my back into a cement partition and sent my body to the ground.

Suddenly the whole world stopped what it was doing and looked over at me.

I buried my face inside my hands in an attempt to hide away my disease, but I was too late and they all saw.

All the deceptions and the betrayals. All the lies I had so cleverly avoided for the last five years had finally caught up with and cornered me on that bridge. I had nowhere left to run, nowhere left to hide. So I just sat there curled up in a cramped hobbit of the structure, spellbound and defeated as I rocked back and forth and allowed the poison to seep into my every pore. My eyes remained dry and fixed as I surrendered over my dreams in a stoic trance to all who bore arms against me.

How long I sat there I'll never know, But eventually I did peer out from between my trembling hands and with a dead stare still on my face, I swallowed in my last breath of freedom, then sent it away. My heart housed no further emotion. There was just nothing left in me. My body was lifeless and cold, and the mean blanket of the city bragged forth another victory as it conjured up a strong wind to overthrow the warm one.

The brisk gale deliberately slapped a chill across my face and it was at that moment that I came to an ultimate realization. It was clear to me now that the guilt I would forever house inside me was simply unwilling to die.

Unconvinced to forget.

This latest violation confirmed that. It was apparent to me now, that I had no choice left but to negotiate a plea bargain with my conscience in the name of mortality. I knew it would not allow my feet to budge until it had an assurance that I would never find my way to this act again. I had to strike a deal.

I had to show the powers that be that I was willing to accept a compromise. There was no way around it anymore. Not surprisingly the penalty for my trespasses materialized quickly inside the walls of my mind and I understood completely the impact of the restitution I was about to bring forth. In the end my sentence was to consist of a mental trade off so-to-speak, a voluntary lobotomy designed to avert any and all further attempts of betrayal.

I had to build the crown a monument, boast its royalty and kneel to its flag. It was the only way. The jury laid down its hard-line conditions in the form of a single word. And as I stumbled like a drunkard off the bridge that day, I didn't waste any time in fulfilling my end of the bargain. I immediately slid down the steep embankment off to the side of the structure and sat down by the river's edge on a large rock while the ominous metal arch of the bridge kept a watchful eye on me from above.

Without a second thought, I took out my old pocketknife and deliberately cut a deep trench into the palm of my hand. I immediately twisted my limb downward and let my blood drip steadily into the murky water of the turbulent gorge. This was the first verse of my restitution. It was a subliminal act of compliance in an effort to render the river satisfied. The pain was sharp and deserving and eventually, when the droplets began to slow, I took off my leather jacket and produced a small disposable lighter.

With my eye's locked in a dead blur, I heated up the end of the blade on my old knife until it glowed red with contempt and began to spell out the single phrase that I would forever bow to on the inseam of my coat. When I was finished I folded up my knife and gazed down at the fresh canvas I had just created in front of me. The letters were still smoldering like the gunshots they represented as I laid my jacket on the ground. I looked up towards the bridge and said the word I had just singed into the material of my bomber for the entire world to hear and know.

UNFORGIVEN.

I ran my fingers across the still curing statement that was now forever burnt into my soul. Letter by letter, I made sure the chains were tight and the locks were sound.

And as I left the river's edge that day with the knowledge that I would never again return, I accepted the fact that for the rest of my days I was to quietly serve out the conditions of my sentence and acknowledge that the ruling I was handed was just and deserved. Then, with my wounded hand in my pocket and my head set low, I slowly made my way up the sandy bank and back down towards the reeking core of the city, back down into the filth and desperation where I belonged.

My heart had been put to death and my feet felt heavy as they scraped their way along the pavement. My thoughts were blank and pointless, but I do remember thinking as I trudged on aimlessly, of how close together life and death really are, and of how I reached a point there on that bridge, where I actually did hover in the minute gap between this world and the next. I knew I had entered a place where so much as a whisper would have sent me to Hell. The line I stood on was so fleeting that I'm sure there had been others who had dared to venture that far, and who had been at that same place, but then decided at the very last moment not to continue on and to turn back instead, to the darkness of this world. But by that time the momentum had already become too strong in its descent and it was simply just too late, for time had broken its own rules and finalized the deal.

I shuffled forward with the aftertaste of this thought bleeding through my mind. Soon I neared a giant mass of skyscrapers and directed my feet towards them. As I did this my body passed by the large bay window of a department store and for some reason my feet began to slow. While I hovered there somewhat confused, I glanced over at my reflection that sat idling in the glass, but sadly, it did not look the same way anymore. It looked more like that of a stranger, the stranger that the old man in the station wagon had so desperately warned me of that day.

I drew my body in nearer to the window in a tranquilized state of shock until the tip of my nose was almost touching it. With sick precision, my eyes began to focus in on the deep lines of anguish that had etched themselves into my brow. I found it so strange that I had never noticed them there before. And my eyes? My eyes too were lifeless. There was no glow or spark to them whatsoever; a dull stare was all that was present. I stood there, hypnotized in front of that glass for a long time, consumed in disbelief by the harsh picture it painted. In a way, my life did end on that bridge, for it was there that my self-proclaimed innocence drew its last breath.

I struggled hard to free myself from the entrapment of that window. My feet did eventually retreat though, and as my stare reluctantly broke, I was officially released back into the custody of the street. And as I continued my downward trek, I did revisit one final memory. It was again, the brief video of the old man in the station wagon. The skeleton of a human being I saw that very first summer long in my past. And it occurred to me then that he was right. He was right to say, to scream, to yell to me to change my ways or pay the price. But I'm afraid his intuitions were all in vain.

He already knew my future.

He already knew I was dead.

The dreams began soon after that. I don't remember the day, but I do remember the night for I was blasted out of my slumber as soon as it was over. I shot up from underneath my covers like a bullet, my heart racing and my shirt soaked. The nightmare was graphic and scary and the thought of being all alone after that was the furthest thing from my mind. So I dove out of my car and started running, running towards light. Towards people.

I finally ended up at an all night coffee shop about ten blocks from where my car was hidden. I sat there perched motionless on a revolving stool clutching a small cup of black coffee like it was my last.

My face remained pale and damp and after a lengthy internment, when I had gathered up enough ammunition and felt like I had gotten far enough away in my mind, I began to let the horrible minutes of the apparition slide cautiously back into my view so that I could study them. So that I could analyze and attempt to shed some degree of reason on the events under the safety of light and consciousness. The nightmare was vague in its message, but furious in its context. The dream was scattered with minced bits of a message, a storyline. But what?

It started out with the sound of trees moving in the wind. Then it shifted immediately to the echoes of a small child's cries coming out from behind a dark oil-stained closet door that sat at the end of a long hallway. The film continues forth as my hand reaches forward and pulls open the door, exposing a sobbing child.

A little boy?

He is sitting cross-legged on the floor of the cluttered enclosure. I ask him if he is okay, and as I say this he tilts his head up towards me, but I cannot see his face for he is wearing a thin plastic mask that is shaped like that of a clown. In his hand too, which is covered in dirt, he is feverishly clutching an odd looking wax figurine that appears to be in the shape of an "I". The letter looks smooth on one side, but jagged on the other. Then his tiny blue eyes meet mine from beneath his mask through the hollow spheres of the brightly painted caricature.

"Are you gonna kill me?" he asks quietly.

With deep compassion I immediately say back, "No, of course not little fella. I would never do that!"

Feeling now that I have possibly gained a little of his trust, I reach down cautiously to remove his mask and expose his face so that I may try to comfort him further. I am confident in my plan as I watch my fingers lightly grasp the oversize red nose on the mask, but then, just as I am about to remove the costume, I notice a small grain-like object fall out from the bottom of it. I think nothing of this at the time and continue pulling off the facade.

Suddenly I spring up in horror as a large clump of maggots spill out the chin from inside the sheath. And as the happily painted mask falls to the floor, I see now the grotesque and decomposed outline of what was once a human face. The shock of this sight hurls me backwards and I find it hard to breathe. I feel my body fighting to keep upright but it is growing more and more weak from its lack of oxygen. I try with all my power to inflate my lungs but it is as if someone is standing on my chest. Then I feel the presence of something in my hand. An object of some sort? I look down and I see that I am holding in my palm, a strange looking trinket. It is small and shaped in the form of an oval. It is hollow with acute points on each end. It appears to be finely-crafted, this thing, and it is covered with a translucent type of stain that is still wet to the touch.

And then it was over.

Almost as quickly as it had begun it was over and I found myself running here, to this place. And now I sit in silence, frozen to my seat as my brain attempts to trap and destroy the many frightful images this nightmare has unleashed on me.

"Hey buddy," a voice suddenly rang out from beside me.

Without warning my trance was prematurely shattered by a mysterious salutation. When I looked over in the direction of the sound, I saw a robust man in a loud sweat suit; he was obviously looking for some conversation. He is overly jovial and has proceeded to sit his big ass down right beside me.

"What's the matter?" he snorted. "Looks like you just seen a ghost."

The rock star then slapped my back and began to giggle on foolishly. I looked straight ahead and did not respond to his misplaced humor in hopes that he would get the hint and go away. And even though the man was probably harmless, I knew in the back of my mind he wasn't wrong. The terrible visions I had endured a short time earlier, I worried, were far from over. This "ghost" was not finished with me yet. It would return.
It would find me again.

In a defensive stumble, I stood up and moved over to another table. One that was set back more in the corner of the place. I'm afraid I wasn't in the mood for socializing.
My coffee was stone cold by now and I hadn't even tasted so much as a drop of it. This didn't bother me too much though, for I knew that the drink was merely acting as a safety rope, an eight ounce anchor that kept me safe and grounded to this world.
Just for the fun of it though, I brought the cup up to my lips and took a little swig. Yecchh! This shit tastes bad enough when it's hot, never mind cold! Feeling a tad ill now, I set the cup back on the table and pushed it aside. Just then, the bells on the entrance door started to dance and my eyes glanced habitually over my shoulder just in time to see the outline of two cops walking into the place.

I'd seen these two guys before, I was sure of it. This was their beat I think, but they never came in here?

Shit. What if they're looking for me? What if someone identified me from the farmhouse or something?

"Christ," I whispered under my breath. "I don't need this shit tonight."

With the speed of an explosion, I dropped my head down towards the table and pretended to read the inscriptions on the weathered cup. I also turned my head to the side slightly to try and shade over my face a little. The wounds to my face had healed up a bit since the fight, but I still boasted an incriminating shiner on my left eye. My heart rate began to speed up and my forehead became increasingly saturated with guilt as the seconds pounded on.

"Just be calm Eugene, just sit tight and ride this thing out. They'll be gone in a few minutes.

I sat there like a corpse, staring down at my stale cup of Joe, holding my breath and waiting nervously for the redeeming sound of the bells reconnecting with the metal door. But my luck, unfortunately, went cold with my coffee.

"Well well! Would you look at the sorry sack of humanity we got here," a man's voice rumbled.

I gazed up from my stronghold and was treated to the snapshot of a short hairless cop in a way-too-tight blue uniform hovering above me.

"Whoa! Looks like we got us a little scrapper on our hands," he scoffed as he stared down at my eye.
"Maybe I oughtta call your name into the station, huh? See if you've been a bad little boy. What do you say to that pal?"

The pint-sized constable reached over to his side and grabbed his radio to further sell his feeble assault.

"Got any ID?" he snapped.

I dropped my head back down to the table and shook it from side to side.

"Didn't think so," he snickered. "Let me guess," he went on to say, "of no fixed address I take it?"

The jaded badge then leaned over me and drew in a big exaggerated sniff.

"Phewwee," he grunted with a deep frown. "Jesus boy, you ever heard of a bar of soap?"

The cop's tone suddenly turned mean as he bent forward and grabbed my chin. "You wanna piece of me?" he snarled as he taunted me under his breath.

My eyes began to water in anger and my fists were clenched and white as he gripped my jaw harder and harder. And just when I thought I was going to lose my cool and nail that cocksucker, a large African man came up from behind the glorified security guard and dropped his enormous hand on the back of the bald man's spine.

I could see the dense muscles in his forearm swell up as he squeezed his partner's neck in a re-directing manner.

"Come on Levi," the big man said. "Let the boy be."

The attacking cop reluctantly loosened his grip on my chin and stood up. "Mr. Personality" barely came up to the brother's chest.

"He's just sitting there," the behemoth of a man said calmly. "Ain't no crime in that is there?"

The tiny officer twisted his neck and broke free from his partner's grip. He stared me down for a moment, but then turned around and walked away in a huff. I looked up at the decent man that had unselfishly come to my aid. The name on his uniform was simple and abbreviated. "T.J. Daniels."

"Thank you Officer Daniels," I said politely.

He did not speak, but he did brandish the smallest of smiles and followed up his courtesy with a nod before he too, turned and walked out the door. I pushed out a huge sigh of relief and let my body slump rag-doll style over the table. Well I'd had about enough of this place for one night, that was for sure, and as soon as I gained my composure a bit, I stood up and stepped back out into the night air. I took my sweet time getting back to my car. The atrocities of the nightmare were still quite fresh in my mind, and I was in no hurry to crawl back into that headspace. Even when I did reach my rig, I still hesitated a bit, but what could I do? It was home.
Within a couple of minutes I was hidden away once more underneath the camouflage of my old sleeping roll and preparing to close my eyes for the second time. I will admit I was afraid. I mean sure, it was only a dream, but the textbook phrase from my childhood was only somewhat comforting.
Something was wrong.
It was deeper than that. I felt it inside, a sense of heaviness, uncertainty.
But why?
Eventually I rolled over to my side and managed to close my eyes. And as the last picture in my mind fell victim to the rumble of the city, I fell back to sleep.

The next two weeks that followed went by slowly. The wounds on my face, it's true, had almost healed completely up. But inside, the deep gashes in my soul continued to fester and swell. The sharp edges of the phrase I had broiled into my coat tore into the back of my shoulders and acted as a constant and harsh reminder to the nature and the duration of my unspoken sentence. My world had turned black, and my heart lay in pieces for all to see.

My walk was no longer quick and directed, but instead was slow and clumsy. Thick whiskers had grown in on my face and my hair had become unbelievably greasy and matted from neglect. I could feel the filth invading my body, but I simply had no more energy left in me to care. On this particular day, I had parked my rig on the north side of the river like usual, and was making my way down to a dry goods distribution warehouse on the edge of the core's border. There was a big row of industrial dumpsters there at the far end of the property that always produced a good cache of pop bottles and I planned on taking full advantage of that scene.

It was the first week of August, a Sunday, and I knew that there would be no-one around the property to bust me. Not that I honestly gave a real fuck anymore. The last week I had been scavenging for empties in broad daylight and I no longer gave a shit who was gawking at me. I really didn't. The warehouse was a fair distance away, and as I shuffled my worn-out boots along the pavement, I came across a thin, scraggly vagrant who was sleeping inside a bus shelter. This type of thing was an ordinary occurrence down in these parts, but today as I walked by him, there was something different about his scenario. It was odd, but seeing him there now, didn't seem so horrible to me anymore. I wasn't disturbed or embarrassed at the sight of him at all. The setting actually seemed to me, almost familiar.

"This is how it begins," I whispered as I passed by. But sadly, I did not linger on that thought very long. I just continued slithering along the concrete en route to my destination. I walked finally, out past the last wave of pawn shops until I could start to see the outline of the buildings in the industrial section. When I arrived at the edge of the property, I crept along the rusty fence of the plant and slid up to the roughly-stacked row of dented-in puke green garbage bins. After a half-assed security guard check, I sauntered up to the first container and heaved myself skyward, balancing on the edge of the metal by my waist. Once I was steady, I took a deep breath and leaned down inside the putrid container and began poking at the montage of bright orange bags, listening carefully for the telltale sound of glass and aluminum rubbing together.

One bag, two bags, three. Damn... Nothing.

With a grunt, I reached back and grabbed onto the side of the metal container. In an awkward twist I pulled myself out and landed back down hard on the ground again. After a brief rest, I brushed off the filth and prepared for round two. Once again I gripped the side of the dumpster and flung my ass up inside, scanning across the rubble this time to see if there were any stragglers out in the open, but that search came up empty too.

"What the fuck?" I grunted. These bins are usually loaded. I was just about to abort the whole deal and move onto the next can, but then I spotted another garbage bag, a big one, over in the far corner. It looked promising, but it was way the hell in there. Morbidly driven, I stretched my body out as far as it would go, but I just couldn't reach it. I had no choice. I had to go in.

"Dammit anyway," I moaned as I braced one hand down into a slimy pile of goop and wiggled my way in. "Why can't this job be easier?"

I inched my body forward until it was extended all the way. By this time, the tops of my feet were resting on the very edge of the container, and my left hand was submerged deeply in a vat of toxic sludge. With a hint of hesitation, I shifted my mass around accordingly to keep my balance and readied myself for the plunge.

The stench of the trash burned a scar into my nostrils and made my stomach heave. "Come on Eugene," I scolded, "Get it over with!"

In a final grunt, I stretched out my right hand as far as it would go and caught the edge of the large sac.
As I yanked a piece of it towards me, I thought I heard something. Or did I? I wasn't really sure so I stopped for a minute and listened. Hmm, nothing now though.

"I wonder what that was." I mumbled to myself, "I hope it's not a..."
"Oh shit! Oh no. No... No! Please God! Please don't let it be a rat! Anything but a rat!! I hate rats!"

Semi- panicked but still wanting what was possibly in that oversized bag, I proceeded on with my grim task and heaved the bulky sac closer. Again, a strange noise echoed out from inside the dumpster. It was kind of like a squeak. No, no it was more like a hiss, a throaty growl of some sort. Well, now I was really getting creeped out. I damn near scrapped the whole plan, but I decided to give that synthetic payday in front of me one more chance. I had to, it sounded like it was a dandy!
So with one last grunt I successfully yanked the bag in question the rest of the way backwards and tucked it away underneath me.

"NYAGG!!" was all I remembered hearing.

I felt a terrified chill dart up the length of my spine and tickle my scalp.

"Sweet Jesus!" I blurted. This can't be real. No way! No fucking way!!!

At that point my whole body became frozen solid. I couldn't have budged a millimeter if my life depended on it, I was that freaked out. All I could do is blankly stare in absolute disbelief at the vision that now sat in plain view of me in that trash can. You know, as long as I live... As long as I feel the beat of my heart in my chest and the taste of the air in my lungs, I will never, never, forget the mental imprint of what I saw before me that day. For in that split second, as my head turned slightly and began to follow the direction of the noise, my eyes suddenly caught the corner of an old ratty white blanket that had been exposed by the recent upheaval of the bag that now sat beneath me. And as my pupils panned the length of that cloth, I quickly found myself staring deep into the eyes of my own kind. What lay in front of me was no a rat, or a raccoon, or anything like that at all.

It was a baby!

A tiny, tiny baby. It was rapped up carelessly within that material and I could see it's little legs and arms begin to gyrate as it lay there sprawled out amongst the rubble with only it's squished-up face peering out from the confines of the urine-stained blanket that loosely bound it. I knew right away that it was desperately trying to cry, I could tell by the pained look in it's eyes.

I'll tell you, for a brief moment there, I actually thought that I was just imagining it all, I really did.

I figured for sure this was... this just fucking had to be a daydream or something. I mean there was just no way this was possible! But as the tiny being snorted in a deep gob of new air into its lungs, it did officially make its S.O.S. known to me, and to the rest of the world for that matter, that it was indeed real, and it would indeed be heard.

"WAAAAAAA!!!!"

A long pissed off cry shot out from its mouth and echoed loudly off the walls of the metal cesspool. It was a sharp angry cry and I understood its point of view completely.

Saliva began to creep down its chin and little tears too, began to roll off its puffy cheeks as the baby started to scream on without pause.

Holy Fuck! You've just found a baby! A baby! Oh my God! OH MY GOD!

My brain shifted into high gear, and my heart followed suit.

"WAAAAAA!!" The infant's cries continued to ring out loudly as its vocal cords broke free from the pungent suffocation of the garbage. Without knowing, without thinking, I scooped up the small child and tucked it tight underneath my chest. I writhed backwards at the speed of light and sprang back out onto the ground. I glanced around quickly for any possible witnesses, but there was no one.

Good, ya. That's good.

I flung open my jacket and carefully wedged the baby into my chest. Then I started feverishly walking back to my car. I wasn't really sure what I was doing at that point, nothing was really getting through. My mind had switched itself off out of sheer terror and the expression on my face proved it. I watched my feet hammer away at the ground steadily as I snaked my way through the backstreets and alley-ways towards my ride. I was acting strictly on impulse, that was it. The baby was still wailing on loudly inside my jacket. I could feel its tiny chest against my shirt expanding and crying, expanding and crying. Crying very loudly. Hmm, wait a sec... crying loudly? Yes... yes that was a good thing. I remember hearing somewhere once that crying was a good sign.

My heart kept the beat with my footsteps as I hurried on. I reached into my jacket somewhere along the trip and with my right hand, began instinctively rubbing the baby's chest, in hopes of easing its fears and calming it down. I didn't want to alert anyone to the baby's presence. It was strange, but I felt like I had just stolen something; I don't know why. Nevertheless, I was fleeing like a criminal on the run. I knew that I was not a convict by any stretch, but I also knew that what I held concealed in my jacket was nothing short of absolute treasure. It was pure gold, and the last thing I wanted in the whole world right now was for someone else to see it and try to take it away.

I made it back to my firebird in record time, flinging open the passenger door like a spaz and setting the reeking child down on the seat inside. I peeled out of that parking lot like a stuntman and hit the juice.. Now I didn't have a clue where I was driving to at first. My actions were simply habitual. But after about ten minutes I did pull off the road into the parking lot of a neighborhood convenience store so that I could re-group my insanely scattered thoughts. I steered my rig into the farthest stall and killed the engine, scoping out the perimeter once again for any passers by. Confident with my safety check, I dropped my head to the seat and took in a long steady breath. Hell, I took a couple.

It felt like I hadn't inhaled once since I left the dumpster. But my escape from reality was viciously short lived for as soon as I pushed out that same gob of air, so did the baby. This time its cries were earth shattering. It had probably been howling on like that for the whole trip, but I don't think I noticed most likely due to the fact that I was in total fucking denial! The piercing scrape of the baby's shriek rebounded off the windows and hammered the shit out of my poor ears. And this time, by God, I heard every single note! My quivering hand instinctively shot over and planted itself right on the little one's chest again as I began mindlessly rubbing away at it in a desperate effort to cease it's unhappiness but it was no use.

"WAAAAAAA!"

Once more the baby's mind-splitting cries began ricocheting off the window and through my skull.
My stress level was beginning to peak! Not only had I just found an infant human being in a garbage can, but that being was now screaming away at the top of its lungs in my passenger's seat!

Someone's gonna hear it Eugene. Then, then buddy, you are screwed!

I knew my third-party intuitions were bang on. There was absolutely no way anybody in this world was going to believe that I actually found this baby. No way in Hell! They would automatically assume that I kidnapped it. That's what would happen. This latest realization kicked my paranoia level up into high gear and forced out a desperate plea from my throat.

"What's wrong little one?" I begged as I stretched my body over to the other side of the car. "Are you OK??? Please... Please, what should I do?"

But my heartfelt words did not phase the thing and it just kept hollering on like a crazy person. Scrambling for solutions, I took off my jacket and placed it overtop the child, like a pup tent, with the faint hope of diminishing the level of noise the infant was producing. I felt a bead of sweat trickle down the side of my cheek as I felt the parking lot get smaller and smaller. Now the reality of the situation I had fallen into was starting to set in.

I continued to rub its chest frantically, trying in vain to silence it, but it just would not cease its message.
I noticed too, during the mayhem, that its tattered coverings were starting to come loose as a result of my circular massages, so I gripped the sides of the saturated linen

and pulled it away from the baby's mottled skin. The shoddy material was soaked right through. Then it hit me!

This blanket is soaked Eugene! It must be freezing to death you dumb shithead. That's why it's crying man, it's cold!

Without further ado, I reached around into my backseat and grabbed a clean bath towel from my ruffled pile. In the span of a hiccup, I sent my coat to the floor and had the rancid piece of cloth that originally cocooned the child tossed aside and a clean towel spun around in its place. I did a quick snugness check and I must say, I was pretty proud of the job I did, I mean you know, for a first timer and all. I followed up my bright idea by cranking over the engine and flicking the heater onto high, directing all the vents toward the infant.

"There," I beamed, "that oughtta do it! Yessirree, no more crying anymore. Nope, nope!" Well, I was on top of my game now, and for about four seconds, I really was convinced that I had won.

"WAAAAA!" Without warning the baby again let out another bone-chilling squeal.

"Jesus," I groaned. "I don't know what you want little one. I don't know what you need. For God's sake, please tell me what you need!!!"

The infant refused my request and continued to pound out its unscripted vibe. The confusion of the situation was beginning to tear down my level of patience at an alarming rate. Suddenly my stomach growled up at me rudely from its usual lack of sustenance and another revelation fell over me. Food, ya... ya, it probably needs food man!!

"Christ Eugene!" I hollered. "Could you be any more stupid?"

I shook my head in anger at my lack of brainpower and in the same breath, jammed my hand into my pants pocket and fished out a pathetic stack of lint-covered coins.

"Be right back OK?" I told the bellowing child and without letting my car out of my sight, I hurried into the nearby store and came out not even a minute later with a small container of milk. I slid back into my car with the life-giving liquid and checked the locks behind me. The heat inside the cab was stifling by now, but I let it blare on anyway. I had no idea just how long that poor thing had been lying in that dumpster so I wasn't taking any chances. The baby was still crying of course, but I intended to fix that very soon. I was convinced that I had recognized the root of the problem. With inhuman speed, I ripped open the flaps on the small container and then stopped dead in my tracks for I felt something subconsciously tap me on the shoulder. It was the little man from the common sense department of my brain.

Oh Eugene. Just how do you think you are going to get the milk into it's mouth hmm? Considering the fact that you don't have a bottle!

"Shit!" I muttered. That's true. How am I going to get the milk into the thing's mouth?

66

"Breasts!" I hollered out suddenly. "I need breasts."

In an instant my mind became happily overrun with the glorious vision of a thousand plump-nippled breasts floating by me. It was a fantasy I had entertained many times before don't get me wrong, but this time, I was thinking about them in a totally new light. I ran through a few ideas in my head, but they all came up duds. I knew I was definitely not equipped for the job, and it wasn't as if I could just up and randomly ask some strange female walking down the street if I could borrow hers for a spell. I needed a mock transfer system and I must say the decibel level of the baby's cries was really speeding up my thinking process in regards to the matter. What do I have that resembles a nipple for Christ Sake? I mean come on! I'm a man here. We just, we just aren't set up for stuff like this!

Nearing the point of a mental collapse, and a total loss of hearing to boot, I buried my face into my palms and began tapping my fingers on my forehead in a thera-peutic twitch. It worked for about a second and a half like most of my ideas, but then only seemed to aggravate me even more. In a stressed-out huff, I started pounding my fingers into my skull even harder and it was then that the answer to my riddle came to me in the form of pain. Unbeknownst to me at the time, it seemed that during the baby's panic attack, I had tapped my nails on my forehead so hard that it had broken the skin and created a wound. I realized this when I felt the thin trickle of blood the poke had caused start to make its way down the length of my nose. At first I was a little freaked out, but when I pulled my hands away from my face, I watched in silence as a lone droplet of the red stuff repelled down from the tip of my tender digit and headed for my palm.

That's it, that's it. I can use my finger! Hell, it's perfect.

With no time to spare I tore open the cardboard container as wide as it would go and cast the index finger of my good hand deep into the hazy liquid. After I felt that it was saturated enough, I pulled it back out and held my breath as I tiptoed my hand over and gently pressed my dripping appendage against the lips of the howling infant. To my immense relief, the baby inhaled my finger into its mouth and began savagely ingesting the fluid that surrounded it. And finally, to the great delight of my poor ears, the crying stopped.

I repeated this process many times over in the next few minutes, transferring the stock liquid into her mouth, via my finger. The baby consumed the milk as fast as I could produce it, and to my continuing delight the newborn's cries stayed away and were replaced by a soft suckling sound. As I fed the child and my mind began to stand down a bit from it's near fatal meltdown, an earlier segment of the whole ordeal started to repeat itself over and over again, stopping deliberately every time on a certain moment for me to ingest.

For me to understand.

It was a girl.

I had found a little baby girl.

That's when my mind stopped relaxing and the shockwave of the last ninety minutes began to steamroll over my senses. My pores began to leak sweat and a stark order jumped out of my mouth.

You've got to turn her in Eugene. You've got to hand her over to the police and tell them how you found her. Do it! Do it before anyone becomes suspicious and turns you in.

My internal warning was followed up immediately by a plan. But you know what? It seems my heart, who had been eavesdropping in on the whole conversation, just didn't quite see eye to eye with it's all-knowing counterpart and began systematically re-routing my train of thought towards a totally different mindset.

Hey Eugene, you just found something real.

Seems my ticker had just raised the bar.

Don't even think about it!!

My mind retaliated, gearing itself up for a fight; but my heart quickly cut back in.

A helpless human being who needs love, who needs a parent, think of it Eugene, you just discovered a little baby girl in a trashcan! An infant. A real live human being! Tossed away and left to die. Abandoned and invisible. The way I see it my friend, it's a simple case of finder's keepers. You found her and now she's yours, know what I'm saying?

Eugene! Eugene, don't you get sucked into any of that hocus pocus bullshit.

My logical side I knew was warning me.

But just think about it. Your very own child Eugene. Your very own little girl! Just think of the magnitude of that for a second.

NO EUGENE! No, no, no, you don't know what you're getting yourself into!

Now my logical side did have a point. I really did not know "what I was getting myself into". Didn't have a clue actually. But that wasn't about to matter much anyway.

"Your damn rights," I screeched, issuing a victorious high five to my softer side. "She's mine!"

And you know, technically she was. I mean if I hadn't have discovered her in that dumpster, the numerical chances that anyone would have were virtually nil. She would have perished for sure.

"Oh my God," I whispered as I looked over at the fidgeting lump of terry cloth on my passenger seat. "She's all mine!"

And then as I muttered those three monumental words over and over in my head again, everything I had come to understand in my life, everything I had finally

68

accepted to be the truth began to crumble away right before my eyes and all I could do is sit there in a numb trance and watch it fall.

Then, just like that, it seemed that all of a sudden my life had purpose. I felt every nerve in my body start to come alive and quiver with excitement. It was an elation that I had feared I would never experience again. I congratulated myself in secret as my incredibly unprepared mind became instantly blasted with a million questions and decisions it had never before even remotely entertained. But I'm afraid history was quick to rain on my recent parade.

Out of nowhere ,my disbarred voice of reason pierced it's long arm in through the sugarcoated bubble it's nemesis had created and hauled me out of paradise valley, dragging me back kicking and screaming to that fateful day not so long ago on the bridge. That moment beside the river when I watched the sacrificial droplets from my hand being fed to the water. I began to feel the word I forged that day begin to cut its reminder into my back. Over and over again the scene played itself out until the sheer weight of it tipped my eyes downward and fixated them on the deep scar in my palm. A lightning bolt of pain suddenly dashed up my arm and quickly reminded me of my crime and the ongoing sentence it provoked. With razor-sharp definition, the bitter reality of my life began to rush back through me, wreaking havoc on my recent jelly- filled attempts at glory and pushed my face back into the dirt.

"Jesus, Eugene, you can't even take care of yourself for Christ Sakes, let alone a new-born child! What were you thinking man? Let's not forget who you are... what you are.

The accusations blared on inside my skull without pause until the very last of my grain fed visions were completely driven off.

"Alright," I finally said. "I give."

It was a cop-out for sure, but it was the truth. A skid like me could never be so lucky as to deserve something like this. With the smile exiled from my face, I looked over at the baby and let out a deep sigh. It felt as if someone had just reached down from out of nowhere and stole my dream away right out from underneath my nose when I wasn't looking. The baby, though, was very docile now. She was no longer agitated or screaming. She was just lying there on the passenger seat sucking on my finger and staring up at me.

That's when I noticed the color of her eyes. They were beautiful. They were blue. Ocean blue.

She spit out my finger at that point; I guess it was her way of saying that she was full thanks. So I slowly pulled my hand away and closed up the half empty container of milk. Then I just sat there for a while and stared over at her in awe. I found myself becoming entranced and hypnotized by her subtle gaze.

God, she was such an awesome sight. And she was as quiet as a church mouse now as she lay there peering curiously up at me.

There was an awkward moment as we stared each other down. I wasn't sure which emotion I was supposed to succumb to, and somehow, I knew she could sense that confusion. It's funny, but it's like we were both sort of taking stock and trying to figure out what in the hell had just happened! I had fallen into the eye of a storm, this I knew. The situation at hand was very delicate but I still realized that I had to do the right thing. I had to make the best decision for the baby. But this meant that I would have to accept the bitterness of logic and cast aside the warmth of the moment. I knew it was the only way, but God, I was tired of being cold.

I felt my heart and my mind lock horns once more.

Ten more minutes passed and although it felt more like a decade, it was all the time that was needed to win the battle and in the end it was my head, not my heart that would emerge forth in victory. I had to take the logical road, no matter how good her soul was making me feel.

With a heavy feeling in my stomach, I reluctantly fired up my wreck and backed out of the stall. I decided right there that the next day, at first light, I would turn her into the first Social Services office I came across and make a run for it. I considered offering up an explanation to whoever was in charge, but I knew when it was all over, I would still end up the bad guy so I made the call to just drop her off and hit the highway.

Once out of the parking lot, I pulled directly into a nearby alley, rolled down my window and tossed away the urine soaked rag that I had found her in. That alone was difficult. And even though it was still pretty early to be bedding down, I started anyway, towards a very special sleep spot over on the east side.

It was one of my very favorites, a place I kept tucked away far in the corner of my highly coveted arsenal.

It never failed me, this spot, and for that reason, I usually only took advantage of it a few times a month to ensure that it would always remain tight and never be spoiled from overuse. Today, I needed that desert island! I couldn't handle any more excitement and more importantly, because of my unlikely cargo, it was imperative that I not be discovered.

I didn't look at her at all as I drove. I wanted to. God! Believe me, I wanted to. But it was too difficult. And the worst part of it was that I could feel her staring up at me the whole trip, endlessly begging me to acknowledge her. But I'm afraid my mind had hoisted up its drawbridge and that baby, to my regret, lay outside its moat, protected now, only by the thin shield of my old bath towel. I had no choice I convinced myself over and over again as I drove on. It had to be this way, it just did.

After awhile, the baby began to gurgle and fuss loudly, I know, in an effort to lasso my attention and make me look over at her. It was harder than you can imagine not doing that, not look over and be drawn into the path of her incredible eyes. I put on a brave face as I sped on, but inside, my heart was still suffering terribly from its recent defeat. I was saturated with guilt. It was as if I had finally found the pot of gold at the end of the rainbow, and now was being forced to give it right back.

After a long solemn drive, I finally pulled off into the parking lot of a small flea market on the edge of an unassuming field. This was one of the safest places I knew.

There were others here like me too. Lots of others. They knew my status and I knew theirs. It was a good place. Everyone sort of watched out for everyone else. It was kind of an honor-among-thieves thing.

Now I have to point something out. You never actually talk to anyone in these circles, or let alone even look over in their direction purposely. Oh no! You don't ever do that. It is considered highly offensive. But even with that rule, there is still an underlying brotherhood in place. It's just never admitted.

In a motion that I had executed countless times before, I routinely stashed my vehicle in between a bleak conglomeration of rust heaps and bent up motor homes, allowing myself as always, a good chunk of breathing room and privacy space. I let the heat blare out and warm up the inside of the car for a few more minutes before I shut it down to ensure the cab was nice and toasty for the child. I did eventually look over at her though. I had to. It was absolutely killing me not to.

She was all smiles and spit by now, her mood greatly elevated by the administration of food and shelter.

"Boy oh boy", I thought, I sure wasn't looking forward to telling her the bad news. While I sat there and watched her fidget, I noticed that she had wiggled her thin little legs free from the snug entrapment of my cheap towel and had begun kicking them up and down. It was difficult, but I did not respond to her theatrics and tried to stay as distant as possible. It had been an especially long day and all the emotional stress I had ingested was beginning to take its toll.

By dusk my eyes were already getting quite low as I pulled out another towel from the backseat and half folded it across her. I wanted to be certain that she would be warm enough for the evening. I followed up this precaution, too, with my own nightly routine of locking the doors, making sure the keys were in the ignition, and of course, setting my hunting knife firmly into the crease in the door. I looked over at the baby one last time. Yep, she was safe too. I mean you know, safer than she was when she started off her day that is.

I released the chewed-up chunk of two by four from underneath the hinge of my seat and let it fall back onto the rear bench, hoisting my own ripped up blanket overtop me in the same motion. I turned onto my side right off and cautiously faced the miracle I had unearthed, lying in the other seat. It was getting dark now, but I was still able to make out the soft contours of her face illuminating off the dim lampposts of the market.

I laid awake for a bit and tried to organize the events of the hours past, but my thoughts seemed loyal only to the current imprint that she was making as she lay there quietly on the passenger seat. I could tell the baby was already asleep for her shallow breaths had become slower and more exact. And her spastic limbs too, had stopped their fidgeting, and were lying dormant underneath the towel.

It was an amazing thing I'll tell you, watching her there sleeping peacefully away without a care in the world.

And it occurred to me in that moment, that this was the first time in as long as I could remember that anyone else had been inside my car with me. I also could not help but wonder in the faint moments before the sandman buried his spade.

Why me little one? Why me?

Not surprisingly, my slumber was cut short and I was unfairly awakened a mere 38 minutes later by the sound of soft steady sobs. As my eyes re-adjusted themselves toward the disorganized heap of cotton on the passenger's seat, I could just see in the minimal light, that the baby's arms and legs were jumping up and down again underneath her odd coverings. She was agitated for some reason and was crying intermittently so I sat up and retrieved the half empty container of milk from the dashboard and prepared to feed her once more. In a half-asleep, half-awake daze, I leaned over and dipped my finger into the lukewarm mixture of white food and pressed it softly onto the outline of her frail lips. After only three helpings of the stuff, she abruptly spit out my finger and refused any further nourishment. "Well that was quick," I whispered to her in a satisfied tone. But I rejoiced too soon and listened in dismay as the tiny thing drew in a supercharged gulp of air and let me have it!

"WAAAAAAAA!!! "

"Oh no! Not this again," I groaned. "Please little one," I begged as she continued on with her long drawn out symphony. "Please stop crying! I give up OK, you win!!"

But the baby, like before, did not deviate from her plan and proceeded to wail on without pause.

OK Eugene, think now. Is she warm?

I ran my hand quickly across her chest.

Yep, she's warm. OK, that's not it. She's not hungry obviously. OK, check! Not hungry.

"Hmmm, oh oh! Wait a second here," I yelped. "What if she…"

I then prepared to face my worst fear, and with legendary caution I slowly tucked my hand underneath the bottom of her towel, expecting to feel a big puddle. Or… gulp, something worse! But to my immense relief, she was dry. That was odd I thought. Confused but undeterred, I leaned back and reviewed the situation. Well, she's not hungry; she's not wet or cold. But she was still crying, I just didn't get it.
And the baby's cries were not subsiding either. In fact, they were becoming louder and louder with each exhalation. The pressure in my cranium was also rising along with that decibel level and I could feel my head begin to throb again. My hand reached over out of instinct and started to mechanically rub her chest in a desperate attempt at peace. But that band aid didn't work and she just kept on howling. I was starting to lose it! My brain was on overload!

What if someone hears her and comes over hear to see what the matter is? What if somebody sees her? What if…

72

I was on the verge of a breakdown. My mind stepped up its pace and began fever-ishly searching for a solution. Any solution would do right now. But alas, nothing came to my head that I hadn't already tried.

Her cries were absolutely earth-shattering by now. I am not kidding, man. She was screaming at the top of her lungs and she wouldn't let up. Not for one second. It was insane!! On the brink of Hari Kari, I leaned over and hollered out a final request to her.

"Please baby," I shouted, "I'm new at this, okay, and I just don't know what I am supposed to do!"

My pleas were forged out of pure honesty, but had no effect on the state of my hitchhiker. Frantic and confused, I swiped the mass of material up off the seat and held the baby up in front of me.

"I don't know what to do," I yelped out in a frenzy. "I don't know what you want!"

And then she stopped. Just like that, she stopped crying. In an awkward and unprecedented move, I slowly lowered the infant down onto my chest and eased my body back into the seat. Within minutes, she was fast asleep once again.

All she wanted was to be held, Eugene, that's all she wanted.

I watched my arms fold in around the baby. This closeness... It seemed so strange to me. So new. I was in uncharted territory and my feelings were upside down. I was angrier at myself than anything else, angry at the thought that I had become so Goddam hardened and bitter that I was unable to recognize the importance of such a basic need. I slumbered there for awhile and pondered that fact. Then, with the precision of a surgeon, I slowly pulled the front cover of my sleeping bag overtop the dozing child and interlocked my fingers across her small body. She was out like a light now, and I could feel her tiny lungs expanding and contracting steadily within my hands. The air passing through her nostrils was producing a hypnotic buzzing sound and her breaths were warm and moist as they flowed across my neck.

I, on the other hand, was wide awake. My eyes were like saucers and stayed fixed on the roof, refusing to even blink, let alone close. This was all so strange to me. But the feeling I had unknowingly tapped into was just so incredible. My body, I knew, had gone into a state of shock the moment the baby's weight had dispersed itself across my chest. And my overrun brain too, had initiated an immediate lockdown of all incoming stimuli out of equal fear.

But my heart. Well my heart was just in its glory.

It was feeding off her every movement and using that potion to repair and refill its damaged hull. And you know it was the craziest thing, but after awhile the rhythm of my own heartbeat seemed almost to adjust and ratio itself to the beat of hers. I lay awake there with the babe sleeping away intermittently on my chest for the vast dura-tion of the night, ingesting every ounce of medicine she offered. I didn't want to miss a single moment of this play. It was almost 4:30 in the morning when I finally looked at my watch. I'd been awake for hours now but it didn't really seem like it. The child fussed a couple of times during the night, but it was nothing a subtle rocking motion and a little milk didn't fix. I must have drifted off shortly after that because I was wakened again at 6:30am to a mass array of feet and arms assaulting my body.

I rubbed the sleep out of my eyes at the looked down at the tangled clump of towels and flesh that lay sprawled out across me. With caution, I lifted up a corner of the cloth and looked down at a small, messed- up, tuft of dark brown hair that was jutting out from the fold. The baby had turned itself halfway around and was facing the driver's door, so I rolled off the top covers and gently hoisted her off my body. As I did this, I felt something small and mushy drop out from the towel and land on my shirt.

"Well good morning to you too," I grunted as I gazed down at her present. The baby did not admit to any guilt and simply looked up at me with glee as a gob of saliva trickled down her chin.

"Well", I continued bravely, "at least all your machinery is in good working order!"

Actually, it was nice to know that everything of hers was working okay, but I was still absolutely mortified by the thought of it. I leaned over and laid her onto the passenger seat, grimacing halfway as my eyes caught the outline of a small greenish yellow pool of fecal matter that had came to rest upon my stomach.
The honeymoon was over!

White as a sheet now, I jammed my hand into the glove box with flawless speed and pulled out a big wad of paper napkins, frantically scooping up the pile of steaming goop off my shirt and firing it out the window like some kind of deadly toxin. In the same state of mind, I thrust my seat forward and hit the engine, double-timing the gas pedal as I fishtailed down the street.

I was in search of a bathroom. Any bathroom!

I drove with one hand on the wheel and on hand on the baby, swerving into the first service station that came into sight. And like a stunt double in a cheesy cop show, I skidded up to the side of the place and checked the restroom door. It wasn't locked thank God, because today, time was definitely money.
The child was fidgeting about quite a bit but she wasn't crying and I prayed for that scenario to continue.
Gathering up a haphazard lump of toiletries and towels into a small clear plastic bag, I kicked shut my car door and ducked inside the shadows of the musty room. I immediately placed the baby onto the sink counter and then stopped to take a long deserving breath.

I hadn't really gotten a chance to properly wake up yet, but my pulse had leveled out to around 174, so I at least had that going for me. After a few minutes I looked over at the child. She seemed quite content actually. She was just lying there, intensely examining her fingers, appearing very fascinated by the way they fit so neatly together. After giving my head a little shake, I began to neatly set out all my accessories.

You can do this Eugene, just don't inhale!

So filling the sink half full of water, I added a small amount of soap from the wall dispenser and stirred it in. I also scoffed a wad of toilet paper from the stall just in case and slowly began the grim task of cleaning up her bottom. I could feel my stomach start to curl and threaten expulsion as I scraped away the goulash, but I resisted and pressed on with the task. After a couple of seconds, I noticed a short piece of dried out umbilical cord dangling from her belly button. It was loosely tied off at the end by a bloody strand of parcel twine. It was at that point that I came to understand that this baby was not born in a hospital, or anything even close to a sterile environment for that matter.

After I had excavated the worst of the slop, I lifted her clammy body off of the towel and eased her into the sink, holding her uncoordinated head steady with my left hand and basting the temperate liquid overtop her tiny frame with the other. Man! You should have seen the expression on that little thing's face when I did that! She actually started to smile and grew increasingly playful as her bath went on. Kicking her feet, splashing the water around with her hands, you know, just sucking it all up. She wasn't complaining one bit about all the attention she was getting and who could blame her for that! And you know something else; throughout the whole bath I didn't once feel embarrassed or awkward like I thought I might. It was all in all a very natural and pure experience. And for the very first time since I'd found her, I actually didn't feel like a criminal.

As I continued on with my maiden attempt at parenting, it occurred to me that no-one had pounded on the door wanting to get in yet. That was odd. Usually the second I turn the locks there was already somebody on the other side trying to open them back up. But not today. The place was totally silent. Only the tranquilizing sounds of the water sifting off the baby's body were present. It was amazing, the whole experience. It was just so calming. So placid. Twenty more minutes went by just like that and still, not one disturbance. That was a real unexpected bonus. Especially today, for I was really due for a break. The last twenty hours of my life had been a real roller coaster ride and I still hadn't had much of a chance to come down from the onslaught of paranoia and adrenaline. The peace and quiet was such a treat, but when the water in the sink had begun to cool, I knew it was time to wrap it up.

I'd been in there for nearly a half an hour without a single disturbance. I couldn't believe it. It was like her and I were the only two people in the world. Well, this kid was definitely clean now, which I'm sure she very much appreciated. And with a hint of sweet hesitation, I slowly lifted her out of the soiled water and laid her back onto a clean towel beside the sink. I picked her back up in that same towel and began drying off her restless body. She had a good thick crop of hair sprouting out from her head, so I pulled the corner flap of the towel over her coiffeur and began rubbing softly away. And as I pulled the cloth away from her face and prepared to set her back down, she, for some reason, suddenly stopped moving. This behavior threw me off a little. I guess I'd become content with her fidgeting. Curious about this latest development, I harnessed my wandering stare and brought it back down towards her to see what caused this sudden docility. But when my eyes met hers, I found to my surprise, that they were already focused in on me.

"What's wrong little one?" I whispered as I brought her motionless face in closer to mine.

At that point, she rose up her uncoordinated arm and placed her tiny palm against the side of my cheek.

Something broke inside of me.

My face became hot and my legs weak and shaky. I felt a renegade emotion escape its imprisonment and I was powerless to stop it, or the ferocious reign of disorder it provoked.

Memories and sensations deep inside of me that I long presumed dead were beginning to rise up and fly out from every nook and crevice of my soul. I became helplessly entangled in her stare, kept hostage by the sheer innocence in her eyes.

I could feel the pressure of a million tears rushing to the bottoms of my eyelids, but I held them back for all I was worth. In a defensive move, I tucked the baby underneath my chin, breaking away from her gaze in a desperate attempt to divert her interrogation just long enough for me to regain my composure. But the baby pushed herself away from my neck just as quick and reconnected her line of sight into mine, refusing to set me free. Refusing to allow me back into the shadows, where I think she somehow knew I'd been hid away for so long.

I was only human. Only flesh and blood.

She would be victorious in her quest, and as my knees began to buckle out from underneath me, I watched as an invisible hand smashed its way through the mortally-damaged wall surrounding my heart, and with great power, ripped my soul away from the mass of thick chains that encircled it, and pulled me into the safety of that baby girl's incredible stare.

And as the tears began to rain down upon me and my limp body slid to the floor with her, I did succumb to all my trespasses and to the sober understanding that I could never again turn back towards the dark for any type of salvation because now I knew that my spirit had become officially tainted with light, and would be no longer welcome there.

I let it all out as I sat there curled up in a dim hobbit of that musty old bathroom with the baby tucked deep into the shallow of my neck. In a hurricane of emotion, my soul began purging out years upon years of sorrow and regret. The proceedings were brutal and intense, but monumental in every way.

The bomb inside me had finally gone off.

I felt ashamed when it was over, after my body had finally stopped vibrating and fell still. I felt like I had let her down, like I had been weak, even though I knew if she could, she would never justify that shortcoming with an answer. In the end though, I did find it mind boggling that after all this time, after all the things that I'd

lived through and survived in my life, my ironclad reign of denial had been effort-
lessly undone by the echo of one simple touch.

Still trembling, I lifted my head back straight and unfolded the child away from my
body. I peered down at her again, but this time with caution, for I knew I was still
quite vulnerable and at her mercy. She had clouds in her eyes as well, but she never
told me why.

I stood back up a few minutes later a different person, a person who was still a
mystery to me, but who was definitely real. After a moment of silence I finished
drying her off, and then set her back down onto the sink counter, cocooning her once
more in another towel. Slowly and meticulously, I cleaned everything back up to its
original condition and then, with the baby in one arm, and a plastic bag in another, I
opened up the door and stepped back out into the world.

It was different too.

You know, I must have been inside that washroom for over forty-five minutes, and
not one person disturbed me. No-one came hammering on the door, not the gas attendant, not a pissed off trucker..... Not anybody. This calamity was almost unheard of
out here. And even when I began walking back to my car, I noticed that the parking
lot, too, was virtually empty, and the streets open and casual.
Another rarity.
It was strange but it felt like some greater power had allotted me this one specific
window in time, free of interruptions, so that I could experience a higher plane.
So that I would see.

Submerged in thought, I carefully set the newborn back onto the passenger's seat
of my old clunker, and then climbed into the driver's seat myself. I didn't turn the
engine over right away. I just sat there for a moment and collected my thoughts. I
was so drained. I knew in my newly exposed heart that what just happened inside
that bathroom was historical and groundbreaking in every aspect. But way in the
back of my mind, that tumor-like voice of reason still throbbed away steadily and
dragged me back to the previous night when the heated battle between my head and
my heart was fought, and logic prevailed.

Facts were facts.

And the true fact still remained that even though it was going to bring me more
sadness than I could know, I still had a job to do. I still had to do the right thing. I
was riddled with guilt. You can't imagine how hard it was to separate my feelings
and turn my back on her ambience. But no matter how much ground I had gained or
lost in the last sixty minutes, I still had to face the knowledge that I was homeless.
It hurt to think that all of a sudden, it really did. Nevertheless, that accusation was
justified and I knew an old rusted-out sports car was no place for a newborn child.

With a sick feeling of loss still in my guts, I spun the key and pointed my car in the
direction of a sterile- looking government building that sat like a tombstone a mere
ten blocks away. I drove slowly and only made it about halfway there, before my

arms broke protocol and steered my Firebird off into an alley.

I just wanted a few more minutes with her. I figured I deserved that. So I pushed the lever into park and reached under my seat to retrieve the last bit of milk that I knew still remained in the wax-coated container.

I wanted to be sure she'd had enough to eat before I handed her over to some geek in a suit to begin her life as a statistic and a case number. In my heart, I knew no amount of time would ever be long enough to render me content, but I'll tell you what, I intended to spread out those next few minutes as long as I possibly could.

As the engine sputtered to a halt, I leaned over and wiggled her off the seat, supporting the length of her spine with my forearm. With my other hand, I began to dip my finger into the small puddle of fluid like before and press it to her lips. She ate her snack quietly. I don't think she understood what I was about to do.

What an incredible sight.

I wondered as I fed her how anyone in their right mind could just toss away something as precious as this. It was a crime that I knew for the duration of my life, I would never understand. I riddled her endlessly with soothing jargon as she suckled the sweet fluid away from my makeshift nipple, and when there was nothing more left in the carton; I knew my time was up. I protested this injustice to her and she backed up my displeasure by expelling a huge gob of frothy white spit from her mouth. The slop crawled its way down her chin and caused her to make a fuss so I cleaned her face off with the corner of my sleeve and prepared to set her back up onto my chest again, a trick I hoped to capitalize on for the second time in an effort to keep her in a happy mood.

But the moment I gripped her torso and began the decent, a supercharged pocket of gas erupted from her stomach and launched out a cannonball of homogenized saliva which subsequently exploded all over my face and shirt. I looked like someone had just dipped me into a huge vat of tapioca pudding. I swallowed hard and fought back an almost unstoppable urge to vomit.

"Be strong, Eugene," I mumbled. "It's only milk."

As I forced open one of my cemented-shut eyes, I saw in front of me a very contented little girl. I guess this was my first experiences in burping a child. Not one I cared to want to remember though. The baby of course, projected forth a very innocent smile as if to say, " Did I do that? Naw, I couldn't have done that!! Not little old me."

I set the child back down in horror and reached into the backseat for yet another towel. It took a few minutes, but eventually I did start to resemble a human being again. Then the baby giggled at me.

Oh you little turkey.

I tried to be put off, but it was impossible. All I could do was grin and shake my head. Unfazed by my sticky initiation, I bravely picked her up and laid her on my chest as originally planned, interlocking my arms around her thin torso for safety

78

as I rocked her back and forth. This was a beautiful moment. It was so very surreal, and I drew it out for all it was worth. Now I'm not sure how long I sat there with her, but I do remember the nauseating lump of sadness that overcame me as I lifted her off me and set her back in her seat. Some may say what I did next was cold, but as I returned her to the passenger's side, I did then erase every single memory of our time together and replaced that void with a jagged stone.

I had to.

It was the only way I was able to exit that world and lift my hand to the key.

With the engine now rumbling away underneath the hood again, I reluctantly engaged my tranny and swung back out onto the road. I knew my destination was close but part of me wished it was still a million miles away. As I crested the last hill, I saw the building I was en route to, up and over to the left of a four way intersection that lay directly in front of me. The light was yellow so I slowed to a stop and forced my signal light downward. I stared straight ahead as I concentrated on the vibration of my run-down engine. I tried not to think about what was next to me, about the life that lay in my passenger's seat, but I'm afraid some wishes were just not meant to come true.

"I'm sorry," was all that I could say.

I peered over at the baby in hopes that she would tell me that she understood, but she did not flinch. Her body was motionless and her eyes remained fixed and down.

"It has to be this way," I pleaded. " It is the logical thing."
"Yes, yes my little friend," I said after a minute. "Logic is the best thing."

I finished off my speech with a nod, proudly satisfied with the lie I had just sold her, then gripped my steering wheel and prepared to execute my turn for I knew that any second now, the light was going to change. I also began to ease the pressure in my foot off the brake pedal, but something pushed it back down.

Suddenly, an angry voice burst into my head and blew apart my all-knowing statue of reason.

Fuck you Eugene! You hear me asshole, fuck you! Take your sorry and shove it up your ass

It was my heart, and it was mad!

Why Eugene, why do you HAVE to turn her in?

With that comment, I prepared to launch a backup squadron into the killing fields, but to my surprise they had already fled away.

Hey Eugene, don't you like feeling good huh? Can't you handle the fact that someone actually needs you?

I could feel my body begin to pressure up as the internal conflict began to heat, and that feeling compounded itself a thousand fold as the shearing blare of someone's car horn suddenly ripped through my eardrums. I looked up at the light. It was green. I tried again to lift my foot off the brake, but I could not budge it.

I will not let you screw this up again Eugene Lauder! No way, not this time.

The damning opposition that lay camouflaged somewhere in my conscience continued bombing away at the base of my decision without mercy, and no matter how hard I fought it, my train of thought just would not steady.

Oh wait a minute, everybody, I know what Eugene's problem is. He's too scared! He likes being miserable. He likes being alone! That's what it is, isn't it Lauder?

"No it isn't, Godammit," I shouted back into the air.
Another horn blast shot out from behind me.

"Come on buddy," I heard someone yell." Make up your fucking mind or get out of the way!"

Alone... Alone... Alone!... Alooone! The unseen demon taunted and cut me every chance it could.

You're a chickenshit, Eugene. Man, you didn't learn a fucking thing back there in that washroom did you?

"But what could I possibly offer her?" I whispered back in a weak defense. Seeing that it had whittled my defenses down to a critical level, the overpowering voice then plunged a great knife deep into the guts of my failing logic and issued me a final lesson.

Hey Einstein. She didn't ask you for anything! You did what you did because you wanted to. Admit it Eugene! Admit it now or forever live with your silence. You took the easy road out before remember? And look where it got you! Hey... LOOK WHERE IT GOT YOU!

I felt a wave of shame rise up high inside me and with it, surfaced the ugly truth of my past failure. I began to envision the sad picture of my mother's face as she crouched behind the terrible stranger in the doorway of our old house that fateful night.

*You can't go back Eugene, you can't help her anymore, but you can help this child. You can make the difference in her life, you know you can! You're being given a second chance here. Don't make the same mistake again, don't you dare! Please, please Eugene. She needs you. Look at her, man. Look into her eyes and tell me that I'm wrong! Look at her right now Eugene! Look at her and tell me that what you see in front of you is not an absolute miracle. Come on, look at her.
...LOOK AT HER!!"*

I felt my head start to turn and then for the very first time, I actually saw her.
In all her glory and pureness I finally saw her, and that vision was nothing short

80

of Godly. Suddenly her little head tipped upward and her limbs began to gyrate strangely underneath her towel. It was as if she had sensed the subliminal shift in my thinking and was now cheering on that movement.

You're helpless without her Eugene. Don't throw her away again. Please.

...Don't throw me away again.

It was right! "Oh God," I cried. "She was right!"

Well that was it! My foot leapt off the brake pedal and crashed down hard on the accelerator. My eyes became wide and my body tensed up as that tired out old Pontiac dug into the cement like it never had before and launched us forward. The tires erupted with attitude as they tore through the intersection.

I drove straight on and didn't even so much as take a second glance over at that goddam government flophouse, for now as far as I was concerned, that structure no longer existed. My mind was definitely made up and I had never felt more in control. And as the RPMs rose, so did my level of confidence.

I looked over at the baby with a big smile. She was still dancing away happily underneath her towel celebrating her win.

Our win.

Her eyes had come back to life too, and her face portrayed the same story. Now don't worry, I fully understood that the decision I had just made was in every way unheard of and crazy, but I also knew that there was no way in Hell that I was about to overrule it either. My heart had made the final call and that was that. I could no longer turn a blind eye to its suffering. However incorrect it was, I christened her my own and stood by that ruling. I figured the baby too, was probably pretty sick and tired of being abandoned. The rest of the day, well I'll tell you, it went by just like that. My thought process became saturated with a multitude of unprecedented questions and decisions. But hey, that was just A-OK with me because for the first time in a long lonely while, I actually felt alive. And my heart too, I soon realized, began to beat again the very second my foot left the brake at that intersection. It was such an incredible feeling to have a purpose again.

Not surprisingly, the very first thing I did was head straight to the nearest drugstore, and with the last of my cash, bought a cheap plastic baby bottle with an enormous rubber nipple on the end of it. Man, you should have seen that baby's little peepers spark up when locked onto the outline of that bad boy. I also grabbed another container of milk and a blueberry muffin for myself, along too, with a truckload of paper napkins I snared from a convenience store that sat nearby. I wasn't the sharpest tool in the shed, but I still remembered what newborn babies were famous for!

I realized though, that those few accessories I had picked up were merely the tip of the iceberg compared to the hardware I would need to succeed in this unheard-of venture, so once I had left the parkade of the drugstore, I pulled off to the side of the road for a moment and jotted down a rough list of supplies I would need in order of importance.

As I scribbled away I found myself staring bravely over at the tiny human that lay in my passenger's seat. The same innocent being who was simply thrown away like yesterday's trash, doomed and alone as she waited silently in the guts of that dumpster for the sound of her death backing it's way towards her.

I made a pledge at that moment.

I swore an oath that from then on, I would never allow any further harm to come to her again. I had willfully taken on this task and for better or for worse I intended to honor that commitment and always put her needs and safety in front of my own. I knew that this was going to be one of the biggest challenges that I would ever face, but with God as my witness, I vowed to cover that bill whatever its price.

I moved around from spot to spot all day and it was dusk before I knew it. I could sense that the child was becoming sleepy, probably due to the 12 or 13 bowel movements she had cranked out during the day. She consumed almost all of the milk I had bought for her and I swear it passed right through her like she was hollow or something. I think her body had taken itself off life support and said," OK everybody, lets rock and roll!"

And believe it or not, I was actually relieved by her consistency. Covered in shit mind you, but relieved.

Spotting a landmark, I steered my jalopy off onto a narrow street and nonchalantly backed up into a row of scraped-up half tons. As I laid there for the second night, this time with the baby perched securely on my chest right from the get go, it suddenly occurred to me that the four-way intersection I had sat at earlier in the day represented a very important crossroad in my life, and did in turn, set in motion any and all the future consequences I would face in the times to come.

I fell asleep to this understanding but was awakened soon after by the echoes of a cry and the assault of miniature limbs against my rib cage. To my delight, she only woke up twice more after that. Not bad I thought, considering her odd environment and her age.

In the morning though, we were both brought out of our slumbers in by the same bright ray of sunshine that cut its way through my side window and gathered in our eyes. That third day, I accumulated money in amounts and ways I never imagined I could with the baby supervising my efforts from her spread on the passengers seat. Cans, bottles, Tupperware, payphones. You name it, I exploited it. I also "borrowed" a roll or two of toilet paper from a couple of neighborhood gas stations. Boy it felt great to be busy, to be working towards something that was real. Something that I could hold.

More and more as the day progressed , I could feel the dark layer of sludge that had coated my life for so long, begin to break up and seep away. I never let that baby out of my sight. No way, not even for a second. It was too risky. She was always within arm's reach. She did cry a lot when she was lacking attention or food but that I knew was to be expected.

I must have cleaned and changed her like six times. She was an absolute crap machine I'll tell you, but even that little chore was already becoming old hat. Heck, the smell wasn't even bothering me anymore. Let's face it, I was turning into a pro, and by the end of that very long day, I had nearly fifty bucks stuffed into my jeans. It was a legendary haul for one shift, maybe even a record breaker.

Now don't worry, I had no illusions whatsoever; I would easily drop the bulk of that loot on supplies for the baby in the next couple of days, but that was fine. And even though throughout my whole life I had heard that "raising kids these days costs a fortune" I remained positive. I was determined to prove that theory wrong.

Actually, I had no choice but to prove that theory wrong!

It would take my level of thriftiness and creativity to a whole new level, but I was primed for the challenge. That evening, after I had made hopefully my last bathroom stop, I drove to another sacred sleep spot and prepared the child for bed, for the moment, on the passenger's seat, cause I had some bookwork to do. I had to get my strategy down on paper. So after she was asleep, or doing a hell of a job pretending to be, I pulled my old sleeping bag down to my waist, and then using the glow from the streetlamp above, I jotted down a list of things to do and buy the following morning. As I whispered the names of the products I would need into the atmosphere, I came to the swift realization that I would have to do some serious corner cutting if I was going to make this whole thing fly.

. For one, flashy name brands were out of the question! The half price bins would be where I would have to do the bulk of my shopping. Now I had already figured out that storebought diapers would be the financial death of me, so I sketched out a couple of crude diagrams and came up with my own line of " Dapper Diapers." Paper napkins from a wide array of fast food establishments and one inch masking tape would become my main mode of excrement containment. I realized that they would probably not be the most leak- proof invention in the world, but I figured if I coupled them up with a pair of those cheap little rubber underwear thingys, they should do the job just fine. Baby powder and Petroleum Jelly were also a must. But a wet piece of paper towel was going to have to suffice for a Cotton Swab.

It was tacky, but I had to cut corners wherever I could. In that same fashion I would utilize my car's defrost heater when needed to bring the baby formula up to temperature, and then sterilize the bottle afterwards using the hot water dispensers sticking out of the coffee machines at the convenience stores. This was a must, for cleanliness and temperature were a mandatory part of the big picture. I planned to visit a Goodwill store I knew of first thing. Towels were just not in style this season and they did absolutely nothing to accentuate my new roommate's eyes. And well, we just couldn't have any of that happening could we?

I did a few more minutes of quick figuring in my head, and then put the meager list away. The baby was sleeping away soundly by this time, so I opted out to just leave her be. If she wanted to be held at any point of the night, I knew I would definitely be the first to hear about it! Being careful not to obstruct her mouth, I decided to shroud her with another towel. It was of the greatest importance that no-one spot her in here, for what I was attempting was totally illegal in every way.

But hey, so was dumping a newborn child into a trash can on the edge of town, right?

When I was finished constructing her house, I leaned over quietly and kissed her on the cheek, whispering a soft good night. Then I lay there on my side with my face to hers and tried hard to shut my eyes. This feat proved nearly impossible, even though I was dead tired from the long day I had put in. And oddly enough, it was my brain that was overruling my body's urge to shut down. You see, it was still playing a little game of catch up with my heart, and to be honest, the whole ordeal had come at me so fast, I don't think I had a clue who was winning what war anymore. All I knew was that I was breathing and still had full control of my bladder. I was one part elated and one part terrified beyond comprehension, you know.

I understood completely though, that what I was attempting to do was a surefire one way ticket to the Looney bin, but I will also say that crazy never felt so good.

I arose before the baby the next morning. She only woke up twice during that whole night. Once to be held, and once to be fed. Now you don't have to be a rocket scientist to appreciate the rarity of that event, however from the smell, I knew that the party was just getting started. The instant I turned the key over, the child sprang to life with a grand howl. In an automatic spin, I fetched the almost empty bottle out of the glove box and with both hands working, I tromped down on the gas pedal and pointed my rig in the direction of water and soap. There wasn't a whole lot of milk left in the bottle, but it was enough to satisfy her momentarily. I rolled down the window as I drove in a desperate attempt to flush out the inside of the car with some much-needed fresh air. I was getting quite used to the smell of shit and all, but that didn't mean I enjoyed it.

The baby calmed down as I drove. I think she was beginning to adjust to the motion of the car.

Things were rolling along as planned, but as luck would have it, I wound up in a small traffic jam and worse yet, got stuck behind a 300 foot motor home to boot! OK, it wasn't that big, but I'm sure it had to be at least thirty-five or so.

And slow! Holy Shit, I don't think the dude in the driver's seat even had the bloody thing in drive! I felt my stress level begin to elevate again, but I quickly doused its upheaval and told myself to chill out. Then me and my passenger just crawled along behind that earth yacht and made the best of it. As I inched my ride forward, I began to focus in on the bumper sticker that was slapped to the frame of the oversized RV

"Sahara Express" read the embossed caption.

Hmm, you're a long way from home, Buddy.

I repeated the words again in my head. "Sahara Express" Then, out of sheer boredom, I began mouthing the rhythmic slogan out loud over and over again, like I was chanting the words to my favorite song.

"Sahara Express, Sahara Express. Sa ha ra Express. Sahara Ex...... Sa..., Hmm, hold on here," I thought.

"Sa hara Ex...press?" Under an onslaught of imagination, I ceased my harmonic interlude and began to break the phrase down.

"Sa hara... Express Su hara. Express... Suara Exp... SU, SUARA...? SARA!!! Well for crying out loud,"

I hollered!

I cranked my head towards the child and looked into her eyes.

SARA!!

That's what I'll call you," I beamed. "Sara... Yes, that's it. That's a great name," I roared. "Sara Lauder."

And as I watched a thick plume of drool creep its way down the baby's smiling face, I knew that she was in total approval of her new trademark. Soon after that the traffic jam broke and we were on our way again but I found it increasingly difficult to keep my eyes on the road though because all I wanted to do was look at her. That baby. The person who now bore the same name as I. Ten minutes later, I came up to an off ramp and veered right. Soon I was creeping around the backside of a random service station with little Sara cocooned up inside my jacket. While I listened to the heavy washroom door close behind me, I felt a slight twinge of fear and déjà-vu hit me. But it scurried off just as quickly and I knew from then on in that I was going to be OK While I carried out the task of cleaning her up, I also took the liberty of stuffing my pockets to the limit with a healthy wad of paper towels from the dispenser. I knew I could never have too many of those things in stock, not now anyways. And even though I was still in my usual hurry up and get out mindset, Sara, it seemed, was quite content to stay immersed in the warm containment of the sink. I thought it funny as I bathed her, of how most people took being warm and clean for granted, yet for us, this privilege had to be stolen.

After I finished up at the gas station, I headed directly over to the neighborhood Goodwill store like I planned. Parking off in the corner, I wrapped my little bambino up in my last bath towel and prepared to take her into public for the first time. I felt a little hesitant about exposing her to the rest of the world, but I didn't really have any other choice. I couldn't just leave her in the car all the time. It was inevitable that people were eventually going to see me with her, that I understood. I knew I just had to keep that kind of exposure down to a minimum. As I booted the passengers door shut, my thoughts fittingly enough, began to rewind back to a particular day in my junior high days when my whole class was issued lifelike infant dolls that we were instructed to carry around with us for the duration of that whole day. I vividly remember the teacher saying that we were not allowed under any circumstances to let that doll out of our sight, not even for two seconds, or we would risk failing the assignment. I did not end up sticking to this iron clad agreement (surprise, surprise) and proceeded to stuff the rubber toy into my locker, and then sneak off to the arcade with the guys for the afternoon.
Man do I wish I had not done that now!

I admit I had been going through a heck of an adjustment period in the last couple of days. I mean let's face it, it had only been little old low-maintenance me inside that miniscule living area up to this point and I guess the sudden realization that I had one of the most responsible and important jobs known to man was, well, quite a large pill to swallow. Now I wasn't about to renege on my contract under any circumstances. No way man! But I'll tell you one thing, I was rapidly gaining a whole new level of respect and admiration for the opposite sex! Oh ya!

The thrift store turned out to be an awesome experience. And when I say, «awesome experience" I really mean, «awesomely cheap experience!" I came in way under budget. I got five fuzzy one piece jumpsuits as well as couple of those little rubber underwear thing's and a nice cozy fleece-lined blanket, all for about thirteen bucks. The cooing store clerk even threw in a couple of brightly colored stuffed animals and before I knew it, I was out of there with an armful of accessories and an ample amount of money to spare. Our next stop was a small neighborhood drug store I had spotted in my recent travels just outside the city's downtown core.

As I inched my way through traffic, their was no doubt in my mind that in the future, that same little drugstore that was now shuffling around inside my short term, would no doubt, wind up becoming a very familiar sight. The store itself was quite old and sat tucked away in the corner of an equally ancient strip mall. It probably had it's heyday in the early 1950's through to maybe the early 70's or so, but then I think, had fallen prey to an overwhelming landslide of corporate super chains and was today, probably just barely eking out an existence from a limited but loyal following of pensioners with sluggish bowels and other various age-related atrocities. It even had the original, but badly weathered neon sign perched atop its flat tar roof, and of course, free parking. With my target dead in my sights, I lurched through a hole in the traffic and snuck my sport scar into the farthest stall.

OK, I need petroleum jelly, white baby powder stuff, baby formula, and, oh ya, some masking tape.

I knew the baby formula was going to wreak havoc on the old pocket book, but plain old milk was just not going to cut it anymore. She needed proper nutrition and that was that. Sara looked pretty good I have to say. Except for her hair which was a disaster of course. Hmm, I have to fix her mop up somehow. I mean I couldn't have her looking like an orphan for God sakes!

Hey, did I just say that out loud? ("Thank You... Thank you very much!... "I'm here all week!)

"Aha!" I said with joy, as I leaned over towards the glove box and fished out a lone elastic band.

"I have an accessory."

Taking the utmost of precaution, I gently gathered up her thick wig into a bushel and fastened the rubber sphere around its base. "That's more like it", I told her as I fanned out the thick parts to make them look even. Then after a quick and negative napkin/diaper check, I held up one of her new bought and paid for jump suits and said, "Yellow OK?" Sara let go a goop filled snicker and the deal was done. Without further hesitation, I slipped the expandable cloth overtop her fidgeting body and gave her a quick spit bath, something I swore in a million years I would never do to a child! With a new jumpsuit and a new attitude, me and my best girl then strolled across the uneven pavement and pushed our way through the double doors. Sara seemed overjoyed at the fact that she was actually out of the car, and she let out an exited squeal as soon as we were inside. It was obvious that she was going to be a shopper!

The confidence I exuded was that of a stallion. I pranced across the shiny tile floor with my head held high and promptly ducked into the aisle appropriately labeled "Baby Needs."

In the span of not even five minutes, three different women walked up to me and asked to see Sara.

Three, ah, hot women, I might add! Now I, too, was starting to enjoy our little shopping trip, and I made a quick mental note to possibly... um, do it more often. I mean, for the sake of the baby of course!

It took me nearly forty minutes to fend off all the curious young beauties and find the things I needed, and by the time I got to the checkout I was pretty exhausted, but very proud! As I stood in line waiting to pay for my goods, I remember looking down at my little bundle of treasure and trying desperately to recall what my life was like not even a half a week earlier, but I just couldn't! The memories would just not step forward. It's strange but in a very real way, I too, felt like a newborn.

After a lengthy wait, I finally got to the checkout and unloaded my things onto the counter.

"Oh what a lovely baby you have there," purred the young, teenaged girl as she began to ring my purchase through the till.

"Thank you," I replied.

"Is it a boy or a girl?" she asked.

"Girl," I said boastfully, dropping my head in an attempt to shorten the conversation a tad and hurry along the transaction.

And as my head tipped to the floor, my eyes caught the edge of the daily newspaper.

"Another Child Missing".

The large bold print headlines jumped off the page and bothered me, but I pressed on anyways and focused in on the fine print that rested below the oversize black letters.

"Another boy has gone missing in the greater downtown area. He was..."

"That will be nineteen dollars and eighty five cents please."

Suddenly the cashier's chipper voice ended my train of thought. In a habitual move, my eyes left the newspaper and my hand instinctively headed for my pants pocket. That is, until my brain actually realized what the Nazi she-wolf behind the counter said.

"Nineteen dollars and how much?" I gasped under my breath. "Holy shit!" I grumbled as I reluctantly pushed my hand further into my jeans. "$19.85...Really?"

The cashier lady nodded her head in confusion, so I pulled in my lip and pulled out my ransom. I was pretty freaked out by the dollar figure she had quoted me, but as my head followed it's target down towards the clump of money in my palm, I also caught a glimpse of Sara's big blue eyes peeking out from the top of her banana-yellow jumpsuit and I knew right then, that this was the best money I was ever going to spend. I set the loot on the counter now with a smile and mentally retracted the whole Nazi she-wolf thing.

As the door to the place closed behind me, a tiny gust of scented air tickled my face as it ran by. It was coming on fall now and the leaves were beginning to change, but still, the sun was resting high above the city and it was shaping up to be a picture-perfect day.

I took my sweet time walking back to my car. My steps were slow, and my breaths were deep and enjoyable. I even stopped halfway and leaned my back up against a cement partition that separated the businesses from each other, so I could close my eyes and let the sun warm my face. I could have stood there forever that way. Even the mere thought of climbing back into the seat of my old car was making my stomach turn. I spent way too much time in that damn thing as it was. The fresh fall air was acting as somewhat of an all natural aromatherapy session and was recharging my body and softening my mind with each passing second. But alas, after about five minutes, Sara reminded me of her presence by kicking me softly in the ribs and with a subtle gesture, I stubbornly felt my feet begin to pivot and turn towards the chewed up lump of metal that sat waiting like a crypt for me in the nearby parking lot.

But then, even to my own surprise, my feet suddenly stopped again a few strides later as I was about to crest the corner of a low budget electronics store. The proprietor was piping out the news onto the sidewalk from a lone, overpriced television set that hung on display in the center of the window. I really didn't intend on stopping again, but something on that monitor caught my attention. And that in itself was strange because I was never really interested in TV, nor did I give two shits about the news. Nevertheless, there I stood, motionless and facing the screen. A pensioner with a well-used handkerchief in his hand had stopped as well and was watching the images through the glass with equal conviction. Now it wasn't the presence of the attractive newswoman that caught my focus. No, it was more due to the desperation in her voice that caused me to slow.

"The latest development in this case brings the missing persons toll up to a total of seven separate disappearances in the greater metropolitan area in the last number of years."

"She must be talking about the same boy in the newspaper headlines."

My legs became heavy as I listened on with sad conviction to the newscast.

"The police believe that this is the work of a serial abductor whose identity still remains a mystery. The authorities are being very tight-lipped about the nature of the disappearances, and even though none of the victims' bodies have ever been recovered, they are all presumed to be dead."

I listened on with a dismal stare, mesmerized and shaken by the impact of the bleak story. I felt my body tense up and increase its safety grip on Sara too. The report continued:

"Police records indicate that the person or persons responsible for these abductions have thus far remained extremely elusive and no one to date has ever reported seeing them or having had any other information whatsoever that may give police any clues to the whereabouts of the culprit responsible for these terrible crimes. The only lead the police have so far is a mysterious trinket, a morbid trademark the authorities say, that is purposely left behind at every crime scene."

Suddenly an enlarged photograph of an object flashed across the screen.

My skin became instantly alive and started to writhe around underneath my clothes, and the bag I was holding onto as well, slipped out of my sweat-laden hands and emptied its contents out onto the barren sidewalk.

"The police are appealing to the public for any leads in this case or any information as to the origin of this strange symbol.

Our sources also tell us that the FBI has now been called in."

The transmission ended.

A hot bead of worry cut its way slowly down the center of my forehead like the tip of a razor-sharp knife.

I knew that symbol.

I recognized its curves and the way it arched up to a precise point at its ends.

"Everything OK?" I heard the old man next to me ask.

I dropped to my knees and furiously began gathering up all the loose items that had fallen out of the bag. My grip on Sara was peaking now, my arms unconsciously wedging her tight against my chest, which in turn, made her start to cry.

"Ya, ya, everything's cool," I muttered in a panic, still held hostage by the image on the screen. I stuffed the last stray can of baby formula underneath my arm, and set the crosshairs of my eyesight dead onto the center of my vehicle, trying my best to calm down Sara as I ran. I dove inside that old white clunker of mine with great speed, forgetting all about how much I disliked it and locked both the doors.

I was fighting hard now to control the tremors that had overcome my body. The trailers of that bloody dream I'd suffered through that dreary night were beginning to show themselves once again, boldly highlighting the eerie symbol I'd seen towards the end of it.

The exact same symbol, I might add, that had just flashed across national fucking television!

"What in the Hell is going on here?" I said, looking skyward. "This can't be possible. Nobody knows about my dreams. Nobody knows what I saw! Something's Fucked up here," I growled. My mind's playing tricks on me, that's what it is...

"I'm losing my fucking mind!!!"

My breathing was starting to max out and I could feel my lips beginning to tingle.

Stop it Eugene, stop it and get a grip on yourself! You're frightening Sara!

Well then my ears opened up. That was the key phrase that brought me around. As soon as I spoke her name, my body got back in line. My lungs began to equalize and my lips too, stood down their alert and became soft. Sixty seconds later my body once more, fell still.

I let my mind regroup for a few minutes as I stared at the dashboard.

Coincidence.

I expelled the last of the tainted air out of my system.

Just a stupid goddam coincidence, that's all it was.

I felt my head tip back and sink into the headrest. My expirations were slower and regimented now, and my nerves trickled back to what my system loosely justified as normal.

I rested there in the parking lot for a few more moments with my hand instinctively perched overtop Sara. She too, was peaceful now. Slowly but surely, the whole ordeal began to dissolve away and that felt good. But I was still baffled as to how this uncommon tombstone, this.. "morbid trademark" of a psychopath went and found its way into my head, even before it showed up in the media. I mean I could understand if it was the other way around, but...

Ah, screw it Eugene. It's over now man, just let it go. It was a fluke. Your mind was fucking around with you. Most likely due to a recent and dramatic life changing experience, if you know what I mean.

"Yep," I smiled, looking over at Sara. "I know what you mean!"

I was definitely relieved after that, knowing that there was a probable explanation for what just went down but I still wish it never had happened. When I finally pulled back out onto the street from the parking lot, I blindly repositioned my hand over towards Sara's chest again as I came up upon a small dip in the road, but instead of acing my target, I landed my palm high and ended up with fingers spanning across her jaw.

Before I could correct the move, Sara to my surprise, had started using my index finger as a nipple again. I found that very interesting.

"I guess she must still acquaint that penny carnival standby to the real thing," I chuckled as I let her chew away at my saturated digit. To be honest, I actually found the simulation quite calming. It was kind of like Sara knew that I was upset and was trying to mellow me out or something. While I drove on and resumed my day, I couldn't help but wonder, even on the off chance, that maybe I was one of those clairvoyant kinds of people. You know the kind that can see stuff before it goes down. But then again, this was the first time that anything like this had happened to me, so once more I found myself at a loss. After another few minutes of curious head scratching, I finally opted out to just forget the whole damn thing. After all, none of it affected me anyway.

I spent the rest of the day tediously working the bugs out of my new and significantly modified routine. You know re-arranging my car, scoping out washrooms with change tables, stuff like that. And oh ya, looking for empties and any other sources of income to replenish my dangerously low portfolio. When seven pm rolled around, I called it a day and stopped at a small park that overlooked the ritzy part of the city. I wrapped Sara up in her blanket and took us over to a shady bench along the edge of the fence line. It was time for some R & R. I had just refilled her bottle for the third time that day and boy was she ever knocking that stuff back!

And as I sat on the park bench feeding Sara and soaking up the beauty of the landscape in the late summer, I caught myself sporting a sappy sort of grin.

"Be careful Eugene, you might start to enjoy this feeling!

After about fifteen minutes, Sara had fallen fast asleep and spit out the gargantuan nipple that adorned the top of the bottle. So being careful not to disturb her, I casually gathered up our things and began the trek back to my car, taking one last swig of the sweet fall air before ducking into the confines of our home.

This night I intended to drive to another one of my favorite sleep spots. It was a flea market parking lot as well, but it was closer to the north side. It was a real cherry, and that's where me and my girl would bed down tonight.

I liked it there. I think it's because there were always a fair amount of people like me in the area as well, so it was pretty safe and hassle free. That was an appealing bonus, especially tonight for I had a big day ahead of me. I had to finish re-organizing my car into a more "baby friendly" one. I had to make it functionable and roomy without tipping off any curious passers by to the true nature of my renovations. I did have a few ideas jotted down from earlier in the day, but in the end, I decided it would be better just to get a good night's sleep and start fresh in the morning. In my usual state of paranoia, I rolled my car to an invisible halt about a hundred feet away from an oversized four door gas muncher of a vehicle off to the right of me.

This place was great. It was not too far out, but still away from it all in the same aspect. I took advantage of it sparingly, as with the rest of the gold stars in my arsenal, and when my engine finally sputtered to a standstill, I began the well-rehearsed task of preparing my own little wandering condominium for it's stay.

As I squirmed and shuffled about inside the cab, I felt my eyes start to drift off and gaze habitually out beyond the windshield of my ride at the desolate graveyard-like setting that lay before me.

I noticed that there were a considerable amount of "associates" here this evening. "Looks like a full house", I chuckled.

But my thoughts ran deeper and more serious than the haphazard façade I presented. I think it was the sheer volume of people here that was causing me great unrest inside, and I couldn't understand why. I mean I'd seen this damn movie about a thousand times before so what was up with me tonight?

I soon found myself arguing with an old demon friend of mine by the name of denial.

It was a heated discussion for sure, but when it was over I did conclude it to be true that lately, I'd begun to notice the base numbers of us out here in the abyss beginning to increase, and dramatically too.

That's what was really bothering me. Because somewhere in my heart I knew that the zombie convention that existed beyond my hood, and that I was way too much a part of, was in reality, an exact and frightening depiction of the way society in general was heading.

The line was getting so wide.
That's a hard thing to face out here. The fact that you are nothing more than a disease in the eyes of society.

"That's the goddam truth," I concluded in a grunt as I sunk my head into my seat and tried to think of something else. It had been another hectic day and all I really wanted was to not be awake anymore! Although I was somewhat fired up from my latest revelation, I did manage to shrug it off and force my eyelids down against their will. But I guess my pupils didn't quite see it that way, and refused to allow the seal, promptly sending them back up to their starting position. After ten more minutes of staring at the tattered cloth on my roof, I once again pointed my stubborn globes in the direction of Sara, hoping to take advantage of her sedative aura to aid in my own quest for unconsciousness. After only a few seconds of watching my little gem's uncoordinated body twitch away underneath her covers, I felt my muscles grow limp as the moon began to ooze its red/black medicine down onto us from the transparent portal in the roof. Before I knew it, the comforting echo of the breeze skipping along my quarter panels finally convinced my body and mind to unite as one and leave the day in the past. My hard-earned slumber, I calculated, was deep but not very long as I was abruptly awakened in the exact same position I went "nighty night" to, by the increasingly familiar and high-pitched sound of Sara's cry's.

"Oh well," I moaned after a quick stretch. "I've been pretty lucky so far I guess."

I think I was starting to get used to her very demanding, but understandable routine. The very first thing I did of course was slide my hand underneath her bottom to check for any surprises. To my relief she was dry as a bone.

Yeah freakin' hoo!

It was a windfall in disguise for I was expecting a worst case scenario to come out of that test judging by the way she was scarfing back her baby formula early on. But Lady Luck decided to grant me a stay of execution it seemed, well for a few more hours anyway. So I went with it. My baby was more than thrilled at the fact that I was awake again too, and judging from the earth shattering scream she suddenly let loose, I figured that there was a pretty good chance she may be in need of a hug or a midnight snack, like ASAP!
So wasting no further time, I pulled myself up and cast my hand toward the glove box where her precious cargo lay. Pretty soon that synthetic home wrecker was brushing against the bottom of her lip.
It took a little coaxing, but eventually my cautious passenger inhaled the well-designed fake and calmed down. After that, the only sound escaping out from her side of the car was the echo of hypnotic suckling.
And in no time at all, that regimented vibration began adding more and more weight to the tops of my eyes. It was impossible to fight and finally, under the influence of her lullaby, I felt my neck suddenly give out.

This must have happened a few times because when I opened my eyes and looked over at my wee angel, I discovered that she was fast asleep and her bottle was lying empty on the floor

"Must be nice," I said as I leaned over and delivered a silent kiss to her tranquilized cheek. "Good night," I told her and with that I crept back over to my side and of our apartment and re-acquainted my worn out body with the equally worn out groove in the driver's seat. I figured I'd be out like a light but just then my own stomach, obviously jealous of it's placement on the priority scale, rumbled loudly in discontent and demanded at least a teaser before it gave the OK for my eyes to shut. Giving in at the sacrifice of a few more precious minutes of sleep, I reached under my seat and pulled out a small bag of peanuts.

I horked back a couple of handfuls then returned the stale snacks into their hiding place.

"Now Eugene you shit head, go to sleep! You know the rules. What are you trying to do? Get yourself sick!"

Big brother, I'm afraid was right; I was looking pretty bad these days. I guess with all the excitement in my life lately, I was forgetting to eat even the meager amount of chow I was used to. But in the same breath, I also understood the consequences of an illness. It was a price tag I could neither risk nor afford. So I did as I was told and closed my eyes. In an attempt to speed up my altered state I used an old trick I had utilized as a kid. I just concentrated on nothing. I spray painted over my minds eye and focused in on the darkness I created. My childhood game was beginning to work and I was three inches away from Never Never Land when the event we all dread out here carved a gash into my spine and hurtled my brain into a state of red alert.

Footsteps!

Coming in loud and clear and ricocheting off the shell of my Firebird like bullets!

Oh Fuck!!

In an instant my muscles began to pressure up and burn with adrenaline.

Someone must have heard Sara crying. Someone must have heard that and now they're coming over here to investigate! "Sonofabitch... I'm screwed! I am really fucking screwed now!!*

I ran over a quick defense plan in my head, but my strategy proved to be weak. My first reaction, of course, was to reach for the keys and get the hell out of there. But as the repercussions of the newest footstep bore through my eardrums, I knew it was all but to late for that little maneuver. Whoever it was coming for me and my little girl was not even three feet away now... tops! With a desperate grunt, I quickly pulled a corner of Sara's blanket over her face, and then disappeared just as quickly underneath my own covers. All I could do now is wait. Wait and try to ready myself for the oncoming confrontation.

Suddenly I heard the vibrations come to a halt. This made my pulse double instantly and caused my left hand to begin it's worm-like journey towards the large hunting knife embedded in my door. It wouldn't be long now, for I knew my assailant was right on top of me. I could feel his angry breaths beating down on the back window. "He knows," I thought. "He knows there is someone in here. He can see us plain as day for Christ Sakes!"

OK Eugene. Get ready! Get ready, he's just ab... Wait. Oh oh. Wait a second here. Back window?

But there's nothing behind my car but bald ass prairie and the odd coulee, I thought.

Ya,... Ya that's right, because I remember backing up to the very edge of the parking lot.
There's nothing behind me but sweet grass and bu, bu... Bush!

Oh fuck! Oh Fuck... it, it was a bush freak! Oh Jesus no. Not one of them! Anyone but them!
Well now I was really flipping out! It was a bush freak that had found me. I knew it! It had to be one of them. There was no other explanation. I had tipped off a greeb and now he was staring right in at me.

"Godammit," I muttered. *But how? How did he make it all the way up here. It's not possib...*

BANG!!

My rationale was suddenly undermined by the unholy sound of dense and exact compressions as they struck the asphalt and made their way around the side of the trunk panel towards the door.
My door!!!
The blanket overtop my face was heavy and thick, allowing me no transparency whatsoever to study my foe. But that didn't mean a thing for in the forefront of my mind I already had a far too realistic picture of what the face that lay only inches beyond the thin barrier of my side window looked like.
I could almost touch the skin of the emaciated psychopath that I knew hovered directly over me now. He was searching for a way in. I knew it. Why else would he approach my ride? I could just about smell his rotting breath as he glared into the cab, but I had a little surprise for this motherfucker tonight! And that surprise was already inching itself out from the security of my door frame.
I winced a little as the tip of the blade abruptly left the steel and plastic sheath of my driver's door.
A place where it always sat and waited for the unique opportunity when it was to be called upon.
That time was now.

I knew my baby was still dozing away peacefully beside me. I knew she was happily surrounded by a dream and was unaware of the incredible danger she was in. Unaware of the predator that lurked within fatal reach of her that no thickness of glass could keep out. A villain however, that was on the verge of being destroyed!

My adrenaline spiked up to an unimaginable level as I heard the forceful expulsions of my enemy's breath drip down the length of the tapered glass not even seven inches from my head. The fury of his exhalations hit the glass with an audible thud. I could endure this torture no longer, so with my heart in my mouth and my hunting knife welded securely in my palm, I boldly held up a picture of the innocent soul in my passenger's seat and taped it to the dashboard of my mind. I would use it as inspiration, as a vehicle to help bring forward every last ounce of courage and strength I possessed to ensure her safety.

And when I figured that I was never more ready to defend she who could not, I sprang out from underneath my sleeping bag with the darkened intensity of a madman and thrust my knife in the direction of my attacker.

The monster I had already come to terms with suddenly reared up in astonishment and exploded away from my car. I watched after that in a state of embarrassed bliss as the intruder darted back into the shadows of the landscape with great speed, its four hoofs and large white tail bobbing to and fro in unison with the ironic message it projected.

The stag was all but a memory in less than five seconds.

Feeling greatly relieved but equally stupid, I fell back into my supine casket and let out a long stagnant gasp.

It was just a deer. Just a bloody deer!

I groaned as I lay their in a haze and stood down from my near-venison encounter. Seconds later I tilted my throbbing face over towards Sara.

She was awake, but quiet. So I leaned over and picked her up, laying her back down moments later onto my chest with my knife still wedged tightly into my shaking hand. We laid their in total silence me and her. Sara was as mellow as could be. It was like nothing at all had happened. I was actually hoping to capitalize on my newborn's placid state of composure again, but strangely enough, it was she that benefited the most from my elevated heartbeat and before I knew it she was fast asleep in my arms. Being careful not to wake her, I tip-toed my left hand that still clenched the knife off her snoring body and slipped the blade back into the thin groove of the door. I replaced my empty limb back overtop her, then just zoned out in a post traumatic haze as I felt the fluctuation of her minute lungs rise and fall with dramatic precision beneath my palms.

With a hint of embarrassment, I referred back to my recent brush with the wild.

He's probably just as scared as you are.

"No Shit" I thought, answering my own question..."No Shit!

It must have taken a good ten minutes for my heart to slow down to a reasonable level. Sara remained sedated and had not been affected in the least by the ordeal, but I on the other hand was well, shall we say, "bright eyed and bushy tailed" if you know what I mean, and about the only thing that I was really sure of at that point was the simple fact that I needed to get the hell out of my damn car for a while! I could feel the already cluttered space beginning to close in on me so I made the call and carefully set Sara back into her crude tent, hiding her away once more from the judging eyes of the real world. Without making a sound I sat up and carefully rolled off my tattered bedspread.

She'll be OK here for a few minutes. I convinced myself. *I'll lock it up tight and not let my car out of my field of vision.* I knew it wasn't the most politically correct thing to do, but I just had to get some air.

Now, actually getting out of my rig without making any noise proved to be fairly difficult. It was a very slow and tedious process, but eventually I managed to wiggle my way outside. It felt great to be free from that space and the first thing I did was suck in a big hit of the night air. The fresh breeze was a welcome change from the suffocating congestion of my sports car. I stretched my arms up to the sky and began to shuffle out into the night, not heading anywhere in particular, but always keeping the outline of my old Pontiac within eyeshot as planned. My stroll was initially intended to be random, but for some reason I found my body being drawn towards the big old four door Buick I had spotted earlier parked underneath one of the huge steel lampposts that littered the lot. As I got closer to the antique sedan, I instinctively slowed up my pace and began lightening my steps. I knew that the vehicle I was approaching had someone living inside it. That was a given. You don't even think of parking out here for the night unless it's the only place you got. It wasn't as if I was under any delusions as to the purpose of the ride, but something seemed different about this car and I couldn't quite figure it out.

I crept a little closer so I could look inside, knowing full well that what I was doing; spying on another transient was absolutely taboo under any circumstances. I should have stopped what I was doing and headed in another direction, but something kept pulling me forward, dragging me closer to that car.

When I did finally reach the side window a sick feeling of regret descended onto me and I knew right away that what I had just done was a mistake. Why? Because what I saw inside was a sight that even for the likes of me, was very difficult to accept. I stood there in shock as I peered down at an entire family. Not simply a lone drifter, which I could more easily deal with. No, this was a whole different ball game. This was one of those images that never really leave you, its memory like a cancer that only gets worse with time.

I could see from the illumination above that the mother and father were curled up in the front seat, while their three young children were huddled up tightly together in the back. One girl and two boys.

It was as plain as day. None of them were over the age of seven either. They couldn't have been. I could easily make out the contours of their innocent faces with the help of a moon ray that was flowing as well, through the glass.

The mother and father had no blankets at all, and it looked like the children were sharing only one. A half -eaten loaf of bread and a box of cereal sat stuffed up against the back window, and it didn't look like there was much else in the form of sustenance in there. I stood like a ghost, and watched them for awhile as they slept. These are the times when as a confessed vagrant, you don't feel so good about your chosen profession anymore because just when you think you've finally seen it all and nothing else can hurt you, something like this happens and your soul hits the dirt again. I felt a great sadness for these people and their situation, even though I too, bled from the same wound.

I wondered if there was ever a time in their lives where they were happy, when they took things for granted and had big dreams and big expectations and how terrible it must have been as one by one, each of those fantasies had to be soberly abandoned.

And the children. They were the real victims in this crime.

And as I watched them dreaming away together on the seat, it devastated me to know that one day in the very near future all their aspirations too will sour, and they'll wake up surrounded by a sea of dragons with no angels left in sight to save them.

I turned away.

I couldn't look at them anymore. I felt like I was going to be sick as I trudged back towards my own coffin. And no matter how hard I tried to block out the atrocity I had just seen, my mind once again went into a distressed state and began pushing forth the same question unto me again and again. The one that I had been trying so hard to avoid.

What the fuck are you doing Eugene? What kind of life can you possibly give a baby? That life back there, huh? Is that it? Is that your "big plan?" A destitute existence chained up in the backseat of a cold car, sharing a handful of cereal and a stale piece of bread everyday to survive. Is that your ten year itinerary boy, because if it is, then you've got real problems!

Did you maybe make the wrong decision? Did you maybe do more harm than good here?

I let my inner caucus battle it out as I drug my feet on towards the white shell of my car. By the time I reached my destination I had successfully managed to sneak away from the damning eye of my persecutors and find some peace, but I knew it wouldn't be long before they tracked me down again. They always did.

And as the battle ensued, I hoped, as always for a stay of execution, but it looked like I was on my own this time. No props in the world were going to help me now. I had to get through this all by myself. I had to fight back the negative thoughts and focus in on the light, for now it wasn't just about me anymore. It was about the miracle that lay in a makeshift bed on the passenger seat beside me. A miracle that I had willfully taken responsibility for and made a pledge to in these past few days. I understood more now, that this decision was going to test me to the limit, but that I would face those challenges with absolute loyalty.

She was worth it.

I mean, when I thought back to how completely despondent my life was only days earlier, compared to the way I felt now, the change was almost incomprehensible. And as I settled back into my car and slid quietly underneath my covers, I solemnly swore that from then on in I would no longer surrender myself to any past levels of sadness or retreat. And whatever the world threw at me I would overcome it and carry on. I would do what I was meant to do.

I would be her father.

I turned over to my side, facing my precious cargo as usual and went to sleep. This transformation happened quite rapidly, but in the span of that ten second trip, I remember thinking of how ironic it was that all of us enter into this life with a pure soul, and then more often than not, spend the remainder of that very life struggling to ensure we leave it in the same way. I wondered, as well in that final breath, if that revelation was to hold the same truth for me.

And what of Sara?

Chapter 2

baby steps

The seven days that followed were definitely an adjustment period for both of us. Sara, mind you, was settling into her new home life in the passenger seat quite well. She rarely made a fuss about her new lodgings except, of course, when she would loudly voice her discontent at me every time I hit a pothole.

I, on the other hand, carried around a little more stress for I was in effect, stumbling through the first stages of fatherhood. And when I say "first stages", I really mean, "The no sleep, being pelted with shit and snot ten times a day under the serenade of a high pitched wail" stages of fatherhood.

They say," what doesn't kill you only makes you stronger." I agreed with that fable 100% now. It's true that my patience was being stretched to the limit every single night, but was mysteriously healing itself over again with each sunrise, constantly widening its range every time. And as the days went on, the onslaught of chores associated with parenting became steadily tolerable and even the decibel level of Sara's cries were becoming less painful. I guess I was just starting to adapt to my new surrounding in much the same way I knew my little girl was in her mobile nursery beside me.

I had designed a rough but surprisingly functional crib slash day bed for her out of two towels that I rolled up and maneuvered around to form a shallow barrier, with Sara's thick fleece "blankee" spread out smack dab in the center. Whenever she wasn't in her bed, I would drape a thin sheet over her sleeping quarters forming a sort of seat cover so if anyone was passing by, they would hopefully not be tipped off to anything suspicious. I also used my sleeping bag in the daytime to cover up all of our clothes and such in the backseat. I had to be very careful about this whole thing. I mean let's face it, what I was doing was the right thing, but not in the eye's of the law. When the time came around to put Sara down for the night or for her afternoon nap, I would take the same sheet and stretch it overtop the bucket seat again until it resembled a tent. She actually loved this whole process and would squeak and fart whenever I did it. I could tell from this behavior that she was going to be a real outdoorsy type when she got older.

Either that or a trucker.

Tell you the truth, the whole inside of my old clunker became slowly transformed into a quaint little apartment for two. It was no different a transformation I figured, than when a single bachelor moves in with his new life mate. You know, things naturally began to change. Heavy metal magazines that had until recently been my only source of literature, were systematically replaced with large print garage sale pop up books with such wholesome story lines as "Hansel and Gretel", and my own personal favorite... "The Little Engine That Could." I was always on a never-ending pillage for pop bottles. I was earning about $12 a day, and although it was tight most of the time, we managed to get by. This baby-raising stuff was pricey by anyone's standards, and even though I had budgeted a maximum of two baby toys in my possession at any given time, (not including her yellow rubber ducky for bath time of course), I ended up in the span of a week with a mound of thrift store trinkets that would have given "Toytown" a run for it's money!

I stashed all her playthings in a black garbage bag underneath her seat so they were always out of sight. I guess it wasn't the most financially smart thing to do, but I never paid more than a dime for any given one so I justified it as an expense.

Besides, Sara never had a problem with acquiring a new toy. I also bought a soother and one of those 69 cent check stand pamphlets entitled, "Your Baby's First Year, What to Expect." But to tell you the truth, I was always too scared to read it. The soother on the other hand well Holy Shit! I'd like to kiss the guy's large hairy ass who invented that sucker! That was the best pacifier I had and I used it extensively. Yep, our little pad was definitely compact, but it was always clean.

The sunroof also doubled as a much-needed vent, thank God. I don't think I could have handled the stench of Sara's regular early morning poop-athons without that standard issue sour gas escape hatch. I went through a ton of paper napkins and plastic grocery bags too. I'll bet a lot of the fast food burger dungeons were noticing a strange increase in their paper serviette budget in the last little while, but hey, technically they were "free", so I wasn't really to blame. Yep, things were going along quite smoothly, and with the exception of unharmed nipples, I pretty much had this maternal instinct thing down pat! How was my stomach holding out, you ask?

Steel baby! Absolute steel!

I was an unstoppable baby changing machine, Jack! And I was getting so good at constructing my own diapers I was seriously considering opening my own line. And for all my labors I was always properly rewarded with things I think, that you can only experience by actually spending time with a newborn. Things like watching her spastic limbs flop around and gyrate as they struggled to get in sync with one and other. Or the way Sara would move her head from side to side and stick out her tongue at me for no reason. You know little things like that. And hiccups! Good God!!... Did you know that newborns get hiccups? Neither did I? Yessir, there were a lot of things I secretly looked forward to in a day with Sara, like the way her eyes reacted to the sound of my voice and the way her body language changed as soon as I picked her up. So many things, so many little quirks and habits she had that were steadily molding her personality - they were all just so... just so miraculous. It's almost impossible to imagine what goes through the mind of a newborn, but boy did I spend a lot of time trying.

The thing I loved most of all though, had to be the sound of her breath at night. It was a totally euphoric experience for me. The hum of the air passing through those tiny nostrils of hers was so mesmerizing, that it soon came to a point where I would wake up in the middle of the night out of a dead sleep if her expirations changed their rhythm for any reason. Now I could lie and tell you that I was not ready for such a massive commitment at such a fragile stage in my life. I could also hint that slowly, I was beginning to feel a genuine sense of connection with that child and that I was starting to be able to pick out the light at the end of the tunnel and all. But you know what, if I was forced to tell the truth, I would really have to confess that since the moment I'd found her, absolutely nothing in my life felt the same way as it did before.

Not one thing.

I knew I was in love with that little girl from the second I laid my eyes on her in the cold sweat of that garbage can. And my life in that same heartbeat was instantly changed forever. The sorrow I harbored in the time before her vanished into thin air the second I heard her cry. She had me at "Hello" and no matter what, that simple fact would never change. Did I worry? Was I afraid? Hell yes!! In fact I don't think that there was a second that passed by in a day where I was not biting my nails and fretting about any one of a million different and catastrophic situations that I was sure were about to happen. But I guess after awhile I came to realize that the only thing I could really do is take this new life day by day and try to do the best I could.

It was early September by now and the fall season was beginning to take hold of the city, embossing the landscape with oceans of browns and yellows. The air was growing a little cooler, and the nights as well, were starting to come about a little faster. It was like summer had disappeared almost overnight. I'd picked up an old wool couch cover at a yard sale for a whole fifty cents and began using it overtop Sara's usual fleece blanket. Her staying warm was more important than anything so I wasn't taking any chances.

By the end of that first week, however, I was in serious need of a Laundromat. I had totally run out of clean towels and my own conservative wardrobe was starting to give off quite an offensive odor to boot.

Now in the past, I had always gone to this big multi-purpose cleaning center on the main drag heading into the core, but now I thought, I'd better look for someplace a touch more out of the way and less mainstream, for Sara's sake. I was still a little leery about exposing her to very many people and after the trip to the drugstore that one day, I realized that my little bambino was a complete and total flirt and was far too capable of drawing attention to herself.

God was I proud of that!

So I decided to check out this small backstreet washhouse I had spotted in the low rent area of the city's west end one day as I drove around and searched for yet another choice sleep spot to add to my collection. After zigzagging up and down a few side streets, I finally got my bearings and caught a glimpse of my destination. Flipping an illegal shithook in the middle of the street, I anchored my beast right out in front of what I guessed, was the main entrance.

Well one thing was for sure, it was definitely quiet and out of the way and by the looks of things, the place was pretty run down and unpatronized.

It was perfect!

It was exactly the type of place I was looking for: unpatronized. Making sure to gather together no less than 80 to 90 pounds of baby supplies and toys, along with the bulk of our dirty duds and of course, my little Sara, I hip-checked the squeaking door to my ride shut, and drug the whole entourage inside. When I fell through the front entrance, I realized that my intuitions were pretty much bang-on. The place was definitely in need of a makeover and a plumber. It was circa 1962 and the number of machines with out-of-order signs taped to them seemed to greatly outnumber the ones without. The carpet was also stained and reeking badly from what looked like many years of chemical saturation and neglect. On the positive side, the machines, although they looked like they'd never been serviced, were dirt cheap to use. It was only ten cents for the dryers and seventy five cents for the washers.

Yep, I was in love with the place already.

Skipping across the depleted section of functioning machines, I luckily spotted two thoroughbreds sitting side by side off in the corner beside a deep, old, well-used scrub sink. Inhaling a solid breath, I let out a grunt and heaved my oversized booty across the last twenty feet of my expedition and plopped the bulging sack onto the floor. I set Sara on top of an adjacent machine with her latest toy while I began to unload and sort our duds.

Without warning, a petite old Chinese woman suddenly darted out from somewhere in the back and quickly descended upon me and my little girl.

"Huwwo," she beamed with a huge porcelain smile. "Huw aww yu?"

"I'm fine," I answered and before I could lay down another word, that hopped-up senior citizen locked eyes with Sara and said as she clasped her palms against her face.

"Wowee, Wha an adowibol wittle tild!"

"Thank you," I said again, taking another shot at actually completing a full sentence.

But nope, it was not to be, for as soon as I finished up my appreciative response, that five foot nothing fireball jumped forward and pasted my tiny angel with a great big Grammy-style kiss. Sara responded back of course with an earth shattering scream! Well that poor old Asian lady reared backwards with the speed of an atomic bomb, obviously crushed by my baby's lack of etiquette.

"She's just shy," I said, quickly applying a mental bandage to the shocked woman's trampled feelings.

"It OK," the lady suddenly yelped back nervously. "Newa fix!! Newa fix evysing," and with that the feisty proprietor bolted away in the same direction in which she appeared and came crashing back through the door again a few minutes later carrying a sinister looking object in her right hand.

"It OK," the woman stated once more, "Newa make evywon happy again."

The notably-flustered, but sincere old woman, then calmly walked over to Sara's side who was by now, vibrating the panels out of the ceiling with her cries, and held up the mysterious article she had retrieved to near proximity of my little girl's puckered face, giving the thing a deliberate twirl with the snap of her finger.

It looked like some sort of charm, the thing she held up. A terrifying-looking sort of a charm to tell you the truth. It was round, flat and about the size of a baseball, but it was surrounded by jagged spikes that were protruding out from all around it. It kind of resembled one of those ninja throwing star things you always see in them old Kung Fu movies and it was attached and hung with a piece of thick braided leather strapping. At that point, I honestly had the urge to grab my little girl and run for my life! But just as my muscles were priming themselves for the dash, something incredible happened.

Sara stopped crying.

Just like that, she became still. I looked down at my child in astonishment and watched in curious delight as the sparse rays from the fluorescent lamps above caught the sharp edges of the deadly-looking trinket and ricocheted them with pinpoint accuracy across Sara's puffy eyes, which were all of a sudden, fixated in amazement on the old world charm. Man, you had to see it. Sara went from hysterical to hypnotized almost instantaneously. Her body stopped seizing and her limbs fell to her side like she'd just been hit with nerve gas!

"You see," whispered the woman confidently. "Newa fix."

After a short pause, I finally broke off the bead of my own stare and said in the most grateful of tones,
"Oh God, thank you sooo much," I joked. I've already lost about 10% of my hearing this week alone!

The wise woman then looked up at me with the most candid of grins and said, "You welcome."

"My name is Eugene Lauder," I said, straightening up my posture and thrusting out my open hand," very nice to meet you. Oh, and this little faker's name is Sara. Sara Lauder.

How did you do that?" I asked, furthering the conversation.

The sweet lady then said with a forced but painfully comical western accent,

"Ancient Chinese Secret!"

We both let out a large simultaneous laugh and from that moment on, it was as if I'd known that sawed-off little rock star my whole life.

Newa Quang, the woman in front of me said, as our laughter began to die down, "Nice to meet you too.
The mother must be wery beautiful," the elderly lady continued to say.

"I... Uh, I... She..." I felt my voice begin to hesitate and skip as I realized the ripple effect of my secret.

"I'm, Uh, I'm her only family," I said after an awkward pause. "It's just... well it's just... her and I."

I then watched helplessly as the frail old woman softened up her smile and guided her hands over toward mine, embracing one of them as it lay sleeping on top a nearby washer.

"She very lucky," smiled the old woman.

I think she was trying to lessen the amount of guilt I portrayed in my sudden apprehensive stance towards the subject. Her touch was genuine and strong and I knew right then and there that I had just made a new friend. A feat I had not accomplished in a long time.

Me and Sara spent the remainder of that afternoon happily tucked away at that backstreet Laundromat getting to know our new acquaintance. She was so cool. She didn't appear to judge me for the way I looked or the length of my hair or anything.

I liked that, for I was all too familiar with the feeling of being segregated, and I think in the back of her mind, she knew that.

We had a great conversation. Choppy, but great. I was amazed at the way she fussed over Sara. At one point, she cautiously asked me if it'd be OK that she held her for a moment.

"Absolutely!" I said, picking up my sweetheart from her nest (whom I would like to add, just loved all of the extra attention.) And as I handed over my squeaking child, I sat back and watched in silent jubilation as that tiny old woman's dim eyes lit up with the intensity of the sun, then sank closed with equal affection as she pressed my baby against her neck. I let Newa have all the time she wanted with Sara for I could see how much the whole experience was rejuvenating her. Eventually, out of innocent curiosity, I asked our host where her family was. Without provocation, the gentle woman's demeanor grew sad and it took a good while before she was able to voice back an answer.

"Husband die," she said quietly. "Kids gone away too. No visit no more."

It was then that I began to re-construct a dismal story of regret and abandonment. I soon realized by the anguish of her last sentence, that the only real thing she had left now was this beat up old out of the way Laundromat and a few scattered memories of an earlier time.

"I'm sorry to hear that," I told her respectfully and shot back with an immediate compliment in hopes of swaying her deep mood.

"Well my little girl just can't get enough of you," I crooned.

My plan was successful, and as a result of my quick wit, a much-anticipated smile raced back to the senior's face and to my relief, stayed there. In an act of celebration, she then hoisted Sara up high into the air and began relentlessly plastering her with tickles and kisses, and some kind of weird Chinese baby jargon.

She also slipped that magical ninja charm into my coat pocket and whispered, "You keep fo go luk."

Well, from that meeting on, Mrs. Newa Quang was simply known to me and my baby as "Gramma", a term Newa was more than delighted to accept. After a lengthy goodbye, sealed with a promise that I was easily persuaded to make regarding many future visits, I packed up my wonderful-smelling clothes along with my equally aromatic child and skipped out through the door. I draped Sara's useful but dangerous-looking charm over the rear view mirror so that she could benefit from its medicinal reflection, but not be able to reach it. I knew my little girl was probably against this move but I'm afraid its edges were super sharp and therefore, strictly off limits to newborns. As I drove off and waved goodbye to our new and unlikely friend, I was hit with an awesome sense of accomplishment. I had gained other adults affections and more importantly, made a lonely old woman feel needed again. It was the best feeling ever and while I made my way back out of that quaint neighborhood with the invigorating scent from my clothes drifting about the cab, I decided that it was my turn too, to get washed up.

So I drove to the nearest hobo-friendly gas station I knew of and packed up my kit. I had already cleaned Sara up that morning so I just laid her there on the bathroom counter beside the sink and let her feverishly chew on her fat little toes while I got ready to scrub my own filthy body down. I lathered up my thick, grease-ridden hair first off with some hand soap from the dispenser, and then worked my way down. The whole process took about ten minutes, a little longer than usual but you know what, I didn't really care anymore. When I was dry I put on my best outfit, which would in reality, would be classified as some normal persons worst outfit. Then, in a move that almost had to be re-learned, I actually combed my hair back and let it set. It was a nice feeling to be clean and have freshly-laundered clothes on again. I felt, well... I felt human.

After I got everything and everybody tucked back into the car again, I pulled around to the front of the service station and threw five bucks of the good stuff in my patient old rig and topped off the sale with a brand new air freshener. "Imperial Pine" Mmm, I loved those ones the best. I rumbled away feeling very confident. Now it was only about 6 o'clock in the evening so I decided that it was high time that me and my number one girl to go out and paint the town red, hobo-style! I mean why not? After all, we were all spiffed up and everything! And I knew just the place too. It was located in this huge shopping mall complex about twelve blocks north of were I was.

It was a garden actually. An enormous solarium and home renovation store where anyone could go and walk around for free. There was a coffee bar there too, and a giant indoor pond filled with grossly overweight goldfish that you could feed if you had no conscience and a quarter for the pellet dispenser. It was an awesome escape, and if you closed your eyes it felt like you were actually in the forest. I didn't go in there very often because the coffee was astronomically expensive and you only got one refill! But hey, that was just okeedokee tonight because me and my Sara were going all out!

The drive over took no time at all and once inside, I purchased a medium hazelnut coffee at the "shoot me in the head with a large gun" price of only $1.50 and picked a spot over by the pond. I sat there happily watching the fish scurry about as I rocked Sara back and forth to the beat of the soothing water. The place was all climate-controlled via computer. It was like sitting by the lake on a warm summer evening without the mosquitoes. It was heaven. We stayed there and enjoyed that serenity for the next couple of hours, but when the soft music abruptly came to a halt, I knew that they were getting ready to close and it was time to leave. With the speed and grace of a sloth, I heaved my pacified butt off the wrought iron bench and took one last sniff of the scented air, then closed my eyes and pictured a campfire with bright stars above it. As I exhaled I said aloud a guarantee to the little girl who lay in my arms.

"One day we will get there sweetheart. One day."

I glanced downward to see her reaction, only to realize that my sermon had fallen on deaf ears for Sara was sleeping soundly away. She even let out a big snort for fun, and then dove back into her slumber.

Why can't I sleep that well? Guess it must be a baby thing.

Walking easily, I thanked the lady at the coffee bar and quietly exited the building. Sara only woke up twice that night but fell back to sleep quickly after a snack and a change. Newa's magical sleep charm played a big part in that success, I might add. All I did was give that thing one flick and the shiny Godsend that hung from my rear view mirror did the rest.

The time that followed after that was like a dream. Our days became full and enriched. I was her dad, she was my daughter, and we were a team. My life now, was definitely in a set routine. But that was OK by me. It was a nice change from the routine I had known in the past. We visited the Laundromat every few days now, sometimes to do our washing and sometimes just to sit and chat with Newa. The rest of the time I was on a pretty tight schedule though, driving around from place to place searching for bottles, applying for credit cards, you know, whatever I had to do to keep the money coming in. I no longer worried in the least what people thought of me, or how they looked at me. The only person's opinion that mattered now was Sara's.

And speaking of Sara, well she became permanently attached to my hip. Boy, if my grade school teacher could see me now! He'd give me an "A" for sure.

It was a tough go at times I will admit, but we had a great game plan in place. Food, sleep spots, playtime, naptime... You name it, it got done and consistently too. I made sure of that. And even though raising a newborn in the passenger seat of a rusty old muscle car was the farthest thing from a normal home life, I worked hard to ensure that it was as normal to her as I could make it. My world was stabilized now, and if I ever became stressed-out or disillusioned about anything, all I would have to do is look over at her, and that was it, the sun would always come out again. She was like a happy pill that I had a never-ending supply of. I didn't think too far into the future. I couldn't really, for I was far too busy being a parent and enjoying the random moments of life as they came at me.

I would read Sara a bedtime story every night and although she could not understand the words, I knew she recognized the rhythm in my tone. It was so ironic to me, the whole bedtime thing now. I could still recall a time not too far back, where I found myself driving blindly towards some dark corner of the city, my mind nervously preparing for and dreading the hours of the oncoming blackness. But all of a sudden here I was in this time, now anxiously awaiting the sun's disappearance so that I could begin my much-anticipated routine of reading Sara to sleep, and then trying for as long as I possibly could to stay awake so that I could profit from the sound of her respirations once again. I loved that, watching her sleep.
It brought me a great sense of peace.
It acted like an herbal cleanse for my soul, every night washing away the many contaminants it ingested during the daylight hours. And the funny thing about those bedtime stories was that I'm sure Sara sort of enjoyed my feeble attempt at public speaking and the crude animation that followed. But the truth be known, I think she actually spent most of the time gazing up at that crazy-looking ninja star that hung menacingly from the rearview mirror courtesy of her "Gramma." She really loved the way the light from the streetlamps would gather at the pointed arrowheads of the charm, then pulse down rapidly and dance across her mesmerized face. Apparently that was way more exiting than my boring old recitals. It was interesting too, how she would totally fixate on that charm, hypnotized and obedient to it's spice until the strange potion it produced finally kicked in and she blinked for the last time. And in the daytime too, if she was ever crying or upset all I would have to do is give that thing a little twirl and boom, she would calm down right away. The charm, I concluded, was magic.

That following week was also a major education period for yours truly. I must have bombarded the poor staff at that neighborhood drugstore with at least a million baby-related questions. I grilled them about everything from diaper rash to hair care, but they never seemed to mind my onslaught of pediatric queries.
I think those ladies at the till were just thrilled to death that a man was actually doing all the groundwork for once. I made up a story that I stuck to right from the start. I told everyone that Sara was my big sister's kid, and that I was taking care of her baby for a while she was down on a course in Mexico. Ya, it was an outright lie, but it had to be that way. Now don't get me wrong. I really did feel bad having to purposely mislead all of those kind folk down at the pharmacy, but it's true that my fable did carry along with it a few subtle advantages.

I guess all the ladies recognized that I was on a very tight budget, being the sole provider for the baby and everything, so more often than not they would sympathize with my plight and slip me the odd free baby product sampler, given to them as well, by eager sales reps hoping to close a contract. Anything I needed for Sara, if they had it in the back, was always given to me when I came in. Yes, I did feel like shit about the whole thing. I felt like I was breaking their trust, but fact was fact. I was on a very strict budget. I mean between gas and baby formula, sometimes there was barely enough money left over at the end of the day for me to eat. All I usually ended up consuming in a day was the sum total of a peanut butter sandwich and a banana. That was it. The rest of my caloric intake sat with the mercy of the sample tables. Oh ya, and I drank a ton of water from the garage washroom taps. It was great filler and all, but man did I piss a lot.

My laundry bill was becoming quite an expense too, but I in no way, wanted nor expected any financial breaks from my friend Newa. It was pretty apparent that she was living day by day off the dwindling forte of customers that still came around and patronized her business as it was.

The whole Laundromat thing was really nice though. I felt a real sense of warmth when I was there and Newa was always more than happy to see us. As soon as we would walk in the door, that 96 pound tornado would run up and give me a big hug, then whisk Sara away into the backroom, which I soon found out also doubled as her living quarters, to begin her tried and true ritual of pampering the living shit out of my baby. Sara somehow understood that Newa was a part of our lives too.

All I would have to do is say, "Hey, you wanna go see Gramma?" And boom, her whole body would start to wiggle. Newa loved Sara I'm sure, just as much as I. You could see the bond between them and it was such a bonus for me to be able to watch that tired old woman's sunken eyes light up the moment she held my baby close. I must admit though, as much as I needed the occasional break from parenting, I couldn't help but feel a little lost at times when Sara wasn't near me. It was a weird sensation, but it was as if an actual part of my body had been amputated. I just didn't feel complete, and my whole world too, seemed so empty and quiet. Needless to say, I was always very happy to get her back, even though I could always see a hint of sadness in Newa's smile as we would walk out the door and wave goodbye. I did take comfort in knowing though, that we were always welcome to return, to begin our joyous ritual all over again.

Happiness, believe it or not, was starting to become a real staple in my life. I was even stopping to smell the roses once in awhile. My world was beginning to have color again. I was alive and well and best of all, I had another human soul to back me up on that. I constantly had the urge to roll down my window and scream my secret out to the world, but I never did.

I always stuck to my original plan and tried to limit Sara's exposure to a minimum as much as I could. It was the safest way. And even though I stuck very close to that decision, one sunny afternoon when me and Sara were driving past the parking lot of a huge mall complex en route to a particular supermarket and bottle picking route that I knew of, (I always tried to marry the two tasks up if I could to save fuel), I noticed a long uncommonly uniform row of flashy-looking hot rods lined up by the entrance. In theory, I should have kept my tires in the direction that they were pointing, but my curiosity got the best of me, and at the last minute I swung my car off to the left and pulled into the huge cement arena to investigate that shindig a little further.

As luck would have it, turned out that the local car club in the surrounding area was hosting a good old end of the season show and shine. Complete with, of course, free hamburgers and soft drinks. Well zippity freakin' do daa!! If that didn't just beat the living shit out of plastic meatloaf! With the speed of an arrow, I quickly parked my rig and got me and my passenger ready to have some fun, and Oh ya, eat as much free grub as humanly possible. Windfalls like this didn't happen every day and when they did, you milked it for all it was worth.

It turned out to be a great time, like I expected. Sara and I just shuffled around at our leisure and checked out all the hopped-up vehicles. There were some real beauties there too. Fords, Chevy's, a couple of import jobbies. Some really classic shit, and all of them souped up to the nines. But after almost two hours of walking around and drooling at all the bodacious rides, Sara felt like she weighed about 700 pounds! It was time to find a place to sit, so I searched across the sea of chrome for a seat, which happened to be dangerously close to the barbeque, (go figure), and nabbed it. God it felt good to plant my ass down. I was exhausted. I must have eaten my own weight in hamburgers too, which I'm sure didn't help. Sara on the other hand, didn't touch her bottle much. I knew that she was probably starving to death by now so I calmly re-inserted the rubber nipple into her mouth, then sat cross legged on the well-used wooden chair and began to feed my growing baby girl the rest of her formula.

The smoke from the barbeque sifted through my nostrils and the low lying sun massaged my face as I drifted away in thought. I found the pictures that came into my head to be ones belonging to the memories of the countless hours I'd spent with my good friends in the Young Frontiers Club. It must have been the scent from the grill that set off that particular recollection, most likely because it reminded me of the campfires we used to have every single night while we were there. We loved those fires and we would sit there beside them for the majority of the evening, charring the piss out of our hot dogs until they were nothing more than straight carbon. But hey, we still ate them, no matter how terrible they tasted.

And all of us guys too, me, Steve, Andy, Ian and Trevor, even had our own special log we sat on that everyone else knew not to go near. We each initialed that twisted old chunk of lumber with the knives that our number one camp leader, Barry "McDrool" had given us. He even carved his own name into that piece of wood, which we were of course, totally OK with. God I loved those campouts. I remember one night that same summer real good too!

It was the time when me and Steve snuck out of our tents in the middle of the night and went around spying on everyone. Our taboo trip ended up, for the most part being pretty boring, that is until we peeked into Barry's cabin! He was in there with one of the female campout leaders from the other side of the lake,... and she was totally naked! Hell, me and Steve near went through the window when we got a look at that scene. She was a knockout too. Huge bazookas, great butt! Yowzers! Barry still had all of his clothes on at that point, but by the looks of it, the highly motivated woman was desperately trying to rid him of that problem. She was tugging on his belt when we got there, but he wouldn't let her undo it and kept pushing her away.

Well me and Stevie thought our good friend Mr. McDool was just plain off his rocker at that stage! Christ!, if that had been one of us in there, we would have been stripped down to nothing in like, three seconds!

Oh well, his loss, we figured. I guess Barry must have had morals or something?

Man, you'd have to have pretty strong morals not to take up an offer from a babe like that. We didn't fault our faithful leader in the least though. Nope, he was still the coolest dude around in our eyes. And besides, me and my pal got to see a grown woman naked! And at that age, who really cares about anything else?

After we'd had our fill and then some of that private side show, we crept back to our tent and shot the bull for the remainder of the night. It was so awesome. We talked about everything, but sonofabitch, we were tired the next morning.

I missed Steve.

I missed sitting in his room and listening to terrifyingly loud music. I missed our conversations too. Hell, I even miss the way his dad would pound on the door and threaten to violently dismember us if we didn't turn that "rock and roll crap" down! Ya, those were the days. I always get kind of sad when I think back about my best friend and the way we parted. But I hope in some way, that he is able to hear me when I often look up to the sky and thank him for all those great memories. All those sacrifices he made and all the times he defended me. I hope that my name too, pops into his head every once in awhile and causes him to grin. I had come to terms with the fact a long time ago that I would probably never see him again, but I still guarded his memory in the center of my mind with fierce loyalty, to ensure that I would always be able to visit those endless days and replay them with the same vividness as the times in which they happened.

With my reminiscent thoughts beginning to blur, I then watched as his spirit made its way back to that special place in my mind where it would forever live, and closed the door.

I sat there after that, basking in a daze and near asleep from my unscheduled trip into the past, until a very loud car rumbled by me and fish hooked my conscience out from its daydream. I felt Sara's tiny frame too, jerk to life as it rolled past. I knew the lines of that particular car. I recognized the acute curve in the hood and the sleek contour of the body exactly.

It was a Firebird. A little newer I think, but just like mine. Mind you this sucker was beefed up to the max! Jesus it was a beautiful car! It looked like it had been restored from the ground up. Custom paint, custom interior, big hood scoop. You name it, that baby had it! And by the way the pressure of the exhaust was rattling my back teeth loose, I think it was safe to say that the motor was definitely... not stock! As I watched that dream machine thump by, I couldn't help but wish my old roadster looked like that. Actually, I shouldn't be so hard on my ride. Hell, that old beater of mine had pulled me through some pretty rough times. And despite being heavily abused and minimally maintained, it still transported me from A to B without fail. And in all honesty I will say, that when I first picked up that bucket of bolts of mine, well, she didn't look too bad. Not too damn bad at all.

It was a very fluke thing actually, how I acquired my car. Especially the trip there to get it.

I was only sixteen at the time. Steve had just scored his Corvette a few weeks earlier and after cruising around in that rocket for awhile, I knew I myself needed a car too. I wanted that sense of freedom.

Problem was, I didn't have any money and that predicament usually quashes any and all dreams of owning a vehicle. But then one day, as fate would have it, I was looking at the For Sale ads in the local convenience store, mainly out of boredom, when I accidentally overheard the middle-aged clerk telling a story to one of her customers about an old widow she had heard of a few hours east of the city.

It seemed that this elderly lady was more than willing to part with an older but running condition "sports- type car", in exchange of course, for the completion of a small amount of chores and fix up jobs that she, in her ailing state of health, could no longer do. Intrigued by this accidentally-acquired information, I waited patiently until there were no other customers left in the store and proceeded to grill said clerk for more details on the trade. After a brief conversation, she drew me up a crude map and a last name and wished me luck. It was definitely a long shot but hey, I had nothing to lose.

Now having insufficient funds to make the trip in style (bus), I opted out to get there the old-fashioned way.

By hitchhiking! So the next morning I took the 6am transit out to the farthest point east of the city it would take me and made my way towards the highway with a beat-up license plate tucked underneath my arm.

Upon scrambling down the steep embankment to the road, I turned my back on the wind, forced out a big shit eating grin, and threw my thumb high into the air. Unfortunately there were not a lot of travelers out there that day who were to willing to share their ride with a long-haired, white, teenaged male in a leather jacket, but I did manage to luck out after a couple of hours and get a lift from a slow moving Volkswagen van filled to the brim with people who were "very high". They eventually dropped me off at this back hills truck stop about ninety miles outside of the city.

After that though my luck ran dry, and I walked all day out into the endless sea of countryside without so much as a second thought brake light. On the plus side, the landscape was scenic and quite relaxing.

It was rich with rolling hills, deep valleys and vast stands of poplar trees which gave the wind a sweet and tasty smell. It was mid-July and except for the multitude of blisters I sustained on my feet, I really didn't mind the walk. But by 7pm or so, my elation was wearing quite thin. I was tired as Hell, and sick of being rejected. After all, I'd been humping it practically the whole damn day and I was still at least 80 or 90 miles from my destination. Besides, it was starting to grow darker and I knew it was high time for me to start looking around for a place to lay my head down for the night.

With no streetlights to reflect off of me, the chances of landing a ride from then on in were practically nil anyway, so I began skipping my eyes across the infinite amount of horticulture before me in search of a hideaway. No spot in particular of course, just a place where I would be out of view. For a while there, I thought I just may have been shit out of luck, because all that lay before me was open prairie, but then I noticed a small hill at the mouth of a coulee over to the right of me. As I rounded a sharp hook in the road I also spotted a small clump of trees jutting out from behind the oddly-situated mound. Well that was it! My search was over.

I would bed down in the seclusion of those trees for the evening and resume my journey in the morning. Wasting no time I left the hard surface of the pavement and stepped off into the gentle earth of the field, plowing my way easily through the knee high grass. When I had reached what I guessed was the middle of my unsuspecting hostel, I did a quick perimeter check and dropped out of sight. A couple of minutes later the back of my head was notched into the groove of my jacket and my eyes stood fixed and hazy as they gazed up at the uncountable array of stars through the whispering portal of the grass. What an amazing sight that was. As to be expected I was out cold in a matter of seconds. That combination of nature and heaven would take down anything. And my slumber too, remained uninterrupted until far into the next morning when a sharp ray of sunshine politely ended my unconscious vacation. I did consider pushing the envelope and sleeping in a few minutes more, but the excitement of my possible "free ride" was too tempting so I slowly forced my body into a stand and within five minutes I was back on the highway with my thumb out and teeth a blazing as I picked up my course and hammered it up for another shuttle.

This time however, Lady Luck was on my side and only three vehicles into my hitch, a big old trucker dude ground to a halt a couple hundred feet down the pavement and waved me in. He didn't say much, which was alright with me, for I was still pretty worn out from the trek I had endured the day before. The trip was slow mind you, and after a while I found my eyes beginning to fall down again. That is until the high pitch squeal of the air brakes engaging cold cocked me out of my trance and shot my head forward.

"This is it young feller," I listened to the burly operator suddenly grunt. "This is where you wanted to go right."

In a daze, my startled eyes slowly began zeroing in on a string of fences surrounding a modest bungalow and quonset combination off to the right of me.
"YA, um ya. This is the place. RR1 and highway 36," I said.

"Yer home free, short stop," the man grinned.

"Thanks partner," I nodded as the text book trucker laid on the horn and eased his big rig to a standstill. A loud blast of air shot out from beneath the tires as I jumped out onto the ground and waved goodbye to my 18 wheeled taxi. I watched the backside of the pup crawl away as I started over towards the bungalow and double-checked my map.

Yep. This was the place the lady at the store spoke of all right. It had to be.

Exercising a touch of caution, I rapped on the front door and introduced myself. The elderly woman was shocked that someone actually took the time out to make the trip, and after a long, fun-filled weekend of what could only be labeled as illegal and immoral slave labor, I emerged out from that rural concentration camp in wheels of my own.
Those being in the form of a filthy, but running-condition 1971 Pontiac Firebird. Paid in full, complete with a shallow dent in the trunk that for some reason, didn't

surprise me. I cruised triumphantly back into the city, overjoyed with the fact that I now officially owned a vehicle. I had no idea however, at the magnitude of that acquisition, or the size of the role that old white sports car would have in my life in the years to come.

By the time I came out of my little daydream, the hot-rod party was starting to wrap up. One by one the dolled-up motorcars were beginning to fire up and rumble away. I looked down at Sara. She had spit out her bottle and was fast asleep. I could feel my eyes starting to haze over too. The smell of the smoke coupled with the memories of mountains and campfires, and of course, that tranquil night on the prairie, were all beginning to take effect on me. With a hint of regret, I complained my way off the bench and started back towards my car as Sara snored away against my body.

As I walked on I passed by a large bay window, one of the many the mall complex housed, I heard my reflection suddenly call out to me.

I became frozen with fear as my heart started to pound. The mirrored glass was holding me to my spot on the dismal tailings of a memory, a horrible one! It was the image of a day. The one not too long before where I stood decimated in front of a similar window in the core and listened to the reading of my sentence. I felt my hands start to tremble.

What if all of this was just a dream? I worried with a serpent of denial now twisting around my body.

What if as soon as I turn around the dream is done and I'm back downtown again, standing in front of that horrible window, only realizing now that I had never actually left it? What if I'd just conjured up Sara and the whole fantasy in the same instant that the gavel fell?

Oh God, Please don't let this dream end!!! Please!, if all this is nothing more than mist, then out of mercy, please God!! Oh please don't wake me up.

I didn't look up when I prayed, I just fixated my eyes tearfully at the dead hollow in front of my feet as I paid homage to the cement. I didn't know what to do, but I was more than prepared to stand there and live out that possible lie for the rest of my godforsaken life if that's what it came down to.

I was there for a long time. I could hear the people begin to point and whisper all around me, but was I where I was supposed to be?

More time passed and the voices just kept getting louder, the accusations the same. I knew I had to look into that goddam window eventually. I saw no other choice. The blurry line between fantasy and reality was rapidly crumbling away from underneath me. It was time to acknowledge my destiny... My fate.

I felt my eyes blink and release a lone captive as I watched my feet pivot towards the glass. I did however, come to terms with the understanding that if all of this had been nothing more than a big wonderful dream, then it was all worth it no matter were I was when my eyes opened.

The moment of truth inched its way up to the brick fascia, and then to the ledge. I could make out the contours of my reflection now. But sadly, they did not seem any different from before.

Sweat oozed out from my scalp and skipped down my cheek. It was a difficult line to cross, but when my field of sight finally lifted away from the stone ledge, I knew right away that I was not sleeping. And the image that rebounded out from the glass was not that of a useless vagrant, but that of a man. A man who was exactly where he was supposed to be.

I walked in closer, anxious to further bask in my victory until the image of my face shone out bravely from the rest of my body. I stared deep into the tempered surface, trying hard to find the scars of hatred that once made their home on me, but they had vanished.

I looked and looked but they were gone. And my eyes? My eyes were not dead like they were before. They were bright and alive, and they ripped into that fucking window like a machine gun!

Sadness and guilt?

Gone!

Strength and determination had run them off. The shell of a human being that infected my thoughts for so long had disappeared without a trace and I knew that I would never have to look up and see that person in front of me again.

Darkness and daylight had gone to war, and in the end, the sun had prevailed.

I backed away victoriously, then paused there a moment and proudly gazed at the man in the reflection.

A decent man.

Satisfied and in control, I turned around and walked back to my vehicle. I drove away that evening with the most secure of feelings pulsing through my body as I happily listened to Sara snore away underneath her covers. Backing into a predetermined sleep spot, I prepared my own body for the night's hibernation and fell asleep to the heavenly outline of my sleeping beauty. It was a terrific night. Sara was only up a couple of times like usual but went back down easily. Three more nights passed on by in the same state but then, for no apparent reason, on the fourth night, our blissful routine was cut short by the occurrence of a second dream. It was somewhat of a sequel to the first. Although this time, it came at me in a much more vivid and frightening manner.

The nightmare started out in the same fashion as the previous one with the eerie sound of trees swaying back and forth. That segment was then interrupted by the echo of the boy's tears and the hologram of the thick door at the end of the hallway. I again reach down and twist open the handle of the closet, exposing the boy wearing the brightly painted Halloween mask that I know, hides away a terrible secret. He is still gripping the bastardized wax letter with his soiled hand and he once more asks me his morbid question.

"Are you going to kill me?" I hear him say. I soften his fears then lean down to pull off his mask, just like I did in the first dream.

Like before, the grotesque sight of the maggots spilling out from the bottom of the mask jars me backwards and I am fighting to breathe now as the young boy's decomposed body falls over dead. My legs start to feel light as I struggle for oxygen. As I fall to the ground I feel something in my palm. Moments later I look down only to see the strange precisely crafted symbol, still wet with stain lying in my hand again but it doesn't stop there. Nope, for as I close my hand around the object and raise my head up in the direction of the little boy's corpse, I discover that it has disappeared, along with the tiny room that housed it. Then all of the sudden it becomes pitch black and I cannot see a single thing. But I do hear something. Music? Yes... I can hear the sound of music playing on somewhere in front of me that appears to be religious in its nature.

And the last thing I remember happening is me looking upwards and seeing the moon.

Then it was over and I found my mind awake again. Shirt soaked, heart pounding on... but awake!

I immediately looked over at Sara. She was wheezing away peacefully underneath her blankets.

I let out a quiet moan, then waited a couple of minutes before I leaned over the console and snuggled up to my little girl. I was safe with her for I knew no demon would dare mess around with a pure soul. Funny, I began to think, of how it was her protecting me now.

Although the dream was equally as disturbing as the last one, it did not haunt me for as long. It was because of Sara. It was because my spirit knew it was not alone anymore. It had an ally. An angel in its pocket to help beat back all the devils that held contracts in the bizzare puzzle.

The nightmare did still shake me up a bit though, but more due to its persistence and disorder now, rather than it's content. Nonetheless, I still found it remarkably easy to shut out its backlash and fall to sleep. As long as Sara was beside me, I knew that I'd be OK

The next morning, after we'd completed our routine visit to an unsuspecting gas station, I decided to pay a little visit to our only friend, Mrs. Newa Quang, down at the laundry. I could tell that Sara was overjoyed at this idea by the way she happily spit up all over the place the moment I spoke her "Gramma's" name.

I think the sudden donation of saliva was her subtle way of saying "Sure Daddy, I'd love to be spoiled rotten for a couple of hours. That sounds like fun!!"

It was great to see Newa again, but after seven cups of tea, three trips to the bathroom, and a whole lot of strange-looking Chinese cookies, I respectfully scooped up my pampered child and said goodbye to our magnificent hostess. Autumn was in full swing now and the landscape was preparing itself for a long winter. The trees were becoming increasingly bare as the leaves continued to fall to the ground. And the air, especially in the morning, was crisp and biting at times. But regardless of all that, it was still an awesome sight. Autumn always sparked me as the most romantic of the four seasons, even though I had never actually experienced it with a woman before.

After leaving Newa's, I concluded that I was feeling much too lazy to resume my normal quest for empties and decided it would be a better idea to take Sara down to the park for a spell instead, the one with a great view of the city.

Fifteen minutes later I pulled up to the playground's edge and proceeded to bundle my newborn up accordingly. Then I carried her over to a special bench, one that overlooked the giant concrete skyline of our home and sat us down. The park was pretty busy which was a little unusual, but whatever.

I began feeding my baby right off. This was second nature to me now. I even felt lost if I didn't have her bottle close by. It felt nice to just sit there and take in the scenery while Sara gulped down her formula. But my thoughts again began to wander off like they always usually did around this time of year and I caught myself secretly fantasizing about a woman, and what it would be like to experience that type of love, the kind I'd only gazed at through the electronic tentacles of a television screen.

I understood that I wasn't a good-looking man. Every time I caught a glimpse of my mug in the rear view mirror, I was quickly reminded of this subtle fact.

I mean, I don't think people ran home and woofed their cookies every time they got a look at me, but I knew I wasn't about to land a catwalk gig anytime soon either. And even though I had always heard that it's what's on the inside that counts, I still couldn't help but wonder if that rumor was really true in this advanced and looks-oriented day and age.

Ah Hell. What am I going on about?

I hadn't the slightest clue what women wanted or what they didn't! I wasn't even sure what it felt like to kiss a member of the opposite sex anymore it had been so long!

Alright Eugene, you're getting all riled up over a dead issue so just let it go!

This was one time that I had no problem agreeing with my alter ego, so I did exactly as it told me to. I released the chains of the whole damn fantasy and watched it run off. After a minute I looked down at Sara.

"Sorry honey"," I said in defeat. "Looks like it's just going to be you and me."

Suddenly, a cool wind blew up out of nowhere and smacked me across the cheek. My arms automatically pulled Sara closer in towards my body. She was definitely an extension of me now, no doubt about that.

"Wonderful day, is it not?" I heard a voice leap up and say from somewhere behind me. In a nanosecond I had Sara covered up and hidden away.

"The warm season is coming to an end," the unfamiliar voice continued on.

I half-turned my body around to see who was speaking, only to be temporarily blinded by the sun to the point where all I could make out was the outline of a long overcoat that rested on the frame of a man.

I then watched nervously as the dark figure sauntered casually around to the far end of my park bench and sat down, arching his back to the sun. He was an older guy, probably in his fifties or so. He had a strange accent and wore a long ranch-style overcoat that supported a single tightly woven ponytail which hung free outside his collar and down his back.

I was instantly suspicious and how could I not have been. In a defensive maneuver,

I rudely twisted my back towards him allowing the intruder only a glimpse of my face and nothing of Sara. Then in a rare tone, I heard my inner voice begin to scold me for being so paranoid.

Come on Eugene. The guy's just trying to be friendly here. Why don't you relax a little?

Maybe the voice was right. Maybe this guy was just trying to be friendly.

"That's too bad," I responded after an uneasy pause. "I'm more of a summer person myself."

The informal conversationalist smiled and reached out his palm.

"Leon Jenkins," he said as I reluctantly eased my stance into his view and shook his hand.
"And who do we have here?" he asked in a jovial tone, inching his body over steadily to try and catch a peek of my baby girl.

I didn't uncover her though. No way! I wasn't about to be that nice. I didn't want to seem like a prick or anything, but this mystery man was definitely starting to invade my goddam bubble, so I chose to stand down the progression of my neighborly antics and adopt a more rigid attitude.

"Her name is Dave," I mumbled, breaking eye contact with the stranger. "Yup, that's my little bundle of joy, " I continued, trying hard to put an end to this unwarranted inquiry. Without breaking my sentence, I purposely dropped my head down towards my child and said with conviction, "And speaking of joy," I said, "I think it's about time I got this little turkey back home for her nap, Um, his nap, I mean, ya."

Riding on the coattails of that prompt, I quickly packed up our belongings and prepared to leave.
Without warning the determined man suddenly cast out his arm and pulled back the flap of Sara's blanket that hid her face. Now I was really freaked!!

"Well well, it's a little girl," the man cooed in a pathetic attempt to remain friendly. "Isn't she just a little darling; I bet she looks just like her mother," the intruder continued. "And where is the mother now?" he asked in the same sentence.

"She's waiting for us at home right now. All 320 pounds of her!" I lied, trying to throw a scare into him.

Then I dug my toe into the dirt and stood up. But just as I was about to walk away I felt the stranger's hand grab my shoulder, stopping me dead in my tracks.

"Leaving so soon?" he mumbled in a sinister tone. "But we were just getting to know each other."

I spun around and broke free of his arrogant grip. With a firm hold on my baby, I backed up a couple of feet and glared a warning deep into him. The creepy imposter brushed off my prompt and folded his arms across his chest. Then, I had an impossible revelation, like I had seen this person before.

"I'm sorry," the man suddenly said out of character. "I didn't mean to offend you."

I refused to acknowledge his feeble apology and instead, severed my offensive stare and turned away.

As my head followed a natural curve across his body, I noticed something on his arm. It was a picture.

A tattoo.

For some reason it caught my attention. It wasn't even very big, but it was odd and quite basic in its nature. The artwork was in the shape of three identical pillars, only with the two outside ones appearing to have collapsed into the center one, now resembling more of an arrow than anything else. I didn't fixate on it for very long though. I knew this weirdo was just plain fucking bad news and it was time to end our little get together. Keeping my damnation current, I backed up to a safe distance beyond his reach, then flipped around and trotted hastily towards the entrance of the park.

"Have a nice day," I heard the man holler out from behind me.

When I reached the gate, I immediately hung a left and headed down the sidewalk, away from the direction of my car and beelined towards a row of newer rigs. The last thing I needed was this freak seeing what vehicle I got into. I mean who knows what the hell was going through that psycho's head, and the last thing I wanted today was for him to acquire a further link to me and my baby, namely my white Firebird!

I pressed Sara close against my chest and speed walked down the road a good 500 yards before deaking across a heavily treed yard and zigzagging my way back.

I took my sweet time in returning too, sneaking finally up to the drivers door about thirty minutes later and diving inside. It wasn't until I'd put a good six blocks between me and that park that I actually started to breath again. After ten blocks, I pulled my ride over and shut down the engine. My heart was still reacting to the encounter so I undid my seat belt and fell over towards my passenger. I could tell by the way Sara's forehead was scrunched up that she too, had not enjoyed the company of the unannounced visitor either.

"It's alright sweetie," I assured her , "You're safe now."

The words I spoke were brave and soothing, even though I still wasn't quite so sure of that fact myself.

"Well it looks like we're just going to have to find a nicer park to go to huh baby?" I said in a more upbeat tone.

This latest statement was actually the God honest truth, and a decision I had instantly made the second that bastard reached out and exposed Sara's face. We laid pretty low for the next couple of days. It's true that what had happened was probably just a simple case of a lonely old man with no social skills, but I still wasn't taking any chances. However, by the morning of the third day of my self-induced lockdown I was beginning to get a little crotchety and so was Sara. She responded in an equally miserable fashion to my uneasiness by crying a lot more and generally being a temperamental little fussfart. After convincing myself that the danger had lifted and it was safe to venture out of the house again so to speak, I packed up my freshly primped newborn along with all of her many accessories and headed toward the big inside garden thingy with the pond and the fish.

I needed that place. It always relaxed me, and that was a pill that was long overdue. I also figured if I was calm, so would be Sara. Once through the doors, I doctored up the least expensive cup of Joe I could find from the quaint little poolside cafe and shuffled over to my favorite bench.

Sara, still pissed at me, began to cry and fuss real loud again so I loaded up her bottle quick-like and twirled the exotic nipple around the edges of her wide screaming mouth. Almost like a switch, my aggravated bundle of limbs became silent the moment she clamped down on that nipple. With Sara's cry's abolished, all that prevailed now were the medicinal sounds of the waterfall and the fountains. Feeling the crisis contained, I leaned back on the bench and stretched out my legs. Now it was my turn to "suck on a nipple" and let the sounds of the manmade paradise break apart the muddy slab of worry that had claimed a stake in my ribcage. I sat there for quite a while, enjoying my coffee and my surroundings. That is, of course, until I watched two distinct figures from my recent past suddenly fling open the glass doors of the humid retreat and stroll on in.

It was the two cops I had unfortunately run into that night in the coffee shop after the first dream.

"Christ," I growled. "I don't need this shit right now!"

With great speed I pulled my legs in and dropped my head down to depict a more conservative stance. I grabbed a magazine that was lying on a nearby table with my free hand and pushed my face into it, hoping it would further disguise me. From out of the top corner of the book, I watched silently as the two officers walked over to the coffee bar. As far as I could tell, the only purpose of their visit was to pick up a couple of coffee for the road.

"Good. YA Ya, that's good. That means they'll be out of here in a couple of minutes, max. OK... Just keep your cool for two more minutes and you're in the clear!

Obeying my rule, I sunk my head into the magazine and pretended to read. The first minute was the worst!

Come on Guys, hurry the Hell up.

My patience was wearing thin but I had no other option but to ride this thing out. I peered out from the magazine to check on their progress. They were at the condiment stand by then, topping up their beverages. The big cop was chatting with a passer by, while the midget was still at the concession booth arguing with the teenage employee over God knows what.

Hold it together Eugene. They're just about gone.

Giving into my alter ego for the moment, I dove back under the canopy of the tabloid and held my breath.

My plan was going along fine. I was just about home free, but then something happened that changed everything. You see, in my centralized quest for invisibility, I had failed to notice that Sara's bottle had slowly inched it's way out of her mouth and therefore had nothing to stop it from slipping past my loose grip. Mind you when the bottle fell away and struck the ground in front of me, my little angel did let me know about it by screaming out a discontented howl that could have easily woken up the dead. Her cries rebounded loudly throughout the place and stabbed into my eardrums as my hand fumbled blindly about my feet trying to retrieve the misplaced accessory so that I could put it back where it came from and possibly save my sorry ass.

"Thank Fuck," I said as my fingers finally brushed up against the hard plastic surface of tube.

Having no choice but to drop the magazine back to the floor, I quickly dusted off the nipple of Sara's bottle and crammed it back into her screaming mouth. The moment the rubber façade touched the edge of her lips it was viciously sucked inward and then at long last, the noise ended. I sat there in a state of shock. I really didn't know what to do. My head was frozen in a southerly position as I stared down at the magazine on the floor that once protected me. "Stress and Parenting", read the fitting centerpiece of the "Modern Woman" magazine at my feet. The cops must have heard that I worried. Hell, Australia probably heard that for shit sakes! I wanted to look up and see if they had already left but I didn't have to.

"Well, Well... If it ain't the greaseball kid!"

Apparently my prayers were not answered, and when my eyes did leave the safety of the floor and begin their ascent, they quickly stopped and became hopelessly ensnared in a showdown with a sawed-off beady eyed shitstain of a man that I had unfortunately locked horns with once before.

"Good afternoon officer," I said politely, attempting to smooth out the situation and not cause a scene.

"OOHH. Now I'm an officer. Well nice of you to finally notice," the half-pint dork responded.

"Hey T.J.," the man scoffed, "Looks like trailer park boy has found himself a babysitting job."

"A bb... babysitter? Ah ,yes sir, officer sir, that's right! I went out and got me a straight and narrow job I did!!" I wholeheartedly agreed with the little man's false perception and sealed up the lie with an even better one.

"And I'm going to go back to school too," I went on! It was a grand plan in theory, but to my dismay, my well-executed pipe dream was only met with contempt.

"Oh ya," the malicious city worker leaned down and said, "What you going to take loser boy? Garbage picking 101? Ha ha, get it? Garbage picking 101!!"

The constable's laughter reached out and touched all four corners of the solarium and cut a deep gash into my embarrassed heart. But help it seemed, was on its way.

"What's the matter partner?" said the giant of a man I only knew as T.J. as he crept up behind his fellow worker and depressed his enormous mitt into the shallow fissures of his partners shoulder,
"Jealous that he's making more money than you?"

I watched in delight as the dominant badge applied more and more pressure to the thin neck muscles of his ignorant counterpart. I could feel an all out laugh gaining momentum behind my pursed lips but I held it in.
Levi swung around in a huff and pried free of his entanglement.

"Why are you always defending this bum?" Levi barked.

"Why are you always coming down on him?" the noble cop warned as he lowered his massive sternum down into the worried eyes of his trembling partner.

Levi, knowing he'd lost again, puffed out his frail chest and offered T.J. a hilarious rendition of someone who was actually tough.

"I'll see you back in the car," he squeaked and with that, he tromped off with the grace and poise of a six year old.

I looked up at my rescuer with a grateful nod.

"Don't mind him," T.J. said in a calm voice. "He was just born three feet shorter than his personality, that's all!"

A relieved laugh finally broke through the barrier of my patient lips and I felt my nerves soften.

"Is this your niece?" the big man then asked as he bent down to get a better look at my now-behaving child.
"Yes," I said, forcing out the lie. "It's my sister's kid. I'm uh... just babysitting her for a while."

I hated lying to him, this decent man who had now come to my defense for the second time. But I knew I had no choice.

"Wow!" T.J. said as he tilted his head to the side. "She's a real cutie ain't she? You must have a very attractive sister, " he nodded.

"Yep," I told him. "My sister definitely got the looks in the family. I got the brains though," I laughed.

The big cop then let out a huge laugh and further cemented my growing admiration for him.

"I don't doubt that, my friend," he said back in a grin, "I don't doubt that at all."

I was great to hear someone say that you know. I mean, to give me the benefit of the doubt like that.

"Car 29, Car 29," blared his radio suddenly. "Please respond to 7818 Laporte Road for possible lead in abduction case, over!"

"Oops, that's my cue," I heard T.J. say as he pulled out a gloss black radio from his holster and brought it up to his face.
"Were on our way," he blurted, quickly retiring his radio back to his belt.

"Well, .. Time to jet! Take it easy fella," he said, and with a courteous nod, he donned a serious look and ploughed his way towards the door.

I wanted to stop him. I wanted to tell him what I had seen in my dream, and what I knew. But that urge was quickly extinguished by the realization of the harsh consequences that could occur with such an action. I'm afraid I had to keep quiet. I had no choice. I had to remain silent for Sara's sake and mine too, even though it was truly killing me inside.
I wasn't in a great hurry to leave after that. I had become freshly stressed out again and all I wanted to do was stay put and let the placid sounds of the water wash away the dense slop that had found it's way back into my chest again. That's all I wanted, and eventually the ambiance of the place, well, ..It did just that. An hour later the dull feeling in my soul had vanished for the moment and my worry went to sleep, keeping in sync, thank God, with my unconscious newborn whose limbs now also lay dormant underneath her blankets. With the rocky start to the day finally behind me, I decided it was time to get a move on. I had a busy day in front of me. There were a lot of places I needed to check out in my ongoing quest for empties, for Sara was getting low on supplies and I was getting even lower on bodyweight.
We spent the rest of the day, me and my little treasure, collecting empties to take to the refund depot. I searched the alleyway trashcans until almost 10pm in order to make up for my lost time. I was on a roll too, hitting pay dirt in almost every can and I milked that lucky streak for all it was worth. I remember joking to Sara as I pulled up alongside another garbage bin.

"Hey sweetie," I snickered, "maybe I'll find you a little brother in this one."

She was not impressed.

The next morning I was at the bottle depot at 8 am sharp. I was on a mission today.
I had to get the bottles cashed in and get some gas ASAP, then head over to that
nostalgic little drugstore to pick up some badly- needed baby necessities. While I
was at the depot, I took the liberty of changing Sara in their washroom.

It was a disgusting place I'll tell you, and that's coming from a homeless guy, but it
saved me some time.

I splashed some water on my hair too. It was all over the damn place. It looked like
I had just crawled out of a dryer or something.

When I steered my car into the parking lot of the pharmacy, I was surprised to see
it so busy. The lot was actually full and I had a bitch of a time even getting a spot.
Before I went in though, I bundled up Sara, fluffed up her hair, and pelted her with
a dreaded spit bath. I must admit I was greatly anticipating being mobbed again by
all those cute young female admirers. And let's face it, if Sara looked good, I looked
good! Giving my hair a quick flip, I rolled into that place donning a confident smile.
My chest was flung out so far I almost fell over backwards, but to my very disappointed surprise, the place was not crawling with hormonally challenged woman at
all. In fact, I didn't even see one female customer in the whole place! It was instead,
crammed wall to wall with old men?

"Well what the Hell is this all about? " I moaned.
But as I looked up at the ceiling, all my questions fell to the ground answered.

"Laxative blowout sale on today".

Well ain't that just typical?

It all made sense now! Damn! And I was really looking forward to all the attention
too! I uh mean, for Sara's sake and all! Leaking out a disgruntled sigh, I dropped
my head and let my chest fall back to its usual concave position underneath my
shirt, then trudged over to the baby needs aisle like a ten-year-old that had just
been grounded. My feet stopped as usual in front of the neatly stacked cans of baby
formula. With one arm around Sara, I began carefully looking over the selection of
goods to locate the best deal.

As I fumbled through the disorganized mass of cans, I was suddenly massaged by
the most wonderful aroma. Perfume to be exact.

"Can I help you find anything?" a woman's voice softly asked from behind me.

Holding back the urge to shit myself, I stood up slowly and turned around only to
wind up staring face to face into the deep green eyes of a beautiful young woman.

"Are you finding everything you need?" she repeated.

"Ahh,... Um sure, uh... I am, th-th-thank you," I twitched.

My response was saturated with all the grace and wit of someone on Thorazine.
I quickly glanced down at the nametag on her shirt, then immediately brought my

eyes right back up to her breast level, I mean nipple line! I mean um... to her eyes! Meridith was her name and holy shit, was she ever a knockout! I stood there for a few moments and just stared at her like a zitfaced fourteen-year-old with a boner, but in a classy sort of way of course. I just couldn't help myself, she was so damn sexy! She was trim ,curvy, and had salon-quality jet black hair that perfectly sun-flowered her naturally tanned face. I mean come on! The woman was a Goddess!

"Well just let me know if you need anything... anything at all, "she flirted. And with that, she unleashed a sassy wink and strutted her sexy little butt out of the aisle.
I hovered there for a minute after she had left, drooling profusely and trying desperately to divert the flow of my blood back to where it was supposed to be.

"Good God," I squeaked eventually. "I gotta start coming here more often!"

The paralyzing scent of her perfume was still dancing about all around me, continuing on with its devastation and I began to feel somewhat weak in the knees. A feeling I hadn't experienced, well... ever.

She must be new here.

It was true that staff in these types of places changed up a lot, but I'm pretty sure I'd have remembered seeing a woman like that. Shaking off the rare cobwebs of the whole ordeal, I quickly grabbed a few cans of formula and pulled myself together. And as I headed toward the checkout counter, I couldn't help but congratulate myself on how cool I acted when I first spoke. "Ahh um... Duhh Hmmm"...

For Christ sakes Eugene, I'm surprised she didn't say something like... "Excuse me sir, your bus is here, you know the short one with the really friendly driver?" Cripes!!!

Rattled all to shit, but curious nonetheless, I decided to strap on my auxiliary set of balls and shoot for some redemption. Taking no chances in the hygiene area, I made a quick pit stop in the men's cologne aisle and sprayed myself with hopefully the most expensive cologne sampler they had on display, and sauntered out of the aisle.
After I let the potency of the fragrance I now sadly realized was named "Karate" dissipate a little, I thrust my puny chest forward once again and headed toward the checkout. I purposely stood in the lineup that she was working, just to see if she was simply trying to be helpful, or if she was actually (Gulp!!), smiling at me for other reasons. I went over about one million hip pick up lines to say to her while I was waiting for the parade of fossilized men in front of me to finish their transactions. And by the time I finally made it up to the counter, I had them all down pat. Or so I thought.

"Hey there, how's it going there? Um, I mean, heh heh, how's it doing there? Um... How are you?"

"Oh, that was real magic Eugene! Oh ya pure gold buddy, pure bloody gold.

"You're 0 for 2 now Danny boy! 0 for 2!"

Feeling like a total idiot once again, I quickly sent my head southward and began memorizing the pattern on the counter. It was a habit I was pretty familiar with, but to my surprise the sexy clerk didn't radio security, or spray me with mace, or anything. She just let go a big smile and politely answered me back.

"It's going fine," she replied. "How's it doing with you ?"she joked.

"It... um, it's going pretty good," I said back somewhat bewildered.

Then I watched the sultry cashier's big sexy eyes shift down towards Sara, who I'm sure was just laughing her newborn ass off at her father's pathetic attempt at courtship.

"Oooo," the gentle clerk purred as she ran her fingers through Sara's thick hair. "What a beautiful little girl you have. I bet she looks just like her mother."

Why in the Hell does everyone think she got her looks from her mother?

"I, I'm not married," I said, blurting out the disclaimer immediately. "I'm single. Yep, you bet ya. Single, non-married guy I am, yessir! This... um. This is actually my sister's kid!"

I finished up my sales pitch with a pursed grin, then subconsciously decided that it would probably be best that I never opened my mouth again.
"Oh I see"," the pretty clerk said. "And where is your sister now?"

"Nnn... Now?" I stuttered. "Oh... um, she's... um, in mmm... Mexico right now! Ya, ya... Mexico!, taking a course in... Sail boating! Right now! Ya... Sail boating course! Yep... she's a big sailor, my sister is!, heh heh!"

I could feel my face starting to turn red with guilt.

Dammit Eugene. You should have stopped talking like you had planned. Now she probably thinks you get coloring books for Christmas every year!

"Well, it's awfully sweet of you to take care of this little angel while your sister's gone," replied the patient woman in front of me, and on that semi-positive note, I swept up what was left of my self-esteem, paid the tab, then issued the cashier a humble goodbye. As soon as I got out the door and around the corner I looked up to the sky and let out a squeal.

"Sonnnofabiitch!" I howled.

Jesus Eugene, could you have screwed that up any more?

I cursed as I slid back into my car. I glanced over at Sara hoping to borrow a little sympathy, but she wasn't about to bail me out on this rap. She was grinning from ear to ear.

"Yep!... She wants me," I laughed eventually as I pulled the shifter into reverse.

I heard my little turkey gurgle as I drove off and tickled her with my free hand.

"Oh well," I muttered." She was too good looking for me anyway."

I felt a touch better after that. I mean, I had to face the facts. A woman like that could get any man she wanted and I was definitely hallucinating if I thought a fox like her would ever give me a shot.
Re-registering myself with the "Single forever" club, I quickly forgot about the whole ugly ordeal and continued on with my day. Sara was overjoyed that I had finally decided to feed her again and kept pretty quiet and well behaved for the remainder of the afternoon. I did, though, catch myself fantasizing about the gorgeous creature at the drugstore a couple of times. I kept on seeing the name, "Meridith Lauder" in my head, and I will admit, it did have kind of a nice ring to it. And even though I knew I had a better shot at being struck by lightning, it was still fulfilling to wander off into that territory for a spell. Kept my swimmers on their toes, know what I'm saying!

The next day was the last Wednesday of the month. This was a good thing for it was the magical day on the calendar where, at a certain Superstore location, all the local food reps in the area would get together and you guessed it... Give away a ton of free food samples! It was plastic cup heaven! A poor man's thanksgiving with the magnitude of the last supper, and me and my baby were going to hit that Shangri-La with a vengeance! Most of the staff there were already way too familiar with me and would begin dishing out their flog of the day as soon as they saw me coming. I showed up there at 11am sharp. The exact time in which their little free-for-all started. In less than 12 minutes, I had already completed my first lap. It was a personal best I believe, so I plopped my ass down at a table in the cafe that the store also leased, and got ready to feed Sara her chow. It was a productive rest for me. Got me in a little digestive time in before I began my second heat. Sara was also eating like a horse lately and her once frail body was starting to chunk out a bit.

She was growing! My little girl was actually growing! I can't tell you how incredible that feeling is, to know that you are playing an instrumental role in helping a living being develop. I'm telling you, it is an aphrodisiac that can only be savored through the effort of time. That understanding also served as a powerful motivator for me when it came to finding money to purchase that life-giving formula.
I heard air begin to trickle through the end of the rubberized nipple, alerting me that Sara, also in record time, had downed her fill, so I set her on my shoulder and gently tapped her back. This motion produced an instant and ghastly productive belch that would have brought tears to the eyes of the most seasoned of municipal workers. It was cleanup time, code blue! But that was an alarm I was very used to and in no time, my little angel was, well, an angel again. When I was done my parental chore, I stood tall and headed back towards my next victim. The strawberry shortcake lady! She quivered in fear as I slithered up to the display table, annihilation and conquest in my eyes.

"That shortcake was so damn tasty," I said in the cheesiest of dialects, "that I couldn't even entertain the thought of not coming back for seconds!"

"I bet you say that to all the girls," the plump concession worker replied back with a smirk.

"OK, you got me," I confessed, shedding away my phony ploy. "But hey, I'm getting better aren't I?"

"Yes you sure are," the kind lady said, and for my unprompted show of honesty the casual employee then scooped out a triple portion of her goo and handed it over.

Without delay I crammed the whole oversized cup of rich sludge into my mouth and prepared to terrorize yet another display.

"You must really love the shortcake here," a calm voice suddenly charged from behind me.

I twisted around in a state of confusion only to wind up standing face to face with, low and behold, that sexy cashier lady I'd seen at the drugstore the other day.

"Oh... Howwo," I mumbled as I casually leaned up against a support pillar and spit cake crumbs all over her. "Fanny menning yu er," I continued as I swallowed down the entire contents of my overextended pie hole in one shot.

The dense mixture of cake and syrup broke a painful trail down towards my stomach. This hurt like a sonofabitch and I felt my eyes begin to water.

Oh God Eugene, don't start to cry. Not now man!... Please, please!!! Any time but now!

I was on the verge of CPR! I'm not kidding! It felt like I had just knocked back an Oldsmobile, but I grit my teeth and pressed out a smile anyway.

"Meredith, right?" I said finally. "From the drugstore. You're the new girl."

"Yep, that's me," she said with a perfect wink. "I'm the newbie.
Listen," she apologized," I didn't mean to bother you while you were eating. I really should just let you be....

"Oh, no! Really, it's OK! I was just, you know, heh heh, seeing what all this commotion was about, heh. That's all. I actually never touch this stuff," I said, looking off to the side.

I heard a loud burst of laughter suddenly break through the lips of the shortcake she-devil somewhere behind me and I felt my veins start to throb.

"So hey, how are you anyway?" I shot back loudly, trying desperately to drown out the giggling bitch to my rear. "You ah, getting groceries or something," I asked dumbly, inching my body away from the sample table.

Keeping up the act, I shuffled over to a nearby shelf and grabbed a couple of random items to make it look good.

"Yes." she answered in a hesitant tone. "Oddly enough I am."

My legs started to grow weak in panic, and for a brief moment my brain began directing my thoughts back to the memories of my recent failures. But for once I said no! For the first time I actually put my foot down and held my inner negativity at bay, just long enough to rescue my battered level of self esteem out from behind its mental blockade and dynamite the doors on the way out.

Because I knew this was it.

I knew that this was a pinnacle moment, this meeting. This was my very last shot at courtship and I had to see it through. I had to play it cool and ride it out. For better or for worse I had to face this right here, right now, or forever abandon the whole idea. In the span of one second, I mentally reviewed and catalogued every single ounce of knowledge and information that I had ever ingested about the opposite sex, most prevalently, the initial courtship part. And then, just as the most attractive woman I had ever talked to was about to shake her head and walk away... it happened.

My mouth and my brain finally shook hands.

"Hey listen," I said for once in a normal voice. "You want to take five and have a cup of coffee with me over at the deli?"

As those unprecedented words left my lips, I waited for what seemed to be an eternity while she tilted her head a couple of times and pondered my offer.

"Sure," I watched her say, "I'd love to."

I was stupefied! I really was. I nearly pissed my pants right there in front of her when she said yes because to be honest, I really wasn't expecting a yes. I was expecting her to say something more along the lines of... "Well, you know I'd love to and all but I have a root canal I'm kind of in a hurry to get to right now, ..So, bye, bye!"

But she didn't. She didn't say that at all. She actually said yes!

I almost asked her to repeat herself just to make sure I wasn't just dreaming it all up. But it turned out I didn't have to because not three seconds after this beautiful and classy woman agreed to have coffee with your basic run of the mill homeless vagrant, who was illegally hoarding away a newborn child in an old sports car, did my precious Sara promptly remind me that, yes, my hearing was A-OK, by immediately ripping out a baby fart that I'm sure the whole damn store heard! Meridith, I could tell, was visibly shaken by the sheer magnitude of my baby's bodily function so I quickly injected a smooth over line into the matrix of our conversation.

"Great," I said, as the sweat rolled down my forehead and the smell of baby shit saturated the vast majority of aisle number seven. "Then I'll meet you over there in five minutes."

And with that, I casually held my breath and walked away with head held high and nostrils a burning. As soon as I was out of Meridith's view, my eyes quickly shifted down towards my reeking baby, whom I might add, was sporting the most innocent of looks on her face.

"Thanks sweetie pie," I said sarcastically. "I should get my sense of smell back in about six months or so!"

I watched half-seriously as a big smirk came across Sara's face.

"You do eventually want a mommy, don't you?" I muttered to her, shaking my head in denial.

Brushing off the embarrassment of the event, I began to focus in on the needs at hand. And that of course, was finding a bathroom and a bar of soap ,which I located with inhuman speed. I had to excavate Sara's shorts and check out my own look. I had to make sure I had no boogers, eye sludge, mouth entrails, you know, that sort of stuff. I also doused Sara with some baby powder, just in case she felt like passing another atomic home wrecker again. Executing one last hair flip, I drew in a deep breath and took a good look at my reflection. It was not too shabby actually. I mean, for a guy who lived in a car and all.

"Alright Eugene. Don't screw this up! This is something that doesn't happen to people like you everyday now OK!

I secretly agreed to behave and boldly strutted my recently overhauled body back out into the aisle that led toward the cafe in the deli. By the time I rounded the corner of the aisle, I was gleaming with confidence and ready to face a single man's greatest fear: the dreaded first meeting. I spotted her right away. She was sitting underneath a large silk fig tree, so with my chest still leading the way, I headed straight towards her and pulled up a seat.

"Eugene Lauder," I said, extending out my open palm. "Very nice to officially meet you."

"Meredith Zebrac," she replied. "Very nice to meet you as well."

"So what's your sister's baby's name?" she asked.

"My who?" I said, momentarily forgetting my own lie.

"Your sister's baby's name? You know, the one who is in Mexico taking that sailing course."

"Oh, that sister's kid," I grunted. "Oh yes of course, I'm sorry. This little gem's name is um... Sara, Sara Lauder."

My words dripped of pride as I picked my angel up off my lap and placed her still-cocooned frame onto the table.

"My my, isn't she adorable?" Meredith beamed.

"Takes after her uncle," I grinned in a joke.
"So how long have you been working at the drugstore? " I asked casually, hoping to get the conversation flowing a bit.

"I just started about a week and a half ago."

"Oh ya that's cool," I said, reminding myself to try and keep the conversation interesting.

Actually, I was quite worried about that. You know, trying to think up witty things to say to this obviously intelligent woman. But happily, as the conversation progressed, I began to feel strangely at ease with this unique person. I was still a little nervous of course, but she never once during the whole meeting, made me feel inadequate or pressured. Our talk was never pointed or overbearing, only objective and pleasurable.
  I learned that she was 25 going on 26, an age I would have never pegged her at for she had such a young and soft complexion, and oh ya, one Hell of a body!! An attribute that I must confess, was quite hard not to stare at. But I managed my demons fairly well, with my eyes only wandering off course once or twice during the whole date. And it was funny too, because even though this unexpected get together was going along so well, in the back of my mind I still expected this way out of my league beauty queen to all of a sudden stand up and say something like....

"Hey! This isn't the post office," and take off.

It's true! I mean jeeze, she was just like... too good to be true man! I couldn't take my eyes off of her, and neither could half the other guys in the place either. I was definitely on top of the world because a woman like this could walk out of the door with any dude she wanted, but for whatever crazy reason, here she was sitting with little old me. And I think it was safe to say that she was at least kind of attracted to me and sort of interested in what I had to say.
  The whole thing was quite surreal actually, but there was no way I was about to jump off this cloud! Even if this was only a one act play, I was going to see the curtain fall.
  But then from out of nowhere, an insane idea snuck its way into my head, an idea that scared me half to death.
  Hey Eugene. Why don't you ask her out on a real date?

This latest rogue proposal sent my nerves into a state of shock, and even though my vocal cords were still acing the game on the outside, on the inside my guts were beginning to shift and rumble again.

Come on man! Ask her out. It's obvious that she is generally interested in you, God knows why of course.

Shut up voice! I thought, trying to subconsciously diffuse the idea.

130

Buk buk buk buk clucked my reckless side.

I was getting frustrated. So far I was holding my own but my alter ego was only getting louder and was quickly gaining the upper hand over my ever supple spine. Hey, don't get me wrong. I'd have to be gay or dead not to want to spend more time with a woman like this but let's face it, I was who I was. I mean Christ! What would I do if she asked to go back to my place after this "date." Say, "...Hop in baby we're here!"
It was a furious battle but the unseen dare kept up the charge on my incompetent nervous system until a blatant phrase suddenly popped out of my mouth, fittingly enough, during a chance pause in a conversation about our favorite foods.

"So hey, speaking of dinner," I said a little nervously, "Would you ah... like to go out and maybe do that sometime, you know have dinner or see a movie or something. I mean you know. With me?"

My proposition ended on a neutral note and I could feel my blood pressure begin to climb as I waited on pins and needles for her response. I now understood that the stress I bore when I asked her out to this low key coffee interlude was all but small change compared to what I was going through right now. This edge of the seat thriller was the real deal and I was clinically flat lined for the sum total of five seconds before her lips voiced an almost unreal answer.

"I'd love to," she said. "That sounds fun."

I don't think I answered her back right away. Can't remember actually. All I do know, is after those few words did make it through the thick walls of my skull, my heart did start beating again and the world around me switched over from slow motion to its regular psychotic pace.

"That's great," I eventually responded as I looked down at the table and checked it for drool.

Now! Now the reality of what I had just accomplished was starting to set in. To say that I was elated didn't even come close to the level of joy I was feeling. I almost ran outside and started kissing people at random but Meridith was starting to don a regretful pose so I stayed where I was and got back into character.

"So um where would you like to go?" I asked.

I left the decision hanging in the air for a few moments while I began desperately racking my brains for a cheap, and I mean cheap, restaurant, that I could suggest where cockroaches weren't a regular part of the decor and you could still have a non-toxic meal for under five bucks. It was an improbability, my dream, and it didn't look like I was going to get off the hook that easy. But to my relieved surprise, the beautiful check-out girl sitting across from me already had done the math on this deal.

"Well," she said, folding her long slender fingers underneath her chin, "Tomorrow there's this free outdoor folk festival down at the Evergreen Gardens public park that

I have been dying to check out. We could go to that if you like."

Now that idea was music to my ears.

"That sounds perfect," I said with a smile and just like that I, Eugene Camille Lauder, had just landed my first date.

Boy I'll tell ya! I was so stoked I could barely speak. Not because I enjoyed folk music in any shape or form. Nope. It was the fact that the whole thing was free that really had me dancing. I'm sorry, but "Free" definitely fit in to my current budget! I purposely wrapped up our little gathering a short time later by saying that I had to put Sara down for a nap. And that was the truth. I really did have to put Sara down for a nap, but it was more to the fact that I was so far ahead by now, that I figured it be best to just leave well enough alone! I didn't want to drag out the conversation any further and wind up saying something stupid, a feat I was more than capable of doing. Behaving like a true gentleman, I politely waited for Meredith to leave before I myself got up and pretended to shop for more groceries.

Actually, I just went around and put back the stuff I had picked up earlier, then grabbed a day old loaf of bread and a small jar of peanut butter before circling back for one more quick round at the sample tables.

Holy shit, I got a date!

I still couldn't really believe it. Me having an actual date?

I don't know how you pulled that one off Eugene old boy, but way to go man!..
"Way to go."

As I inched my way towards the cashier, still riding a cloud, I spotted the daily newspaper and instinctively glanced down at it.

"Another Child Disappears."

The blunt headline sent a chill through my body and instantly knocked me off of my short-lived pedestal.

"Take it easy Eugene, they're just words man... just words. They can't harm you.

With a dose of caution, I began to read:
"The Mystery Abductor appears to have struck again, and the police still have no leads in this terrible case that has advanced the missing persons toll now to an unnerving total of eight. The latest victim, eleven year old Tommy Anderson, disappeared while walking home from a friend's house last night in a quiet suburb of the city's south end. Once again, a mysterious hand-made symbol was left behind at the crime scene. This time it was placed deliberately on a swing set at a small neighborhood park not even two blocks away from the boy's home. Authorities are once again asking for the public's help in solving this case. If you..."

I forced my eyes away from the paragraph and looked up. An eerie feeling began to ooze forth into my stomach as visions of that Goddam symbol that so ruthlessly controlled my dreams started to flood into my mind and chase me around.

Was I a part of all this craziness?

It was a question I could no longer run away from.

Maybe I was the bloody killer and I didn't even know it. Maybe I was blacking out and committing all of these horrific acts without any recollection.

Suddenly, I felt an invisible hand of logic rise up and interrupt me.
Wait a second pal ,there's no way you could be doing those things. Do you know why? Because Sara would wake up and start to cry the second you opened the car door, that's why! No way buddy.! It couldn't be you. Think about it. It's just not possible.

My intuitions, I agreed, were correct. Sara would have definitely woken up and let me have it like right now if I got up and left the car. Unless of course, I was really quiet and tiptoed my way out. Naww... not possible, I concluded. There's just no possible way.

Relax Eugene, you're a lot of things, but you're no killer.

I let out a pent-up blast of air from my lungs, then drew in a fresh supply and let it go to work.. I was relieved in a way, but also sick and tired of worrying about it too. In a selfish move, I chalked the whole thing up to a rare coincidence and moved on. I surrendered to the notion that I had probably seen that symbol before in a book or something and just simply forgot about it until now, until all of this shit started going down. I did hash over a few more remote possibilities as I inched my way forward in the lineup, but in the end came up with nothing.

After I had paid for my goods, I walked back to my car and settled in. I knew Sara was getting tired. I could tell by the way her eyes lay fixed at half mast and by the lack of enthusiasm in her limbs. I decided this time, to drive a few blocks over to the west and shut her down in a strip mall for a while, so that Sara could have a snooze in peace. I was pretty low on gas anyway, and I too needed some downtime. After Sara woke up from her afternoon nap, I fed, changed, burped and rocked her, then spent the remainder of the day scouring the alleyways for empties. Even though I knew the concert itself was free, I still realized that I would have to buy my lovely escort a soda, or even a, yikes, an actual drink or something crazy like that while we were there.

"Man," I grumbled as I picked through yet another trash can. "This dating stuff is expensive!"

But on the upside, at least I had one now.

The next morning I was up at the crack of dawn and all I did was search for bottles, like hardcore! This was the day of my big date and I was really starting to worry about my cash flow. Mind you, by two in the afternoon I had managed to collect about fifteen dollars in returnables. Not a bad haul by any means, but I still wondered if it was going to be enough.

What if she orders some food or something? Shit, then I am in trouble!

I tried not to think about all the "what ifs", that could accompany this ritualistic get together and instead, mulled over what I was going to wear. I mean, most of my clothes were shit! I mean real shit!!

I also wondered what she was going to say when I showed up there with Sara. I realized it wasn't "kosher" to show up at a first date with another person, baby or not, but what other option did I have? Nope, I'm afraid this new girl was just going to have to accept the fact that I was a package deal, and that me and Sara were sold as a unit. I was nearly ready to sign my name on that fresh law when a tiny spirit climbed up onto my shoulder and whispered something in my ear.

What about asking Mrs. Quang to take care of Sara for the afternoon?

No way. Uh, Uh. Forget about it. I couldn't do that. ...No way! That would be very selfish.

But why not? I bet she would love the company.

Stop it! I couldn't possibly do that. It's just not right.

I fought back the idea on the grounds of not being a nuisance, but the seed that was illegally planted in the soil behind my eyes was now sprouting up at an alarming rate. I offered up my usual weak resistance, but after a while, and the more I thought about it, well... the more it actually started to sound like not a bad plan.

I mean Newa. Well jeeze! She loved Sara, there was no question about that. And I did completely trust her too. But what if she tells me to get lost or something. What if she?... I mean...?

Ah what the Hell Eugene, give it a shot. Maybe she would like the extra company. And hey, if she says no, she says no. Won't change your friendship any. Won't change it at all.

Reasonably confident with my decision, I spun my wreck in the direction of the old Laundromat and lay on the gas. As soon as I walked up to the front door, Newa was already on the other side of it to open it for us.

"How my two favit people?" she chanted happily.

"We're great," I replied, more relieved now by her demeanor. "And how's your day going?" I asked back.

"Wondofol," she said kissing Sara on the forehead. "Como in."

I stood there with my baby on a nearby washing machine and prepared to deliver my speech.

But no sooner had I drawn in the required amount of breath to ask the favor, did Newa jump forward and say, "You come in back to my home. YA Ya, you come!" and without pause, she hastily snatched up Sara and darted towards the rear of the business.

I followed in behind her, struggling hard to keep up. She was pretty quick for an older person and after a short jog, I chased her through a semi-hidden entrance that appeared to be the doorway to her living quarters. Tapping it shut on the way through, I watched then as the animated old woman gently sat Sara down on an easy chair and began relentlessly showering her with affection once more. After a minute, my eyes started to acquaint themselves to their new surroundings and sadly began to uncover another depressing chapter to her tale. The place, I saw, was very run down. It was even worse than the front half.

Thick cobwebs embossed the frames of ancient black and white photographs I assumed were impressions of her immediate family. The ones that ,"No visit no more". The off-white roof tiles were badly stained from a series of long neglected leaks. And the carpet too, was thin and worn right through to the wood in some places, probably due to it's age. I understood immediately, that the measly collection of nickels and dimes she gathered up from the daily take of the few working machines was her sole source of income. And by the looks of things, that sum wasn't very much.

Making sure to keep the mood jovial, I threw on a big smile and said, "Wow Newa, this is a great little bachelorette pad you got going on here young lady!"

"You sink so," Newa said carefully.

"Oh ya," I said convincingly, "this is all a person needs. Really, it's very cozy."

"Oh sank you," she blushed and I knew right then that I had put her mind at ease about the state of her surroundings.

Hell, I lived that same drill, and I was all too familiar with the mental side effects of poverty. An average person's level of self esteem to begin with is usually very fragile, and judging by the amount of dust I saw clinging to all those old pictures, I knew hers had already taken a beating as it was.

After chit chatting with my friend for a few minutes, I finally built up the nerve to pop the question.

"Listen Mrs. Quang, I mean Newa. I was just wondering if you could um... do me a little favor."

"Now you don't have to if you don't want to... like it's no problem if you say no and all."

Pull it together Eugene! You're starting to sound like an idiot!

The sweat was beginning to work it's way down my scalp and I suddenly felt embarrassed asking for help. But I'm afraid the ball was already rolling on this disaster, so I just came right out and said what I was trying to say.

"Newa, I was just wondering if you wouldn't mind babysitting Sara for a couple of hours later on tonight. I um... asked a girl on a date and I was just wondering if, you know, you could watch her."

I stopped talking and waited for her response. Newa grew uncharacteristically quiet and covered her hands around her mouth. Now I was really wishing I had never thought up this stupid idea in the first place. But I did and now I had to face the music, which so far sounded pretty bad.

Newa kept silent for quite a few seconds which did even more damage to my conscience. I dropped my head down in embarrassment and when it could take no more of the uncomfortable silence, my brain started to feverishly backtrack and scheme for a way out. A scapegoat. Anything to reverse and iron over the sentence I had just spoken. When I finally looked back up to initiate my withdrawal of terms, I was surprised and caught off guard to see that Newa was now slowly making her way over to me.

Oh shit. Here it comes. I'm going to get a fresh one, I can just feel it!

Dammit Eugene! You probably insulted her heritage or some shit! Now you're going to get a tune up and you'll probably wind up without a friend to boot!

I was so disappointed in myself I could have just screamed, but there was no time, for Newa was now directly in front of me. I braced my body up for the oncoming trauma. From the slit that still remained across my eye, I could begin to see her hand rising up towards my face.

OK Eugene, here it comes! And remember, you deserve this for being so damn selfish.

My body jumped a little as her hand made it's initial contact with my cheek. But the blow was not sharp or reprimanding. It was soft. I crooked open my one eye in a state of confusion. Within seconds her other hand had cupped my vacant cheek and my eyes now, stood staring down at a caressing smile, not a frown. And my face, I was happy to discover, was being supported, not punished by Newa's frail palms.

"I wo wuv to," she said with a hazy smile.

A great sigh of relief left my throat. "Thank you Newa," I gasped. "I was worried because I didn't know if you were busy, or if I made you mad, or if I offended you, or...?"

Newa pressed her finger over my babbling mouth and said carefully. "It would be my pweasure."

It was official. It was stamped in stone that our friendship was still very much intact and now even stronger. I watched happily after that as the serious look on Newa's face quickly disappeared and was overthrown by her usual spastic expression that I

was used
to and had grown to love. Without missing a beat she bounced backwards and
dropped to her knees in front of Sara, rambunctiously informing my child of the
good news.

"Sawa stay with Newa tonight ,"she sang. "Yes, Sawa and Newa gonna have goo
times. Ha Ha!"

Then my Asian confidante began initiating her tried and true avalanche of affections
onto my child as I leaned up against the wall and took in the show. After a few minutes
of this ever-evolving sitcom, I came to understand that it was more the idea that
someone had finally trusted in her again. Someone finally took the time to look past all
that dust and see the kindness she was so capable of and willing to give. I knew that
was the main cause of her joy and I can't tell you how good that made me feel.

That evening I dropped Sara off at Newa's at about 5:30pm. I also left behind a
good cache of formula, squeaky toys, hand-made diapers, and of course, her very
favorite possession, the ninja sleep charm.
Newa was all ready for us when we got there. She had cleaned up her place from
top to bottom and laid out a special blanket for Sara smack dab in the middle of her
front room. She looked so happy, so re-born, a feeling I could now relate to. She
wasted no time in snatching up my baby and whisking her away either.

All I got was a little punch in the arm and a "Hawa goo time!" and she and my baby
disappeared into the never-never land of the front room.

Feeling quite alive, I hopped back into my white roadster and sped away. Me and
Meridith had agreed at the cafe to rendezvous by the concession stand at the downtown park at exactly 6pm. I always knew of that park, but rarely went there.
Once in the vicinity, I parked my car in a familiar spot on the opposite side of
the river and began making my way towards the festival. My gait was hurried and
anxious, even though I was trying very hard not to seem desperate or easy.
I got there at ten to six on the nose. Just enough time, I allotted, to hit the can and
check out my look.
After a quick hair flip and eyebrow groom, I strolled out the bathroom door and
scouted the surrounding area for the concession. I made out the place in question
over to the right and thankfully, I also saw Meridith standing in front of it.

I was relieved as soon as I laid eyes on her because every man that has ever had a
first date I'm sure, is always in the back of their mind, a little nervous at the very real
possibility of being stood up. But today thank God, that did not happen.
As I drew closer, I found myself becoming increasingly entranced by her slender
figure and for a second, started to wonder just what a woman like that was doing
going on a date with me. My pessimism was short lived though for I was riding a
thundercloud, and there "weren't nuthin" that was going to get in the way of this
little hoe-down! No bloody way! Confident and surprisingly relaxed, I rolled up to
her and let go my best smile.
"You made 'er, huh?" I said with ease.

"In the flesh," she grinned.

"Hey, let's get a seat before it packs up," I said perfectly. "Would you a drink or something?"

My words were bold and undeterred, but behind my rough and ready monologue, I was secretly bracing myself for her almost certain and economically destructive answer. Something to the effect of... "Sure, I'll have a double Paralyzer with a beer chaser to start and then we'll go hard from there!"

But to my grateful relief, all she said was, "No thanks I'm fine. Brought my own," she gaffed in a sneaky voice as she brandished a liter sized bottle of soda water from the depths of her handbag.

Oh thank Christ.

Now them were the words I wanted to hear!
"Are you sure", I repeated, still pushing forth the option to make it seem like I wasn't a cheap SOB.
"Yep", I'm fine, she concluded.
"Where's Sara?" Meridith then asked curiously.

"At her babysitter's right now," I told her. "She's being spoiled rotten by her um... Gramma, as we speak."

The word "Gramma", rolled very easily off my tongue which was a nice feeling. I saw Meridith kind of smile back too in a familiar agreement with my statement.
We did, for the amount of people there, manage to find a pretty decent pair of seats. These freebee concerts, from what I had gathered, were usually quite packed and it was common to see people standing on the sidelines to catch a glimpse of the show. The folk fest itself was pretty good. I think it was anyway. But to tell you the truth, I wasn't really paying too much attention to what was happening on the stage for I was far too busy thinking about what to talk about during the brief pauses from the band and of course, trying to the best of my ability, to make my chest appear bigger than it actually was.

And besides, I was a head banger. Non-practicing at the moment, but nevertheless, still a head banger!
And it was true that my main stream of joy this day, was emulating out from one source, and one source only. And that windfall was Meridith. The drop dead gorgeous drugstore clerk that for reasons I couldn't even begin to explain, was sitting right beside me. Of her own free will I might add! That's what was really blowing my mind. And the smell of her perfume, the same magical potion that grabbed me by the short and curlys in the pharmacy that day, was once more inebriating me with it's poison. It's probably not that difficult to imagine, but in all my life I was never really that much of a lady's man, even before I became a skid.

I was just never able to make the connection you know? I'm afraid the whole girl/

boy thing sort of passed me by. And with the exception of the odd beer-induced kiss at a house party and a tragically awkward one night stand, I had never really been on an actual date before. I knew this was mainly due to my odd living circumstances. I mean, when you live in a car, the last thought you ever entertain is actively "playing the field". Actively sleeping in a field sure, but that's about it.

But this. Now this was the real thing! This was a bona fide interlude. And not surprisingly, I was still having a little trouble with the fact that this woman beside me was in no way without legitimate prospects. Yet, here she was sitting next to me. It was just something I was almost scared to even think about.

The concert seemed to fly by and was over before I knew it. I did try to extend our outing a bit by offering to buy her a coffee and a muffin somewhere as we made our way down the grandstand and out onto the street, but she politely refused saying that she had a big day ahead of her and needed an early night.

As we neared the corner that would separate us in the direction of our vehicles, I ended the date like a complete gentleman. I didn't try to hold her hand, or snare a kiss, or pull any other of that grade nine dance hall shit. Nope, I just thanked her for coming out, and promised her that I would see her again at the drugstore. Then, after a casual handshake, I bid her farewell and turned away.

The date was fantastic, but it flew by so quick. Hell, I didn't even remember the trip back to my car.

But the next day, and throughout the days that followed, all the quiet conversations and subtle dialogues of that wonderful evening began to play themselves out over and over again for only me to see and enjoy.

It felt like she was all around me. Wherever I went, whatever I did, it was like she was right there beside me. The potent mustiness of the many decaying leaves did not seem to faze me anymore, for that aromatic time slot was now occupied solely by the memory of her perfume that appeared to have saturated itself deep into the pores of my skin. And for the first time since I could remember, the river in my mind, usually flowing hard in a rampant state of survival, was now beginning to recede and slow and I caught myself just relaxing on the banks of it for once.

October 1st announced itself with a drumroll of cold rain. It only lasted a few hours until the bright fall sun gobbled up the swollen clouds that supported it, but I knew that this was still a subtle warning of things to come. Cold rain eventually turned into snow, and snow worried me. Snow always worried people like me, especially now. But as the sun continued to heat up the city, my worrisome thoughts lessened and the memory of my sacred interlude with Meridith continued to flow about my veins, causing me to brandish a stupid grin from time to time.

With our morning wash, bottle pillage, and chow down session already completed, I decided it was about time that yours truly began some post secondary education. So with the radio blasting away loudly, I put the hammer down and screeched my car onto the freeway. I was in a great mood so I cranked up the stock boom box a little and let the power of the airwaves saturate my ears.

"Another industrial early morning, da na na na..."
The overplayed song thumped on sharply as I sped down the road and out of the

corner of my eye, I noticed that Sara had pushed off her thin camouflaging and was keeping in sync with the rhythm of the tune, flailing her chunky little limbs up and down to the stark vibration of the base drum.

That's so weird. I didn't think baby's picked up on things like music.

"That's it my little dancing queen," I urged. "You go girl! You become a movie star and make daddy rich now."

A contented montage of squeaks and gurgles spilled out from Sara's mouth as she accepted my challenge, as well as of course, about seven gallons of sticky drool.

Babies are drool machines in case you're wondering. I'm sure they produce their own weight in spit every hour, but hey, what are you gonna do?

We drove on happily listening to the radio and jiving away until my breaks came screeching to a halt directly in front of my latest idea. The library. Yep, you heard that right. I, Eugene Lauder was sitting in front of the library, and I was more than ready to expand my somewhat atrophied mind. This whole literary expedition actually started when I overheard a conversation at a coffee shop between two obviously seasoned mothers. They were going on about how, if you were a parent, the book service was free.

At first my intentions were that of thrift I admit, for I'm sure Sara was getting pretty sick and tired of the same old stories. So I figured what the heck. I mean I didn't have the budget to buy her any more new ones, so ya, it's true that this whole library thing was initially about cost.

But to tell you the truth, the moment I held up that freshly laminated membership card I really have to say that it felt pretty good. I guess it was just the fact that I was a member of something. Something legit.

Beaming with sophistication, I pocketed the card and snatched up a small handful of brightly colored pop up books, then strolled over to the common area and pulled up a seat. One by one I read Sara the simple plots, which she seemed to enjoy immensely. It was probably just the familiar hum of my voice that she was drawn to, but as long as it made her happy. But whatever the case may have been, the fact was that she sat there as quiet as a church mouse the whole time. That was sweet! Now after about the fifth book, I noticed that Sara had nodded off, so I carefully stood up and walked us over to a nearby couch. The hard plastic chair was starting to kill off my back anyways. Once repositioned on the inviting cloth of the new furniture, I set Sara to one side and stretched out my arms.

Ya.. I liked this place.

It was quiet and warm and most of all, no-one was really paying any attention to me. That was the best part.

Letting my eyes wander about, they eventually stopped dead on a particular heading on the bookshelf off to the right of where I was sitting. "Ancient religions and their Trademarks", read the binding. Well, that was a title that no doubt sparked my interest, so without waking Sara I carefully eased my body off the couch and grabbed the thick encyclopedia. Sitting down in the same slow fashion, I began to flip through the pages of the dusty bible. I was a little apprehensive at first as I slowly pulled apart the musty pages, but I'm afraid it was high time that I found

out if I could, just what that Goddam symbol thingy was all about! I searched and
searched through the thick manual until my eyes finally found a match.

Almost in disbelief, I cautiously ran my fingers across the all to familiar emblem on
the page. Yep, it was real. And it was the very same object that had been deviously
slipping through the cracks of my sanity.

After a minute I broke my stare away from the high gloss drawing and tipped my
head downward to the writing below the picture.

"The Mandela, or 'Mystical almond' as it was better known by, was an ancient
pagan symbol for that of purity," the caption explained. I kept chipping away at the
historical blurb for a little longer but basically the whole paragraph said more or less
the same thing. The object on the page and in the news was simply just a letterhead
for "Purity"?

Well that sure as hell didn't make any sense,

And I'm sure the police felt the same way about that definition too. So what then?
I mean why would an ancient symbol for "Purity", be left behind at the scenes of
such horror? Evil and Innocence? That just didn't add up, no matter what way you
looked at it, it just didn't. I pondered the confusing evidence at hand for a little
while longer, but it was pointless. Good and evil just kept on canceling themselves
out again and again until I got to the point where I could no longer rationalize my
findings. Maddened by my lack of fortune, I closed the book hard and leaned back
into the chesterfield. My brain was spent, but eventually I did lean forward again
and re-open the text. This time though, it was solely out of boredom. The pages I saw
now were all the same. Just a bunch of weird drawings that were weakly supported
by a layer of cheap philosophic propaganda. Crayons and bullshit to narrow it down.

Watching the last set of pages fall away from my thumb and flutter downward,
my eyes accidentally caught a glimpse of something obtuse. In an instant my hand
became rigid and my fingers began nervously flipping back through the chapters
under stark orders from my memory to retrieve the setting they had just flagged.

Within seconds my pupils had found what they were looking for and my limbs
fell quiet as I sat staring curiously down at another meager symbol that I had also
come into contact with. The sketch I now was fixated on was that of the three pillar
like fonts, standing upright in which the two outside lines were purposely collapsed
inward and resting against the center one. It was the same description of the artwork
I had noticed on the tattooed forearm of the eerie stranger that I had ill-fatedly
encountered in the park that day. The same forearm that coincidentally, reached out
and rudely attempted to get a look at the face of my baby. I felt a bad vibe snake
through me as I looked at that drawing. Up until now, I had all but forgotten about
that unpleasant encounter, but my curiosity was now peaked at the reinstatement of
the memory, and my eyes dropped quickly down towards the caption at the base of
the modest picture.

"The name of the above caricature is called Awen," the print went on to say. "It was
a coveted symbol of the ancient cult society known as the Druids.

The Druids were a Celtic tribe, mostly consisting of highly educated men and woman who were believed to have carried out numerous human sacrifices in praise of a highly sacred species of tree known as "Druis", or... "Great Oak", as it is translated in modern language. These sacrifices apparently took place all throughout the year, but the majority of these deadly ceremonies were usually held around the end of the warm season, or "SamHein", as the Druids called it. This was the time when they believed that the veil between their reality and that of the otherworld was the most easily accessible. Mistletoe was also highly prized among these people and was widely used in their rituals. Some experts believe that the Druid society still survives in great numbers and continues to carry out their dastardly ceremonies to this day, operating in the utmost of secrecy in small, but well established sects."

The words in front of me suddenly disappeared as the book caved in between my shaking hands and hit the floor. A stark gust of fear raced across my hot skin. I was paralyzed. The words 'Human' and 'Sacrifice' were holding me fast to that couch. That weirdo in the park was not just another lonely person in the big city.

He was a goddam cult member! A "Druid", or whatever the fuck they called themselves.

He had to be, I mean why in the hell else would he have that same marking inked into his skin if he wasn't involved with them in some way?

"Sonofabitch," I mumbled.

The phrases from the book kept surfacing over and over again. 'Warm season, SamHein, Mistletoe'
What the hell were they all about, and furthermore, what did they have to do with my little gir...

OH,... Oh Christ no, wait a minute here. Jesus Christ... SARA!!!! They're after Sara. Good God, that freak's after my baby!

My hands vibrated with fear as my breathing started to jar. In a state of utter disbelief, I began to slowly comprehend and come to terms with the grim repercussions of my terrible discovery.

He knows.

"Fuck," I growled! He must know Sara is a stray. A ghost. An undetectable Jane Doe that no one would ever miss, or come looking for. He must know that or he wouldn't have approached me. But how? How could he know?

"Fucking Hell, That's why he wants her. He wants to sacr..."

I could barely say the word, the word "Sacrifice". It was like the world around me no longer existed anymore, I was that scared! I swallowed hard and for a moment there, tried in vain to wash away the conclusion of my findings and invent a less horrible machine. But the bleak truth of the situation would not uproot itself and the more I pondered the riddle I had just solved, the more it made sense.

The end of the warm season, the tattoo, his accent?

That's why that Bastard kept asking me questions about the mother. It was his last clue. My stomach started to turn and swell as an avalanche of recent headlines from the media began to paste themselves up to the bulletin board of my mind.

"He's the one," I muttered, holding back the urge to puke. "He's the Motherfucker that's kidnapping all those kids!!"

The man at the park? Holy Fuck Eugene! He's the serial abductor! He's the one they are looking for.

There was no question in my mind now. None whatsoever!
The symbol, the fact that winter was on it's way, the "warm season coming to an end"...

Fuck!!.... Fuck, he's collecting them - the children for his sacrifices. That's what he's doing! And now he's got his eyes on my little girl!

With deadly precision, the whole puzzle suddenly fell into place and sent me into a world of terror I never in my life believed I could feel.

I had solved the mystery.

The lethal riddle that kept the city at bay, and that I now held a stake in.

This was all just too much for me to take, and I began to suffocate under the weight of that knowledge. It was time to get some fresh air into me and pronto! With the grace of a bull, I snatched up Sara and headed for the door, forgetting altogether about the free books and the general purpose of this visit.
Falling out the front door of the place I'm sure never to be welcomed back again, I drew in a huge and diluted mixture of air and car exhaust and let it refurbish my starved lungs. After a few minutes, an oxygen-induced lucidity masked the trauma of my ordeal, but the mountain of evidence I had just uncovered in that library still rendered my nerves a war zone.

I convinced myself that I had no other option but to head directly to the police with what I now knew. But as before, my ever-present alter ego had a much different take on the whole situation.

And just what exactly do you really know Eugene old boy? Have you really uncovered something they don't already know, or are you just panicking?

Think about this my friend. All you are really doing by going to the cops is furthering your risk of losing Sara. Am I wrong, huh? I mean am I?

The voice continued to bellow on and I tried so hard not to listen. I wanted so badly to hold my ground against this domineering poltergeist but the numbers, I'm afraid, just didn't add up. The evidence I'd unearthed could easily be dismissed as coincidence. And even though I had gained a lot of ground from an educational point of view, when it was all said and done, the end result still materialized as nothing more than a couple of wild dreams and a rude middle-aged loner with a pony tail. The only real crime I had a concrete fix on was my own.

I was still sold on the fact that there was some sort of connection to everything, but I also knew that if I were to come forward with my findings, regardless of my good intentions, the final tragedy would ultimately wind up being me losing Sara. And that was a risk I was definitely not interested in taking. ...ever!

So I gave in to the voice as usual and laid down a battle plan. From now on, my day to day life would be much different than before. I would need to become much more elusive, that was a given. But I would also have to streamline my leisurely outings with Sara as well and be very careful to not to draw any extra attention to us. The rules had changed and the stakes were high. It was time to immerse my already uncommon life into a state of further deception for the welfare of my child. There was no other alternative. Once settled back into my car, I pulled out onto the crowded side street and waited in line for the light to turn green, mentally categorizing the numerous safety precautions I would now have to integrate into my routine. I was confident in my ability to carry out those immediate changes, but that optimism was about to undergo a lethal test, for on the corner directly adjacent from my vehicle, stood none other than the mysteriously-tattooed man himself.

It was Leon Jenkins.

The very same man I had read about not ten minutes earlier was standing there on the opposite sidewalk, sporting his trademark overcoat and ponytail and bobbing his head around from side to side with great intensity. He was looking for something.
He was looking for me.
In the blink of an eye, my body erupted again in fear. My limbs froze and a huge dose of panic rushed through my veins. Now on the positive side, he could not see me from where he was, but that cover would be blown out of the water as soon as the light turned green. For then, I had no other choice than to follow the natural flow of traffic, and that path would lead me right past him.

Godammit, Now what do I do?

I briefly entertained the idea of flipping a shithook and bolting off in the other direction, but I knew if I did this, he would spot me for sure and it was absolutely crucial that he not recognize me, or more importantly, my car. For if he did, I knew that I would never be safe in this life again. I watched in agony as the swinging bulbs changed from dark to light and the vehicles in front of me started to move forward.

"Do something Eugene," I howled. "Snap out of it and make a decision you dumb fuck. Do it now!!"

144

In a desperate maneuver I quickly jabbed my hand underneath my seat and grabbed my ball cap. In the same breath I also donned a thick pair of sunglasses and covered Sara up completely with the other half of her blanket. My heart was pushing it's way through my shirt as I cautiously idled past the evil man in the oilskin shroud. I pretended to look over at the opposite street sign as I drove by in an attempt to further shadow my identity. When he was a good three cars behind me, I finally tipped my eyes toward the rear view mirror and let go a stagnant belch of relief. The Druid was still shifting his head about aimlessly, never once fixating his line of site toward my ride.

"Fuckin aye," I growled.

Without hesitation I began to aggressively depress my accelerator. It was high time to put some distance between me and that psychopath. It felt good to hear those RPMs climb. It felt good to know that my plan had worked.
I crested another block in the span of ten seconds and let out a long breath.

Man!... That was too fucking close Eugene! Too close!!

Now, with nothing in my rear view mirror but pavement, I reached over and uncovered Sara with my still shaking hand.

"I'm sorry about that Sweetie," I murmured.

I was fully expecting at least some form of audible wrath, but she never let out so much as a peep. She was just laying there attentively examining her fingers as usual. She was so calm. If she only knew the extent of the danger that lurked beyond her dream-like world.

Over the next forty-eight hours, I plunged myself into a deep state of hiding. I didn't pick bottles; I didn't visit Newa. I didn't do shit. I just laid low and watched over my baby, leaving the safety of my car only to discard Sara's dirty diapers and to take the occasional alley-side leak. Luckily, I had stockpiled enough formula to last the two days, but as for me, I'd run out of food on the first one and I was becoming terribly weak from hunger. By the third morning I knew I had to get back out there and get on with my day to day routine. Just because I had stopped living for a couple days didn't mean Sara had stopped eating. She was down to her last can of formula, and I was down another pant size. It was high time to resume my so-called life, only this time under the mindset of modesty and restraint.

After a slow and unremarkable start to the morning , I eventually got back into the swing of things and came across a nice ripe pile of beer bottles around 10 am. Three full garbage bags worth.! I found them in a residential alley. It was an amazing score, but I'll tell you, I didn't envy the poor bastards who sucked back that amount of booze in one shot. They must have been wishing for death at that point! As soon as I cashed in my morning haul, this time opting out to patronize a recycler in a different part of town to keep in check with my unspoken promise of stealth, I then headed over to the Laundromat and had a visit with my friend.
God it was nice to see her again. You never know how much you miss someone's

company until you haven't access to it anymore.

We had a great chat, me and Newa. I told her that I had been very busy the last couple of days and was unable to stop by. I wanted to ask her if she'd mind looking after Sara for the afternoon, due to the fact that my two day hiatus had left me seriously broke but I was hesitant, even though I knew it was imperative that I equalize my losses by expanding my refundable search into an area that would yield me a big score.
A windfall that would put me back in the race.
That area, however, lay deep in the wretched alleyways of the core, which was no place under any circumstances for a newborn. I had crunched a few other ideas earlier on, but they all led to the same conclusion. The only way I was going to recoup my losses from my layoff was to go down there. I let my conscience battle it out for a while during the course of my visit, but finally decided that asking her to baby sit again would constitute pushing my luck, so I just quashed the whole notion.

That was, of course, until Newa sprang up in the middle of a sentence and said, "You wa me to ta care of Sawa fo you again? I no mind. You lo like you need a bwake."

I was stunned by my friend's sense of intuition and unconditional generosity.

"Would you mind?" I asked cautiously.

"Of cose not! I would wuv to," she smiled.

"God Newa," I gasped. "That would be such a help to me. Are you sure I'm not putting you out here?"

Newa didn't say anything else, she just smiled and booted me out the door, issuing me a reassuring wink and a pat on the back before she sent me packing.

"Yes!" I howled as I jogged down the alley to my rig.

Now I would be able to get caught up and not have to stress about Sara's well being. I drove off with a great sense of security, basking happily in a much-needed ray of hope as I sped toward the parking lot down by the river. I cleverly stashed my car in between two large cargo vans and began my trek.
I felt a little nauseated when I first picked up my once-familiar trail that snaked its way down into the pit. In a way I kind of felt like a reformed drug addict who was being forced back down to an old flop house to re-visit his seedy past. But the uneasy feeling I had started my journey with quickly faded away to thoughts of my Sara and how she needed to eat. After that little flashback, my feet only became steadier, and my focus only stronger. I was here to make money for my family and that's exactly what I was going to do!

By the time ten to five in the evening rolled around, I was feverishly sorting through four and a half completely full garbage bags of empties at the main downtown bottle depot. I was in quite a hurry because I knew they closed at five. As I organized my bounty, I came to the proud conclusion that the day's take was a new all-time record. You know, it's amazing what you can do when you have someone to do it for.

Inside the span of fifteen minutes and the odd "Thank you for letting me cash in so late" speech, I walked triumphantly out of the extremely well- used doors of the place with an impressive fistful of cabbage, which I quickly stuffed deep into my jeans. "Out of site, out of mind." And in this part of town, that little proverb held a lot of weight.

During my long trip back up to my well-hidden vehicle, I decided to take refuge in a semi-enclosed bus shelter for a few minutes. I was pretty tired out from the pace of the day and needed to catch my breath before I began the second leg of my sprint. After about ten minutes of ass time, I reluctantly got up off the hard wooden bench and prepared to leave. But just as I was about to exit the narrow opening of the cubby, I was suddenly stopped dead in my tracks by a short bald man in a very cheesy suit, who appeared out of nowhere and blocked my escape.

"Where do you think you're going?" he growled in a stern but obviously rehearsed voice.

Now at first I admit, I was generally concerned and maybe even a little worried about this new situation. But the stress I had endured over the last few days was seriously affecting my level of restraint, and without even thinking twice, I immediately cocked back my fist and prepared to knock that pompous little motherfucker's head clear off his shoulders.

"Hey, Hey... Easy now buddy boy," the little man yelped back as he quickly shielded his soon-to-be dismantled face with his arms.
"No need to get all rough and tough on me now," the suit said. "I'm just here on a little business."

Holding my offensive stance where it was, I watched the man in front of me carefully reach into his breast pocket and pull out a neatly folded leather wallet, which he then opened up and raised toward my face.
"Department of Social Services - Child Welfare Division" read the government issue badge.

"You see," the man responded with an appointed smile. "I'm strictly here for work related purposes.
"My, my," he continued. You sure are a hard person to track down.
Have a seat," he gestured.

"No thanks," I said. "I'll stand."

"Suit yourself," he said in a quasi-professional manner and without ado, he eased his slight frame down onto the bench and cupped his hands over his folded legs not even four feet from where I was standing.

"My name," he said out of the blue "is Jeffrey Simmons. I'm from the Social Services office, just in case you can't read and all."

His tone was steady, but reeked of weakness.

"What can I do for you today Mr. Social Services Prick?" I blurted meanly. "It's past 5:30 now. Aren't you paper-pushing government whores off duty for the day?"

"Au contraire," he grinned back deviously. "I myself am never off duty, that's just the thing.
"And by the way," he continued, "from this day forward you should permanently etch that little tidbit of information into that grossly-uneducated mind of yours. You dig?"

"Listen…" I warned.

"No you listen," the puny man shot back out of character as he stood up and attempted to match my threat with a better one.

But his little show ended abruptly as I grabbed the end of his collar and drew back my arm, this time with full intention of releasing it in his direction. Knowing that his physical prowess was no match for the anger that sat ready in mine, he did then shrug off the grip I initiated on his coat and decided to use the only weapon he had at his disposal, his big mouth. I listened half-heartedly as he rambled on and pummeled me with an entourage of fancy adjectives and scary subtitles. Thankfully though, after about five minutes, he finally shut the fuck up for two seconds and prepared, I guess, to plant his teency weency sword into the center of my unscathed chest.

"I'll tell you what Trailer Park," scoffed the underpowered man as he inched his beet red face ever-so- cautiously towards mine. "I'll do you a favor and cut right to the chase.
You see, I know you have a little secret that you've been hiding away. I know this for certain," he continued as he directed his finger towards my skull.
"Now unfortunately, I just can't just simply knock you over the head and drag your guilty ass off to jail. Nope, I'm sad to admit that even lowlife scumbags like you still have rights... For now.
No, I'm afraid the only thing I can do at this point is... Well,... How do I put this? Ah... persuade you I guess, to confess your sins of your own free will."

The odd-looking little man then squeezed his twig-like fingers into a ball and made them crack. This pre-empted show of fierceness, well, you know, just scared the shit out of me and all, but surprisingly enough I didn't start to cry!
As I stared down the pipsqueak below me with grave intent, I think he finally realized that I was not about to cave in to his forceful approach and after a few seconds, he stood down his last shot at glory and instead, reached into his jacket pocket and produced a white business card, which he purposely set face up on the bench beside me. He then took a pen out of the same pocket and proceeded to encircle a particular sequence of numbers.

"I can be reached at that number anytime," he snarled. "That's my private line. I've highlighted it there so that whenever you are ready to 'fess up, well, you just give me a call and we'll, you know, work out all the details."

"Like I said", he continued. "We don't have to get the whole entire world involved here. If you want, I'll be the bigger man and give you the option of walking away from all this scott free. No criminal record, no jail time... no nothing. As long as you cooperate with me, you'll walk away from all this unpunished. But you must cooperate with me fully or I swear I'll have you face down in a holding cell so damn fast you won't know what hit you. You got that tough guy?!"

I did not answer him. I just held my ground and kept glaring at him unrepentantly.

"Think about it," he said, as he deliberately brushed by my shoulder and pranced out of the bus shelter.
"But don't think about it for too long asshole," he warned as he looked back and flashed me a cold stare,
"Cause I'll be watching you boy. I'll be watching you real good you hear?"

Then with a smug look on his face, the stranger casually turned and disappeared into the crowd.
Now my nerves were officially back on high alert. It was bad enough that there was a possibility I was being stalked by a psychopathic cult freak, now I had the government on my ass too!

Fuck anyway!

I stared down at the glossy card that lay in front of me. Just for a laugh, I picked it up off the bench. I mean, I had absolutely no intention of ever handing Sara over to the all-knowing wisdom of the Social Services System. Nope... No fucking way! I had already thrown out that option, but that card found it's way into my hand anyway. I left the bus shelter soon after that and hurried back to my car.
On the way to pick up Sara I slowed down for a corner and noticed a roughly-painted sign on the front door of a large turn-of-the-century house.
"Moving Sale in Alley" it read.

And even though my head was filled to the max with its usual overload of worry and confusion, as soon as I saw that sign I swung my rig around to the opening of the carport and stopped. Even as I manhandled the shifter into park , I still couldn't believe I was able to entertain the idea of looking for yet another toy for Sara, but I guess I was just acting on impulse. Ducking into the musty shack, I immediately saw an elderly man perched in the far corner of the place chewing down hard on a wooden pipe. He was comfortably nestled in amongst the numerous piles of age-old trinkets and bargain bin castaways. Announcing myself with only with a weak smile, I began to routinely bob my head from side to side in search of anything that was really cheap and geared towards infants. After only a few seconds, I quickly realized that baby toys were about the last thing I was going to find in this open-trenched landfill, so I haphazardly thanked the still-mute attendant and swung my body back towards the door.
And I was just about out that door when an object that was sitting atop a mass of worn out hand tools jumped up and caught my attention. It was an object I never in my whole life, thought I would ever take a second look at.

It was a gun.

A pistol to be exact. It looked like one of those ancient, western six shooters, and it was pretty beat up too. In a surreal trance, I watched my hand reach over and pick it up.

It was heavy and unbalanced but it felt good resting in my palm, and I purposely let that eerie sense of power flow out the cold steel handle and make its way into my spine.

I liked that. That feeling of dominance.

"It ain't a real gun anymore," rang out the old man's voice from behind me. "Had the barrel welded shut a couple of years ago. Had to," growled the senior. "Goddam government was going to make me get a license for the thing.
Just for display now," he said in a deeply jaded tone. "Just a goddam paperweight!"

The tainted veteran then let loose a wheezy cough-laden snicker, but I didn't acknowledge his justifiable complaint right away for I was too submerged in the hurricane of power the once-lethal weapon was bestowing on me. The gun felt like a supernatural guardian that was sworn to obey only the holder.

God, that was some feeling.

Now, I don't think I was actually serious about buying it when I asked him the price, but he made me an offer I simply couldn't refuse.

"Gimme a dollar and you can have the damn thing," he snarled.

The crumpled-up bill almost flew out of my pocket on it's own.

I don't know why I bought it, the gun. I mean it wasn't even real. It was, at best, like the old man said, nothing more than a glorified paperweight. But it made me feel strong while it lay in my hand.
In a way like I had just acquired an extra defense shield against all who sought to harm me and my child, most notably, that psychotic cult-freak. He was the one whom I feared the most. He was the monster that lay under my bed. But holding that decommissioned pistol in my hand, letting it further inject it's soothing venom into my veins, caused my body to begin a well-deserved reincarnation. And even though the piece of iron that lay curled up in my palm was not real, the courage and willpower it was restoring within my mind was.

That was the gig. If my mind stayed strong, my body would follow suit.

Now keeping on the subject of foes, I must admit that I honestly wasn't too worried about my recent run in with the peckerhead from the Social Services office. He was nothing. He was just a lowlife, cubical-pawn justifying his inflated paycheck by running down a chance rumor he must have caught wind of. There's no way he could have connected me to Sara. This city is way too huge to support those odds. But the cult guy on the other hand... I believed he was capable of anything. People like that are lethal, in any form.

After flipping the old timer the note, I stuffed the piece into my jacket and steered my rocket in the direction of the Laundromat to retrieve the treasure I coveted the most.

In the days that followed, everything I did, I did with the stealth and planning I'd subliminally agreed to. I kept to the alleyways and avoided the streets. I rotated my bottle routes on a daily basis and shuffled up my sleep spots. I did everything underneath the radar. I kept my head low and my eyes sharp, always looking behind me as I drove to make sure I was not being followed by any particular vehicle. I was neck deep in a lethal game of hide and seek, but I was winning, and I planned to keep it that way. I ended up leaving Sara at the Laundromat during the day two or three times a week now for safety's sake. I'll tell you, that precious old Chinese lady was really turning out to be my saving grace. I think she somehow knew I was in trouble too, but she never questioned me on the matter, and always welcomed me and my little girl into her home with open arms.

I didn't use the front entrance to the Laundromat anymore either. Newa invited me to use the side door to her apartment instead. This was a good thing for it was nicely hidden behind a thick mesh of bushy trees and you could access it from the alley. I also stashed my car a good two to three blocks away from Newa's place as well, randomly parking it in a different location every time. I then walked in the rest of the way through dirt alleys and abandoned yards to eventually end up tucked away and safe behind the living wall of brush that guarded the secret door to "Gramma's house." I wasn't taking anymore chances. I couldn't afford to. The stakes were too high.

A full week passed by without incident. I had chiseled down my newly adapted invisibility to nothing shy of a masterpiece and for the first time in a lot of days, I finally began to feel that Sara and I were once again, on a safe journey. I hadn't seen hide nor hair of "Mr. Cult Dick", or had any altercations with that sawed-off little geek from the government office either. You see, that's the neat thing about not being connected into the system, it makes you virtually impossible to locate. It was a long week though, and by the finish of it, I did come to the realization that I had been far too careless in the way I went about things. I had become unknowingly flamboyant in the way I was showing off my little secret and that oversight may have been the whole bloody cause behind my unwelcome wave of popularity.

I guess I just loved the amount of attention Sara generated, but in the end, my selfishness only wound up jeopardizing her safety. I was wiser and more efficient now and I was not about to revert back to my sloppy ways. But in the back of my mind the truth still remained that I greatly missed Meridith. I couldn't help it. Her memory would not fade. I hadn't seen or talked to her at all since our last date for I had been avoiding the drugstore in an effort to keep in sync with my plan to shop randomly. It was a logical maneuver, but it hurt. And even though for me, pursuing a relationship at that point should have been the absolute farthest thing from my mind, I still felt a great compulsion to go in and see her again. I eventually gave into my softer side and decided to go visit her. I mean, Sara was already safe and sound at Newa's house, so with that main detail taken care of, I felt a tad more ballsy. And to be honest, I knew I had to go over to that run-down pharmacy and find out if she still even recognized me, or had chosen to forget I existed altogether.

That's one of the things I believe that was poking at my conscience the most because I still had no clue how she felt. For all I knew, she may have already written me off.

When I walked into the drugstore I spotted Meridith immediately. She was at her usual till and appeared to be quite busy. She didn't notice me come so I took advantage of this little windfall and darted my easily-hidden frame off into the baby aisle. Scrounging around in my jeans pocket I scraped together enough loot to purchase the sum total of two cans of formula. Then after a short and deliberate pause, I held my breath and crept out of the aisle. The moment I stepped into her lineup, she looked up at her present customer and spotted me with her other eye. Right away she twisted her head around and flashed a big smile. I felt a heavy blanket of relief surround me as I set free the stale lump of air from my lungs and cracked a guilty shrug.

When I reached the counter the first thing I said was, "Hey, did you miss me?"

My dialogue was initiated with the intent to provoke humor, but to my surprise, was returned with the comment of a more serious nature.

"I've been waiting for you to come see me all week Eugene! Where have you been?" she whispered.

"I'm sorry Meridith," I said, feeling somewhat ashamed now. "But I've had quite an eventful week."

Man, if she only knew how true that statement was.

"Listen," she said as she tore off a blank chunk of till tape and scribbled a series of numbers down onto it. "Here's my home phone number," she said in a hurried tone. "Call me tonight, OK?"

"OK," I told her in an absolute state of shock. "I'll call you at about eight or so. Is that alright?"
"That's perfect," she grinned. And that was it! I paid for my formula and turned away.

"Don't forget!" I heard her say again.

"I won't," I mouthed and with that I backed into the glass double doors and fell out onto the street.

As I floated towards my car I instantly forgot about all my problems and once again, found myself skipping happily down the main highway to la-la land. I didn't hear or see a thing the whole way back. All I could make out in front of me were the magical group of numbers that Meridith had written down on that piece of till tape. Actually, it was nothing short of a miracle that I didn't get run over or lost, I was that high.
Now I understood what was missing in my life the last week.

It was her.

Dusk had conquered the city by the time I finally snuck around to the side door of the laundry to pick up Sara and do my chores. This was another part of my newfangled routine, my chores. You see, after Newa had closed up shop, I decided that in exchange for all the gracious babysitting Newa had been doing for me, I would (at no charge) clean up the entire front of the store, including the bathrooms, and fix (if I was able to) any of the machines that were out of order. I always ended up doing more cleaning than fixing, but I knew it was all good to her. She would shut the blinds tight on the big windows as soon as she was done her collection and let me at it.

It only took me, at most, an hour or two from start to finish, but I knew it relieved a great burden off her shoulders, which I'm sure were not fit to lug around heavy pails of mop water anymore. After my duties were complete for the night, I had a quick cup of tea with my friend, then packed up Sara's kit and stuffed my sublime child into my jacket for the trip back to my car. After a short and uneventful three and a half block jaunt, I slid Sara down into her tent in the passenger's seat and tucked her in.

By 8pm my innocent child was fast asleep and I found myself sitting quietly in my car facing the dim outline of a lone payphone on a dark nameless street.

I was just sitting there looking down at Meridith's phone number, running my fingers across it again and again, making sure it didn't run away or vanish into thin air. The glow from the street lamp above me was purposely illuminating the heavenly sequence of digits like a black light against a moon-colored sheet. Gathering up my courage for the last time, I casually looked around for anything suspicious, then ever-so-quietly, pushed open my car door and walked up to the receiver.

I took my time dialing in the row of numbers that I had instantly memorized the second I laid eyes on them.

"Hello," I heard a woman's voice say.

"Hello... um, Meridith? It's... ah... It's um, me... Eugene here. How, uh... "How are you?"

I could make out the faint sound of expelled breath hitting the mouthpiece at the other end of the electronic line.

"I'm so glad you called," she said, "I've been waiting."

The conversation, I know, began directly after that. But those first few words that she spoke, that first sentence where she said that she was "glad" I had called and that she was waiting... Well I'll tell you, that sentence would be forever engineered into the framework of my memory.

"I'm sorry I didn't call you earlier but I had some running around to do," I told her. "You know how it is."

"That's OK," she responded.

Her voice was so placid, so reassuring that I could feel my eyes start to become heavy and drunk. We continued to talk. She was so easy to converse with and for the first time, I no longer caught myself stuttering or searching for something to say. I also made up a story that I had been out of town all week and was unable to get by the drugstore to see her.

It was a lie, but that's what I was living.

She didn't appear to be mad at me, only concerned. She asked me if I would like to join her on a walk the following evening which I agreed to instantly and after a few more minutes of idle chit chat, we made arrangements to meet each other at a cozy little coffee shop she knew of a few blocks north of the pharmacy. Once a time was set, I thanked her for the gab session and said goodbye, then listened with a grin as she returned the gesture.

Stumbling forward like I was on dope, I tipped open my car door and sank inside. I sat there for a long time and relaxed to the serenade of my baby's respirations, the whole time replaying the tape in my mind over and over again of Meridith saying goodnight.

It was my new favorite word.

As I drove off toward a pre-determined sleep spot, I allowed my mind to wander about at will. It needed that. It deserved a break. That noggin of mine had bore a lot of stress lately and it felt good to let it go out and play for a while. Thankfully, Sara only awoke twice during the night. This was a nice change from the once-every-two-hour telethon I had persevered with the last little while. I knew Sara was somehow ingesting my tension and in turn, was becoming more agitated. In the wee hours of that following morning, while I was changing and feeding her for hopefully the last time, I noticed that her favorite yellow jumpsuit was becoming quite difficult to stretch across her always expanding frame. This was both good and bad.

Good because, well, she was growing. And growing was always a healthy thing. But bad in the sense that I didn't have any extra money to go out and buy her a larger one. Every spare cent I had was now going straight to baby formula and supplies and there was virtually nothing left over for much else.

Oh well Eugene. I tucked in my little angel once again. *At least she's cutting you a little slack on her toy habit.*

The next day I didn't show up at Newa's house until almost four in the afternoon. I was usually there to drop off Sara a lot sooner but lately I was beginning to feel very confident about our revised safety regimen and I really wanted to start spending more of my own time with my baby. It had felt so strange the last little while without my little girl beside me as I pressed on with my day to day procedures. I mean, she was such a huge part of my life. Hell, she was my life, and I was beginning to suffer from the occasional case of separation anxiety. And even though I was technically breaking the rules a bit, nothing happened and we ended up having a great day together with no surprises. Just like old times.

I would stop the car to check out a promising bag of trash and Sara would just sit there quietly and shit herself.

It was heaven!

The moment I knocked on the door though, Newa was right there to whisk my little girl away into paradise. I explained to her as she riddled Sara with belly button kisses, that I had another date with that same girl again and if it be alright that I start my cleanup duties a little earlier than usual.

Newa ceased her bombardment of affections on my baby for a brief second and said with a grin, "It OK, you a good boy! I give you night off OK?"

"Thank you Newa," I said softly. "I can't tell you how much I appreciate having you in mine and Sara's life"

I saw the smallest of tears rise to her eye as she gently stood up and began walking over to where I was standing. Without warning she wrapped her arms around me and began to squeeze. She didn't say anything to me because she didn't have to. She just smiled warmly and walked me to the door.

Once outside though, I was mortified, but definitely amused as I felt her boney foot connect jokingly with my ass. This was followed too, by an uncharacteristic remark that I knew would be quite hard to forget.

"Go ge her, yu big stud!" the dainty oriental grinned as she pulled her pointy shoe back out of my butt with a giggle.

As I made my way back to the car, I couldn't help but laugh at Newa's unforeseen shtick.

When I had rediscovered my Firebird, I used the gratuitous window of time I didn't think I would have and checked out a couple of more trash cans, then packed it in for the night and raced over to the designated coffee shop where I was to meet the lovely Meridith. Parking around back, of course, to justify my daily, "I don't actually exist" quota, I ended up strolling into the joint a good fifteen minutes early. You know, for all my obvious shortcomings, I will yank my own cord a bit and brag that I was rarely ever late. Ya sure, I never really had too many places to be and all, but if I did, I always got to the church on time.

Once I was inside, I grabbed the smallest coffee the place sold and planted my aching bones firmly into a seat that boasted a clear and unbiased view of the main entrance. Not ten minutes later and looking as sexy as usual, Meridith walked in the door, wearing a light-colored pair of viciously snug hip-huggers and a matching sweater that fit the same.

I didn't even finish my coffee. I just stood up like I was attached to strings and eagerly glided over to her.

Trudging through a few awkward moments of small talk, Meridith out of nowhere grabbed my hand and said, "Come on Eugene, let's get out of here! I've thought of the perfect place for our walk. It's just up the river a bit. You'll love it! Come on."

Well hell, what was I supposed to do? Say... Jeez Meridith, I'm sorry, but as a homeless fugitive who's being stalked by a wanted cult leader, I've made it a rule not to socialize with normal people.

Nope, I wasn't about to do that anytime soon. Actually, I doubt I even had a choice in the matter judging by the way she nearly tore my arm out of it's socket yanking me out of the cafe and into the side door of her sporty little turquoise import. Hot girls always drive those types of cars, I've found. But having said that, I was quite relieved that we were taking her vehicle because I was sort of wondering just what kind of story I was going to make up if we had ended up taking mine. I mean my car, well, it wasn't really a car anymore.

We sped away from the cafe and headed north. I geared my brain up intellectually for what I thought was going to be a chatty ride but Meridith, instead, fell strangely quite on the way up to this so-called "perfect place of hers."

This struck me as an odd transformation from the giddy woman who first greeted me in the cafe. But hey, that was alright I guess. I mean I still felt a little nervous around her anyways, so it's probably a good thing that we both resembled deaf mutes for awhile. By the time we pulled into the parking lot of what looked more like a glorified jogging trail, it was already getting fairly dark outside. But undeterred, we both set out down that trail with only the glimmer of a half moon to guide us. We did talk a bit, but the conversation was consistently shallow. Smalltalk was the only meal on this flight I'm afraid, but I didn't contest it.

During the course of the quasi-romantic stroll, I had come to the realization that Meridith was not really the happy-go- lucky, life-of-the-party type I think she really wished she was. I mean she had her moments and all, but I think deep down she was a hopeless introvert. This was not a bad thing, for I figured the less we talked, the less chance there was of me unknowingly ramming my foot in my mouth, a common ailment I regularly suffered from. There was one definite thing we did have in common though - our admiration for Mother Nature. I picked up on this by the way she would occasionally tilt her head over to one side and snare the beauty of a natural scent that had already coated the lining of my own nose on its way by. And when we reached what I logically assumed was the junction point for another path, we came upon a well-utilized log that was fossilizing over to the left.

"Let's sit down for a sec," I said to my timid companion.

Meridith agreed with a hint of relief and down we went. The limb was nicely grooved, further evidence of it's popularity.

"So how was work today ?" I eventually asked her.

"It was long and boring," she replied in an exaggerated whisper. "Hair color was fifty percent off today and that place was literally wall-to-wall with short, white-haired people. It looked like an outtake from the Wizard of Oz."

I laughed out loud at my date's out-of-character insert and understood once again how absolutely clueless I was as to her true nature.

"Listen," I said after a minute, "I really did enjoy our first date and I am very sorry I did not come into the store to see you sooner. It was inconsiderate of me, but I was just run off my feet, you know."

Meridith accepted my apology, but then fell silent again, so I decided to revamp the whole direction of the conversation back to a method of communication that had never seemed to fail me. Bullshit that is!

"And besides," I cracked back swiftly, "It's not easy, you know, ...me being the big playboy that I am and all, to remember the babes I'm obligated to grace with my presence.
You understand don't ya honey-bunch?"

I heard a faint giggle creep out of the lips of the girl next to me, but she didn't follow up her admiration for my rapier wit with any other show of approval. She did though, send in my direction a short but effective "Oh Please" gesture, which I heeded squeamishly. But in the end, my off-the-wall sense of humor proved effective and managed to reboot the jovial setting that this whole nature expedition started off with. For a spell after that, the conversation began to flow on rather nicely. The topics were still characteristically thin and non-specific, but that was OK Just being around her was a good time in my books .We also successfully filled up the dead spaces throughout the light innuendo by taking turns throwing stones into the slow moving body of water that paralleled the path.

As I bent down to retrieve another bullet, Meridith suddenly intercepted my reach and said, "Hey, why don't we walk some more OK?"

I agreed with a grin and we were on our way, now breaking trail down the considerably more narrow sub-path off to the right. After about twenty more minutes of this latest safari, we jointly decided to turn around and head back to the car. Meridith said that she was really enjoying our visit and everything, but her feet were starting to get pretty sore due to the fact that she had spent the better part of the day perched on them.
When we finally got to her car and began driving back in the direction of the coffee shop, I found my brain scrambling away trying to think up something else to do. I mean the night was still relatively young and I didn't want our date to end just yet. Call me crazy!

Even as we pulled into the cafe parking lot I still hadn't come up with anything concrete that her and I could do that didn't involve peanut butter and feathers. It's true, a few perverted thoughts were swirling about my mind at that point (the southerly one), but I quickly blocked them out and got my head pointing in the direction it was supposed to be. If I was nothing else, I was still a gentleman. I heard the clicking of the floor shifter give way to the force of Meridith's slender hand, eventually coming to a stop beside the illuminated abbreviation for park. After that there was no sound inside the cab except for that of uncomfortable silence. I was desperate. I needed more time, just enough to conjure up a feasible, but not too pushy, game plan to keep this party going.

A few more long seconds passed by and then, fearing the ding of the bell, I finally said to her "Hey, do you want to go inside and have another quick coffee or something?"

It was a weak ploy, but to my knock-me-on-the-ass surprise, Meridith turned and gave me the best answer to a question like that any male in the world could ever hope for.

"I've got a better idea," she said. "I've got fresh coffee at my apartment. Why don't we just go there instead?"
Well I'll tell you, you ain't ever seen a smile come across a guy's face so fast.
In a state of blissful shock, I humbly accepted her offer and we were again, on our way. The butterflies in my stomach were going mental as we drove towards her place. This was just too good to be true. I mean I just saved another two dollars here!!

As we drove onward, I would have been lying if I didn't say that I'd never been so happy, or so nervous in my entire life! I mean she was inviting me into her home, so I knew she was at least somewhat attracted to me. After a series of undocumentable twists and turns, we finally ended up in front of a modest but newer- style row of apartments in a part of town I never even knew existed.

"My place is pretty small," she warned, as she fished her keys out of the ignition. "I hope you don't mind."

"Don't worry," I chuckled way too honestly, "you should see mine!"

After passing through a security door that would have made the pentagon jealous, we walked up two flights of stairs and veered off to the left into her suite. Apartment #327.
Her pad was meticulously neat and smelled of jasmine. I had really come to appreciate the smell of clean air in the last month or so. Go figure!
Contemporary artwork adorned the walls too, and a moderately priced stereo lay waiting over in the corner. Yep, it was definitely your basic bachelorette pad in every aspect - conservative in a way, but stylish nonetheless.

"Come on in," she said as she hung up her fine suede jacket on a solid oak hook. "Just throw your coat on the sofa if you like and I'll get the coffee ready."

I shed my boots and did as I was told, happily planting my homeless ass onto her soft leather couch. Five minutes later she returned from the adjacent kitchen with two steaming cups of excellent-smelling brew and sat down beside me. Man, the smell of that coffee alone near made my whole year! I was so used to the toxic waste they loosely referred to as gourmet caffeine at the all night swill baristas, that the thought of a real cup of Joe was almost too much. As we lounged on the sofa, the topic again was light and user friendly, and I couldn't help but wonder just why she never wanted to talk about anything meaningful or important.
I tried to shift the flow of our nattering down a more in-depth path, but every time I did this she would always detour it back to the weather and the bloody price of gas!

I was beginning to wonder if she was just extremely shy, or if I was just terribly boring. I asked myself many questions about her in that thirty minutes, and towards the end of our little gab session, I did stumble upon a very possible answer to my silent query. Actually, it happened more by accident as I pounded back the last swig of my exquisite beverage and set my empty cup on the matching coffee table beside us.
As my eyes carefully followed the cup in my hands, they also picked up the edge of

a small but delicately framed picture of what could have only been Meridith's imme-diate family. It was a photograph of a man and a woman, looking to be in about their late forties or early fifties. They were standing behind two other people amidst an artificial, cloth backdrop. The first person to the right kneeling down was obviously Meridith, but at a little younger age, like probably nineteen or twenty. She looked pretty much the same as she did now, but she was a bit chubbier in the picture. She had definitely lost weight and toned herself up since then.

And standing next to her was a shorter, neatly-dressed kid. He was younger looking, but you could still see the genetic resemblance in his eyes.

Must be her little brother.

He was a good-looking dude. He kind of looked like one of those famous child actor types, you know?

All in all it was a really nice picture and after a while I spoke up and said, "So, hey, who are all those good looking people?"

I pointed briefly at the picture, then dropped my arm and waited for her response.

"Oh," she said quietly. "Umm, that's... that's my family."

Then without warning, Meridith suddenly put down her coffee and crammed the photograph underneath the couch cushion, blurting out something to the effect of, "God, that's got to be the worst picture I ever took" as she did.

Her actions took me somewhat by surprise so I tried to cover over her obvious embarrassment with an equal show of far to realistic honesty.

"I look like a convict in all my photos too," I smirked ,and after a few awkward minutes the conversation started back up again and everything was fine.

But it was clear to me now that the possible root of Meridith's on and off persona was most likely linked to either a serious lack of self esteem on her part, which I seriously doubted, or more probably, the presence of an underlying and deep-rooted sensitivity within her seemingly unremarkable family structure. Whether it lay in the past, or in the present, something was wrong with that picture.

Now I was beginning to understand why she acted so aloof most of the time. Maybe she had some structural issues that were eating away at her, like most families do. Maybe she hated her dad for not being around enough, or maybe she hated her mother for being around too much. I mean who knows, but I decided that it be better if I just played it cool and change the subject.

"So how about those Yankees?" I said off the cuff.

"I don't know, "Meridith answered back. "I never watch football."

We both let out a little chuckle at my couch mate's hack and I secretly breathed a sigh of relief. The conversation was kept easy after that, and even though I was kind of surprised at Meridith's reaction to me seeing her family portrait, I did, for the first time, feel somewhat of a connection with her now. I guess I came to realize that she too, underneath that perfect exterior of hers, had a few demons of her own that I was sure she wasn't proud of. She was to my great relief, human.

Now, we have something in common.

When the coffee began to run shallow, I made the unconscious decision to thank my gracious host and call it a night. Our evening had been a success and I wanted to end it in the same fashion. No use jeopardizing a great save by dragging out the game you know.

"Well," I said, pressing my hands onto the tops of my knees. "I guess I had better let you get some sleep."

Meridith nodded with a half-yawn and walked me to the door. I thanked her once more for the great coffee and even greater company. I told her that she need not drive me back to the cafe for it was just as easy for me to snare a bus. She argued a little that she didn't mind giving me a ride, but I insisted on the bus. Personally, I would have loved the lift, but I didn't want to seem like a burden. I wanted her to think I was one of those low-maintenance guys. Man, if she only knew the extent of that little statement!

There was an awkward moment at the door, but I covered it up nicely with a couple of random lines of admiration towards the furniture in her apartment, but after that I knew it was time.

That time! The moment for the first kiss thingy to happen.

Seconds ground by like hours as I stood there frozen to my spot like a teenager waiting for the strap. I wanted to kiss her. I mean, God! did I want to kiss her! And I think that maybe she even wanted to kiss me too, but I had gotten such scattered vibes from her during the course of the evening that I wasn't really sure just where I stood. I quickly decided that a peck on the cheek was all that I would chance tonight, so I leaned forward and slowly tilted my head over to the side. For a split second there, I could feel her hesitate slightly, but then, just in the nick of time, she turned her head slightly and accepted my ground level show of affection.

"Thank you Meridith," I said as I pulled back. "I really had a nice time."
Meridith didn't say anything. She just stood there with a sort of confused look on her face, which did not help my ego one bit.

Oh shit. Maybe I shouldn't have kissed her yet. Maybe it was too soon!

I quickly spun around and grabbed the door handle. I knew I had done enough damage for one night and it was time to hit the road. Red alert flags were going off all over my body as my hand began to squeeze the cold steel knob, but suddenly I felt Meridith's hand grip my shoulder.
Now I was really confused.
And my confusion only tripled when she turned me back towards her and planted me with a real kiss that would have restarted a dead person's heart! And this play

wasn't just a one scener either, for just as I thought she was going to pull away and let my body drop to the floor in a pile of post-sematic goo, she slid her arms over my shoulder and continued on with her good intentions. When her lips finally separated from mine, I was pretty much fucked.

I did, though, hear her say in a stag film-type slur, "Now that's how you kiss someone mister, don't forget that OK?"

"OK," I mumbled as she poured me out into the hall.

"We should hang out more often," she said.

"Oh yes," I told her with a cheesy grin." I think we should too!"

I stumbled out of her apartment complex like I had just downed a 26er of vodka. I don't think I was able to walk more than about five feet at a time without tripping over my out-of-synch legs and bashing into the sides of the walls. The whole trip out of her place took quite a while and I'm sure I woke half the place up in the process. It seemed Meridith's Hollywood-style kiss was wreaking havoc on my coordination, as well as my reproductive system! I almost knocked on someone's door and asked them to spit in my eyes so I could blink again.

When I finally made it back to the Laundromat and retrieved my snoring little angel, I remember Newa looking at me with a... "Well look what the cat dragged in smirk on her face" as I floated through the side door.

"Loo like you have fun," she said as she crossed her arms and shook her head.

"Did I ever!" I smiled back devilishly. "Did I ever!"

Newa didn't say much after that. She just giggled and muttered something in Chinese as she followed me back to the entrance, Sara now tucked securely into my jacket and fast asleep. I waved goodbye to my dear friend and slid back out the side door into the night air.

Me and Meridith saw a lot of each other over the next several days. Our meetings were pretty casual for the most part. We mainly just went for short walks after she got off work. I guess she really loved touring around the city after nightfall. We did talk a little, but we mainly just took in the sites of a big city. Our conversations were still light and superficial, but that didn't bother me anymore. I understood all too well that when she was ready to tell me more about herself she would. I was in no hurry to push her though, for I was having far too much fun just being around her. I think she was even beginning to enjoy my company as well.
I was sort of living a normal life, believe it or not.

I was also feeling very safe lately. I hadn't seen hide nor hair of the cult guy, or the social services dick, or anybody for that matter. I knew that didn't mean they weren't still out there, but it did mean that my plan was working. My regular day usually consisted of me searching for bottles with Sara supervising the operation in the passenger's seat, and then around 5pm I would cash in my take, then head over to the Laundromat to begin my nightly cleaning duties. After I was finished I would surrender Sara over to Newa's waiting and eager hands, and head out the side door to go and meet Meridith as usual behind her apartment complex to begin our nightly excursion.

I always parked my car at the farthest end of the parking lot for I didn't want her to discover the real purpose behind of my ride. I knew it would be over for us just like that if she found out what I really was. Meridith asked about Sara a lot as we would stroll along. I told her that Sara's grandmother babysat her at night to give me a little bit of a break. She protested this arrangement often and would passionately insist that we "bundle that little girl of mine up" and take her with us on our nightly safaris. I did briefly entertain the idea a few times, but concluded in the end that it was just too risky and always declined Meridith's offer.
I could never tell her why.

I felt bad about that. I mean virtually everything I told her was a complete lie. My past, my family, my living arrangements... all lies. And sometimes, it was even difficult trying to remember what lie was what. It was like the old saying goes: "One lie leads always leads to another." Boy, I could vouch for that these days! I told Meridith, as well, that I was staying at my sister's place until she got back. Meridith hinted casually as to what part of town I lived in, so I flipped a coin, picked an area and called it home. When she asked me what I did for a living, I told her that I worked in the recycling business, which, in my own defense, wasn't really a lie.

Unfortunately though, everything else was.

Every other goddam word out of my mouth was total bullshit. And lying to her so often really bothered me. But what else was I supposed to do? Tell her the truth? Tell her that I was a fake and a criminal? No bloody way! I was never going to do that. She wouldn't understand, or want to have anything more to do with me again for that matter. Nope, I wasn't about to ever risk the thought of doing that. I just couldn't chance it.
I mean, God, she made me feel so good when I was with her. She made me feel like a man again and I didn't want that feeling to ever go away.

I needed her. She gave me the courage and self esteem I needed to overcome all the daily hurdles I faced when it came to raising a newborn baby out of the moldy guts of an old car. It was like I was being nourished by two separate streams. Meridith re-enforced my confidence, and Sara fed me love and gave my life purpose. What more in this fucked-up world could anyone ask for? I was whole again, and I was able to return the love I received - something I once feared I would never be able to do.

Me and my movie star girlfriend would finalize every evening with a kiss behind her apartment, beside a boxwood shrub in the far corner of the cement lot. At first our alleyway interludes were relatively short, but as the nights progressed I found that our affections would stretch on longer and longer each time, with Meridith now, not me, initiating the playoffs. I guess I was OK with that. Yes sir, I really looked forward to that nightly routine and I would always show up at the Laundromat to

162

pick up Sara afterwards with a big shit-eating grin slapped across my face. Newa could only just snicker.

"Someone is fawing in wub," she would say. And you know what, I think she was right!

I was really in debt to that sweet old lady. She was a total lifesaver and I would send my thanks up to the stars every time I crept out that old side door.

As Saturday night drew to a close with the culmination of mine and Meridith's usual back alley kissathon, she suddenly asked me of I would like to go with her to another one of those outdoor folk festivals that was being put on the following day at lunchtime.

"Sounds like a plan," I said and we agreed to meet in the same spot as we did on our first date, over by the condiment stand.

This time she told me the music was that of a more Maritime venue. This was fine by me for I had always heard that Newfoundlanders were a fun-loving bunch and that they always put on a good show. I closed the deal by stealing another kiss.

"Hey buddy," Meridith quipped half-seriously. "One per customer."

"Yes Ma'am," I said in a quick salute as I smiled and sauntered away into the dense foliage of the alley. "See you tomorrow."

That night was a good one. Sara slept like a rock and so did I. Although when she did arise for the day, I noticed in the most traumatic of ways that her customized diaper was packed to the rim with liquid shit.

"Yeecch," I groaned. "This was a real bad one."

I decided right then and there that it was time for me and my little girl to treat ourselves to a little splash time, hobo-style. I loved bathing Sara anyway. It was like a form of therapy. And lets face it, I was a poster child for therapy! But this bath was going to be a special one for I , Eugene Lauder, actually spent three whole dollars and rented a private shower at one of those big truck stops. There would be no rushing our cleanup time today. I intended to spend some quality time with my baby and I had a key and a receipt as insurance.

After I had thanked the nice lady at the till, I walked into what I thought was the biggest one, locked the door behind me and began setting out our stuff. With Sara cocooned up on the floor by the sink with an extra towel underneath her for hygienic safety, I hopped in the adjacent shower first and had a quick shampoo and rinse off. Once I was out and dressed, I discarded my baby's annihilated diaper and ran the water in the sink to begin a ritual that I had come to cherish. Sara squealed with joy as I immersed her tiny body into the warm liquid. We took our sweet time that morning. No-one was coming into this bathroom until we were damn good and ready to leave it!

Sara was surrounded by her toys as I basted her clammy skin back to a shine. Her favorite toy of the day turned out to be her tried and true rubber ducky, which she had latched onto and was trying to consume. As I leaned over the sink and scrubbed away at my little excrement factory, the long, still wet locks of my own hair fell forward and jiggled away with the repetitive motion of my arms, about five inches above her face.

This intrigued my baby and she suddenly spit out her rubber birdie and began fixating on the tail ends of my dirty blonde locks, reaching up for them and giggling sporadically. I teased her for a few minutes, pulling my hair away at the last moment before she was able to catch it, but boy I'll tell you, when she did finally get hold of me, I honestly thought she was going to snap my neck. Her grip was amazing!

Sara loved her bath time. I knew it was because of the warmth, but I think too, it was probably due to the fact that she got to make a huge mess. I sifted the water over her uncoordinated frame for a long time, refilling the sink from time to time to dispel the bad and refurbish the good. My overgrown locks acted like a protective wall, like a hallway to her where her face was the only thing I saw. Things became a little surreal after that and I felt my heart become heavy with emotion. I think it was because all this time, since the day I found her, I had been somehow trying to put a measure on things.

On love.

To rate it on a scale with a formula, a theory.

I guess in my own way I was trying to prove to Sara just how important she was to me, and how scared I was of ever losing her. Why our paths crossed in the first place I guess I was never to know, not on this plane anyway, but whatever the meaning I knew that I must never take the treasure before me for granted, not for one second. For this child, in my whole life, was the single greatest gift I would ever be given.

And it's true, that there were some days, when I wasn't completely sure if my sanity was still intact.

But those days were becoming fewer and fewer all the time, and her reality was beginning to take the reins for good. I did though, as I drifted in and out of bliss, find it absolutely mind boggling that I had actually spent the better part of five years stuffed away in the bowels of an old car, pathetically hiding myself away from the world, always starving for something. I was always struggling with my conscience to accept a reason for it all, but never sincerely willing to take a chance and reach out for the door handle. And now suddenly here I was, standing in a bright clean washroom, staring down at this baby. This miracle. Feeding off her every move, her every gesture. My soul was no longer hungry and my eyes no longer closed.

The weight of that knowledge was so humbling and so powerful that I watched a single drop of water leave one of those open eyes and splash down into the sink below me. It was then, at that exact moment that I realized something very important about love.

I realized that you could not measure it.

You could not chart it or buy it. It came with no guarantees, or rule books, and no matter how hard you try, you would never be able to contain it or attach it to reason. Love was, and could only ever be. Unconditional.

And I believe it was the sheer magnitude of that understanding that constituted the last piece of my puzzle. It was the secret password that freed me. I also came to know that my longstanding fear of that emotion had, in turn, prevented me from opening the door to the daylight world, a passage I had for so long dreamed of seeing.

That's what was wrong in my life. That was the magic key.

I told Sara about all of this, about what I had just learned and the summit I had finally reached. I also assured her that I would forever be there for her, and I thanked her for all the wonderful nights she let me listen to her fall asleep. I talked to her about a lot of things as she splashed away and listened on patiently to my ramblings. She was a great listener, Sara was, and as we conversed away, the topics we covered varied a lot.

At first we dashed over the vast matrix of human emotions and how they usually tended to bungle up the whole girl-boy thing. Then we discussed in great detail, the grossly inflated price of baby formula and how it should be 100 percent subsidized by the government. That was a real scorcher of a discussion I'll tell ya, but all in all, it was a very productive chat. I did also apologize at that point, for leaving her at the Laundromat so much lately, but she downplayed my concerns and told me that she was just happy that I was finally getting out there and socializing more with a member of the opposite sex.

Personally, I think maybe she was just looking forward to the very real possibility of one day being around someone with functioning nipples.

But hey, who was I to knock her for a request like that?

Knowing that I still had a little more time on the clock, I purposely drained out the now-cooler water in the sink and replaced it one last time with fresh stuff, then happily continued basting my little turkey. My mind was finally still, which was a wonderful feeling and all, but it did have one small disadvantage. With no stress-appointed barriers to protect it, a few pessimistic thoughts were able to sneak themselves into my head, and what started out as a peaceful demonstration, quickly turned into a congested free-for-all, jam-packed with all sorts of rogue nail biters emptying out their swollen complaint bags as to what was going to happen in the near future. I was not prepared for this confrontation, but I knew there were questions lurking about my mind that had been waiting ever-so-patiently for answers.

For starters, winter was on it's way and it would be here a lot sooner than later. That was a major issue. I could feel the days becoming shorter and the nights growing colder more and more all the time. I had picked up another two blankets for cheap over at the Goodwill store and so far that trick was working. In fact, Sara's bed had begun to take on a more igloo type appearance than a daybed. But this, I knew, was a short term answer to a long term problem for there were times in the middle of the night when I could almost see my breath as I fed Sara her snack. Luckily though, the temperature inside her little flat was still nice and toasty, due to the insulation of her own body heat, but how long would that last?

I had gotten into the habit as well, of letting my car run a few times a night to keep the heat as constant as I could, and this practice was expensive. Necessary, of course, but expensive, and to compensate for the extra fuel loss I was forced to cut down on my own sustenance. Most of the food I was taking in lately came mainly from the sample ladies because Sara's formula and gas for the car were consuming the rest. Did this lack of grub bother me? Not a bit. I had made her a promise and I intended to keep it.

Another infidel that raised it's boney hand was the fact that I couldn't keep imposing on Newa. Even though she had assured me over and over again that it was alright, I still knew it wasn't, and I feared that I would one day wear out my welcome and wind up losing her as a friend. It was a possibility that I could not chance. I felt too strong of a connection with her these days. I needed her wisdom and under-standing and I couldn't imagine not having her in my life. I didn't want to risk not being able to watch the ever-evolving transformation my newborn was responsible for in my elderly friend. Newa had become a totally new person. You could see the fulfillment and the joy in her eyes. They were alive again and they burned through the darkness of her past like a gothic sword, slaying all previous misconceptions about the quality and range of her heart. A heart that I knew was cast out of pure gold. They all were guilty, all the people who should have been there beside her. They were all at fault.

But that all changed the moment I asked of her a favor: the moment I asked for her trust with a life I valued more than my own. From that point on I believe my elderly friend was finally able to summon forth the strength she required to pick back up off the floor that amazing heart of hers and let it begin to heal.

And heal it did.

With each passing day I could see it getting stronger and stronger, the beauty of it's finish gleaming out from behind her eyes. I knew she coveted her new position of "Gramma" with fierce devotion, and as a testimony to this, she literally changed the entire outlay of her modest little apartment in the back of the laundry to suit the needs of my baby girl. Her house now resembled more of a nursery than a senior's dwelling. But I think too, that the bright decor and the scent of a new life, also helped in guiding her away from the thick cloud of depression she'd been surrounded by.

Yep, Newa was brand spanking new again, and I could never get enough of the way she would fuss over my baby. Sara had given her a whole new lease on life, as she had done with me, not so long before. She allotted a broken down old woman a second chance to prove to all the world that she was indeed a good mother and a good person - one who could be trusted and confided in. Every time I watched her pick up my angel, I knew that deep down she was secretly celebrating another unspoken victory against the many skeletons that lay waiting in the closet of her mind. Kiss by kiss, hug by hug, I watched in blissful silence as they all fell dead at her feet. Newa was family now, and I hoped that she would always remain a part of our uncommon circle in some way.

As my thoughts came to a close, I reluctantly finished up Sara's bath and began to dry and dress her.

I warned myself too, that the future was bound to be riddled with many unseen hurdles and setbacks, especially now. But those were challenges I was ready for, and neither a psychopath, nor a snowflake was ever going to get in the way of that future. My mind and body were finally at peace again, and with Sara now comfortably fitted in an ever-expanding jumpsuit, I casually packed up our things and loaded them back into the car. It felt so great not to be rushed and as I pulled out of the parking lot I had a feeling that the day was going to be a smooth one, but as usual I went ahead and spoke too soon. For the moment I veered out onto the freeway heading east, I glanced out my side door mirror to check for traffic, and guess who was right on my ass.

It was none other than my old pal Jeffrey Simmons from the Department of Social Services. Child Welfare Division, I believe, driving an ugly little shitbox of a car.

"Why hello Assface," I said aloud to him through the reflection.

He returned my dirty look and began frantically waving his arms, motioning for me to pull over. I cupped my hand to my ear and pretended I couldn't hear him. I continued this torture for a couple of more minutes, then, with the widest of grins on my face, looked him directly in the eye and gave him the big old " You're number one" sign with my middle finger, then mouthed the symbolic request in his direction.
I wasn't worried about this dork in the least. I mean, he was a joke, just a loser trying to justify a bunch of big words on a little card. I continued gesturing obscenities to him for I knew he couldn't see Sara. Like he could catch me in that tin can anyway!

In a sudden pocket of traffic, I heard his underpowered engine begin to scream as he pinned it and slowly pulled up beside me. I didn't speed up because I found the whole thing quite entertaining. Once he was parallel to me he began inching his tin can closer and closer towards my door. I guess he thought he was intimidating me or something. Then he shot his car forward a few feet and tried to bluff me into thinking that he could jump ahead and cut me off at any second, but I could tell by the way his overpriced little dinky toy was revving that he was shit out of pedal. I teased him for a while longer just for sport, easing off the gas and letting him get a half a car length ahead of me from time to time. But eventually I grew bored of his pathetic illusion of dominance and I decided to wake him up. I purposely edged my rig over in his direction, coming within a mere three feet of his passenger's door. Then with fire in my eyes, I glared over and stabbed a deep warning into him.

"Leave me the fuck alone!" I hollered in a voice I meant. Then I pressed my fist against the window and hit the gas.

That old car of mine might have looked shit, but it had about 300 more horses under the hood than his did.
The front end of my Firebird responded accordingly to my generous offering of fuel by gearing down and lurching forward, quickly leaving my unwelcome escort in a tapped-out cloud of dust.

"Shop American, asshole!" I hollered triumphantly as the image of his vehicle swiftly vanished from sight.

I kept my speed fast and steady for a few more minutes, just to make sure I was well out of his view. Then taking one last gander in my rear view mirror, I darted over three full lanes and disappeared down an exit ramp that led back to the suburbs. As soon as I ground to a halt at the first stop light, I turned my attentions to Sara. She was already celebrating our recent checkered flag by farting and burping uncontrollably. In a parallel act of victory, I reached my hand over and gave her a quick high five, then quickly rolled down the window and tried not to pass out. That half pint's arse was becoming a real weapon, I'll tell you.

I took a different path towards the laundry again like usual, zigzagging my way in and out of streets and alleyways until I was about two blocks away. Then I hid my wreck and walked the rest of the way in. When I did eventually duck my head through the side door, baby and supplies in hand, Newa was bent over a pot on the stove, religiously stirring the contents of the cast iron tub with slow even strokes.

"What's on the menu today chef?" I asked.

"Fiss heads," she cackled with an exited grin. "You wanta some?"

"Jesus no," I coughed back in a terrified voice. I mean I was desperate, but I wasn't crazy!

Newa rested the ladle on the side of the pot and gave me a sneer.

"Fiss heads goo fo you," she preached. "It bwain fruid."

I kept the frightened look pasted to my face as Newa walked over and snatched up my baby girl, administering to the child, her usual dose of affections. I resisted Newa's persistent offers for a taste of her "bwain fruid" a few moments longer, then thanked her as always and backed out the side door to fish head safety. I was feeling very anxious as I pulled off into the parking lot by the river. I could hardly wait to see that sexy cashier today. I knew I was really beginning to fall for her, and I will admit that my ever- growing feelings for Meridith did at times frighten me because my heart, although on the mend now, was still quite fragile and prone to injury. But Meridith, I assured myself, was different. She had a tranquility in her eyes that was almost impossible not to be drawn into. There were times though, when I was sure that I saw the edge of a ripple splash up against the banks of those eyes, but the mist, even in that state, would still emit a soft echo.

My thoughts stayed on my lady friend until I reached the edge of a narrow brick path which I instinctively followed up to the entrance of the stadium. I saw Meridith standing over by the edge of the concession stand just like we had planned.

Sneaking up on her the best I could, I crept up from the side and planted a firm kiss into her left cheek. After watching her blush ever so slightly, we began making our way up to the top of the old wooden grandstands to claim an empty section of bench we had spotted from below. After a solid 45 minutes of listening to a host of theatrical computations about dead herring, I caught my eyes starting to wander secretly away from the stage and begin skipping subtly over the crowd. Randomly at first, but eventually they began to fixate on the image of the concession stand over in the corner which sparked the memory of mine and Meridith's first date. I remembered

168

looking over and seeing her standing there, looking so... so beautiful, waiting there patiently for little old me. A girl like that, waiting for a guy like me. It was almost too crazy to comprehend.

I daydreamed away happily while Meridith sat strangely enthralled by the near cartoon-like performers, but my fantasy, as soothing as it was, ended up being abruptly switched off by the debut of the very last person in the world I wanted to see today!

It was fucking Levi, that asshole cop with the worst case of short man's syndrome I'd ever seen. He'd ended up at the coffee bar for some fucked-up reason and was now attempting to strike up a conversation with the young girl at the till. He was followed in closely behind, thank God, by his much more honorable partner, and my personal hero, Officer T.J. Daniels. My head twisted forward immediately and I pretended to be very interested in the show again. I kept the act up, watching closely out of the corner of my eye as Levi, freshly shot down by the young prospect, had now begun to focus his intentions instead, to what was happening within the crowd. T.J. had left the condiment table by this time and was scoping out the situation too.

Godammit, I thought. I don't need this shit today! Not with Meridith here. If that little prick sees me, it will be suicide for sure.

I knew Levi wouldn't be able to resist the urge to pick on me. He didn't have it in him not to, especially in front of an audience!

Relax Eugene. They're probably just on a routine patrol and will be on their way in no time so just sit tight and don't make any sudden moves.

For once I didn't challenge my alter ego and I did what I was told. I sat there like a stone with one eye one the stage, and the other on the two cops. I could tell by his head movements that Levi was looking for a fight, probably due to the fact that he had just been shut down by another female. And my heart rate rose even more as I watched the short man's head begin to bob up and down the length of the grandstands, searching for a misdemeanor to reboot his ego. Then it got bad ,and I watched in a state of denial as Levi's head froze it's position in my general direction. I also saw big T.J. tilt his head up toward me too.

No! No! This is not happening, not today, not today!!

My nerves began to peak as Levi's hand began to raise up in a pointing manner, but then his antagonistic quest was suddenly diverted to the south by the dark sinewy forearm of his larger workmate. For some reason, T.J. had strangely rerouted his partner's stubby limb in the opposite direction. I turned my head slightly to get a better look at the scene that was unfolding below me. Not a lot, but just enough to get more of an idea as to what was going on. T.J. had his hand on Levi's shoulder and was pointing his other arm off toward something beyond the stadium. In an instant, the tiny corporal darted off in the direction of his partner's rigid palm and exited the stadium all together.

I let out a long-concealed sigh of relief and felt my head pivot. With the threat now gone, I treated myself to a full view of the concession. My unsung hero was just standing there looking up at me with big sappy grin spread across his face. I flashed him a heartfelt thank you nod and he returned my gesture with a subtle thumbs up. He didn't follow in behind his apprentice though, he just leaned himself up against a neighboring tree and began taking in the show while he casually sipped his coffee.

"I gotta go visit the little fireman's room," I said as I turned my head back towards my date. "Won't be long."

"When you gotta go, you gotta go," Meridith whispered, temporarily peeling her eyes away from the show.

I started at first walking towards the bathrooms, but then backtracked my way over in the direction of the concession. I wanted to talk to this cop who had three times now saved my skinny little ass. I wanted to thank him.
I wanted to ask him why.
He noticed me coming towards him underneath the bleachers and he too, began to make his way over to meet me.

"Thank you again," I said right off the bat." I saw that great detour job you did back there. You see, it's just that... Well, I'm with a girl you know, and I'm sort of trying to impress her."

"No problem my young friend," he said with a smile. "I kind of gathered that too. That's why I sent Levi packing."

"He took off pretty quick," I said with a snicker. "What in the Hell did you say to him?"

The big man leaned in closer to me and said with a wink.

"I told him that I thought I had seen a female streaker heading towards city hall, and that he should check it out immediately!"

My God did I laugh. It sent T.J. off too, and me and him stood underneath those bleachers for a good five minutes and chuckled on at his great trick.

"Listen," I told him after our adolescent sputtering died down, "I can't tell you how much I appreciate you sticking up for me. But I have to ask why?
Why do you go out of your way to help me? I guess I'm just curious that's all. I mean, things like this don't happen to me a lot, you know."

T.J. then looked down at me and said in an easy voice, "Gut feeling I guess."
"Besides," he continued, "I know what it feels like to be judged simply by the way you look."

"I'm down with that," I said as I stuck out my open hand in front of him. T.J. completed the honorable transaction and we said our adieus.

I walked back up to my seat that afternoon with something I'd never had before: a formidable ally, not to mention another friend. The concert finally wrapped up around 3pm and I was damn near a vegetarian by the time it ended. Now don't get me wrong, I have no problem with easterners. I just wish the people who booked these things would give Van Halen a call once in awhile.

As the masses began to make their way down the creaky wooden bleachers and head toward the exits to decide where to go next, I found myself entranced in thought with that same idea. It was still so early and I wasn't ready to say goodbye to Meridith just yet. So I brainstormed once more for scenarios that didn't involve money, but my options like usual, seemed pretty limited.

As we walked past the now boarded-up concession, I saw a little woman. She looked very old and she was rummaging through a trashcan off to the side, obviously looking for empties. I felt my heart sink down and was reminded once again of who I really was. It made me sad to see her there. It hurt me to know that I played with that same fire, but it bothered me more that she still had to. I dropped my head in respect and kept walking. When we reached the intersection that divided up the core, I still hadn't nailed down a concrete idea of what we could do that didn't involve money. I was growing very tired of worrying about that all the time and I'll bet Meridith was beginning to wonder when I was going to take her on a real outing.

"Hey," I heard my date suddenly say. "Are you hungry?"

"No," I said back quickly, trying to sway my girlfriend's train of thought into a different direction. "Are you?"
"God, yes, I'm starved!"

Oh shit.

I became terrified by the implications of her latest answer, but I knew this moment was coming. I'd known it for a while now. It's not that I didn't want to take her out, it's just that I couldn't. I had maybe six dollars on me and most of that had to go to formula. If I spent that, Sara would suffer. No way Sara was going to suffer! I had to say something. I couldn't keep putting her off, but then again, I couldn't tell her the truth either. Meridith went to speak but I cut her off and prepared to tell her something that for once, wasn't a lie.

"Listen, um... Meridith. I... I have a confession to make."

"What is it?" she asked with a concerned look.

"Well it's just that I don't, I mean, well, it's just that I don't really have a lot of money right now."

Meridith did not say anything, nor did the expression on her face change either. A couple of more seconds went by and I felt my body become saturated with worry. Panic was descending on me fast and I didn't know what to do, so I did the only thing I could. I just kept talking.

"But work might be busy tomorrow and then maybe we could go out, you know. Tomorrow, and then we could eat, like tomorrow, how's that? How's tomorrow?"

"Sshhh," I watched her say as she harnessed my flailing hand and steadied it inside her palm. "We don't have to go out anywhere, Eugene," she told me in a soft voice. "We could just have a sandwich at my place if you like."

I felt so ashamed as she spoke to me; I was so mad at myself for being the thing that I was.

"You deserve better," I whispered in a rare surrender. "You deserve so much better."

I felt my eyes shade over with guilt as I dropped my head. I didn't want her to look at me. I didn't want her to see. Meridith drew her face close into mine. She didn't say anything, she just looked up into my eyes and unfolded my hand across her heart.

"It's OK Eugene," she whispered. "I never said you had to be a millionaire."

I was so humbled that I could not speak. I felt so fragile, so unsteady, but she never let me fall, not once. We held hands all the way back to her car, walking through the leaves whenever we could.

She drove me back to the parking lot by the river and dropped me off about twenty feet from my Firebird at my request. I followed her back to her apartment and once inside, I began helping my girlfriend retrieve the necessary supplies out of the refrigerator. We sat at her kitchen table under the soft glow of a candle and proceeded to chomp away at the montage of bread and meat. As I reached for a second sandwich, I tilted my head up slightly and noticed that the same picture of her family I had seen on my first visit was now sitting in exile on top of the fridge. It was jammed into the far top corner of the appliance and hidden out of the way.

Feeling obviously remorseful, I said in a careful way, "Hey Meridith, I'm really sorry I was asking all of those questions about your family the last time I was here. It was really none of my business."

"It's OK," she said back, to my relief. "I'm sorry I acted so strangely too."

Feeling more confident now, I brandished an easygoing smile and said, "I'll tell you though, you sure do have a great-looking family, and that brother of yours, he sure is a handsome fella too. Boy, I'd love to meet them sometime!"
Suddenly, Meridith's head sank forward and without warning, she dropped her arms and put her half-eaten sandwich back on the plate in front of her.

"I'm just going to have a quick shower," she said, standing up quickly and leaving the room. Then she disappeared down the hall somewhere and shut a door.

"Oh way to fucking go Eugene. Do you always have to open your goddam mouth so much? Now look what you've done? You think you might have learned your lesson last time but I guess not hey?

172

I got up from the table and let my sandwich hit the plate. I was so angry at myself. I couldn't believe that I did the same fucking thing twice! Now, there was nothing else I could do but wait. So I walked over to the couch and began plotting away as usual, just how in the Christ I was going to fix my latest fuckup. I sat there for what seemed like an eternity. Meridith was taking anything but a quick shower. I must have really upset her this time. Restless and submerged in worry, I got up and began feverishly pacing about the room. Finally after about a half an hour, I heard the shower nozzle turn off. A few minutes later Meridith came out of the bathroom and walked up to me with her head facing the floor.

"His name is, was, Ben," she said in a lifeless voice. "But you can't see him because... because he's dead."

I shook my head in disbelief and embarrassment as I watched Meridith slowly walk over and sit on the end of the couch, her eyes still low and her face still empty. At that point, I hadn't a clue what to do next, beside walk out on the balcony and hang myself of course. I mean, God! What do you do you say in a case like this? After a moment , I inched my way closer to my upset companion. It took a while, but eventually I eased my body next to her. I was sick to my stomach. I knew I had screwed up big time and was now feeling the effects of that crime. I wouldn't be surprised if she booted me right out on my ass for this. And you know what, that was exactly what I deserved. I did not speak as I sat there. I just shut up for once in my life and examined the floor.

"That explains her sometimes odd behavior though - her shyness, her moods. It all checked out now.

She was suffering from loss. The loss of a sibling.

"Meridith," I said quietly. "I'm sorry, I didn't mean to pry, I um..."

"It's alright," she interrupted. "It was a long time ago. I should be over it by now. I should be..."

"Listen," I cut in gently." It's OK Meridith. You don't have to explain. Really, it's not necessary."

I felt my girlfriend's body settle in closer to mine after I spoke those words and a welcome feeling of acceptance finally began to flow across me. We sat there in silence for a minute, and then I asked her the question that I knew she was expecting.

"What... um. What happened to him?" I asked gently.

"Meningitis," she said after a long pause. "We didn't catch it in time." I heard my girlfriend let out a long sigh. "It was a long time ago," she finally said. "I just don't like to think about it you know."

I backed off my innocent query immediately. Meridith got up and walked back into the kitchen. I heard the tap turn on and then there was nothing but silence. I wasn't sure what I should do next. Should I leave, should I follow her into the kitchen, I mean what? I considered going to her, but I figured I'd caused enough damage for one day so I just stayed where I was for the moment. Eventually though, I did get up and walk carefully into the kitchen. I had to, the silence was killing me.

"I'm sorry," I said as I cowered in the archway. "Meridith I'm just... really sorry. I didn't mean to upset you."

Meridith was standing with her back to me at the sink and did not acknowledge my apologies. This in turn, fueled an even greater fire. I needed to do something. I needed to fix this situation, so in one brash move I walked up behind her and secured my arms around her waist. She hesitated for a second and attempted to pull away, but I stood my ground and finally,... finally, her body became docile and fell back into my own.

"I miss him". He was so young. It wasn't fair," she sobbed.

I didn't say another word to her. I believed that to be the best thing that I could do. I just listened. I held onto her tightly as she grieved. This was her time. I was there only to bear witness and understand. After a long while, Meridith drew in a deep breath and set it free. She was all done. She wiped her eyes, then led me back into the living room and proceeded to shut off all the lights on her way before repositioning us both back down on the sofa. She leaned forward before she settled and lit another candle. From the flame's light, I could see that Meridith's eyes were red and puffy.

"It's been years," she suddenly said without emotion. "Why can't I just forget?"

She went to look away, but I placed my hand onto her cheek and brought her face back into mine. A bloated tear left her eye and streaked down her cheek.

"We are all fools," I said to her in a comforting voice, "if we ever think for a second that we are strong enough to forget!"

I wiped the tear away from her cheek and guided her head to my chest. I held her close as she tried to curtail her emotions, but her rugged intentions did not hold and she started to cry. It was the first time since we met that I felt I was seeing the real Meridith. She really opened herself up to me and it filled me with a great sense of privilege. She was no different than I was. Just a normal person with a sad past.
She was just like me.

Meridith did not cry for long though, and after a few minutes she braced her arms against my ribs and pushed herself away. She told me that she was disappointed in herself for "spilling her guts" and acting like a child. I assured her over and over again that it was OK to acknowledge a fear, for that was the only thing that made us human.
Meridith stopped her sniffling for a moment and looked over at me with a long, sad frown.
I didn't ask her anything else. I just sat with her on the couch and rubbed her back while she pulled herself together. I felt very connected to her now. She opened the door to her heart and in turn, advanced our relationship to a higher level, a place

I think we both needed to get to. Within a few minutes Meridith had settled down again and I asked her if she was going to be alright. She told me not to worry about her, and from the steady tone in her voice, I accepted her answer.

"I had better get going," I said.

I wanted to stay a little longer to make sure she was really OK, but I had a feeling she wanted to be alone, so I made the right call and stood up. Meridith stood up too and walked me to the door. After giving her a tiny hug in the archway, I bid her goodnight and promised I'd stop by the drugstore in the next day or two. With a hint of regret, I fired up my beast and began driving back towards the laundry. It was only around 5pm and there was still a lot of daylight left, so I made up my mind that when I picked up Sara, I was going to treat her to a little quality outside-time. I guess my girlfriend's heartfelt tale had made me realize the importance of time well spent.

It was true that me and my baby had not been out of the house for quite awhile now due to the obvious safety issues that had surfaced regarding my eerie discovery at the library. But I hadn't seen the long-haired psycho in the overcoat for quite some time now, so I figured I had more or less given him the shake.

It was 5:30 by the time I retrieved my spoiled child from her "Gramma's" house and found my way back to my vehicle. It was hidden pretty good so I decided to just leave it where it was and make the trip on foot. Just as a precaution, I bundled Sara up in an extra blanket and filled up her bottle. I knew she would need that.

I kept a decent pace as I bopped down the alley en route to a tiny playground I had driven by a couple of times that week.

Actually, it wasn't really so much a playground. It was more of a fenced clearing that was half surrounded with trees. But that was good enough for tonight. Besides, it was nice and low key. It was about six blocks away and in the direction of the river. I guess I could have just driven, but I fantasized that all the fresh air Sara received on our walk would make her sleep through the night. I made it to the park with a good amount of daylight still left hanging in the sky. I was happy to finally be engaging in some R & R with my baby outside of that damn car. I'm not trying to sound like a whiner, but it got pretty cramped in that thing at times and it was nice to stretch my legs a bit.

When I arrived at the glorified putting green, I plopped my tired ass down on the first bench I came to and fished Sara out of my jacket. I rested her on my knee and promptly twisted the oversized rubber nipple into her mouth, then prepared to enjoy the rest of the day. I loved fall. If I had to pinpoint the one thing I enjoyed the most about it, I would have to say it was the smell of the leaves. I'm not sure why.

"Hey Sara," I said peering down at my lap, "what's your favorite season?"

She did not answer. She was far to busy annihilating her fresh bottle of formula so I looked back up again and focused my attention on the horizon. The sun was sinking at a steady pace, but still doing its best to keep the city lit. It had been an educational day, I mean with Meridith and all. It was so nice to see a different side of her, that, to be honest, I didn't think she had. I sat there and pondered my life for a bit longer, but soon decided it was time to hit the road.

I had the motivation of someone in a coma as I packed up our gear. I was pretty relaxed by then. It felt great though, this mini-vacation. It was a much needed break from my usual routine.

After a quick glance around, I made sure I hadn't forgotten anything, then stood up and repositioned Sara back into my leather bomber. I was getting really good at that, but no sooner had I begun lifting my foot towards home, did my ears ring in agony from the sound of screeching tires that were tearing up the road somewhere behind me. I spun around in a panic, thinking at first that a fender bender had just occurred or something, but my eyes only picked up the image of a lone car as it ground to a halt in the middle of a deserted intersection to the rear of me.

You know... My arms instinctively gripped around Sara. *It's assholes like that who cause accidents!*
And he's stunting in a playground zone for Christ Sakes!

For a second there, I almost yelled out and told him to slow down, but to my heart-stopping realization, the person in the vehicle already knew who I was.

I succumbed to a hurricane of denial as a middle-aged man with a long overcoat and a ponytail suddenly leapt out of the car and began running hell bent and determined in my direction.

I whipped around with the force of a bullet and made my break for the gate at the opposite end of the park, bracing Sara tight against my chest as I fled. By the time I stormed through the wire mesh exit, my stress level was off the charts. I looked back mid-spin and to my dismay, saw my extremely determined foe racing towards me at full steam, quickly closing up the gap between us. He still was about 150 yards away from me, but that number was becoming less and less by the second.

I kicked the gate shut as a weak deterrent, then bolted out onto the road and dove into a nearby alley. I briefly thought about heading back towards my car, but a positive vehicle ID was definitely out of the question, and besides, my ride was behind me, and right now, that direction didn't exist. I didn't look back for anything after that. I just kept hauling ass through yards and alleys trying to escape. Sara's bottle had been jarred out from her lips during the course of the pursuit and she was now wailing away frantically from inside the cramped hollow of my coat.

"I sorry sweetheart," I grunted down to her as I ran. "I'm sorry about all of this."

After about fifteen minutes, I ditched left out of a back yard and snuck up alongside the wall of a vacant house, then spilled out back into the street and beelined toward another dwelling. I peered inside my jacket from time to time as I zipped in and out of the shadows en route to God knows where, and assured my heavily agitated passenger that everything was going to be OK The tone in my voice echoed confidence.

But I knew right then that I had just told Sara her first lie, for the man behind us was a cold-blooded killer and he fully intended to exterminate me, an untraceable nobody, then sacrifice my invisible newborn to some twisted version of a God. There was no denying that fact anymore and I'd never felt so afraid.

Fortunately, nightfall was overthrowing the horizon at a vicious pace and that was good. I knew my chances for survival would be greatly elevated under the cover of darkness.

When I felt I had successfully put some distance between myself and my aggressor, I stopped behind the dim corner of a large house and check out the landscape behind me. I had a good overall view of the street from where I was hidden so I took advantage of the situation and used it to calm Sara a bit. I, too, grabbed a couple extra breaths as I rocked my cocooned child back and forth inside my coat and scanned about the perimeter. It was clear for about thirty seconds or so, but then in the near distance, I began to pick up the faint silhouette of an overcoat flailing in the wind. He was still coming on strong, but he was more like 200 yards away now and I knew I was finally leading this race, even though I feared it's ending.

But I could not just keep running, this I knew. Eventually he would catch up with me.

I needed a place to hide.

I couldn't go back to the Laundry for that meant going right back through the path of my enemy, and besides, that would also risk putting Newa in danger which was totally out of the question. I glanced down at Sara in my coat. She was still crying. She was scared, just like me.

Think Eugene. Think for fuck sakes!

I was trying not to panic but it wasn't easy. I had to find some cover, bottom line. And I had to find it fast.

It was the only way I had any chance of shaking this bastard.

I needed a goddam place to hide.
Wait a minute... hide?

My brain suddenly rewound it memory tape back to a particular day in my past, then flashed that information across the screen in my head and without further delay I was off. My feet automatically pivoted themselves towards the imprint of the great bridge that bordered the river. I ran with all my might in the direction of that familiar landmark, but it was not there that I intended to evade my predator. No, it was actually below the giant structure in the deeply woven thickets that lined the shore. Yep,.. I was heading straight in the direction of the Greeb Hell!!

I had no choice.

The bush dwellers' lair was the only place I stood any kind of a chance of leveling out this mortal playing field. I would have to venture back into their territory and hope to God that I picked the right rabbit hole to tumble down into, one that was uninhabited to be more precise.

It was dark by now, and as I rocketed my body closer to my preset destination I understood all too well the inherent dangers of my plan. But at that point, I was shit out of options.

I bolted out from the concealment of the last alley like an animal and made my break for the bridge. I could see the curvature of the immense metal arch from the thin row of street lamps that came to an end at it's base. The bridge looked like a spaceship rising up from the water, and it was there, underneath the darkness of that platform, that lay my uncommon utopia. I was fully out in the open now and the boulevard lamps easily highlighted my position, but there was no other way to safety except through that overly vivid corridor, so I just kept running.

I glanced back at the midpoint of my lethal dash and saw what I feared I would. Leon had closed the gap between us somehow and now, he was not even half a block behind me and picking up speed at a breakneck pace.
But that was OK, for I had finally made it to the bridge.
The sound of my boots echoed out loudly as they repeatedly struck the steel grate below me. My oxygen levels were all over the place, but my legs, thank God, were holding out well and propelling me on.
I crossed that river in record time and became briefly airborne for a second as I leapt over the concrete boundary and skidded down the shale-ridden banks of the other side. I could see the faint density of the stunted shrubs about a half a minute run away over to the left of me and I wasted no time in getting to them.
This was the last leg of a deadly race I had to win. I had to reach the mass of interlocking thickets and quickly disappear into their maze before Leon left the structure's boundaries.
It was my only chance.

I heard the sound of gravel giving away to the pressure of my attacker's feet a split second before I fell to my knees and dove into one of the many random openings on the waters edge. Jenkins was not far behind me, but now the odds in this crap shoot were finally even. He was in my world now, and I prayed it showed him no mercy.
I braced Sara and began to scroll my way forward, using only my right hand as a blind guide. The tentacles of the dense circuitry snaked out in every direction. If I was to elude my aggressor in any way tonight, it would to happen in here. After I had made it about twenty feet into the living tunnel, I lucked out and stumbled upon a deliberately pruned-out part of the brush, so I scurried into it and flipped onto my ass, focusing my attention back on the way I came in.

From what I could tell, I had ended up inside a crude dwelling. It was a hollowed-out circular room, about six feet by six feet and high enough to stand up in. It was loosely attached to an endless network of similar crawl shafts and most importantly, it was uninhabited. I took in a deep breath, then opened up my jacket and checked on the state of my baby. She had been amazingly quiet crossing the bridge, but as soon as the impact of my necessary leap hit her, she began to cry out loudly again.

"No Sara, no honey, sshh baby," I pleaded to her, frantically searching inside my jacket for her bottle. I knew that if I couldn't settle her down we were doomed. I ransacked the inside of my coat but came up with nothing.
Goddammit! Her bottle must have fallen out when I crawled in here.

I almost went back through that prickly corridor and tried to find it, but I stopped myself immediately for I realized that action would only produce a grave consequence.

It was too late. Where I sat is where I stayed!

Sshh baby... SSShh sweetheart, please!

I tried in vain to calm Sara down with a wafty strain of well-injected baby jargon, but she wasn't buying any of it. She had been through more than any infant should ever be subjected to and the only thing she wanted now was her goddam bottle. Nothing else would do.

I was out of options. I had no bottle and her soother was still in the glove box of the car where it usually sat. And as the seconds pounded on in sync with the horrified muscle inside my chest, the solution to my problem suddenly began to speed back toward me in the form of another memory. I was taken on a lightning fast tour back to the first day that I found Sara, to the part where I was sitting in the parking lot of the convenience store and thrusting my milk-laden finger into her wailing mouth in a desperate plea for peace.

Now I knew that I had no milk to barter with, but I still had my finger. The idea was at least worth a shot, so I quickly wet my trembling digit and began feeling around for my child's screaming mouth. It didn't take long for me to locate that volcano, and the moment my bull's eye became established, I instantly began wiggling the mirage across her vibrating lips in a nervous attempt to mimic her absent bottle.

Suddenly, I felt Sara's muscularly little jaws grip tightly around my finger and to my mind-altering relief, a blanket of silence fall over the room.

"Oh thank God," I gasped as I began rocking my baby back and forth to cement our deal. I also whispered to her another proposition.

"Sara," I whispered, "If you are a good girl and stay nice and quiet for daddy, I swear I will never complain about your crying again, OK?"

I closed the offer with a quick peck to her forehead and readied my legs for a quick departure if that need arose. From where I was crouching, I could see the outline of the river as the moon recorded it's steady flow. I sat there in a shadow and tried to become as invisible as I could against the brush.

I knew the outcome of the next few minutes was going to hinge solely on my ability to remain hidden.

It felt like I was sitting their for a year, but not even a half minute later, the moment of truth in this deadly game suddenly materialized as I began to hear the sound of footsteps scrambling over the same patch of dirt I had just passed. I could hear them getting closer and closer to the doorway I had just entered.

This was it.

I sat there suspended in agony and watched as the dense outline of a human being frantically passed by the ground level archway in front of me. Leon's mass briefly eclipsed the moon, but it did not stop.

Yes, Yes... He did not stop!

I rejoiced in silence as the terrifying sound of scattering earth started to become harder and harder to hear.

I kept my breath secured in my lungs for a bit longer, waiting patiently for the last distant sounds of his footsteps to drift away before I blasted the hot stale air out from my throbbing chest.

"It worked," I said down to Sara eventually. "It worked!"

My little girl however, was not paying to much attention to me. She was to busy trying to extract fluid out of my impotent digit.

Well Eugene, you might just live to see another day after all.

I let my head fall back limp and rested it on a clump of branches behind me, staying in that position for quite awhile. I was in no real hurry to leave that spooky cavern at that point, even though at one time, it was a place I greatly feared. My stress-inflicted coma was kind of nice, but was bluntly disrupted by the pissed off sobs of a double-crossed baby. Sara had recently spit out my finger and was now protesting my treachery with great contempt.

"OK honey," I said, peering down into the fold of my jacket. "You're right, it's time to get out of here."

I eased my body up to a stand and let my legs twist out a well-deserved stretch. In one well-rehearsed maneuver, I repositioned Sara back into the paunch of my coat and prepared to drop to my knees and exit the musty bubble. I snorted in a quick serving of air to power up my lungs, but spat it out immediately in a disgusted grunt. For some reason, a pungent stench had drifted into the tiny room's air space and was wreaking havoc on my nasal passages

"Yeech," I grumbled under my breath." Must be coming up from the river."

Having had enough excitement for one night, I held my breath and tilted my head forward in the direction of the hazy entrance. But I froze dead in my tracks again as I felt a hot gust of moist air scrape the skin off the back of my neck.

Oh Shit!

The strike came quickly and sent my body reeling face-first into the wall of sharp brush. The pain shot down my spine and paralyzed my knees, toppling me sideways towards the dirt floor. I felt my hand instinctively rise up and cup the fresh wound on the back of my skull and it wasn't long before I heard my assailant's evil snarl begin to close in behind me. In a desperate move, I flipped onto my back and attempted to fend off the oncoming attack, but I was too slow and was unable to avert the second wave of brutalities. A rainbow of obtuse stars exploded in front of me as I felt the blunt end of a stick pierce my forehead and spill blood down into my eyes. My arm automatically barricaded itself around Sara who was now screaming obscenities at me from inside my bomber.

Get the fuck out of here or you are done for Eugene.

So with my veins now engorged with pain-suppressing adrenaline, I rammed my heels into the soft earth and did my best to get back to standing. I was halfway up the sharp pillar of thorns behind me when I felt the pressure of a rotting body pin me to my spot. I winced in terror as the greebs boney fingers found their way up to my neck. His breath, now in my face, was as black and rotten as his teeth, and with the help of the moon's unbiased glow, I watched in agony as the pus from those charred grinders danced about his swollen gums. He pushed out a growl through the phlegm and the spit in his throat and I writhed in denial as a thin stream of that diseased ooze streaked out from his cracked lips and connected with my cheek. The warm sputum spiraled down the length of my neck and trickled across my windpipe that was, I might add, being critically jeopardized by the presence of his surprisingly powerful hand. My thoughts started to become unstable, weakened considerably by the lack of oxygen I was receiving and my eyes too, began to cloud over and sting.

You gotta do something quick Eugene. You got to find something and hit him with it for Christ Sakes!

It was true. Time was running out for me in the form of air and I only had about ten seconds to relieve the pressure on my trachea. After that, I knew it would be all over.

With my consciousness steadily fading away, I unhooked my protective grip from the howling cargo in my jacket and feverishly began tripping my palm across the cool floor beside me searching desperately for anything that would suffice for a weapon. A branch, a stick, a bottle.

YA, ya, a bottle?

A distant glimmer of hope mirrored across my near-doomed eyes as my hand suddenly brushed across the thick glass contour of what could only be an empty liquor container. Without wasting another second, I securely hooked my fingers around the tubular features of the canteen's neck and heaved the large end of it up in the direction of the monster's delusional head. It made a sickening but victorious thud as it ricocheted off his mite-infected scalp and almost instantaneously, I felt his filthy hand cease it's tyranny. The emaciated shell of a human being then tumbled off of me and landed face first off to the side, his body limp and his brains temporarily scrambled.

"I'm outta here," I groaned as I braced my arms back around Sara and flipped onto my stomach.

I quickly wormed my way back out the narrow tunnel towards the rabbit hole opening that got me into that mess, and prepared for a speedy exit. My body was vibrating with trauma as I penetrated through the spiny portal and spilled out onto the rugged banks of the great river. I could still hear the greeb moaning away loudly from somewhere within the uncharted maze but I didn't care.

Moan away you Motherfucker. You're damn lucky I didn't finish you off for good!

I stumbled to my feet and scurried back across the uneven landscape towards the end of the bridge. My head was gushing out blood and manipulating my vision with a red hue, but I ran on at full speed anyway, catching equal air off the other side of the structure as I fled. I kept my pace at full too, and not until I reached the temporary safety of the nearest alley did I slow down to catch my breath and wipe the blood from my face. It took me nearly an hour and a half to get back to my ride and God did it feel good to slide back down into the driver's seat. I was already idling down the road before I eased Sara out from the confines of my jacket and set her back into her crib beside me. She was still very agitated, but considering the circumstances, she was holding up fine. I really had to give that little trooper credit. I mean Hell, most adults couldn't have put up with that much stress!

When I finally convinced myself that I was far enough away from whoever in the fuck else wanted to make my life miserable, I removed my heavy foot off the gas and pulled over to the side of the road.

I took a minute to collect my thoughts, then reached around behind my seat and fished out a clean towel to put over my wounds.

While I nursed my cuts I instinctively felt inside my bomber for Sara's bottle and realized that it was not in my Mickey pocket where it usually hid.

Of course it's not there Eugene. You left it back there in that tunnel.
Shit! That's right, it is still back there.

And it was "back there" that I knew it was going to stay! No way I was ever going to poke my head into that world again. But Sara cries were not diminishing either, so I leaned over and picked her up, methodically rocking her back and forth while I tried to think of the best way to tell her the bad news.

After ten minutes she still was crying so I injected into the equation the only ace I had left up my sleeve, the ninja charm.

With uncommon speed I watched with glee as the time-honored antidote began to work it's magic. My hands eventually went limp too, courtesy of the ancient sedative, and there me and my little girl sat. The blood from my wound was still dribbling onto my shirt a bit, but at that point I didn't care. I was too busy being hypnotized by Sara's toy. I sat there in a daze for a while, but was brought back to life by a sudden memory. Her soother.

Yes, I still have her soother. It's in the glove box.

In the span of a few seconds I had that thing out of the cubby, cleaned off, and into her mouth. This gracious addition, along with the anesthetic from the charm, secured my quest for peace and finally my mind became still.

It was over.

This crazy night was finally over and I felt my heart rate adjust it's rhythm to that understanding.

But I also realized that I had been stupid. I got too complacent and suffered the consequences. From now on I knew I would have to revert back to my original blueprint of safety. I had to play this gamble straight up from here on in. No more fucking around!

Eventually, Sara did fall asleep so I carefully reconstructed her personal igloo and once my cargo was secure, I sat upright and decided it was time to have a look at the latest round of damage I had sustained. But cranking the rear view mirror towards my face was something I should have rethought.

It was nasty!

My "Greeb" friend had done quite a number on my already-homely face. I winced in pain as I ran my fingers across the deep, wet ravine that was now sliced into my forehead. I also felt the presence of a notable goose egg behind my ear, but it wasn't opened up so I just concentrated on the gash to my noggin.

The cut itself was about two inches long and was purging out an odd-colored fluid. Not knowing much about dealing with this level of injury, I blindly reached around for a second time and retrieved another towel which I dragged slowly across the full length of the cut to clear away the majority of goop. This was a bad move, for all it did was break apart the microscopic dyke that had already formed there and proceeded to cause a fresh surge of blood to spill down my face again.

The damage already done, I learned the hard way that direct pressure was the only way to fix my problem.

With one hand on the steering wheel and one hand now pressing against my forehead, I restarted my beast and drove away, weaving through the dark deserted streets in search of a safe place to bed down. When I found the situation I was looking for, I silenced my rig, locked everything up, and slid my hunting knife down into it's bed in the door. I was asleep right away, my blood-soaked towel still jammed into my forehead. But into my slumber a short ways I came to the unconscious realization that this was definitely not my day, for I began to dream.

It was an apparition I was all too familiar with.

It was the same one I had been mysteriously exempt from for so many nights prior, but sadly tonight, had managed to somehow find its way back into my soul.

This time it really shook me up. It was brutally graphic and merciless in every way. It followed the exact path of the first two, only this time it was played out ever-so-slowly, ensuring that I not miss one single gory detail of it. It was like the dream knew I had shrugged off its apparent teachings and decided to make me pay for that mistake.

It started out the same way with the trees bending in the wind and the sound of the toddler crying from behind the door at the end of the hallway. The nightmare then evilly portrays the maggots spilling out from behind the brightly-colored clown mask as I remove it and expose the grotesque contour of what was once a human face. As before, I cannot breathe at the sight of this and I begin to feel the muscles in my legs start to give out. Watching my body crash hard onto the ground, I feel the still-wet wooden symbol that I now have learned represents purity bulging inside my hand.

Suddenly, it is pitch black again and I am treated to the angelic hymn of a religious lullaby, but now those rhymes have become tainted with the evil pitch of a shovel stabbing the earth. I notice too, that my hands are held up high in apparent rejoicement and I can see the moon shining down on me like before. But it's not over yet, and without warning, my head suddenly shifts over to the right and focuses in on a door. As I walk towards it, I feel my head brush up against something hanging from the roof and then a thin stream of something warm runs down the length of my forehead. The dream pivots there and I find myself running wildly through the empty streets in the dead of the night, finally ending up walking slowly through the large main gates of the one place in my memory that I covet the most.

Central Park.

My eyes shot open after that and I found my body sitting upright, fighting as usual to control it's respirations. I immediately looked over at Sara. She was sleeping away peacefully. She was OK

I let out a sigh, then reached over and put my hand on her torso just to make sure she was indeed real. I had to rule out the possibility that this latest development was not just another deranged twist to the already confusing nightmare. My mind let down it's guard the moment I felt her diaphragm begin to expand and fall. My body followed suit and sent my ribs towards the steering wheel. I did lay back down eventually but it was no use. The claustrophobia of my Firebird, coupled with the lingering images of the dream, were wreaking havoc on my ability to get back to sleep. My eyes just would not close in fear of another subdural asskicking.

I needed light to scare off the darkness I had suffered. I needed people to surround and hide me. It wasn't long before my eyes began focusing in on the brightly-colored neon sign of an all night coffee shop.

With the tiniest sense of belonging, I picked up my sleeping child from the car, blanket and all, and headed into the lone building. I spotted an empty booth way in the back of the joint by the payphone and trudged toward it.

I fished around my pockets for some change and scraped up just enough loot with a couple of quarters to spare to purchase one regular coffee. It felt good to be around humans. It felt safe.

Once unloaded at the table, I maneuvered Sara and her posse of blankets so that her snoring face was towards me on the bench.

It was just a matter of time before she woke up in need of attention and I wanted to be ready.

Well, ready came fast and no sooner had I thought those words when I noticed a slight change in her breathing pattern and boom, she was up.

I knew I had nothing in the way of a bottle to offer her, so I just began dipping my finger into an open coffee creamer, and low and behold my plan was a success. Sara settled down just like that and once she'd had her fill, fell right back to sleep again. I was relieved of course, but I also understood that the staple my baby had just consumed was going to find the way out sooner or later so I cautiously loaded up my jacket pocket right then and there with a huge wad of paper napkins from the chrome table dispenser, then sat back and started to doctor up my own drink. As I slowly sipped my brew, I found my mind suddenly overrun with various images of a certain drugstore clerk. I attempted briefly to focus in on the problems at hand but Meridith's imprint refused to fade. No matter what I tried, it seemed that she was there to stay. I really wanted to fight my own battles regarding the dream, I really did, but I was losing ground by the second.

All I could think about was her.

Man, what I wouldn't do to see that gorgeous face of hers right now. That would squash the memory of the dream for sure!

Well why don't you call her then stupid?

I glanced over at the clock on the wall. One thirty five... A.M.

"Fuck that," I grunted. "It's the middle of the bloody night. She'd lose it on me!"

I leveled the flames of the rogue thought for the moment, but in the end, was unable to put out the fire.

No matter how much water I poured on that crazy idea there was always one red hot coal that refused to die, and the more the minutes ticked on, the brighter the ember became.

I was screwed. A huge part of me was yearning to see her and it showed no signs of backing down. But it was so late. I mean Christ, it was nearly two in the morning. My senses argued back and forth as usual, but as my feet began to lift up, I knew I'd lost the fight. With a twinge of hesitation, I reached into my pocket and pulled out the crunched up sliver of till tape that held her precious number. With the speed of hair growing, I eased my body away from the disaster of blankets that held my child and walked over to the phone. With one eye on the booth, and one eye on the dial pad, I dropped in a lone quarter and spun through the mesmerizing sequence. As soon as I heard the ringing sound begin on the other end of the line, I began to panic and question my decision.

This is fucking crazy Eugene. She is going to slam the phone down right in your ear, you watch.
She will be bloody pis...

"Hello," I heard a sleepy voice say.

The echo of my girlfriends response instantly silenced my train of thought and left me hanging there for a moment.

"Hey," I said after a short pause. "How are you?"

"Eugene?" I heard her whisper.

"Ya, it's me," I answered, now feeling ashamed for waking her up. "Listen I'm sorry to bother you, but I had this freaky dream you know, and I just can't shake it off and Um... Oh God Meridith. Dammit... I'm sorry.
I'm so sorry I woke you up. It's just... It's just I can't sleep that's all."

I halted my ramblings and silently waited for her retaliation. After a few seconds of antagonizing silence, my brain started to renege on its doped-up idea and began scrambling for a way to save face.

"Ya, well you know," I said, shooting back a cold stream of spin control, "it's not a big deal or nothing."

Then in an arrogant tone, I voiced an escape: "Well I guess I'll let you go. See you around sometime, huh."

With that, I pulled the phone away from my ear and prepared to smash it into the base.

"Wait Eugene," I heard Meridith's faint voice call out. "Don't hang up!"

After a second, I slowly brought the receiver back up to my ear.

"It's OK," I listened to her say through the tiny holes in the plastic. "I wasn't sleeping that well myself."

Now I felt like a damn fool. I didn't really know what to say, but eventually my pride, realizing it's mistake, stood down it's rude defense and issued a less threatening response.

"Meridith," I said quietly. "I am so sorry for waking you up. I guess I just needed to hear your voice that's all. I had this horrible dream you see, and then I tried to get back to sleep, and then I..."

"Where are you?" she asked out of the blue.

"I... um, I'm at..."

I quickly pulled the receiver away from my face and looked down at the address stamped on the phone book.

"I'm at The Coffee Cave," I said finally "over on 188th and Aberdeen. I couldn't sleep so I just thought I'd hang out here for a bit, you know."

"Why don't you come over here," I heard her suddenly say.

I was totally caught off guard by her response. Even a bit shocked, and as usual, I became mute.

"Eugene, Eugene are you still there?" Meridith said a few moments later.

"Um, ya, I'm still here."

"Do you want to come over here?"

"God I'd love to Meridith, if... if it's no trouble and all."

My state of shock was definitely over now, and I wasted no time in recovering the lost ground. But then, the vision of Sara sleeping in the booth to my right jumped into the picture. I worried briefly about what my gracious host might think when I showed up at her house with a baby, but we were a package.

"Listen Meridith," I said carefully. " I have Sara with me of course, I mean she's already asleep and everything, and when she's asleep she's really good, like she only wakes up a couple of times a night so it's not a real big deal and she..."

"Please do," I listened to my girlfriend say in a beautiful and sentimental voice, "definitely bring Sara along. I'd love to have her."

I felt my heart swell up and begin to fly when I heard those words and I watched in deep jubilation as the evil spirits of the dream began to run for their lives, terrified beyond belief at the powerful new emotion that had suddenly broke down their door and put the chase on them.
It was a done deal. I thanked her sincerely and told her that I would be there as soon as I could.

"Just get here quick OK?"

Riding a velvet wave, I eased Sara up out of the booth and we were on our way. Throughout the whole trip over to her apartment it was all I could do to keep my car under seventy-five miles an hour. God, I was on such a cloud! Pulling up behind the bushes in Meridith's alley, I could see a light on through the window of her balcony.

"That one's for me," I bragged out loud." That one's for me!"

I quickly threw together a bag of Sara's supplies and then without waking her, I slowly dislodged my dozing child out from the heap of blankets on the passenger's seat and pressed her against my chest.
After buzzing apartment #327 and pulling open the thick metal security door, I walked up the stairs and down the hallway still riding a thunderbolt and rejoiced about how safe I actually felt now that I was behind that bomb shelter- like entrance. When Meridith opened the door to her apartment, I know she was unsuspectingly treated to a pretty sobering picture.

There I was, standing in the hallway with Sara cocooned up in a massive ball of fuzz in one arm, and in the other, my hand gripping furiously onto a tattered plastic supermarket bag filled to the limit with squeaky toys, paper napkins, and a couple of cans of baby formula, one of which was already opened up and leaking.
And smack dab in the middle of all that, stood none other than good old, busted the-fuck-up me! That must have been quite a shock for her, waking up out of a dead sleep to a sight like that. I was amazed she didn't slam the door right there in my face and pretend that it was all a dream. Mind you, the first words out of her mouth were a tad pointed.

"Jesus Christ! What happened to your eye?"

I paused for a second and gave her a confused look. I guess with all the excitement of my rare invitation I had completely forgot about the wound on my head I had suffered at the mercy of that crazy bush fuck.

"My eye, oh ya, mm, my eye. Ya. Um. Well you see I uh, hit my head on a tree branch," I lied. "But it looks worse than it really is."

Meridith shook her head and took Sara's bag of goodies out of my hand. I could tell she was very shaken by the site of my wound, but the damage to me was already done.

"Make yourself at home," she said in a still-disturbed tone. " I've laid down a foamy for Sara on the floor next to my bed. She should be OK there for the night hey?"

"Oh ya, she'll be fine," I nodded.

Then I watched Meridith's eyes light up as she pulled back the flap of blanket over Sara's face and exposed my sleeping beauty.

"She's so adorable," Meridith cooed as she gently plucked Sara out from my arms and disappeared through the door at the end of the hallway. After a bit, she came back out of the room and walked over to me, gazing systematically into the open gash above my eye.

"Must have been some tree," she mumbled in disbelief.

I stripped off my bloodstained jacket and handed it over at her request, but instead of hanging it up, she donned an unimpressed frown and disappeared into the bathroom. I listened attentively as she turned on the shower head and rinsed off the evidence. My girlfriend emerged out of the tiny room a few minutes later and descended on me with a frightening command.

"Now it's your turn Mister!"

I winced a little as she grabbed my arm and hauled me too, into the overly-pink bathroom. I caught a glimpse of my freshly sterilized leather jacket hanging from the shower nozzle as it dripped slowly of dark red fluid, moments before I was hit with another stern ultimatum.

"Sit!" she demanded, pointing to the edge of the tub. I did as I was told and nervously awaited my punishment. Meridith turned away briefly and began fumbling through the bottom drawer of her matching vanity, quickly producing a compact first aid kit. Without missing a beat, she spun around and began saturating a big white pad with iodine. My girlfriend was almost ready to operate when I saw her face pivot down towards my neck and squint up in disgust. Seems the blood from my wound had leaked down the side of my neck and stained my t-shirt in the process.

"This has gotta go too," she scolded.

I did as I was told, but the process was slow due to the painful umbrella my body was under. Meridith noticed this ailment and began to assist me with the task. At first she was OK, but as soon as I was half naked, it appeared that my textbook nurse became caught a little off guard. I even saw the hue of the slightest blush form on her cheeks.

Well this was new.

I just chalked it up to mystery and kept my mouth shut. During the course of my treatment, I slowly looked up into her eyes and whispered forth my admiration.

"Thank you Meridith. You have no idea what this means to me."

Meridith leaned down and gave me a tiny kiss.

"Don't thank me until you get my bill. "

I let out a small chuckle to, but it was run off immediately by a painful moan as my unusual nurse pressed the uninviting disinfectant into my cut.

"Still want to thank me?"

"Yep," I grunted, trying not to bawl my brains out.

She doctored that forehead of mine up with the competency of a surgeon. I couldn't believe how fast and precise she was. She was a total pro. When she had finished up her artistry, she put away her trauma kit and led me into the kitchen.

"Would you like some tea?"

"Love some."

Within five minutes we were curled back up on the couch in the living room sipping away at our drinks with only the somber dazzle of a candle burning on the coffee table to reflect our thoughts. I didn't say much. I could have I guess. I could have carried on for a full hour apologizing to my hostess for waking her up in the middle the night and all that, but somehow I didn't feel Meridith expected that. I felt very at ease with her now, like I'd sat close to her a million times before already. Our unconscious therapy session however, was interrupted a short while later by the familiar sound of my hungry baby waking up for her usual midnight snack. Before I could react, Meridith jumped up like a mother of six and darted off in the direction of the bedroom, returning a couple of minutes later with my discontented child and her bulging entourage of supplies. I stood up immediately and held out my arms to accept my parental responsibilities, but to my surprise Meridith walked right by me and plopped herself and my little girl back onto the end of the couch.

Okeedokee, I guess I'll just sit this one out.

Meridith rifled through the overfilled grocery bag for a moment then suddenly twisted her head over in my direction and said with a concerned squint, "Where's her bottle?"

"I... uh, lost it today. Don't know where. I was going to buy another one first thing tomorrow whe..."

"Oh that's OK," Meridith said cutting me off. "I have an extra one."

Well now I was confused, but my couch mate quickly reconstructed her statement as she saw a bewildered look park itself on my face.

"From when I babysat my cousin's kid," she added.

"Oh good," I replied mindlessly, even though I did find it strange that my girlfriend never mentioned anything about having a cousin before.

I was not about to complain though, due to the fact that in the back of my mind I was still racking my brains trying to figure out just how in the Hell I was going to budget in another one. Meridith then directed me to a thin cupboard above the stove. I opened it up only to find, you guessed it, a brand new baby bottle with a custom-ized, oversized and a near fatal-sized nipple sitting on the end of it.

Jeeze, Sara's eyes are going to pop right out of her head when she gets a look at that sucker!

Hell, my own eyes just about did that! I brought the plastic device back into the living room and once again held out my arms to receive my baby. But low and behold I was denied a second time, for Meridith did not surrender my child and instead, snatched up the container from my hand and began loading it up with the open and sticky can of formula that was stuffed recklessly in the sac. I knew now, that I was in no way going to be allowed any participation in this ritualistic feeding whatsoever. This was ladies night only, and it occurred to me that Meridith had fully intended to front this time honored task right from the start. God, that was a nice feeling.

I watched my girlfriend begin to dance the gargantuan-sized button around the edges of Sara's open wailing mouth then collapse back into a maternal ball as soon as my baby took the bait. All I could do after that was watch in a state of blissful paradise as the woman I adored instinctively nourished the baby I loved. What a magnificent sight! Meridith became consumed in Sara's gaze, a gift I too had been blessed with many times prior. I didn't disturb the woman at the end of the couch for anything. Meridith had earned the right to witness my newborn's mystical powers as much as I. She had gone beyond the call of duty for us tonight and I just could not help but feel an overwhelming sense of unity between the three of us as we sat there in silence on the couch.

When the sad sound of liquid meshing with air finally broke me away from my wonderful movie, I watched with equal bliss as Meridith gently hoisted my baby onto her chest and lightly tapped her long slender fingers onto Sara's back. A large belch echoed through the darkness of the modest room and was followed by a similar expulsion from another orifice. I heard my girlfriend chuckle and commend Sara on her valiant effort.

I too laughed under my breath, but then said numbly, "I guess it's my job to change her though, huh?"

"Yep, it is."

She quickly handed over my ripe infant to me, now without hesitation, so I took Sara into the bathroom with her bag of goodies and cleaned her up. I asked permission before I set one toe into Meridith's bedroom to put Sara back down for the night, a request that was cheerfully granted. Once I had tucked my sweetheart in, I returned to the living room and prepared to thank my gracious hotelier with a good-night kiss to the cheek before I respectively chose a spot on the living room floor and hit the sack, But the moment I executed said procedure, I received a totally different reaction, one I don't think I was actually ready for.

With my knee's a-knocking, I watched in a state of erotic terror as Meridith set down her teacup in an ever-so-ladylike fashion and crawled overtop me like a giant cat, seductively pinning me to the sofa.

OK Eugene old boy. You're not in Kansas anymore!

Meridith followed up her Saturday night wrestling move with a mind-blowing lip lock that involved no less than 90 percent of my internal organs. She meant business and I'm not kidding. That was no goodnight kiss she just hit me with. Hell, it was going to take a good half hour to untangle my tongue for God's sake!

Nope! That sexy cashier had only the worst of intentions in store for me and I became instantly afraid!

Don't get me wrong, I'd have to be in a coma not to be enthralled with this latest and unexpected development, and I was!

I really, really was!

But the truth be told, the fact was that I had only been with one other woman my whole life, and that alcohol- inflicted one night stand I had suffered through in my teens was not about to go down in silver screen history as the greatest love scene of all time, if you know what I'm saying! And let's face it! This was not your average horny teenage girl either.

This was your average full-grown horny girl!

And from the demonic look that lingered in her pupils, I understood all too well that this woman was about to reduce me to nothing more than a spastic ball of nerves and saliva!

Be strong UGH! If there was ever a time in your life to be the Man, it's now!

Shaking like a ten-year-old in the principal's office, I subconsciously strapped on the biggest set of auxiliary balls I could find and let her have it! I ran my fingers across the small of her back and down the sides of her slender hips, returning her passionate kiss with an even stronger one of my own. Then I gently knocked out her footing and let her body fall into me, flipping myself over in the same smooth motion as I boldly repositioned myself on her. After that I showed no mercy.

I began to run my lips without pause up and down the length of her neck. She flung her head back in ecstasy and made sure I didn't miss a single inch of her hot, agitated skin. In another daring maneuver, I dominantly grasped her hands and carried them above her head, still forcefully massaging her shoulders and her bosom with my lips. Without warning, she suddenly flung me off of her and stood up.

"Would you like to see more of my bedroom?" she purred.

"Hell yes!"

Then, as we sprinted neck and neck in the pitch black towards the door at the end of the hallway, Meridith suddenly tightened the grip on my limb and darted out ahead of me. She told me to wait for a second which I did, and a few moments later I heard her tightly close a door somewhere in front of me, then sprint ahead again towards her own room. I listened on with perverted glee as my ears picked up the telltale sound of clothes being removed. I heard a candle being lit and moments later Meridith appeared at the end of the narrow corridor sporting a very see-through outfit.

"Come and get it big boy," she taunted as she waggled her index finger playfully.

It took me less than a nanosecond to reach my destination and I swallowed hard as she tiptoed backwards and inched her way towards the bed that was now pleasantly illuminated by the glow of the lone candle.
Her body floated backwards onto the mattress, her finger still edging me on, and our naked bodies soon met and became one. What happened after that is pretty obvious, and I'll tell you this, what I did, I did in style.
I didn't apologize to her, I didn't ask her for permission or if it was too soon or anything. I just made love to her. Like a man would.

The sex was brutally passionate. It was obvious that she had been suffering from a few pent up emotions. She didn't hold nothing back and neither did I. She was amazing, that woman, and as I watched the hazy contours of her nude body slowly blend into mine through the vortex of the candle, I no longer felt awkward or guilty about our relationship. Our bond was now official. We laid their sensuously entangled in one another when it was over. I felt no more pain as the heat of her skin warmed my soul and repaired my every wound. I fell in love with her that night.

I fell hard and it wasn't because of the sex either. It was because this woman took me and my baby in from the cold. Without hesitation, without persecution, she opened up her heart and her home and locked out all the bad things that relentlessly sought to do me and my little girl harm.
That single act, what she did, was something I had been waiting for someone to do my whole life.
And it was in turn, also responsible for delivering the last blow to my self-imposed solitude, an execution that I was very much in favor of.
I lay there and watched in a sleepy daze as the dying flame from the candle finally

192

flickered it's last light and disappeared.

I felt my own eyes surrender to that notion too, as the photograph of Meridith's already-sleeping face began to slowly develop in the folds of my mind.

I was sleeping like a rock, that is of course, until nature called.

I eased my body out from the bed slowly. I didn't want to wake up Meridith for I knew she had to work in the morning. Once standing, I crept around to the other side and knelt down beside my sleeping baby.

She was out like a light and snoring away soundly. It was nice to see her sleeping in a normal environment for once.

I leaned over and kissed her cheek. She had been through a lot this evening, but she was tough. God, she was tough! Sometimes I think she was even stronger than I was. Hearing my bones crack a bit, I stood back up and left the bedroom, shutting the door quietly behind me before stumbling my way down the dark passageway in search of the bathroom. My boney frame scraped it's way down the textured wall until my hand finally connected with the trim around the door. Slipping inside I braced my eyes and flipped on the three million watt bulbs that sat above the mirror. My retinas screamed out in agony as they tried to compensate for the sudden trauma and when they did I was treated to a terrible case of deja-vu.

The gash that was carved into my head from my earlier altercation was oozing forth a wretched green filth from out beneath Meridith's textbook dressing. A few negative images from my impromptu boxing match at the farmhouse began to find their way back into my brain again, but I quickly ran them out and told them never to return.

With a deep sigh, I turned away from my reflection and did what I'd come there to do. After I was finished I reopened the bathroom door and went to kill the light. But as my fingers applied pressure to the switch I noticed the outline of another door that sat adjacent to the room I still occupied, the one that Meridith had strangely closed up tight earlier on.

Don't do it Eugene.

Apparently my conscience already knew what my curious side was thinking.

That's none of your Damn business in there.

Then, just like that, the whole inside of my mind turned into a giant war zone! You know, good fighting bad. Right attracting wrong, shit like that. But the battle quickly swayed itself in the direction of wrong and as the last angel I had toppled sideways, I began steadily walking towards the unknown entrance using the light from the bathroom to guide me. Then, as quietly as I could, I twisted open the handle of the heavy plank of wood and pushed it away. Once again the bright rays of the restroom light paved my way into the small cubbyhole and uncovered an eerie and very confusing sight.

I found myself standing smack dab in the middle of a windowless encasement, staring blankly up at a wall behind a meager desk that was plastered to the hilt with strange posters of every shape and size. And there were also books. Books scattered everywhere. On the floor, on the desk, in boxes. They were all over the place. Upon closer examination, I determined immediately as to what the general theme of this misplaced library really was.

It was dedicated mainly to the study of witchcraft.

At least that's what most of the literature and artwork in there was geared toward. Witchcraft and Voodoo. Well this was definitely odd.

OK I understand that everybody has a hobby. But this shit? Witchcraft? Voodoo? I mean come on. That just didn't seem like Meridith at all. I scratched my head in denial as I began searching the far perimeters of my rational thought for some sort of visible connection that would match up Meridith's personality to this Gothic path of madness, but I could find no such evidence to support it. And when I finally reversed my legs back out of that room, I found myself still in a very uneasy place. A place mind you, I did willfully enter into, even though I knew goddam well it was wrong.

I didn't go back to sleep right off. I just couldn't, for my head was still trying desperately to make some kind of sense as to the eerie way of life that lay poised in that room. Now I knew why she didn't want me to see in there and I couldn't help but wonder as to why she was possibly misleading me as to what type of person she really was.

Hey Eugene you hypocrite, while you are on the subject of lying, do remember that you haven't actually told Meridith one single thing that was true in the whole time you've known her? So let's not get all high and mighty here OK?!

I didn't answer my subconscious back for I knew it was right. I was the one who was misleading her, and she wasn't under any obligation to tell me anything that she didn't want to.

Well now I felt bad. After all Meridith had done for me and Sara I go and do this. I felt my guts begin to shift. I stuck my nose where I shouldn't have and was beginning to pay the price for that mistake. The guilty sickness only became worse as I carefully spooned my body against my girlfriend and felt her sleepily accept me. Eventually the feeling of remorse subsided a bit, at least enough to allow me to get back to sleep, but I warned my jealous side to take heed of the lesson it had just learned or suffer the consequences.

Surprisingly enough, my sleep was OK, and it wasn't until the morning sun broke through the thin shading of the rose-colored curtains that I began to hear the faint protests of my baby coming up from her comfy spread on the floor. And as my eyes cracked open I was treated to the same awesome view I had closed them to. It was the picture-perfect outline of Meridith's body curled up tight against me that would begin my day. Her eyes were now open slightly too, due I'm sure, to the intermittent sobs of my newborn.

My girlfriend's nude contour shifted away from me momentarily as she stretched out her arms above her head and casually asked, "What time is it?"

I glanced upward and focused in on the alarm clock the sat on her headboard.

"Ten after six," I said.

I knew Meridith had no reason to get up this early so I made the call to get a move on so that when she did awake, it would be in peace.

"It's early," I whispered, running my fingers through her hair. "You don't have to get up. I'll just pack up Sara and let us out. That way you can catch a few more zzz's before you have to go to work, OK?"

Meridith mumbled something then closed her eyes.

I lay with her for a few more moments then very, very reluctantly, pulled my body away from the warmth of hers and got dressed.

After I was all together I knelt down to Sara, who was still blubbering away and whispered "Good morning sweet pie."

I snuck a kiss to her puffy cheek and she actually stopped crying for about two seconds, but resumed her podium speech shortly thereafter and increased the volume a touch.

I think she was trying to say something like, "So where the Hell were you asswipe, and where is my breakfast? And boy, do I have a big surprise for you in my diaper pal!"

Ya, I think it was something like that. Further investigation of course, proved all Sara's charges against me correct. Especially the last one! So I scooped up my little treasure and headed straight for the bathroom. Five minutes later I exited out from that cubicle with a clean-smelling, freshly-dressed tot as well as a dry and blood-free jacket. I crept back into the bedroom before I went to leave, to give Meridith one quick kiss goodbye, but she was not there. And the bed we had shared the night before was already made up and ordered with like 400 pillows. Her housecoat too, was gone from its hanger behind the door and this exposed a very tiny set of lingerie. My carnal thoughts however, were quickly overruled by the tantalizing aroma of bacon fat and charred bread so I followed the heavenly scent down the corridor and into the kitchen.
Meridith, believe it or not, was bright-eyed and bushy-tailed as she laid down two sets of dinnerware onto the kitchen table.

"Hungry big fella?" she said.

"Oh ya. Worked up an appetite last night you know."

Meridith dropped her head for a moment and grinned innocently.

"You didn't have to make us breakfast," I said, feeling like the world's biggest freeloader.

"There are a lot of things I don't have to do," she responded, and with an engaging grin she motioned me to the table.

As she divvied up the chow she asked, "Did the little one sleep alright? A rolled up comforter on a foam cushion isn't really the most comfortable thing around."

"I'm sure she slept just fine," I said, holding back a grin as I envisioned Sara's usual crib. "She's pretty tough that girl."

We all sat down and ate a big tasty breakfast. This was a habit I could easily get used to. Sara continued to break in her new bottle while me and Meridith crunched away at our hash. I ate quickly though. I figured our kind chef had to get ready for work soon and I didn't want to be in the road. She had gone so far out of her way as it was. Finishing off my meal I set my dirty plate in the sink and started for the door, thanking Meridith once more for her incredible hospitality.

"Last night..." I said as I crooked my head slightly downward. "Last night was um... unexpected, but awesome."

I waited patiently for her response, but she too, judging from her body language, was feeling a tad shy.
This was, I'd like to say, quite a remarkable turnaround from the risk-taking seductress I had witnessed the night before. But that's to be expected I thought. Daylight has a funny way of taming people.

"Are you OK with what happened?" I asked cautiously as I prepared to leave.

I wasn't trying to bottleneck the conversation or anything, but that was a question I really needed an answer to. Meridith remained silent, but issued me an acceptable answer in the form of a deep kiss.

"I feel the same way," I whispered, and with my query now accounted for, I knew it was time to go.

Driving straight to the Laundromat, this time parking a healthy four blocks away, I found it nearly impossible to wipe the smile off my face. When I finally criss-crossed my way through the long maze of alleyways and rapped my knuckles against the secret passageway to Newa's apartment, I will admit I was pretty worn out. But that was OK A game plan is a game plan and I was going to stick to this one like glue. I didn't care how long of a walk it was.
When Newa came to the door, she was still in her housecoat.

"Newa, it's me," I said quietly as she peered out through the six inch crack in the door. "I'm sorry to bother you so early. Can I come in?"

Newa didn't hesitate for a second and before I could say another word, she swung open the door and waved us in. I heaved my posse through the entrance and set Sara on the couch. Newa fetched her glasses and walked up to me with a curious scowl.

She peered up at the bandage that was stuck to my forehead and said with a squint, "Wha happen to yu?"

Newa's arms remained folded across her chest in suspicion while she waited for my excuse.

"I got into a fight," I muttered in a guilty voice.

My Asian friend stared me down for a couple of seconds, but then purposely broke the awkward run of silence and said with a smirk.

"So who wa she?"

The old Chinese lady then tromped away giggling at her joke. Newa's slapstick rebuttal was pretty funny, to tell you the truth, but somewhere behind that cackle, I knew she sensed I was in trouble.

I left Sara at the Laundromat all day, just to be on the safe side and throughout my travels, I stuck mainly to the alleys and avoided the freeways whenever possible. I was doing what I had told myself I was going to do. My "Everything will be alright" attitude was long gone and had been replaced with a rigid outline of security measures. The wound above my eye sealed that contract.

Leaving Sara with Newa helped out a lot when it came to work too. It was nice not to have to worry about her safety as I pillaged the city for empties. It allowed me to cover more ground and that was a good thing, for I was seriously broke. Even more so than I was used to. Sara was nearly out of formula and her supplies were dwindling away as well. I needed to put my nose to the grindstone and get some cash together like pronto! Throughout the day, a million questions about the night before raged through my brain.

Was it to soon? Did I offend her? Did she do what she did out of sympathy?

The list went on, and every question was followed closely by a landslide of garbled answers that only furthered my anxiety. Now personally, I did not regret what happened, but I feared that maybe she did.

I came to the conclusion that I would not bother Meridith at all today. I wanted to allot her some breathing space that I felt she greatly deserved. I would need to pick up a fresh stock of formula tomorrow as it was, so I figured I would just hold off and talk to her then. It was a mental game of abstinence really, but I wanted to make sure she wasn't feeling smothered.

The next morning came quickly enough anyway, thank God. I already missed that woman immensely and it had only been one bloody day! I dropped Sara off at the laundry at ten, then weaved my rig onward and strolled through the front entrance to the pharmacy sporting a confident grin, spinning left after a few paces and darting into the baby needs aisle. I scooped up only four cans of my baby's mainstay. That was all I could afford at the moment until I cashed in another aluminum paycheck. My mood though, even under its usual amount of worry, was untouchable. I honestly could not get the smile off my face.

I strutted out from the isle like a rock star en route to Meridith's till and descended upon her with a vibrant wink.

"Hey sexy lady, you looking for some trouble?"

I followed this ad-lib come on with a cocky laugh, but I shouldn't have, for it was not met with the same.

In fact, Meridith did not say a word as she hastily began to ring my order in to the cash register. This deliberate silence caused an instant end to my spontaneity and confirmed my biggest fear.

Christ. The sex was too fast.

I knew it! I knew right away that's what was wrong.

Godammit Eugene. You should have waited!"

At that point I wasn't sure what to do. I mean, how do you react to something like this? After all, I was pretty new to all this shit as it was.

"Just kidding," I shot back immediately, trying hard to erase the memory of my unrehearsed comment.

"No problem," Meridith said mechanically, still avoiding eye contact with me.

"What's the matter?" I asked quietly as I set my change onto the counter.

"Nothing," she said finally looking up at me. "I'm just very busy OK My boss has been on my back all morning that's all."

I didn't know if it was warranted or not, but I apologized anyway. I wanted to keep talking to her but her body language told me to get lost. And when I went to say goodbye, I wasn't even able to get the coined phrase past the end of my lips before Meridith beat me to the punch.

"Call me later or something," she mumbled as she scooped my change up off the counter and threw it into the register.

"OH, OK," I stuttered, turning to the door in a state of shock.

I was so crushed by her frigid welcome that I found it hard to speak.

I shouldn't have called her the other night.

I realized the damage of that mistake immediately. I mean, Christ, I woke her out of a dead sleep, then went over to her apartment in the middle of the night and mauled her like a fifteen-year-old hormone junkie.

"Ya, real gentleman- like, Eugene old buddy! Real smooth.

I trudged down the street towards my hidden car for a couple of more minutes and

198

mentally disciplined my selfish actions. But not even a half a block later my feet suddenly came to a halt. They were told to. They were obeying my conscience now, and it was insisting that I march right back there and apologize and that's exactly what I planned to do! It was time to suck up my pride and make things right. She deserved that.

My body near fell over as it spun a one eighty and began trotting back in the direction it came. I was furious by my lack of consideration, but I was also determined to correct it.

Barging through the pharmacy doors for the second time, I veered left toward the checkout right off. I was hell-bent for redemption, but soon realized that Meridith was not at her usual post. Undeterred, I angled my feet starboard and one by one, began searching the aisles. About midpoint in my quest, I scaled up the length of the stationary corridor and was preparing to take on the rest. But as I twisted around the natural corner, my search came to a sudden end for kitty corner from where I stood in pause, was the backside of what could only be my girlfriend. She was leaning up against the far wall of the next aisle. My right foot lifted briefly under the direction of my remorseful conscience, but was instantly grounded by the sound of a man's voice, a deep voice that was reverberating out from somewhere in front of Meridith.

In an instinctive maneuver, I stepped back out of view and pretended to read the greeting cards. I knew it was devious to eavesdrop on her and all, but I was already in the doghouse as it was, so I figured I didn't have much left to lose. I tried to hear what was being said, but from where I was standing, I was just out of earshot and the only sounds coming through were muffled and incomprehensible except for the obvious distinction between male and female. I thought about moving in closer but decided it was too risky. I didn't need to add invasion of privacy to my already swelling list of convictions. Not quite knowing the rules of this game, I shuffled my feet dangerously close to the edge of the aisle in a desperate attempt to pick up what was being said, but that little stunt was short lived, and I quickly retreated back to my original position as I heard Meridith's low profile heels begin to strike the floor. Her stance was changing, and that fact coincided with the sudden clarity in her voice.

"I'll call you later," I heard her say to someone as I abandoned my post and prepared to confront her at that same corner.

But as her footsteps became softer, I realized that she did not take the path I thought she would and instead began walking in the opposite direction from where I was hiding. Still holding my cover, I cautiously inched my head out from behind the greeting card section and watched wearily as Meridith led a strange man with long scraggly hair down the back row and out the side door. I couldn't see his face, but it made no difference anyway. I heard what I heard.

I felt a thin layer of distrust begin to coat my body.

'I'll call you later.' What the fuck is that supposed to mean? Is this another boyfriend or something?

In an instant, my innocent guilt was demoted into jealous anger. With my face now hot and flushed, I began to creep along the length of the aisle towards the front of the store. I watched in secret as Meridith returned to her till. She couldn't see me for I was standing behind a large Halloween display and camouflaged under a mountain of suspicion. I contemplated going over to her. I wanted to walk right up to her and tell her to go to hell! That's what I really wanted to do, but I resisted. I didn't lose my cool at all. I just waited calmly until she was looking the other way, then slipped back out the main doors.

A gross, unsettled knot formed in my guts.

That's why she hurried me out the fucking door in the first place. That fucking guy must have been waiting for her in there and she didn't want me to hang around and see him.

Oh now I was mad, but just out of habit I began to run through no less that a thousand different scenarios of why Meridith would need to phone that guy. Some of my answers were legitimate, but most of them just kept turning the knife. Was I being played here? Was I just a charity case or something? Fuck I was mad!!

I didn't know what to think anymore, not now. One part of me was protesting wildly and pressing for a motion to ditch her ASAP, but the other side of me, oddly enough, stood firmly in her defense. Rubbing my scalp in confusion, I decided to put the whole situation completely out of my mind and concentrate on the reality at hand.

Money!

I had started this day with a financial goal in mind, and I intended to achieve that figure no matter what it took. I spent the remainder of the day in a totally different suburb of town. I rummaged through dozens of big dumpsters looking for empties. I was on a mission today and I kept a picture of Sara purposely highlighted on the front page of my mind to make me work harder. She was my rock, my constant, and she never let me down, or for that matter, talked to any other guys. Driving all the way out to this recently-built subdivision was costly, but I wasn't taking any more chances. No way! I had none left to risk. My self-implemented defense strategy was put in place for a reason.

The whole day dragged on horribly, just like I figured it would. You know it's funny. When you are in a good mood, the hours fly by like seconds, but when you feel like shit, time stands still and rubs your face in it.

By 8pm I'd had enough. Call me what you will, but it was driving me insane, not knowing who that guy was. I had just finished up my chores at the laundry so I pushed the envelope and asked Newa if she would mind looking after Sara for another hour or so. I told her I needed to go and straighten some things out with someone. Newa, as usual, accepted with smiles.

I drove like an escaped convict towards Meridith's apartment. Speeding was a stupid thing to do I admit. I couldn't afford so much as a gumball, let alone a bloody speeding ticket but I couldn't help myself. I wanted to see her and clear all of this shit up, whether I looked like an asshole in the end or not.

When I got to her place, I parked my car in the alley behind some trees and walked around to the front entrance.

After a few minutes of staring numbly up at the intercom board, I reluctantly reached up and depressed her buzzer.

"Hello?" Meridith's voice echoed.

"Hi," I muttered, trying hard to disguise my anger.

"Eugene... is that you?"

"Ya it's me," I answered, and quickly followed up my less than optimistic opener with a cover-up lie. "Listen, I was just in the area visiting a friend, so... um, I thought I'd just drop by and say a quick hello. Do you mind?"

"No, not at all. Come on up."

Meridith's tone of voice now, was a heck of a lot different from our last meeting.

Without warning, the piercing sound of security latch bounced off the walls of the cramped porch and released the heavy door.

When I walked into her apartment, I donned a fake smile to match hers. I knew we were both putting forth a brave face.

Now I didn't have the faintest clue just how I was going to ask her if she was seeing someone else. I mean fuck, how do you do that? But I intended to try.

She guided me into the living room, then disappeared into the kitchen. I leaned my body back on the now infamous couch where we had made out not too many nights earlier, and tried to revisit a few choice memories from that monumental event, but my thoughts were too clouded with distrust and I could not find my way clear to enjoy them. After a minute or two, Meridith came back to the living room with a couple of sodas and sat herself right beside me, delivering along with the beverage, an exaggerated kiss that I was not expecting. She was carrying on like nothing had happened.

"How was your day?" she asked.

"Oh fine. How was your day?" I asked back, secretly setting her up for the kill.

"Oh, it was shit," she groaned out of character, "Just shit! My boss was riding me all day and he wouldn't let up.

Plus it was stock day," she went on, "Which is a pain in the ass to begin with, you know?"

I sat there after she was finished with a stunned look on my face. I had never heard Meridith talk so frankly before. Usually she was quite restrained.

"Well that's no good," I replied, still a little shell-shocked. "I figured you were in a bad mood when I came in," I continued to say in hopes of riding the coat tails of her unprecedented momentum.

"Ya, you definitely caught me at a bad time," she mumbled playfully. I could tell that she was sort of trying to sweeten up the path of the conversation a bit.

"Listen Meridith," I said in a more serious voice. "There is something I want to ask you."

"What is it?"

"Well, um, you see, after I left the store this morning, I sort of sensed that something was wrong, so I uh..."

"There wasn't anything wrong," Meridith suddenly interrupted. "I was just busy, that's all."

"Yes, Yes, I know you were busy," I cut in. "I mean now I realize that, but at the time I thought you were mad at me for some reason so I..."

"Oh Eugene," Meridith said as she interrupted my speech once more in a reassuring tone. "If I was mad at you this morning, wouldn't I still be mad at you right now?"

I felt her hand reach over to encircle mine. I couldn't take it anymore. I was losing this fight in a big way, so I just blurted out what was burning a hole through my heart.
"So I went back to talk to you, but you were busy talking to this guy with long hair and then you said you were going to call him or something."

Actually, that's not what I really wanted to tell her.

I really wanted to look her in the eye and say, "So lady, are you screwing anyone else but me? I mean, am I just a bloody science experiment or something? I mean what is this, sleep with a homeless guy and win a prize or some shit?"

That's what I really wanted to say, but I guess the governing body that controlled my vocal cords didn't really find a whole lot of humor or productivity in that particular speech.
Meridith fell silent and dropped her head for a moment after I delivered my edited blow, which only fueled my suspicions further.

"He was a supplier," she said finally, looking back up at me with a convincing stare. "Just an ornery supplier who forgot to send us some stock so I told him I'd call him when I received it. Really Eugene, that's all he was."

I then felt her second hand reach over and join her first.

"Oh, I see. I thought you were mad at me or something," I said as I painfully shrugged off my inquisition and anchored a smile onto my face.

To be totally honest, I wasn't really sure if I believed her story or not. I mean for all I knew, he could have been "just an ornery supplier", who was I to say any different?

But something inside me told me otherwise.

Nevertheless, I ended our little discussion on a positive note, only due to the fact that I had no more real evidence to bring forth. I didn't question her any further. I had nothing else to say.

Eugene. If you are ever going to succeed at this game, you have to learn not to sweat the small stuff OK?

The attitude adjustment was warranted, and I did feel somewhat at ease. Well, as much at ease as I was going to get, that is. So I decided to ask Meridith the question that was equally tearing away at my conscience.

"Hey," I said carefully. "About the other night, was it um, too soon, you know, the sex thing?"

Meridith did not voice her answer and she instead proceeded to douse my fears with another deep and provocative kiss.

"OK... I give!

"I'm sorry I was so cranky today," she whispered as she completed her seductive peace offering.

"That's alright," I moaned back in a stupor. "I'm sorry I was so worried about it."

I left her apartment complex that night feeling a little better. There were still a few demons buzzing around inside my skull for sure, but the hard fact of the matter was that I hadn't a leg to stand on. I had absolutely no concrete evidence of any wrong-doing on her part and all the guilty fingers seemed only to be pointing, as always, on me. I guess I could have hashed over all the pro's and con's of the situation as I headed back to the Laundry that night to pick up my princess, but the effects of Meridith's wheelchair lip lock were still flourishing within my veins so I chose to just remain sedated. After I had picked up Sara and bid farewell to her gramma, I cranked up the heat and set off towards another pre-determined sleep spot. Once we were happily docked and all the necessary precautions were met, I turned over to my side and tuned my hearing into the frequency of my baby's quiet breaths as they traveled through her nose. And it was through her music that I eventually came to realize, as I did every night, that even though my relationship with Meridith had just experienced an unscheduled tremor, my love for Sara was never-ending.

Chapter 3
the promise

A frozen wind engulfed me as I opened the car door to retrieve my baby for her morning wash. It bit deep into my skin and caused Sara to let go a squeal. Mother Nature had officially issued her warning that winter was on it's way. I had begun sleeping at night with my jacket on underneath my blankets. This was a ritualistic move I always adopted in the late fall as a supplement to my usual covers. It kept my body heat in a little better. I also started running my engine to heat up the cab of my car about four to five times a night as well to ensure Sara was good and toasty. It was flu season in the land of the less fortunate and it was of the utmost importance that I take every known precaution to make sure neither of us came down with anything.

It was a wise call, however the extra fuel cost was seriously jeopardizing my already paper-thin budget.

I'd been desperately looking for a safe power source to jack into so I could utilize my electric heater under the dash, but due to my extremely sensitive cargo, I had to be very selective in this quest and thus far had come up with nothing. In an attempt to compensate for the increase in my gas bill, I had no other option but to cut down on the food I was buying for myself and gain sustenance mainly through the select offerings of the condiment stands, since it was becoming unfeasible to drive to all of the supermarkets to take advantage of the sample carts. As a result of this protocol, my body had become very thin, even thinner than it usually was and my clothes were beginning to hang off of me like the rags they were.

The last few nights I hadn't slept worth a damn and neither did Sara. This put us both in a difficult mood, and to top things off, I hadn't talked to Meridith either. I thought about phoning her the evening before, but decided against it. I also considered swinging by the drugstore to say hello, but my pride and suspicion kept me at bay. I had been in this funk every since our little tiff earlier in the week.

Something was just not right about that woman and I just couldn't put my finger on it. This strange feeling in my gut would just not go away, and it kept festering inside me.

After I had left my freshly laundered tot in the safe and capable hands of her Gramma and stashed away my car, I set off once again to begin another fun-filled day of bottle picking. The morning turned out to be very productive, which was fantastic for it bumped up my standard of living by a notch and momentarily took my mind off all my problems. Namely my troubles with Meridith. By 2pm, I had exploited most of the refuse bins in the area I had driven to, so I decided to pack it up and check out a couple of ripe dumpsters I had spotted the other day up on the north side. But when I approached what I thought to be my well-hidden vehicle, my eyes became fixated on a neatly folded piece of paper that was stuck underneath one of my windshield wipers.

It was a note?

A delicately crafted note that smelled wonderfully of perfume. I opened it slowly and read the simple caption inside.

"Please call me Eugene, I miss you," and it was signed neatly at the bottom, Meridith.

It was the craziest thing, but as soon as I read those words, I felt an enormous weight lift off me. My recent depression, I now understood, was largely due to the absence in my life of the woman who wrote them..
It's funny how two-faced the heart can be. One minute it's standing behind you, the next, it's running you over. Nevertheless, I didn't waste another second of thought on the matter, I just hopped into that old beater of mine and drove like a NASCAR trainee, hell-bent and shamelessly without my spine, in the direction of the drugstore.

She must have delivered the note on her lunch break I figured, but how on earth did she find my car?

Well, Eugene old boy, guess you're not as sneaky as you think you are!

Parking only a block away, I tumbled into her workplace after a short jog like a swat member into a war zone and trotted directly up to her till. The store was quiet and there was no-one in line so Meridith, brandishing a wide grin, jumped out from behind the counter and met me half way. We exchanged a flurry of hellos and I miss you, as well as a lone apology from me for not coming by to see her sooner.

"How the heck did you find my car?" I asked her curiously at the end of our dialogue.

Meridith cleared her throat and said with her hands supine.

"It was just by fluke actually, I had to deliver a bunch of prescriptions to a house-bound lady on my lunch hour, and I saw your car parked there in the alley. It was really weird," she told me. "But the bottom line," she continued, "was that you got my note. That's all I care about", she beamed.

Suddenly, my girlfriend's eyes burned of mischief as she carefully glanced about the store and grabbed my arm. She led me back into a small photocopying room on the opposite side of the pop machine and then, making sure the coast was clear, she yanked me into the narrow enclosure and near laid me out with the kiss she hammered into me. We sucked face like a couple of teenagers at a drive-in. Her lips systematically annihilated any and all of my shortcomings I'd had about her and filled my body once more with adrenaline and commitment.

"I had better get back to my till," she whispered as she released me from her passionate grip and wiped away the residual lipstick from my shell-shocked mouth. "Are you going to do a little more shopping before you go?"

"Yes," I answered back, still dizzy from her kiss. "I need to pick up a couple of cans of baby formula before I take off."

"Great, I'll see you back at the checkout then".

"You got it," I assured her. "I'll see you at the till."

Still in a fog, I snatched up two cans of formula for Sara and headed back to the front of the store. This time my luck was not so good and I found myself stuck way at the very end of a slow-moving lineup that was like six people deep.

Where did everyone come from?

I could see Meridith above the crowd, faithfully manning her till and wildly pounding away at the keys on her register in a desperate attempt to clear out the sudden gathering. Letting go a slight frown, I bit my lip and assumed a position behind the docile train of shoppers. As I waited in line I watched a little old lady with perfectly formed hair squeeze in behind me. Her arms were overloaded dangerously with sale items so I stepped out of the way and gave her a smile.

"Would you like to go ahead of me?" I asked.

"Why yes, if it's no trouble," she said.

"Absolutely not, " I grinned, and with that, the frail senior inched her way in front of me with the speed of growing grass.

And upon her arrival, a good sixteen inches from her original spot, she then coughed up a giant greenish- colored lung nugget and spat it into her handkerchief. You know, there was a time when the sight of someone doing that would have sent me screaming into the night, but nowadays, after dealing with the many graphic expulsions of a newborn which I had, the elderly woman's little circus act didn't faze me in the least.

"Terrible thing that happened to that little boy isn't it?" she said as she stashed the phlegmmy prize into her purse.

"What boy?" I said back.

"That poor little boy that was kidnapped the other day, the one in the papers. Snatched right out of his own back yard if you can believe that," the frail woman continued to say.

Suddenly my brain hit the emergency brake and issued me a vivid glance of the past, at the exact same interval that I looked down and caught the headlines of the day's paper.

"VICTIM NUMBER NINE DISAPPEARS."

"Fuck!" I screeched, as the reality of the newest tragedy began to infect me.

My ill choice of vulgarity caused the whole lineup to crook their heads around in astonishment.

"Sorry," I mumbled in a mass apology.

Even Meridith was giving me a confused look. The headlines, I noticed after the tension of the situation softened a bit, were also decorated with a composite sketch of an all-too-familiar oval symbol. The "Mystery Abductor" who sadly enough wasn't a mystery to me anymore, had claimed his ninth soul. I felt woozy and weak as I read the captions.

When the fuck is this going to end Eugene, when? How many more innocent children are going to have to fall before you tell the authorities what you know? Huh? How many?
For Christ Sakes Eugene. This has gone too far!
And how long is it going to be before Leon catches up with you?
Think about that godammit. Think about it.

"No," I said unconsciously. "I can't think about that right now. I just can't!"

I was well aware of my predicament, but I was also still in control of the situation.

I am still in control. I fired off a silent rebuttal in the direction of the voice. *Now leave me alone.*

I was proud in a way that I had finally stood up to my negative sidekick, but I also understood that this freak, this "Druid", was not about to go away anytime soon either. Anxious and flushed, I arrogantly cast the whole problem aside and waited with great patience as the senior in front of me slowly handed over the last of her change to Meridith, who now stood in plain view at her till. I watched her sneak me a secret wink as she politely bagged up the lady's goods and waved me forward. As I plopped my meager purchase onto the counter, I took one last glance down at the newspaper that had so rudely attacked my jovial mood and let out a disconcerting sigh.

"Are you OK?" Meridith asked.

"Ya, I'm alright," I nodded.

"Hey listen. Why don't you bring Sara over to the apartment tonight and I will make us all dinner?"

Well that was an offer I didn't have to think about too much!

"I would love that."

"Great, then I'll see you at eight."

"Eight is perfect. See you then."

My brakes squealed to a halt at the specified time behind Meridith's apartment. I had raced like a madman to finish my chores at the laundry and got them done in record time. I even had time to do Sara's hair before I arrived.
Sara knew she looked great and she was chattering up a storm in the passenger's seat as I pulled up.

"I'm exited too," I said as I leaned over and gave her a happy-go-lucky smooch on the forehead.

When I walked into Meridith's place, my baby tucked securely under my arm, I was greeted with a kiss and massaged with the tantalizing smell of simmering chicken. Then to my delight, Meridith leaned down and delivered a similar show of affection to Sara, which of course, swelled my pride up even larger. We all sat down at the kitchen table and ate like a family. And as I spoke that word in my mind, "family", I felt a wave of euphoria flow through me and rush to my eyes, but I fought back the emotion and painted on a smile. I didn't want Meridith to see me weak. I wanted her to see a confident man.

But it was true that my globes were experiencing a definite transformation. I think it was due to the sight of Meridith and Sara sitting so close together, coupled along I'm sure, by the tranquility of eating a meal at a table, in a house. It was an event that up until now had been nothing more than a fantasy to me and my newborn. It was almost too much for me to take. I had reached an unprecedented level of joy in my life, and now, was finding it quite difficult to remember even one of my many problems. When I had finished up my restaurant-quality meal, I instinctively reached over and plucked my little girl out from her makeshift highchair in the seat beside me and began my usual job of twirling the plastic nipple of her new bottle around the edges of her mouth. After a few minutes of this, I looked up and noticed that Meridith had put down her fork and was now just sitting there with her hands on her lap, entranced it seemed, by the sight of me feeding my baby. I knew right away that the suckling noises that were drifting out from Sara's cheeks, were beginning to have a hypnotic effect on my girlfriend.

"Be careful," I warned the mesmerized woman in front of me." Don't stare directly into her eyes or you'll fall in love."

Meridith slowly broke away her stare and looked up at me with a gleam that, I understood, constituted a threat of equal intensity. You know, there is not a straight man in the world who does not lay awake at night and dream of the day when he can look up and catch a woman staring back at him like that. It's a look people sometimes wait their whole lives for. But tonight, that lengthy time slot did not apply to me for I had already spotted my pot of gold. It was sitting right across from me.

Once we had finished our dinner, I offered to clean up the dishes, but Meridith, I quickly found out, had a completely different task for me to carry out that evening. Without explanation, she suddenly disappeared into the back bedroom and returned to the kitchen a few minutes later with an armful of brightly colored material.

"I picked you up a new outfit," she said with a heavenly smile." I hope you don't mind."

I was speechless! I was literally reduced to ashes by her kindness.
"Meridith," I gasped as I closed my hands under my chin. "Really, oh boy. You really didn't have to do this," I told her, feeling like the world's biggest freeloader. But my Juno speech was halted instantly by one bold instruction.

"Just hush up and go try them on."

The order was polite but stern, so with a giddy expression smeared across my face, I jumped up out of my chair and whole heartedly accepted her unexpected gift.

"If they don't fit," I heard her say as I closed the bathroom door behind me, "I can take them back and exchange them."

Within seconds I was in the buff and sorting through the neatly pressed pile, soberly realizing the extent of my mate's generosity. She had bought me a whole entire outfit! New jeans, good quality socks, heavy wool sweater, even a funky pair of underwear inhabited the stack of crisp apparel. The name labels were still on, but the price tags had been removed. The clothes she bought me were taut and fresh and once dressed, I looked down at the stained clump of duds I had just shed, and for some strange reason, my heart fell still.
I don't know why, but it was so difficult to look at my old clothes. It made me sad somehow. It felt like I was abandoning an old friend.
Shaking off my odd despair, I turned my attentions to the mirror and after a quick hair flip, I walked back out into the kitchen with a profound gleam riveted to my face. A satisfied grin also swept across Meridith's face as I entered the room. I was very comfortable in my new apparel, but could not shake the feeling of vulnerability in them.

"You look fantastic Eugene," Meridith purred in approval. Her saucer-like eyes boiled with victory as she came over and began adjusting my garb. That is definitely a girl thing.

"Meridith," I said in a somewhat embarrassed tone, "You really didn't have to go to this much trouble. I mean, you have done so much for me and Sara as it is. I just, I…"

"Shhhh," Meridith said raising her index finger to her lips. "I know I didn't have to, I did this because I wanted to."

My girlfriend then finished up her heartfelt monologue by brushing a soft kiss across my cheek, and all I could do was stare at the floor in a hazy stupor. The remainder of the evening went as smoothly as its start, and after a bit of TV, we all retired to the comfort of Meridith's bed, Sara snoozing away in the middle of us now. I purposely waited until both of the girls were asleep, before allowing my own eyes to fall. I felt it my duty to protect them both now, even though in reality, it was probably the other way around. And I thought in that moment, that I wouldn't have been at all surprised if I were to suddenly wake up inside my car right then. Cold and alone. Tucked away in some dark corner of the city, realizing to my dismay that all of it had been nothing more than an incredible fantasy. A dream that my fading mind allowed me to briefly enjoy before it threw me back to the wolves again.

But it wasn't. What I was experiencing was real. And when I did awaken in the morning, I was treated to the same loving imprint that I had gone to sleep with. It seems my delusions of fantasy were being slowly replaced with an almost undeserving truth, and that's something you don't mess with.
I watched Meridith's eyes pinch open stubbornly as I lay there warming up my thoughts in the early sun. I brought my arm across her, then walked it back over her naked body and retired it on my baby. Meridith glided her hand over as well, and weaved it into mine and it was at that moment that I understood how blessed I was, how precious that union was.

We lay there for quite a while, just smiling, just staring at each other as we felt the pulse from our fingers join in a symphony. And it wasn't until Sara announced to us that her day was about to start, that I felt my muscles begin to contract instinctively in a stretch. I delivered a couple of kisses to the warm cheeks of my bed mates, then reluctantly pried my body out of it's seductive mold and got dressed. When I finally left my girlfriend's apartment that morning I could almost see my breath. And while I let my old clunker warm up, I glanced out of my side window and saw Meridith standing up by the patio doors in her housecoat waving goodbye to us. Man, you can't buy that kind of satisfaction. You have to earn it.

A half an hour later, I pushed through the tangled maze of bushes that hide away the secret entrance to the Laundromat and gave the weathered door a few raps. As the plank began to open, I cut loose my usual smile and prepared to be greeted by the same, but I was not?
Instead Newa, whom I'd known up until now to be quite upbeat, could only find the strength this morning to muster up a sincere but somber nod. She waved me and my baby inside, still trying desperately to carry on the act of her wilting demeanor, but then uncharacteristically disappeared after that into her bedroom and shut the door.

"Make yo sef a home," I heard her say quietly from inside her room.

"OK," I told her, still dumbfounded by the situation.

I walked over and set Sara down into her crib. Newa's mood was very odd. Very sad. And for a minute there, I fully believed that me and my girl might have finally worn out our welcome. But then again Newa didn't seem frustrated or angry. Only sad? But why was she so down? She usually lit up like a Christmas tree as soon as we got there. But not today.

Hmm, I wonder what's wrong.

I paced back and forth for a spell and momentarily turned my feet in the direction of her bedroom, but halted them immediately in fears that I may do more damage if I persisted. I didn't have the foggiest clue what was bothering her, but I was relatively sure that it didn't have anything to do with me or Sara, which made me feel a bit better. I wanted to further my inquiry and try to cheer her up, but worried that I may only upset her more.

With a large dose of apathy, I then said in the direction of the bedroom, "So, um, I'll see you later then, alright? And by the way, thank you so much again, you know, for everything."

I listened up closely at the end of my sermon for any type of acknowledgment from the sweet old lady that I had come to care for so greatly, but I heard nothing. It wasn't until I was almost out the door that I finally made out a faint reply from somewhere beyond her private entrance.

"OK, I see u lato."

"Oh, thank God," I murmured under my breath.

I was happy to hear a response from her, but my heart was still covered in soot by the sudden onset of Newa's uncommon despair. Maybe I was beginning to wear out my welcome. It was a real possibility, but even as I hashed over that theory for a second time, my gut still did not sign off on it. Confused as shit but out of answers, I walked over and gave Sara a quick smooch, then pivoted back in the direction of the way I came in. As I neared the passageway, I walked past a small wooden side table that I had set my car keys upon. In mid stride, I bent over and snatched up the leather pouch. As I executed this maneuver, I accidentally knocked over an open letter that was also making it's home there. Muttering incoherent obscenities, I shook my head, then crouched down and began fumbling around the floor to retrieve the fallen document.
That's when my eyes saw something. That's when they caught a glimpse of a cheaply etched catch phrase that inhabited the contents of the unsealed envelope.
"Happy Birthday Mrs. Newa Quang," read the computer generated headline.
The title words were highlighted in red and followed up by two or three paragraphs of commercial jargon. The letter was dated October 20th.

Yesterday.

It was one of those bulk mailers that large marketing corporations sent out to unsuspecting consumers who usually tended to be seniors. They use someone's birthday which they acquire from a lowlife hacker at a nominal fee, to break the ice and better their chances at winning that person's trust in an attempt to flog whatever the "deal of the week" might be. It was a heartless and criminal invasion of privacy, but to the head honchos, it was just another surefire way of increasing their bottom line. But even with this new evidence, I was still a touch thrown off as to why an event that was as significant as this, would send my dear acquaintance into such a depression? I mean hell, it was just a stupid letter. But things all began to make sense as my eyesight left the page in front of me and started to focus in on the thick layer of dust that was accumulating on Newa's rotary-style phone. It was a device that was, ironically enough, decomposing at the same rate as the row of freshly dusted pictures beside it, the ones of Newa's immediate family. I became sick with anger as one by one, I mentally executed every single one of those heartless bastards within those frames for their lack of respect on the one day of the year when everyone in this world at least deserves the courtesy of a goddam phone call!

A layer of mud covered my soul as I stood there for a moment and mourned for my friend. But that heaviness was quickly lifted by the arrival of a marvelous idea. Without saying anything more, I quietly tiptoed out of the Laundromat and began sub-consciously planning a surprise birthday party for a golden spirit. All morning I scrounged hard for empties. I had the numbers from a price tag I had seen earlier bouncing about my head. They were attached to a particular item, one I had unconsciously spotted a couple of days prior in the window of a gift store not far from the drugstore.

After cashing in my haul, I ducked into the west end of that business and snatched up my pre-chosen token, taking advantage as well, of the happy clerk's offer for a complimentary gift box. As I walked out of that cluttered store and into the custody of the late fall air, I reached down and pulled from a bag, an exquisite container that housed an item I would proudly present to Newa that night.

"World's Greatest Grandma" read the caption underneath the clay character of a bubbly senior engulfed in three dimensional hearts.

I ran my fingers across it and smiled. It was perfect! And I couldn't wait to see the look on my friend's face when I gave it to her.

Stashing my purchase back in it's holder, I darted towards the well known pharmacy that lay within eyeshot to finish off my shopping spree, this time in the form of a real birthday card! When I broke through the doors I looked over and saw that Meridith was not at her till. Not worrying much about that sort of stuff anymore, I spun right and disappeared down the greeting card aisle, returning out a few minutes later with an equally honorable compliment to my unique statue. As I paid for the gift, I casually asked one of the other checkout girls if Meridith was around. I was told that she had left the building at noon to go on her lunch break.

That's weird.

I remembered Meridith telling me once that unless she was on a delivery, she preferred to eat her lunch downstairs in the lunchroom to save the fuel it cost to drive back to her place.

"She'll be back at one o'clock though," a stock boy suddenly interrupted. "You can wait for her here if you like."

I declined the teenagers offer and backed out of the store. The clock on the outside wall said 12:25pm. Thirty-five minutes was way too long a time to stand around and look like a desperate fool. I did intend to come back at one, though, because I really wanted to see her, but I opted out to wait for her somewhere else. I ended up kicking back in an adjacent alley on the opposite side of the street from her building, an area that conveniently faced the warm sun. I recalled the memory of an old bench where the working class people from the strip mall occasionally took a break and had a smoke on. I only had to wait a half hour anyway, which in the scope of things was nothing, especially if it meant seeing Meridith. I found the seat I was looking for and plopped my ass onto it, happily soaking up the inviting rays of the sun while they were still around. The time flew by quickly as I relaxed there and before I knew it, that half hour had disappeared.

Stretching out my limbs I sluggishly rose to my feet, and thanked the gas-engorged sphere for its charity.

Setting my course again for the drugstore, I stumbled out from behind the far side of the building I had just stole some privacy from and wound up seeing Meridith in the same stride. She too was emerging out from a shady corner on the opposite side of her workplaces parking lot. I raised my arm up to catch her attention, but terminated my inviting gesture just in the nick of time when, to my great surprise, I suddenly caught the image of a familiar import shitbox of a car pulling out from the same parking lot behind my girlfriend. It was that prick from the Social Services office, Jeffrey Simmons! I quickly dropped my hand to my side and darted back around the corner of the concrete building that I had recently exited from.

"What the hell is that sonofabitch doing in this part of town?" I wondered as a nervous heat rose to my skin. "Can't people just leave me the fuck alone for two seconds?"

After a long tense pause, I finally crooked my head past the corner of the structure where I was hidden and scoped out the landscape. Looked like the coast was clear! The dope from the draft board was long gone and Meridith was obviously back inside the pharmacy.

"Goddammit!" I hollered as I bolted across the street. "I'm so bloody tired of being followed it's not even funny. It's a good thing I didn't have Sara with me," I growled.

When I got back inside, I saw Meridith standing back again at her station and I gave her a secret wave before slipping quietly into the first aisle. I was only in there a couple of minutes when I heard a sweet and familiar voice drift out from behind me.

"Can I help you with anything Big Boy?"

The smell of my girl's perfume began to wreak it's usual havoc on my loins, but I manage to respond back with an equally witty poke just the same.

"Why yes," I replied without turning my head. "I'm looking for a beautiful green-eyed nymphomaniac who poses as a cashier at a local drugstore so that she can pick up unsuspecting men and perform a bunch of crazy experiments on them. Know where I could find anyone like that?"

I felt Meridith's hand sting my shoulder as I turned around and was met with a weak display of non-verbal punishment.

"Hi baby," I said as I leaned into her semi-amused face and snuck a kiss.

"Hi yourself," she purred back, discarding her charade and wrapping her arms around me.

My other half was in an uncommonly playful mood. I figured this out in a hurry as I felt her hand connect with my body once more, this time in the general vicinity of my ass!

"Ouch," I yelped as she directed me out of the aisle. "What was that for?"

"Nothing, nothing at all."

Her actions were quite spastic and juvenile which I found refreshing. There was no-one in the store so I took advantage of the situation and began to openly flirt with her.

"What are you doing later?" she asked as she flung her elbows onto the counter and shimmied them up to mine. Without speaking I pulled out Newa's birthday card and tipped it upwards.

"I'm throwing a birthday party for a friend, " I said.

Meridith dropped her eyelids down in an exaggerated huff and pushed out her bottom lip.

"But I'll definitely take a rain cheque on that offer," I said in a smile.

Meridith continued on with her melodramatic pout and extended her lip out even further.

"Aww come on little cowpoke," I teased. "I'll saddle you up tomorrow, how's that?"

A productive giggle forced it's way past Meridith's puckered lips so I followed up my exceptional monologue with a more sincere one.

"I will sweetheart OK? I promise, I'll stop in tomorrow."
Meridith didn't say anything else, but I could tell by the understanding look in her eyes that I was off the hook. I checked for witnesses then planted an extra strong kiss on my lover and ducked back out of the store, waving goodbye through the mosaic of the window. I felt bad for not visiting with her longer, but I didn't want to chance staying around just in case the goon from the welfare building was still in the area.
With a little bit of hustle in my walk, I snuck back to my car, and with the last chunk of my money, picked up a blueberry muffin from a nearby bakery and coaxed a lone wax candle out of the store owner for free. The stage was set, and after finishing up my chores as usual, I pretended I had left something of Sara's back in my car and nonchalantly slipped back out the side door of the laundry to retrieve the surprise package that I had stashed in the bushes.

Newa was in a slightly better mood but I could still tell her heart was in disarray. Mind you that all changed the moment I waltzed back through that same door singing Happy Birthday. I strolled in holding her lit muffin in one hand and her "Worlds Greatest Grandma" figurine in the other and all the way, happily chanting out the words to the time-honored jingle. In an instant, I could feel her wounds begin to heal up and close. It was such an amazing sight to watch the expression on her face suddenly burst back to life again. Setting down the pastry at the end of my song, I then motioned with my hands for her to make a wish, but by the look on her face, I think it was safe to say it had already been granted. After she had extinguished the tiny flicker of the candle, I held up the Disney-like character in front of her and said from my heart,

"Newa, this is from me and Sara."

I watched the old woman's eyes begin to swell with joy as she reached out for her present.

"How di yu no?" she asked tearfully.

Taking advantage of this rare opportunity, I leaned softly into my friend and said with a grin....
"Ancient Chinese Secret!"

A rogue snicker escaped from her body and without warning she shot forward and gave me a grand hug.

"Thank you Newa," I whispered. "Thank you so much for all you do for me and my baby girl, I can't tell you how grateful I am."

With the deliverance of my latest compliment, that frail little senior bumped up her affection and near snapped my spine with the increased pressure of her embrace. She was much stronger than she looked I'll tell you! We all had such a great time that night. It was such an excellent party. Newa even fired up her pre 1950's record player and let the scratchy transcriptions rip it up in honor of the occasion. I didn't have a clue what the musicians were saying because it was all in broken Chinese, but she danced up a storm to it anyways. At one point, Newa suddenly disappeared into her bedroom and came back out brandishing an equally archaic camera.

"Smile," she chirped as she prompted me to pose with Sara.

She took a few shots and then I said purely out of fluke, "So when are me and Sara going to get a picture of you huh?"

Newa became silent for a moment and I worried that I might have somehow tripped off another bad memory. But my Asian confidante was not upset at all. The mist that occupied her eyes was only that of joy. Before I could say another word, our Gramma spun around and began rummaging through an old wood desk behind her. A short spell later she let out a high-pitched squeak as she rose up an old white bordered photograph into the air. She was blushing ever so slightly as she pivoted

sideways and handed it over to me. It was a 6 by 5 black and white picture of what
was obviously her but at a slightly younger age, maybe fifty or so. She still basically
looked the same though. I guess the rumor was true that Asian people never looked
their age. I accepted her gift with smiles.

"This will go into my family album," I said, even though I knew that particular
book never existed in a material form.

Not yet anyway.

That night as I sat their sipping tea and happily watching Newa fuss over Sara,
her spirit officially repaired, it began to sink in just how dear she was to me, and
how important she was to my family structure. A secret grin erupted across my face
as I thought back to the day when she first descended upon us from the backroom
with that crazy-looking ninja charm. I could laugh now, but at the time that ancient
heirloom really freaked me out, mainly because it looked more like a lethal weapon
than a newborns plaything. But however menacing it appeared at the time, I soon
learned it's medicinal importance. It was easily the single most effective tool I had in
my arsenal for calming Sara down. One flick of that oriental skull splitter was all it
took. The charm had an equally mesmerizing effect on me too. Many a time I felt my
own limbs fall weak to it's poison. Yes sir, from the very moment I met Newa I had a
funny feeling that she would end up being a very special part of mine and Sara's life.

As the time flowed on and the festivities drew to a close, I lazily bundled up Sara
and said goodnight to our Gramma and our friend with the execution of a long
heartfelt embrace. She was one of us now, and she always would be. As I made my
way to my favorite flea market parking lot that night, a place I hadn't patronized in a
little while, I briefly pondered over the thought of telling Newa about my situation. I
knew in my soul that she deserved to know the truth. I wished everyone could hear
the truth actually. Hell, there were some days when I wanted to walk out into the
middle of an intersection and start yelling out my sins to the whole bloody world, but
in the end I knew that decision would not only jeopardize Sara's safety, but it would
ultimately end my relationship with her too.

Once hidden away for yet another evening, I locked down my mobile fortress and
kissed Sara goodnight.

And as I lay there underneath my covers and stared out of my windshield into the
immense blanket of sky, I found myself becoming very anxious to see Meridith
again. My unconscious jubilation was cut short however, by the untimely arrival of
my favorite sidekick.

So when do you plan on telling Miss. Meridith about who you really are huh?

I did not answer the voice, for just like in the case of Newa, I had come to accept
the hard fact that if I opened my mouth to anyone I would wind up alone again. That
was the bottom line and that fact never weakened. No thanks. I was never going to
chance that again. My eyes shut.

Sara only awoke twice that night for her usual chow and change combo, but settled
quickly each time. When I arose the next morning the inside of the car was already

216

beginning to heat up a bit. The sun, it appeared, was offering forth its last stand against the oncoming colder temperatures. After I had cleaned Sara up at a passing convenience store, I dropped her off at Newa's and turned my tires in the direction of the drugstore. While I drove I began to worry about just how much babysitting Newa was ending up doing for me lately. That was starting to eat away at me, but I'm afraid the Laundromat was the safest place for my baby during the day, at least until they caught that Leon freak and things calmed down a bit. I knew I was being selfish but I had no other choice.

In the highly volatile game I was playing, pride would always have to take a backseat to safety.

I stashed my hotrod about four blocks away from Meridith's workplace and began trudging towards the store. I looked back every couple of minutes or so just to make sure there was no-one on my tail, and for some reason, the decrepit still of that old white clunker decided to stay with me for most of the trip. And even though my miled-out Pontiac was really beginning to resemble something you'd normally see in a bone yard, I really had to give that baby a lot of credit for what it had got me through. But the rust! Man, it was getting so bad I could almost see the road through the floor boards!

When I eventually rounded the corner of the block that housed the nostalgic business, I fished around the insides of my pockets and retrieved all the change I owned, which, I calculated, would be enough for a total of three cans of the good stuff.

That is of course, if they were in the half price bin. So twisting to the left at the last second, I hopped across the weathered asphalt and set my sights for the entrance. As soon as I jumped back up onto the sidewalk again, I caught a glimpse of a big black Mercedes Benz pulling out from one of the parking stalls in the shared compound. I stood their like a stone as it began to exit with my tongue hanging damn near to the ground.

Man, what I wouldn't do to live in one of those babies!

The jealousy continued to ooze out of me as the sleek four-door rolled on by. I tipped my head down at the driver with a double-edged sliver of respect and hatred, but to my surprise, he wasn't that much of a stranger.

"Wait a minute," I growled, as the lone operator flashed me a cocky grin and squealed away under the contempt of his thick dark sunglasses" I know that prick! That's the long haired supplier guy I saw Meridith talking to the other day. It was him, I was sure of it."

"What the fuck are you smiling about asshole?" I hollered as he tore off down the street.

"Goddammit," I sneered as I watched him speed away. "That's a pretty flashy ride for a bloody toilet paper salesman!"

Boy, now I was pissed! Why the fuck was he smirking at me anyway? He doesn't even know me, that sonofabitch! I slumped there on the side of the street and watched the expensive sedan fade off, and even though he was out of sight long before I entered into the pharmacy, the suspicious lump he had planted into my chest was beginning to grow at an alarming rate. I tried momentarily to sever their mutating roots but they were just too thick. When I walked through the front doors of the business, I purposely avoided eye contact with my so-called mate and disappeared quickly down the baby needs aisle right off.

Was Meridith cheating on me? Or was this all just a figment of my jealous imagination again?
Christ, I am getting so sick and tired of this emotional roller coaster shit."

I didn't head to the tills right away. I just hovered in the narrow aisle for a moment and let my conscience battle it out. The mere thought of her playing me was causing my body to vibrate, but then again, what if he was just another "ornery supplier?" To tell you the truth, I had absolutely no idea what was real and what was not anymore. But the one thing I did know was that it was time to confront her about my fears, and hold my ground until I got an answer. I had no other alternative. Ya, it was childish, but it was the only way I could once and for all oust this sick feeling of mistrust that was constantly invading my heart. Whether it was right or wrong, whether Meridith blew up in my face and never talked to me again, I just had to get this thing off my chest. I needed to know if I was the only one in her life.

With a touch of hesitation, I eased my way out of the aisle and saw Meridith standing as usual, in front of her till. Her face lit up the moment she saw me, ironically enough, so I forced out an authentic smile of my own and walked over to her.

"Hi,... how was your night?", she grinned.

"It was great. Listen Meridith," I said right off, "I really can't stay long right now because I have to get back to work. But I was wondering if I could like swing by your apartment later and talk to you for a bit."

"Sure," Meridith said curiously as the smile on her face drifted away.

"Seven o'clock OK?" I asked.

"Seven o'clock is fine, she said quietly."

And with that, I politely wrapped up our little meeting and left the store.

I felt bad for putting a damper on her initial mood, but what else was I to do? The feeling inside me was too heavy and not receding, and there had to be some meaning behind that.

The remainder of the day dragged on miserably as I sifted through the dumpsters and carried out my daily evils.

By 6:45pm I found myself sitting back inside my car on the side of the road about a block away from Meridith's apartment compound. My guts were still churning with unrest like they had been doing all day.

As I sat there, I went over the framework of what I planned to say to her, but when the time did come, I still knew that my studied inquisition would probably just spew out in an incoherent strain of riddles. My heart was lying in my heel when I

"Come on up," I heard Meridith say in a blank tone.

Meridith greeted me with a cautious smile as I stepped into her apartment. It wasn't too hard to see that I was upset.

"I had better make some tea," she whispered as she closed the door. "Looks like you've got something on your mind."

We both sat down at the kitchen table and it was me who initiated the topic of conversation with a bold statement.

"Meridith," I asked soberly. "Am I the only one... you know, that you see in that way?"

I watched her eyes slowly fall down to her cup, but they immediately rose up again and met mine with a sincere answer.

"Yes Eugene. Yes you are. You are the only one."

Well the cat was definitely out of the bag now and I decided quickly that I need not even bring up the debonair supplier. If I was being two-timed, I wanted her to tell me on her own. I had nothing to lose anymore. I waited patiently for some more words to come out of her mouth, but Meridith, it seemed, was struggling to find them.

"Because if there was someone else," I blurted, trying desperately to keep the topic intact. "I mean, cause if you are seeing another guy, well, I just don't know if I'm alright with it, that's all."

I ceased my verbal cues and entered into a vigil of silence. I had made it as easy as I could for her. Now all I could do was wait. After a long pause, Meridith finally got up and pulled her chair up to mine. It was a risky move for her I knew, but she pressed on and eventually drew my body into her embrace. I wanted to resist her. I wanted to scream out so loud at her but my voice would not rise. She just felt too good next to me and without resistance, I watched my rigid stance begin to loosen and crumple under the incredible weight of her affection. I let her console me for while, but this spineless action, I knew, was seriously jeopardizing my chances of a fair trial. I had to know the truth godammit!
I had to see it in her eyes.

I kept the docile charade up for a few more seconds, then without warning my heart broke free from its altered state and took back control of the situation, openly condemning her attempt to sugarcoat the evidence. I wanted an answer and I wanted it now, so I wiggled free from Meridith's grip and laid it all on the line.

"You've got my heart now," I told her. "Please be careful with it."

My girlfriend knew that my request was final, so she slid her hand overtop my own and doused my fears with a whisper.

"You've got mine too," she said. "And please believe me when I tell you that I will never betray that."

Meridith's response was soothing and sincere, but it was followed up with an equally pointed favor.
"But you are going to have to start trusting me. You have to trust me Eugene or all we have is a lie."
Meridith ended her speech with the delivery of a long honest kiss, which easily swallowed up the remainder of my suspicions and freed my untrusting spirit.

"I'm very sorry Meridith, it's just that I am so new to all of this and sometimes it just overwhelms me, that's all."

She didn't respond back to me in words, only passionate acts of confirmation were issued, which suited me just fine.
With our necessary tiff in the past, we left the stark atmosphere of the kitchen and sat ourselves back down in the living room. I didn't stay very much longer. I couldn't, for it was nearing Sara's bedtime, and I still had a few chores to do at the laundry. I felt good though. The demons I had come there with would not accompany me back. The last kiss at the door ended their reign.

Although I felt renewed in my relationship with Meridith, my life once more, took a whole new twist in the week that followed.
For God knows what reason, Jeffrey Simmons, the nerdy-looking prototype from the Social Services office whom I actually feared the least, began to mysteriously pop up everywhere. It was insane! My whole entire world became transformed into a city-sized game of chance.
He was relentless and somehow, was always one step ahead of me. I kept Sara at the laundry as much as I could, but it was still open season on my baby and I the rest of the time, which forced me to further mix up my already taxing array of deception.

During the day when I could keep moving it was OK But at night, now that was a different story.
At night I was always on high alert. As soon as the sun fell, my body would tense up and stay that way. I rarely slept for more than twenty minutes at a time and more often than not, I would end up changing sleep spots two and three times in the same evening just as an added precaution. This system, for now, seemed to be working, but my body was beginning to shut down and become ill from its lack of sleep. I had been too weary lately to make much of a dent in the bottle trade and that added breakdown had put a serious squeeze on my already jeopardized income. I was down to eating only once a day, scavenging my base diet from whatever stray condiments I could get my hands on at the coffee shops and convenience stores. It was true that this latest consequence had withered me down to nothing more than a tower of skin and bone, for most of the money I was able to get went directly into Sara's formula fund and the rest went into my gas tank.
Meridith was continually commenting that I didn't look well and would sneak me

chocolate bars from the store whenever she could, but I always downplayed her concerns.

This was my fight and I would see it through.

The last weekend of October came around far too quickly. It was a Friday, but not just any Friday. It was a particular day that I had been dreading for the last couple of weeks now. It was the date on the calendar when my insurance and registration officially ran out on my car, and I of course, had no possible way of renewing it. God I was broke. I'll tell you, in the last ten days I had really given the word poverty a whole new meaning. And there was another financial time bomb creeping up on me too. Clothing! Not for myself, but for Sara. She had porked out so much in the last two months that all of her jumpsuits were skin tight. I even had slit open the material on the arms and legs to make sure her coverings weren't jeopardizing her circulation and all. But this quick fix would not suffice for very much longer. Sara would need a completely different wardrobe very soon and I had absolutely no idea just how I was going to pull that little magic trick off. But today mind you, had nothing to do with style. No sir, today I was on my way to a certain store outlet to sadly pawn off my wristwatch.

I knew it was coming. I needed to play some financial catch-up here and beside's my car, my watch was the only other real thing I had of value. It wasn't that big of a deal actually. I mean I still had a clock built into my car stereo, but I think it was more due to the fact that I had always held onto the vague idea that as long as I had that watch, I was still real. Don't know why.

When I got to the place, I just covered Sara up and locked the door behind me. I didn't want to take her into a public place, especially a convict-ridden hole like that. As soon as I walked through the door, I looked over at the big greasy heart-attack-in-the-making perched behind the thick glass counter and let out a sigh.

This should be fun.

The store owner was as fat and slimy as the cheeseburger he was inhaling and I knew right then that I was about to get the royal shaft. But I judged my opponent too soon I guess and I nearly keeled over in front of him as he nonchalantly dished me out a whopping thirty dollars for my unremarkable timepiece. I was maybe expecting ten to fifteen bucks tops! But I wasn't about to question him on it or nothing. I just scooped up my loot and headed for the door, just in case he started to have second thoughts about the deal.

I unlocked my door and immediately told Sara the good news. I still couldn't believe it and the first thing I did as I drove off was set the clock on the radio while I still had a ballpark idea what time it was. While I performed this task ,a great song suddenly came over the airwaves so I cranked it up a touch and began to groove.

After the song was over the DJ changed the format and shifted his party-style voice back into a more newsworthy one. I listened on blankly as the faceless announcer read out his spreadsheet.

"The local police and FBI are still searching for the latest victim of the infamous Serial Abductor. Twelve year old Justin Clemmant recently disappeared on his way to school in an upscale suburb of the city's west side, bringing the latest number of these abductions to a shocking total of nine. The authorities assure us that whoever is responsible for these crimes will be brought to justice one way or the other, but to date, they still have no legitimate leads."

I let the transmission play out for a few more seconds, then shut it off. The dismal story had been all over the news lately and it cast a shadow of despair across the mood of the entire city.

"Who was it?" I would hear people say. "What kind of animal would do such a thing?"

I would drop my head in secret as I listened in on their conversations and it made me sick to my stomach to know that I held the remedy to all their fears, but chose to let them burn.

But I loved Sara too much and I would not break my silence. I coveted her with all my heart and no matter how wrong it was for me to stay anonymous, my loyalty always sat with her and my quest to remain her guardian.

But there was something different about this latest crime. It was hugely publicized. The cops, the media, the Mayor, and everyone else in the know seemed to be focusing in on this recent atrocity with great interest.

The kid's parents must be rich.

It was the only thing that made sense to me. You know it's funny how the almighty dollar speeds up the order of priority in an investigation. People are greedy these days, especially people in power. Personally, I don't think anybody in those circles really gives a shit who's missing unless of course, they are financially motivated to. And I admit I have had the odd vision of my own in the last little while. It's actually a picture of someone looking down at the day's headlines and seeing the images of me and Sara painted across them with the same headline above us. But I knew that it would never go down that way. For if anything ever did happen to us, no-one would ever know about it. Why? Because we were poor. Because we were nobodies in the eyes of the world. We would simply just disappear and that would be the end of it.

The grim realization of our place on the food chain sent a cold shiver down the length of my back. I guess it was the basic understanding that mine and Sara's whole existence could be wiped clean in an instant, that caused my insides to suddenly twist. That same demoralizing thought terrorized me for the remainder of the day, and subsequently, I didn't end up accomplishing much of anything in the form of work. I mean I picked up the odd can here and there, but for the most part I just drove from spot to spot and hid us away. I was becoming increasingly paranoid. I felt like I was always being watched, followed.

My health was also declining. My joints never stopped aching and my throat was always red. I'd have greatly welcomed a night on the couch with my nurse, but Meridith had told me in our last conversation that she had a lot to do in the days to come and a get together was not possible. Because of this hiatus, I ended up having ample time to starve to death and ponder over my life, and just how crazy it had all become.

I knew that when I made the decision to keep Sara there would definitely be challenging obstacles. I didn't however, expect that those difficult times would include being hunted down by a psychotic cult member or a promotion-hungry government worker. Nope! Never saw that coming, but it held true that I had to face some cold hard facts about the future now.

I would never abandon Sara, no way. That wasn't even a distant option. I had made a promise to her and I intended to keep it. But sewn into the fine print of that same document, there was also a clause that stated that I would keep her warm and fed too, and lately that particular task was becoming more and more difficult to uphold. I was confused towards the end of the day, but I did come to a final conclusion about one thing.
Meridith deserved to know the truth.

For better of for worse, I had to spill my guts as to what me and my baby really were. I had to tell her everything. She had earned the right to know. And Newa too, for the same reason. But Meridith, I decided, would be first, for it was becoming so hard to keep up with the incredible charade of lies I was entangled in, that some days I wasn't even sure just what the truth was myself. Now the decision to spill my guts did not come about easily, for I knew all too well that once I did tell her the truth, she might very well brand me a fucking liar and walk away, a move that she had every right to do. That was my number one fear, that she would leave me and I would lose the trust and devotion of the one person who chose, in this undiscerning world of vanity, to look past all the ugliness in my life and seek out the man I always hoped was there.

I was taking a great risk in telling her, I knew that.
But I was also taking an equally dangerous chance by not, either.

And I knew it was lame, but I did opt out to confess my sins to her in the form of a note. It was chickenshit I know, but I was so bloody scared to face her. I mean after all, every single thing she had learned about me and hopefully come to admire was a complete pile of shit. I was ashamed of myself. And there was just no way I could look her in the eyes and tell her that. So I ended up devising a plan where I would drop by the drugstore and see Meridith just before it closed. At that point I would casually set a date to meet with her the following afternoon at a side street cafe not far from her apartment. The next day was a Saturday, and I knew it was her day off. Once inside with her, I would hammer back a quick coffee and pointedly emphasize just how much she meant to me. Then I would wrap up our meeting with a long sincere kiss, give her the note and get out of there.

After that, I would let her be for a day or two so that she could let all the things I confessed to her sink in. Then, if by some strange miracle she still wanted to continue a relationship with me once she discovered the real facts behind my life, well, I guess we could hook up again sometime and start fresh. No lies, no deception. Just the truth from then on in. Like a new beginning.

With a nervous heart, I put on my bravest face and headed in the direction of the old pharmacy. I was sticking my neck out that was for sure, but in the same sense, it did feel immensely liberating to know that I would soon tell her something that wasn't a fairy tale. My legs were shaking with fear as I stumbled towards Meridith's till. I set a couple of cans of baby formula onto the counter and prepared to tell my only girlfriend one final lie.

"Hey, do you work here?" I said goofily.

Meridith didn't answer me back, thank God. She just looked up at me and smiled in a "Don't quit your day job" sort of way. After she rang through my purchase, she spoke the heavenly phrase I had been waiting for too many days to hear.

"So what are you doing later?" she asked, as she closed the till and leaned toward me with her beautiful face.

It was a sentence that both healed and hurt me at the same time. On one hand, it was such a high to know that I still held a position somewhere in her heart, and that my jealous inquisition in the days prior had not compromised that.
But it was also true that I had to now take that freshly repaired trust and challenge it once more.

"I, uh, I'm just going to take it easy tonight and try to get rid of this sore throat you know. Gotta nip it in the bud."

Meridith again pushed out her lip and began to disagree. "I was thinking you could bring Sara by and we could all go out for a walk in the park or something," she said optimistically.

My girlfriend's provocations were starting to wreak havoc on the loose mosaic of my plan, so I feverishly began to search for a backup excuse. I had to politely resist her very tempting offers for it was imperative to the big picture. It was true that I needed the extra shuteye to combat my illness, but it was more to the point that I needed the extra time to draft up a finely-tuned and well-constructed letter explaining to the woman in front of me that I was a total fake.
But a total fake who had fallen deeply in love with her.

"I'd love to," I balked sincerely. "I honestly would, but I really have to attack this damn cold tonight you know. But hey," I said, executing the first phase of my master plan. "Lets get together tomorrow afternoon over at that little cafe down the way from your apartment. You know, the funky one with all the paintings in it. We can hook up then and do coffee, how's that?"

Meridith drew out her shtick for a few more seconds but then released her grip on my conscience and said the words I was waiting for.

"OK Mister, I'll let you off the hook this time, but don't let it happen again."

"Aye-Aye Captain," I agreed, snapping my hand toward my forehead.

It was all set up. She bought my story and agreed to meet me at the coffee shop at 2pm the next day.

I left the pharmacy, my task a success, and started toward the Laundry to pick up my little girl who had been in the affectionate care of her Grandma since noon. As I drove on, it did give me some comfort to know that from now on, I would no longer have to tell Meridith any more fables. One way or the other, this lie would end.

After I had finished my cleaning, I sat down with my friend and had some tea. The wonderful feeling of security I always gained when I walked through that old side door had once more worked its magic.

I enjoyed an unprecedented sense of connection with Newa nowadays. I had never really gotten to know my own grandmother for she died when I was very young. But by getting this second chance, this gift of a no longer lonely old widow, I occasionally caught myself wishing I had somehow been able to enjoy more time with my own. So I could see what she was like. So that I would know how she lived and the things she cherished. Nevertheless, I was still grateful to the powers that be for providing me with such a worthy substitute to trust and to learn from.

As I sat their and sipped my drink, I just couldn't get over how much better Newa looked now, as opposed to when I first met her. She just looked so rebuilt. Her clothes were neater, her hair was trim, and her eyes twinkled with joy. It was a look she had long deserved. As our visit drew to a close, I packed up my angel and gave Newa a long deep hug, and once out the door, I set a course back through the extravagant series of pathways towards my hidden Firebird that I had mapped out earlier on. It was tucked carefully away under a willow tree about four blocks to the east, and when my eyes reconnected with it, I stood in the shadows for a minute by the corner of a sleeping house and scanned over the perimeter, just to make sure.

It was clear. Only a quiet empty street stood in my way now.

After a short and uneventful sprint I was inside my car, had it started, and was already driving away.

It was dusk. Seven twenty pm to be exact.

It would be dark in about twenty minutes or so, but that was all the time I needed to get my ass over to a secure sleep spot that lay in waiting approximately fifteen blocks to the north and shut her down.

I came upon a yellow light about halfway to my destination and decided not to chance it.

After all, I was driving an uninsured, unregistered car with an illegal child residing in it so, you know, I made the call! I was only stopped at the light for about five seconds when a long, wide-bodied car made a sudden left turn and drove past me.

As my eyes met the driver's, my blood froze solid and I watched in horror as the man who boasted himself a Druid, locked sights with me and proceeded to visciously swing his car into my lane, a mere two cars behind me.

It was the one and only Leon Jenkins, and he was hot on my trail. And worse than that, he now also knew what I drove.

"Shit!" I hollered, as I began desperately trying to absorb the severity of the situation and plan my escape.

Don't panic Eugene. Think it out man, just think it out.

But the moment I figured I had pulled it together enough to handle the task, I was hit with yet another blow.

A police car suddenly ground to a halt at the edge of the crosswalk directly across the intersection in from me.

"Jesus Christ!" I yelled again, "Is this ever going to end? I'm done for, this is it!"

If that cop runs my plate, he'll pull me over for sure. And if that happens Leon will surely get us because that the cop will automatically ground my car once he learns of it's illegal state. And then he will force me to get out and walk.

It was protocol! The cop didn't even have a choice in the matter. After that, all Leon would have to do is wait in silence for the right moment and wham, it would be all over! He'll ace me in a heartbeat and nab Sara for sure.

I felt the pressure in my veins skyrocket as the intensity of this new development began to take root, and my chest became even tighter as I secretly watched the stone-faced badge tilt his head down towards his computer while my car idled helplessly in direct view of him.

Fuck! He's doing it. He's running my plate. Godammit Eugene, how could you let yourself get into this mess?

With my life now in pieces, the only thing I could really do is sit and wait.

Wait for the hammer to fall.

I looked over at Sara and fought hard to regain my composure through the stillness in her eyes but it was too late.

The light had turned green.

My future hung dangerously in the balance as I let my foot off the brake and slowly accelerated forward. I didn't make eye contact with the cop as I passed him because that was just suicide, but out of the corner of my eye, I did see his own head tilt over at me as we passed.

I couldn't take anymore! I thought about just laying on the gas and making a break for it, but I knew that was a race I would never win. Without moving my head I dropped my eyes down to the side mirror, and in a wave of disbelief, I watched the amber glare of his brake light suddenly come on.

Keep your cool Eugene. Just keep it together and try and put some distance between you and that cop!

Slowly and deliberately I began applying more and more pressure to the accelerator. After a few seconds I glanced into my rear view mirror again to face the music, even though I had a pretty good idea of how that song was going to sound.

But to my great astonishment I did not see the outline of the squad car flipping a one eighty.

Uh Uh! Nope, all I saw when I stared into that mirror was the ass end of that black and white getting smaller and smaller, its brake lights now terminated. I near pissed myself in relief, but my rejoicing was short lived, for I still had a murderer on my tail and unfortunately, he was not about to just drive away.

Shifting my eyes back down to the side mirror, I zeroed in once more on the reflection of Leon's boat.

He was still dangerously close but just as I began to re-align my vision, I also picked up on an intermittent signal that was chattering away in front of him. It was a light. A signal light!

Turns out the mid-sized station wagon that separated me and my foe decided to make a left turn at the last second. Now I don't usually subscribe to karma, but tonight I had no choice but to accept the fact that it did exist. And I wasted no time in taking advantage of that beautifully-timed Godsend by laying on the juice.

I knew Leon was not stupid enough to suicide pass someone at a major intersection with a police car in the area, so with a steady but lightning pace I leaned back and watched the intersection that held my enemy at bay become farther and farther away.

When I crested the top of a nearby hill and lost complete sight of my attacker, I immediately spun my rig off onto the first side street I came to and disappeared deep into the armpits of that neighborhood.

I drove in a zigzag pattern, weaving steadily back in the same direction from which I just came. I figured Leon would never expect such a brash move from me so that's exactly what I did, and within fifteen minutes I was back on the freeway with no trace of my aggressor in sight. I drove out into the night towards a backup sleep spot in a quiet, family-oriented district. It was a district that I had not yet exploited, but it seemed safe.

Once there, I puttered around the medium-sized suburb for a while until my eyes spotted a favorable scenario.

It was a dark cubby hole burrowed into an alleyway that would house my family tonight. It was nice and private and you couldn't even tell it was there from the street. After backing my crypt into the said spot, I killed the engine and allowed my pupils to adjust to their new surroundings. My heart rate was slower now, but the presence of one horrifying detail was still keeping it's rhythm strong.

He saw my car.

Leon saw my goddam car! I repeated the sentence in my head over and over again until the words grew muffled.

Now the game was different. Everything was different and the odds rested heavily in Leon's favor.

Now that he knew what I drove it would be far easier for him to track me down. The only thing I could do is keep running. Keep moving and hiding like the wind, and hope to hell that I was just as impossible to catch. I didn't sleep a wink that night. I didn't even put my seat back. All I did was sit there, stone-faced and upright like a soldier as I guarded my precious cargo. The hours drug on slowly, but that, for once, was OK, for it gave me lots of time to lay down my extravagant confession to Meridith. It also gave me the solitude to sit back and take a good long look at my life. It was something I really needed to do.

I confessed everything in that note. I didn't hold back one single detail. I also apologized to her relentlessly, but at the same time, backed up my apologies with constant testimonials of my love for her.

I told her that was the one thing that I never had to disguise.

I said that I would understand if she decided to sever our ties and never speak to me again. It was an honorable move, but I knew in my heart that I would never recover from such a blow.

I wrote and wrote for the better part of the night. I explained to her that I would leave Sara at the Laundromat during the day and go out in search of bottles and cans, and that was my actual job. Not the puffed up engineering by product I boasted about when we first met. I let it all out. I didn't want to feel guilty or ashamed anymore. She was going to get the straight and narrow and that was that.

After I had read over my finished confession for the last time, I have to admit I felt so much better. It was like this huge weight I had been carrying around suddenly turned into air and floated away.

"The truth shall set you free," I said to the face in the mirror, and I prayed that saying held merit.

Dawn announced it's presence with a sharp ray of sunlight that broke over the horizon and pierced my eye's.

My baby woke up shortly after that so I fished her out of her bed and quietly fed her. I loved Sara.

I loved her far beyond the borders of this world. I was eternally bonded to her spirit with a kind of connection that could only be achieved and enjoyed by the person who puts in the commitment to grow it. And even while my mind was struggling to sort out all of the psychotic events of the previous hours, I still caught myself being carried away by the sheer power of her mystical stare.

It was uncanny how they never dimmed or let me down. No matter what the situation was, her tiny eye's would always make it through the smoke and find me. We sat there and watched the sun come up, me and my baby. Eventually, I peered down at the note I had prepared for Meridith and let out a tired sigh. I had an uneasy feeling about venturing back into that part of town and handing over to my girlfriend, the damning piece of paper I held in my hand. And there was no question too, that Leon Jenkins would be initiating a relentless crusade to apprehend me now. Now that he knew what my car looked like.

But I just had to go back in and give Meridith that note. That was an important step in my life. To come clean with her, then hold my breath for the outcome.

We stayed in our hiding place until half past noon, and after changing Sara for the last time, I dumped the excrement out the window, then eased my car back out onto the empty street. I stopped at a gas station on the way to clean myself up a bit and I also gave Sara a good scrub as well.

As I neared the coffee shop in question, I could tell from a good block away that there was absolutely no parking available beside the restaurant. It was a Saturday afternoon and the little cafe was packed to the gills so I pulled off into an empty space on the side street leading up to the place and checked the clock in my dash. "1:35pm".

I was early, but I decided to go in and try to get us a table anyway. After tucking Sara underneath my arm, I reached for the note on the console, gave it a quick once over, then neatly folded it up and stuffed it into my side pocket. I wasn't really worried about our safety today, not here anyway. This was a public place and there were enough people walking about to easily conceal me and my little girl away from the eyes of our enemies.

So, depressing the lock on the door, I slowly made my way down the street. My feet were heavy from the sleepless night I had just endured, and my eyes too, blurred with ease. But I walked on unfazed, determined to set things straight. As I started to get closer to our meeting place, I spotted the hazy outline of two people standing side by side in the parking lot beside the coffee shop. I thought nothing of it at first, except for the obvious jealousy I housed towards them in finding such a close stall. But as my body shuffled its way closer, the identity of the two figures became crystal clear.

It was Meridith, and the slick, long-haired playboy she had sworn up and down to me never existed in her personal life.

In a disgusted frenzy I changed my course and crept up on them, ducking behind a large white cargo van that sat not far away from the happy couple to try and hear what they were saying. Was I upset? You can't fucking imagine. But I was also in a position to finally hear the truth.

With my back sucked up against the van, I strained my ears to the max, but there was just too much traffic going by to pick up any of their conversation so I inched my head around the back end of the van and began to spy on them. Meridith had her hands in her pockets and wasn't saying much. The arrogant salesman whom I had come to despise by now, had both of his hands on her shoulders and he appeared to be flirting with her.

Meridith was just taking it all in with a dazed look on her face which did nothing but enrage me further.

I turned my head back into the safety of the van and examined the ground. I didn't know what to do. I was so furious I could have spit fire. Do I walk right up to her and tell her off, tell her she's a fucking liar? She definitely had that coming! Or do I leave it alone and just wash my hands of her? My brain was in a state of emotional disarray, and once again my heart lay dead in my soles. I briefly searched around for my old friend Hatred in hopes he would ease some of my pain, but he had deserted me long before and I'm afraid I was on my own this time. I peered around the end of the van again and saw pretty much the same scene, only this time, Meridith's secret acquaintance had taken off his sunglasses and was closer to her.

"Ya", he was good looking. And his clothes oozed of money too. I had to face the facts. He was everything I fucking wasn't.

Worried that I may be spotted, I went to draw back and wait for another opportunity but I was too slow and the stranger that held my so-called girlfriend suddenly caught me spying on him. I then watched as the unnamed man donned a smirk, then passionately embraced my ex-lover in a kiss.

I turned away.

I had to for I felt a gag reflex suddenly come up from the back of my throat. But my sadness was murdered in an instant by my anger and without mercy, I bolted out from my cover and yelled out to Meridith at the top of my lungs.

"You told me you would never betray me," I screamed. "You told me godammit!"

Sara was now crying away loudly and deep inside, so was I. Meridith suddenly brandished a surprised look on her face as she spun around and pushed the dashing man away from her in disbelief.

I saw red. I saw red and fire and my eyes began to purge forth that poison.

With Sara still bawling away in one arm, I pulled out the neatly folded note with the other and crumpled it up in front of her. Then I threw it in her face.

I looked over at the man who stood beside her. He still had a smug look on his face that reeked of enjoyment at the unfolding situation. I turned around and fled away. I could no longer bear that sight.

As I ran off, I could hear Meridith yelling to me in the background.

"Wait Eugene. Wait," I could hear her say, but I ignored her pathetic apologies. I had seen all the evidence I needed thank you very much! I understood it perfectly now.

When I reached my car I jumped in quick and hit the engine. As I rounded the corner by the cafe, I saw Meridith there alone on the boulevard with her arms crossed in shame, but I did not look at her as I passed by. Nope! My heart would not allow it. I simply turned the corner and sped off.

I drove like a madman, keeping my speed high as I fishtailed back onto the freeway and headed north. I kept my gauge pinned as I drove. I wasn't exactly sure where I was going, but I was certain that Saint Anger was in full control of the gas pedal. I sped towards nowhere for a long time. I had to get out of the city. I had to get away from Meridith and the pain her infidelity was inflicting on me.

I finally pulled over about thirty miles up the highway into a truck stop and shut down my livid car. The sorrow attached to the event I had just witnessed was starting to oust its angry ally and a million questions began to race through my mind, but only one stark fact ended up making the final cut. She was kissing another man. I had to come to terms with that knowledge. The sobering fact was that Meridith had been unfaithful and that I was never the only one in her intimate life. The truth had just played itself out right there in front of me and I realized then, that I'd been living out someone else's fantasy.

Loneliness and betrayal immediately morphed back into hell-bent rage as the little voice in my head began to call me out.

You see Eugene you stupid fuck! You see what relationships bring you huh? Pain, you hear me, pain!
I thought you'd have learned your lesson by now but I guess I was wrong wasn't I?

The overpowering entity continued to crucify me without end and I just let it. I didn't try to challenge it at all because it was absolutely right! I was crazy if I ever thought that an upper crust woman like that would ever seriously consider drawing her ship in for a shiftless fuck like myself.

"You can take the man out of the gutter, but you can't take the gutter out of the man," I yelled.

I knew I fully deserved the wrath I was presently immersed in and as I drifted
in and out of emotion, I looked down onto my body at the crisp new clothes that
Meridith had purchased for me. But they didn't feel the same way as they did when I
first put them on. They felt like they were lined with thorns now and I began ripping
them off my body as quickly as I could, replacing back to my skin the worn out rags
that never should have left my homeless ass to begin with.

After a while I looked over at the clump of flashy material that now lay dead on the
passenger floor beside me and accepted one simple fact:

Eugene, did you really think that a new set of clothes could really change your life?

In a fit of rage I then bent over and gathered up the tragedy that occupied the
passenger's side cubby of my rig and coldly threw the flashy duds out the window.
After that my nerves fell still. I hadn't a clue what my next move was. The only thing
that I knew for sure was that my heart had been seriously wounded and was now
pushing out tons and tons of thick red blood with my every breath.

I needed to disappear.

I had to get back to some uninterrupted place so that I could heal up and get my
head back on straight again. With no set destination in mind, I pulled back out onto
the interstate and headed towards the serenity of the mountains that lay in front
of me. It was time to escape the grave mess I had all too willingly created and
re-acquaint my soul with an old friend by the name of Mother Nature. I wanted to
ask her for help. I needed her to provide me with the strength and wisdom I would
require to overcome this latest round of genocide.

I knew that I was I was just running away. Running away from Jeffrey, from Leon,
from everybody.

Even, I thought, from myself.

But I desperately needed to regroup and be alone with Sara again, like it was in
the beginning. Before everything went to Hell. I was looking forward to letting my
baby's innocence recharge me and replace the pieces of my heart that had been deliberately torn off. I drove on and on, deep into the concealment of the majestic hills,
and I began to think back of how good it would feel when me and Steve would go
out into the woods for our summer pilgrimage when we were kids. I remember the
elation of leaving the meanness of the city behind and drifting out into the countryside. The memories were surprisingly intact. And the visions too, of me and my best
friend exploring the valley in the middle of the night also remained vivid.

Everything was so alive and fresh back then. The animals, the trees, the earth. They
would all wake up and prowl around with us. It was like hearing a million voices,
but never seeing a face.

Eventually my dreams of my youth began to slowly dissolve as my left foot woke
up out of its slumber and crawled over to the brake pedal. I was well into the forest
by now and had come up upon a narrow dirt road off to the right which I took. It led
me like an angel deep into the secluded perimeter of an old manmade campsite that
lay dozing beside a small creek. Pulling carefully onto the side of the open nook,
I felt the wheels jump over and grab the shallow indentations of the last vehicle to
visit this place and I followed them in. Now it was time to set up camp and believe

it or not, I was... well, semi-equipped. I had an ancient tent stuffed underneath the mountain of filth in my trunk. It was full of rips and stains but from what I could tell, it was still functional. I tried to pawn it off a long time ago, but the second hand dealers would just laugh as soon as I walked through the door, it was in that rough of shape. This would always piss me off, but now I understood why. I guess everything happens for a reason.

Once I retrieved and laid out the archaic web of nylon, string, and poles next to my car, I was almost ready to gather it up again and throw it right back where it came from, it was that bad. But patience ended up by my side and after about forty minutes, I stood there leaning up against my Firebird, staring down in awe at the finished product. My old tent was terribly ugly, but it was livable. As soon as my sleeping bag was added to the construction, I gathered some sticks and twigs and arranged them inside the roughly assembled fire pit that was already adorning the center of the clearing. They lit up easily and the smell from the smoke began to work it's magic. It was five o'clock now, and with all my work complete it was time to fetch my tot and give her some din-din.

I spotted a small log not far off in the trees which I uprooted and dragged over to the fire to use as a seat. Sara was very curious and fussing about. I knew she was wondering just what the heck I was up to so I loaded up her bottle and brought her out beside the fire. She fell quiet the instant I wiggled the King Kong sized nipple in front of her, and with her calm, rightfully enough, came my own. I was beginning to wonder who was feeding whom here. We had an awesome evening. Me and Sara just sat in front of the ever- consuming fire for hours until we watched the last morsel of flame surrender itself to the atmosphere and fade off. It had been a long time since I'd done anything recreational and it felt great not to look over my shoulder every five minutes.

We slept that night like a couple of stones. I kept my big hunting knife within arm's reach and tucked Sara in close beside me just to be on the safe side. But it wasn't needed, for Mother Nature, a person who I was again indebted to, did her part to protect us. She also provided us with a little chow too, when late in the afternoon that following day, as my stomach rumbled on in protest, a curious fool's hen graced the outer edge of our campsite. It flew into a nearby shrub about twenty feet from the car.

"I'm sorry Mr. Chicken," I said honestly as I grabbed a fallen stick. "But I am very hungry right now so please don't take this personally."

I told Sara to shut her eyes and as I crept up behind the wild bird and delivered my blow. The animal did not suffer. I killed the native fowl in one swift arc and then began to pluck it eagerly. I was no Great White Hunter by any stretch, but the fact remained that I was starving ,and I was sick. My body was in desperate need of nourishment in order for it to acquire the strength to fight off all of its infections. And when the task was completed and the last clump of feathers drifted to the ground, I cooked up that softball-sized carcass using my hunting knife as a spit. I silently thanked the animal too, for giving me it's life, for dying so that my body and my health could benefit from its much needed nutrients. After I was done my supper I found a spot in the creek

232

where the water was spilling over the rocks and took a swig. In a victorious rumble I felt my body start to break down the meat and skin it had just consumed and begin to transporting it hastily throughout my rundown frame.

Within minutes I started to feel better. My joints stopped aching so much and my energy level rose a bit too.

The overhaul was long overdue and throughout the rest of the day and into the night, I mainly just sat there, perched on that log, and watched over Sara as the smoke from the fire kept me sedated.

I knew my little girl was very much enjoying her vacation, and God, so was I. And you know, the more I stared across at the awesome mountain formations, the more I realized I needed them in my life. I wanted to feel their presence and inherit their wisdom. It took awhile, but after a long, long serenade underneath the majestic hue of those giant hills, I did come to a final conclusion.

I had to leave the city.

It was quite an emotional decision, believe it or not. I mean after all, be it good or bad, I had called that dirty old cement shithole my home now for so long that however crazy it might have sounded, I still felt like somewhat of a deserter. But since everything had fallen apart with Meridith, I could feel my loyalty to it notably lessened.

My verdict of course, was also heavily influenced by the unending game of cat and mouse I endured on a daily basis with my newly-acquired foes. That was the main reason. I mean Christ, if I wasn't dodging Simmons, I was running for my life from Leon. It was utter madness and I'd had enough. Maybe me and Sara would have better luck in a smaller community. Then I might have a chance at landing a steady job or going back to school or something. Yep, a fresh start in a new environment could be just the edge I needed to get back on track. To find the daytime world.

I concluded the idea was excellent and the foundation of it really gave me a long overdue shot in the arm.

I immediately began planning for my departure, coming to the conclusion that I would venture back into the city the next day for one last purpose, to say goodbye to my dear friend Mrs. Newa Quang. In theory, I could have just driven back out onto the freeway and continued heading north en route to the new life I now dreamt of, but I had to tell my friend of my plans in person. She deserved that for all she had done for me and Sara. I also knew that it was going to be a very long time, if ever at all, before I saw that wonderful senior again, and if that was to be true, then I wanted to be in her gracious company at least once more.

I wanted to talk with her and let her hold Sara so that I could witness the joy, so that I could see the love that my baby always brought to her eyes, just one last time.

Before the dawn broke the following day, I was already packed up and ready to roll. I was so excited at the fact that I was about to start over that my eyes sprang open before the sun. Firing up my wagon, I waved goodbye to the therapeutic clearing and idled out of the forest. It was Monday, October 31st.

It was Halloween.

A vision of the evil mask that occupied my dreams briefly made an appearance behind the mirror of my eyes, but I didn't ponder it's haunting for too long for I had grown tired of it's unwarranted pursuit. I set a course back towards the city and settled in for the drive. I could still smell the smoke from the campfire on my skin and it made me smile. I felt thoroughly refreshed. The unlikely dinner I had roasted the night before turned out to be all my body needed to begin its repairs. The tranquility of the countryside had a lot to do with it too, and I secured a pact as I drove, to do that sort of thing more often in the future, when I was back on my feet again.

I arrived two blocks away from the Laundromat at exactly 8:05am. Not bad timing I thought, considering the morning traffic and all. While I crept through the alley in the direction of Newa's place, a trickle of despair began to overcome me. I was sad because I knew how desperately I was going to miss her, this wonderful spirit who had played such a major role in mine and Sara's life. I definitely planned to keep in touch with her by phone no matter what. I mean that was a given, but I guess it was just the fact that from this day on, our lives were going to change. It was not going to be like it was. I was not going to be seeing Newa on a regular basis anymore like I had done in the past. It was a habit I had grown very fond of and I knew I was going to miss her giddy laugh and terrible English. But most of all, I was going to miss her, the loving old woman who nobody in the world took the time out to trust except for the likes of a homeless bottle picker and an abandoned baby.

Pausing the avalanche of memories I was currently reviewing, I pushed my way through the thick brush and fell out into the hollow space in front of the side door. I raised my hand up to give it a few knocks, but to my surprise it was already open about five inches. That was strange I thought, for Newa always kept her doors locked when she was inside. Maybe she didn't close it hard enough, I figured.
Cautiously sliding my body through the opening, I started to call out her name.

"Newa?" I said quietly. "Newa, it's me Eugene. Are you home?"
She did not answer?
Maybe she is still asleep? ..."Shit, I mumbled". I hope I didn't wake her up!
I tiptoed in a little further as my eyes focused in on the imprint of her bedroom door. In a squint I realized that it was wide open and her bed was already made. Hmm, that seemed even stranger.

"Oh wait a minute Eugene," I said aloud. "She's probably in the laundry emptying the money out of the machines."

Confident in my judgment, I then turned to the right and prepared to walk toward the entranceway that separated the two entities. That's when my eyes caught sight of something.

Something horrible.

It was a scene that I know my mind was never going to let me forget. Newa was lying on the floor face first with her head halfway underneath the coffee table. Her hands were secured behind her back with nylon ties and her body was stiff and life-less. A coagulated pool of blood loomed beneath her open throat and her eyes were glazed over and dull.

She was dead.

Oh God... Oh my God!! Newa was dead. She was dead and I knew exactly why.

I knew right fucking then that it was because of her involvement with me.

"Oh Jesus, Oh Jesus no," I said as I began pleading up to the heavens and begging the higher power to reverse the clock and make things right again. But God did not turn his head and acknowledge me.

"I'm sorry Newa," I cried as I knelt beside her in agony. "Oh God I'm so sorry."

I set Sara in her bed and embraced the lifeless body of my friend as I wept on without pause for her return.

Things got blurry after that, but when I eventually did come out of my warranted state of shock, I found myself sitting back inside my car, idling quietly in front of the deserted parking lot of the very same coffee shop I had camped out in my first winter as a nameless man. I don't remember even starting my car, but there I was. I recalled as I peered up at the old dwelling how it had gone bankrupt a couple of years earlier and been boarded up. The only evidence of its life now, was the heavily vandalized and burnt-out sign that lay decomposing above the entrance of the long abandoned venture.

"Mocha Heaven," read the once robust caption.

I thought my mind might soon be full of sentimental residue at this sight, but in the end, all I saw was a cheaply-made rectangular bubble with red paint on it.

I was there for a long time, that I am sure of. I just kept rocking Sara back and forth, back and forth. It must have been a good hour and a half before I was even able to speak, and the first word out of my mouth was Police.

I had to call the Police.

But you can't do that. You call the cops and you go to jail, get it? Do you think for one second that they are going to buy your cockamamie and unproved story about a crazed baby-sacrificing cult? Huh? Do you?

No way Eugene. You will be handcuffed and in the back of a squad car so fast it will make your head spin.

And then you'll be up on a murder rap.

The voice disappeared after that, but I knew it would be back in an instant if I persisted in challenging it.

The time ticked on painfully as I struggled to keep my emotions together and try to find even a speck of rational thought within me. It was true though, about the Police. If I did call them, there was no way that they'd believe me. My situation was simply too unreal.

And the voice also had another good point. Newa's murder would definitely be pinned on me. That was also a fact. It was just too easy, too cut and dried, and the authorities wouldn't be able to resist it.

And I was just about to sign off on that virtue, when another uninvited spirit barged it's way into my skull.

"Godammit Eugene, Newa is dead for Christ Sakes! Doesn't that say anything to you? This has gone too far. She's dead Eugene, DEAD! And you and Sara are next. If you care in the least about the little girl you are holding, then you must do the right thing, and you know what that is.
Godammit Eugene... You know!

I let the wise voice yell on at will because what it was saying was the truth, and I could no longer convince myself that everything was going to be alright. That fantasy was now lying dead on the floor beside Newa.

It was at that moment that the single most devastating fact I was ever about to accept came crashing through the gates of my soul, and with one almighty blow, did annihilate my entire world.

Sara was no longer safe in my care.

The brutal truth had finally surfaced and I felt my heart begin to die. Its disease quickly spilled down into my stomach and forced it to retch and abort. I flung my car door open in a mad frenzy and let the putrid evidence spew out and stain the pavement below me.

My dream was over.

And all the groundbreaking triumphs and honest intentions I had persevered with for so long were now relentlessly ambushing me from every direction. Sara, no matter where I ran, or what new town I was in, would forever be in danger if she was in my presence. For now, not only was I untraceable, but I was also a witness to a murder. I was a legitimate echo in a trial, and a voice that would eventually be silenced.

I heard my baby begin to make a fuss and start to cry, but I couldn't move. I was paralyzed with guilt. I tried to look down at her, but my conscience refused the action.

It refused to allow her to look up at a failure.

Sara didn't see it that way though and continued to wail on loudly, trying desperately to get my attention and tell her side of the story.

After a few minutes, my body was no longer able to contain it's sorrow and it fell over onto the passenger seat. I buried my face in the tangled web of blankets that Sara had called her home now for so long and let go. A tidal wave of agony rushed out of me as I surrendered unto my angel, every last ounce of wisdom I had left.

The time that went by from then on was very much like a hallucination. Everything started coming at me in slow motion. Hazy shades of incomprehensible sights and sounds flowed through me at random.

It was as if I had broken through into another dimension, an anesthetic purgatory where I felt nothing. No pain, no thought.

Nothing.

The only thing I could make out for sure was the dull rhythm of my heartbeat. My euphoria however, did not last as long as I would have liked it to because no matter how high you get, the fact remains true that there is always the cold hard ground waiting for you below. And that frigid dirt caught up with me it seemed, just as quickly as it left.

As my sedation began to wear off, the harsh reality of what just went down began to reboot it's gruesome images back into the framework of my mind. And even though I was struggling hard to keep my sanity, I definitely had no further hesitations anymore as to what I had to do.

The man who killed Newa was also the very same force who viciously sought to do harm to me and the great treasure I held in my arms. And this horrible beast of a man, I knew, would never, never give up his search for us. He would not have a sudden change of thought, nor would he eventually adopt a different agenda. I was his only witness and he would keep pushing forward until he had ahold of my little girl. No matter what, someday he would find me and when he did, he would find Sara.

It was check mate.

In a blind state of shock, I let go of my little girl and sat upright. With a dead stare on my face I reached into the consul and started numbly fishing around for a business card with a phone number on it, a phone number that at one time I was convinced I would never look at again. It was the same calling card of the man from the Social Services Office, Jeffrey Simmons, the one he left at the bus shelter. As my fingers brought the glossy salutation up to my face, all I could do was hover there and repeat the code etched into that card over and over again. It wasn't about winning or losing anymore. It wasn't about pride. It was only about Sara now, and what was best for her.

So without any more delay, I started up my rig, drove to the nearest payphone, and made the call. The secretary robotically put me through to his office, and when Simmons answered, he was ecstatic to hear that I had finally,... "come to my senses". He assured me that he would keep the law out of it. He also called me a sneaky little sonofabitch and warned me that I had better not stand him up, or else!

He instructed me to meet him at exactly twelve noon at an old park approximately seven blocks from the government office where he worked. He gave me precise directions and told me to meet him over by the merry-go-rounds. I agreed quietly and hung up. When I got back into my car, I glanced down at the gas gauge and it read what I expected it to. Empty. So I drove to a service station and put the last five bucks I had to my name into the tank. After that, I pulled into a strip mall and shut my old clunker down.

It was 10:05am.

I only had two hours left to spend with Sara. God, even the thought of that seemed impossible to comprehend. But I held my head up regardless and tried to remain strong. For her.

Once my engine sputtered its last, I looked over at the gyrating bundle of arms and legs that lay beside me and began to direct my vision towards hers. Without warning, my memory began racing back through time and came to a screeching halt at the exact moment when I first looked down at her as she lay covered in filth in the dumpster that fateful Sunday afternoon on the edge of town. A bittersweet feeling of harmony and loss swept over me as I picked up my angel from her crumpled nest of blankets and began to cradle her underneath my chin. I understood then without remorse, that if I never again felt so much as one second of happiness in my whole life, I would still be one of the luckiest men alive for ever being allowed the gift I was staring down at right now.

With a deep sigh, I slowly reached over and loaded up the last can of baby formula I had into her bottle. And as Sara chomped away at the sweet liquid, I began a final speech to my precious child.

"I'll say my goodbyes and I love you's now," I told her, "for it was such an incredible privilege to have your beauty in my life. Even if it was only for a short while. You Sara, you were my light."
"You were my daytime world."

I bit my lip hard as I felt a rush of water start towards my eyes.

"But there comes a time," I continued. "When a person has to do the right thing. Even though it just tears that person apart inside."

I could hear my voice start to break up, but I fought back the emotion with all my might.

"This is the best thing for you," I said as my vision began to blur. "You'll get to live in a proper home, with proper diapers and a proper bed that's always warm.
"You deserve that, sweetheart. You deserve the best."
We gave it our best shot didn't we? We had a great run, but now I have to do what's right for you, OK?"

My attempts at bravery were quickly beginning to fail. I tried so hard to curb my emotions so that I could make this last moment of ours last, but I could not and the water began to jump out from my eyes and spill across Sara's cheeks. Giving in to the massive outcries of my heart, I let Sara's bottle fall down between the seat, then embraced that child with everything I had. I packed a lifetime of devotion into those next few minutes as I hid there in that parking lot.

"I love you Sara ," I cried openly. "I will always love you."

Time stood still at that point and I prayed to God he let that dream last just for a few more seconds, even if it meant that in the end, I would never again own my mind. But he was still asleep, God was, and in a surreal fog, I slowly released my grip on Sara and let her sink down to my belly. She wasn't making a fuss or carrying on like I was. Nope, that little trooper was the stronger of us two. She was just lying in my arms and gazing up at me with her wide beautiful eyes. I guess I should have remained in misery, knowing that very soon my angel was going to be gone forever. But you see that was the thing about Sara. Whenever you looked at her, it was almost impossible to feel sadness.

It was like looking up at a clear summer's sky, where everything below it seemed to vanish.

That was her gift.

We talked for a little while longer, me and her, reminiscing, laughing, and whispering. Sara assured me that she would keep in touch and write. She also promised me of course, that she would not date any boys until she was thirty-two. It was a plan that I fully agreed to. Yep, we just hung out there for a bit like we always had. I dreamt of how wonderful her life was going to be and it made me feel a little better. It made me smile to know that she was going to be normal and not end up like me.

Eleven o'clock rolled around far too quickly.

It was time to go.

I had to gather up the last bit of strength I possessed and get her to the drop-off point. It was important to remain strong now and not let my emotions get in the way of the transaction, for I wanted Sara to remember me as that. As a strong man who made an even stronger sacrifice.

I followed the directions I'd been given and parked my car a few blocks away from the park. I wanted to walk the rest of the way there so I could stretch out what little time we had left together. As I gathered up a couple of her favorite toys and stuffed them into my pocket, along with her soother and her empty bottle, I kept on mentally repeating my vows to stay focused and not break down, even though I fully understood that what I was about to do was one of the most heartbreaking things a person could ever go through.

I was just about to shut the car door when I caught a sun-charged glimpse of the ninja charm that Newa had given to Sara that first day we met in the Laundromat. With the tiniest of smiles I gave it a flick and watched the light rebound off it's pointy ridges. Suddenly, everything Newa did, every look, every smile, every word she spoke to me and my baby began to rush forward from the depths and mystic of that charm.

"Watch over your Granddaughter," I asked silently as I steadied the pendant. "She will need your guidance."

I then lifted Sara's gift away from its longstanding home on the rear view mirror and carefully put it into my side pocket. I knew my baby would appreciate having her good luck charm around to aid her in her sleep somewhere down the line. But more importantly, I knew it was to be the only gift she would have ever received from her Gramma.

We took the long way to the park. I was in no hurry to get to that place.

And as I forced my feet on, I tried hard to comprehend just what my life was going to be like now without Sara, but I'm afraid at that point, I was only existing within the fleeting realm of the last valuable minutes I had left with her. And I began to wonder as I stumbled on, if this whole thing had actually been real.

Were the leaves that surrounded my feet now the fantasy, and the nightmares I'd been having constituted my reality? It was a justified riddle, but by the time my legs had made it to the entrance of the place, I did finally come to terms and even found a whisper of peace in my heart. I had humbly been able to congratulate myself on all of my efforts and managed to face down the majority of the demons that surrounded me. I was all done.

And after that my mind just sort of lapsed into a sublime state of lucidity. By the time I reached the edge of the grass, I wasn't happy, or sad. I wasn't really anything at all. I was just another empty face.

I looked up in silence at the sealed clock that was attached to the side of the white cement washrooms. It was only 11:35am. I was early. I guess the clock on my dash was fast, which I might add, was just fine by me!

And the surprise fact that I had another twenty-five minutes left to spend with my little girl played a major role in knocking me out of my self-imposed trance and re-instated the smile back to my face.

I decided to just head directly over to the merry-go-round and have a seat while I waited for the victorious man from the Social Services office to show up. There I could bask in the last of the season's sun and shower Sara with another thousand acts of affection before Jeffrey showed up.

Staying parallel to the cold rock latrines, my body emptied out at the north end of the playground, not far from the meager assortment of brightly-painted steel and stone amusement rides. My eyes skimmed across the landscape in search of the correct ride and found it sitting off to the right.

But my eyes were also awarded the agony of an early tip-off to a conspiracy that, if I had a million years to live, would have still never saw coming.

You know for a moment there, I wasn't really sure that if the outrageously twisted plot that was unfolding right in front of me was actually happening, or just another exaggerated figment of my imagination.

It was to be a lethal grievance, for in the near distance, I saw the outline of Jeffrey Simmons, the man I had come here to meet and surrender my child to, standing where he was supposed to be over by the circular ride. That was OK But the part that was quickly setting in as sheer disbelief was the fact that his hand was firmly planted into the palm of another. An extremity belonging to the one single person on the whole planet whom I feared the most,

Leon Jenkins.

I watched in horror as he stood there grinning proudly with the two-faced government employee firmly attached to the opposite end of his handshake. His dark, trademark overcoat and ponytail flopped about in the breeze as the pair greasily congratulated each other on the upcoming success of their sinister partnership, a contract obviously forged by Leon in a final attempt to gain access to my child. My body froze. I was immobilized with fear from the grim realization that I had just fallen into a fatal crossfire.

Move Eugene. Move godammit, it's a trap! Back away, back away slowly and get the hell out of there.
Come on Eugene, do it now!

My mind kept laying down the framework of its escape plan, but my body wouldn't respond. All the muscles in my legs were locked up solid in a state of denial and they

240

just wouldn't budge.

Sara, think of Sara. Just move back ten feet and you'll be out of their view. Ten lousy steps old buddy. "You can do it! "You can do this Eugene!"
Then it happened.

I felt my left foot begin to leave the magnetic pull of the earth and start to drag itself backwards. My right foot followed suit as well and my silhouette began slowly inching its way back to the corner of the shithouse. I could hear the jubilation inside my skull as my adrenaline kept it's magic potion on standby and waited patiently for the signal to kick in its power and put some distance between me and this insane discovery.

You're going to make it Eugene.

I celebrated as my heel brushed up against the ridge of the narrow sidewalk that encircled the small brick building, the one I was nearly behind.

Five more feet to go. Just five more steps to go Eugene.

I steadied my pace and prepared to cross the finish line of this morbid race.
One step, two steps. That's it man, keep going. Three....

Suddenly a sick thud followed by the loudly-publicized sound of breaking glass echoed off of the thick concrete shell to my rear and officially knocked me out of the playoffs. The two men in the foreground instantly whipped their heads upward and over in my direction. My heel, it seemed, had blindly dislodged an innocent pop bottle that was sitting on the edge of the same cement pad I had just rejoiced about seconds earlier.

"Fuck!" I yelled as I watched the outline of the two men crouch down and spring forward. The courtesy of subtle movements was over. It was time to shift into high gear, like right now! So I braced Sara into my chest and burst away from the edge of the park with my two sworn enemies following close in behind. My lifelong pal adrenaline cut loose its only product and injected my skinny legs with a blast of power. I spied over the landscape for the absolute quickest route back to my car and kept up the charge. I could hardly comprehend the scope of what was happening, but it did all make sense. Jeffrey and Leon had struck a deal, and now there was really only one thing left for me to do.

Run!

And run I did. I found strength and speed in my weakened body that I never knew existed. I kept Sara sucked tight into my chest as I fled off and tried feverishly to get back to the safety of my vehicle before my pursuers caught up with me.
I threw in an extra jump as I emerged out from behind a modular house and laid eyes once again on my old white roadster that now resembled more of a golden chariot than an early 70's sportster. Yessir, that beat-up, Detroit staple was in every way a rocket ship, eagerly waiting to transport me home, and once at it's tail,

I skidded up the length of it like a stuntman, and quickly flung myself inside. I plopped Sara into her seat in the same motion and rammed my keys into the ignition, hitting the engine with an avalanche of relief.
But wait... nothing happened.

What the fuck is this?

But not even a click from the solenoid was audible from underneath the hood.

"Christ," I yelled.

I tried the ignition one last time but my car,... my car was dead.
Looking to the sky, I boldly attempted to extend my warranty once again.

Oh God. Of all the times in the world for my rig to break down, please don't let it be now.

I brought my head back down to the steering wheel with a faint glimmer of hope and was just about to spin it over for a third time when I noticed something strange on my hood. I squinted my eyes and zoomed in on the front end of my ride a little closer.
Pry marks!

"Oh shit," I yelped as I struggled to grasp the reality of my worst fear.

I shot out of my Firebird like an arrow and threw up the hood, holding onto my sanity for dear life as I looked down into my engine compartment.
It was destroyed. The spark plug wires were all cut and laying off to the side and the ignition coil too, was smashed to bits and dangling helplessly on the firewall. The whole electrical system was basically ripped apart.

Jesus Christ! This can't be happening!

All of a sudden, the advancing sound of feet striking the pavement rang out from somewhere behind my lifeless ride. My head sprang up in shock and to my horror, I saw the outline of Leon and Jeffrey's outerwear flopping in the wind as they rounded the corner at the end of the block.

"Get moving motherfucker," I heard something say, but this was one time when I didn't need any help in deciding my next move.

It was time to disappear and that's exactly what I planned to do! I dove back inside my deceased vehicle and snatched up my unsuspecting tot from the bulky comfort of her bed and quickly stuffed her inside the security of my jacket again. As I zipped up my coat and prepared to abandon ship, I noticed the butt end of the fake army pistol I had bought off the old man at the garage sale sticking out from beneath my seat. In a mindless blur, I grabbed it too and stuffed it down inside the top of my jeans. I don't know why I took it. I mean the thing was, nothing more than a boat anchor the way it was, but at that point I wasn't really rationalizing things a whole lot. I was simply

riding out a huge surge of fear-inflicted commands. I then shimmied out of the cab
and spun my head to the right, only to be hit with another blow.

The two men were not even fifty yards away from me now and were closing up that
gap at an alarming rate. Even as my heels ground into the asphalt and began to point
my body in the opposite direction, I understood that I was not going to be able to
evade my enemy for very long.

That is, not on foot anyway.

I knew my chances for survival in this deadly match up were greatly leveraged on
me finding a faster mode of transportation For a split second, I considered seeking
out an idling vehicle and momentarily stealing it, but the streets at that moment were
quiet and time was something I didn't have. I thought I was doomed for sure, but
the instant my legs had completed their turn and straightened out, I spotted a lone
ten-speed leaning up against a tree on the other side of the street.

A bike? "Hell ya, that will do? That will do just fucking fine," I screeched!

It was a two-wheeled Godsend and by the time I'd mounted that old bike and
secured my coat into my jeans, my attackers were almost right on top of me. I could
even hear their labored breaths rumbling out from their lungs as my legs inflated in
an explosion of pressure and launched me forward. I didn't look behind me after
that, not even for a second. I just stared straight ahead and hammered away at those
stiff old pedals with everything I had. My legs burned in agony as the resistance of
the pavement nibbled away at the thin wheels.

For a second there, I thought I was done for because the vibration of the two men's
footsteps behind me did not seem to be getting any further away. But that squeaky
old transporter refused to let me down and finally I was able to reason with the gear
shifter and adjust the power transfer to a ratio that lent itself more to my favor. I
felt the back tire bear down and chirp a bit the instant the rusty chain curled its way
around the correct sprocket. I glanced over my shoulder and unleashed a smug look
in the direction of my pursuers as that ill-acquired petal bike suddenly lurched away
from them and began to fly.

A twinge of satisfaction rushed across my skin as I watched the imprint of the two
men behind me shuffle their unconditioned masses to a standstill and fall to their knees.

I actually laughed out loud at them as I sped on, but my celebration was a tad
premature, for a short spell later I began to hear the on and off roar of Leon's four-
door ocean liner as well as the buzz of Jeffrey's import as they gained speed and
initiated their motorized charge on me and my little girl. It was time to re-instate my
anxiety attack and hit the gas, so I launched that bike into the first side street I came
to and laid into the frame. I still had no real clue where I was going but I worked
those pedals hard anyway, and only paused my charge to periodically speak down
the odd sermon of wisdom to my brave tot, who was now hollering away madly
against my chest.

I was so scared. So completely lost in terror that it was difficult to pinpoint any single emotion. But they say that during a person's darkest hour, he or she is always drawn back to someplace in their past where they once felt safety. I understood how completely true that statement was as my legs instinctively rotated the frame of my unusual chariot back a degree towards the south end of the city, and began picking up speed again. It was as if my brain had switched itself over to auto pilot, and I knew right away what destination it sought.

I was heading straight in the direction of the forgotten park that lay hidden away within the deep crevices of the musty coulee that me and Steve discovered as young kids so many years before.

I hadn't been there in years, since me and him were teenagers. But amazingly enough, I was still able to spot all the landmarks and shortcuts that I had relied upon as a youth. The coulee, unfortunately, was deep in the south end of the city. It was a good hour away by car and I estimated that it was going to take me a solid three hours to reach by bike. I briefly thought about flagging down a cop, but after what I'd just witnessed, I didn't know who the good guys were anymore. The only person I trusted was T.J. Daniels, and he was the only one I would surrender to.

Taking advantage of my downsized mode of transportation, I ducked that bicycle in and out of yards and alleyways in a way that I never could have dreamed of attempting in my Firebird. I fled on without pause through the backyard of the city as the straw-filled goblins bobbed back and forth in a deadly sway. It was eerie. It felt like the decorations were plotting against me, mapping out my course and selling it to the highest bidder.
The race hurtled on.

Sometimes I could hear the screeching of tires behind me, and sometimes I could not. But I didn't worry too long about the severity of my situation. There was no time left for that. I just pedaled on as fast as I could and focused in on my final destination.

After the most strenuous two and a half hours of my life, I could finally begin to make out the shale-ridden cliffs of the precious ravine that safely housed my child-hood memories. And that was a good thing because by then my body and lungs were on the verge of collapse. I hadn't heard the high-pitched whirl of Jeffrey's import since shortly after this goddam Indy 500 started and within the last forty five minutes or so, nor did my ears pick up the sound of Leon's sedan either. I took advantage of this windfall and stopped for a second to catch my breath.

Sara, who was wailing on spastically at the start of this game, had unexpectedly calmed down a bit in the last hour and seemed to be now, with the exception of the odd squeal or two, more or less just enjoying the ride. Easing her out from her cubby, I showered her with about a dozen kisses to her forehead and began apologizing to her over and over. After that I slowly set her back into my jacket and began steering that two- wheeler back down the road. I kept myself parallel to a ten foot high cement freeway barrier until I came up to the end of it. As I crested the ominous wall I let out a sigh of relief, for about 200 yards over to the right of me stood the crumbling stone entranceway to my most sacred haven. Jackson's Coulee.
I resuscitated a flood of great memories back to life the moment I laid my eyes on

those decrepit archways.

"We're home sweetheart," I said happily as I peeked inside my jacket again.

I stood there resting at that pinnacle for a moment and stretched out my legs in an attempt to disperse the many pins and needles that had overcome them. I had to be careful they didn't cramp up on me for that would constitute a death sentence in the face of this horrific double-cross. Then, not one second after I began to press back down on the pedals to complete the last hurrah of my grim voyage, my ears picked up the faint sound of a large vehicle spilling out from around a corner. I spun my noggin sideways and squinted my pupils in the direction of the noise. In the far distance behind me, I began to make out the grisly silhouette of Leon's massive car.

It was engulfed in dust from its recent skid, but still coming on strong. He had spun out onto the street from an adjacent alley and was accelerating steadily in my direction. But just as I suspected, there was no Jeffrey following in behind him. Now this didn't mean that two-faced bastard wasn't still on my trial, it just meant that Leon's car was faster.

"Time to roll," I grunted madly as I drew in a fresh breath and mounted the pedals.

The entrance of the coulee was about two telephone poles away and I estimated that it would take about forty-five seconds to get there if I really walked on it. I knew that if I could just make it past that gate before Leon emerged out from behind the cement barrier I recently occupied; it would give me just enough footage to avoid being spotted. You see, the park was off to the right a fair ways and the gates to it lay at the bottom of a short gravel ramp which was not at all in sync with the flow of the main road. I figured if Leon did not see me before I dropped into that obscured driveway, there was a great chance that he would just keep on to the left, possibly anticipating that I was trying to escape the city altogether and use the surrounding countryside as my cover.

It was a move I would have actually considered, if I still had my car, but being basically on foot, there was no way I'd chance it. My reasoning seemed just and I also realized that once I was inside those gates, I was officially back in control of the situation. This was my territory and I knew every nook and cranny of that prehistoric riverbed. And if there was anything in the world that was going to deliver me out of this latest mess, it was my knowledge of the surrounding landscape that was going to do it.

But no matter how much I fantasized about the odds that sat beyond those walls, the game I knew, was far from over. The fact remained that I still needed to make it to the end of that stone guard first. Airborne once more, I zeroed in on the target that lay before me and hit the juice, letting the semi-recuperated power in my legs wreak their havoc on the pedals once more.

The front tire reared up in defeat from the sudden surge of energy I had just unleashed on the chain, so I shifted my weight forward and resumed my course in a dead heat towards the thick interlocking shrubbery that surrounded the front of the parks inlet. I was half way there before I knew it.

But so was Leon.

I could hear the scream of his engine hurtling its cargo in my direction from out beyond the other side of the cement barrier.

Come on Eugene. You can make it. Just don't look back.

I bore down on those pedals with all my might as the edge of my sanctuary became increasingly closer. The rattle of Leon's engine was still muffled so I knew that he had not yet crested the edge of the wall. This was a good thing, for me and my baby's mortality was hanging ever-so-loosely on the positioning of us and that car. It was going to be a close one that was for sure, but I was determined to be victorious, as the granite portal in front of me grew larger and larger with each passing second.

That a boy Eugene. Just five more yards now and you'll be there... three more yards... two more yards... One... Yes!

I had made it to the gate, and with one final burst of power I launched that stolen ten speed at Mach 4 through the ancient concrete arch of that time-honored coulee and landed down hard onto the safety of the other side. I damn near lost control of that rickety artifact when I landed, but I shifted my body accordingly and came away with the big save. I was well inside the security of the park when I heard the sharp echo of Leon's sedan fishtail out from the corner of the cement wall and dive back onto the main road, still hell-bent for redemption in this deadly pursuit.

But he was too late.

For I was already hidden deep behind the living wall of the coulee and stretching out that void with every breath I took. I veered off to the right after about seventy-five yards or so and sped across the grass. Within seconds I had ditched the bike behind a bush and was fleeing once again through the intricate maze of creeks and canyons I had once mapped out many years before as a young boy. The paths and gullies were exactly as I remembered them. I couldn't believe it. I mean sure, the park was desperately run down and grown over, but I was still able to pick out all of the familiar trail ways that loyally guided me along as a kid.

At that point in time, I was almost positive that I had given Leon the shake. But as the eerie sound of metal scraping pavement ricocheted about in the near distance behind me, I soon realized that the game was still on, for Leon Jenkins was also inside the park.

I didn't obsess about why or how the evil cult fuck had managed to figure out my strategy. That wasn't important anymore. What was important was me being able to successfully evade him while he was there, at least until it got dark enough for me to find my way back to the main road without being noticed. That was the goal and my feet, now understanding the full scope of their latest order, dug themselves into the soft earth even harder and began their journey towards another destination.

This time, however, I knew exactly where my legs were taking me. They were instinctively heading in the direction of the old ball diamonds at the far end of the park. The ones that lay hidden on the other side of the rusted out steel culverts that once fed the reservoir it's water. They were my only hope now. The city had built new playing fields a number of years before, even prior to mine and Steve's time, closer to the main entrance of the place for obvious reasons. The wild grass had long since decimated the field, but they never destroyed the old dugouts. They just left them there, I think, as sort of a memorial to the modest beginnings of the place. There were not a lot of people around who even knew that those weathered old monuments existed, but I knew they were there.

I remembered way back when about how me and Steve stumbled onto the ancient pathways that led to them one day as we bravely made our way into no-mans-land, as it was nicknamed by the rest of the kids. We had always been sternly warned by our mothers to never go beyond the tree line of the last knoll, but one cloudy Saturday afternoon me and my ace pal decided that we were definitely old enough, or stupid enough, to traipse into that great unknown. Without fear we pushed our way past the ghoulish barriers of the willow trees and carefully made our way through the intimidating waterless tunnel to boldly explore the legendary wasteland and all of its monsters that lay in waiting on the other side.

But once we did look death in the face and venture through that dark tunnel, we surprisingly-enough, did not encounter cannibalistic aliens or any other hardships for that matter, and were rewarded handsomely for our valor with the reclamation of our own private paradise in the form of those old ball diamonds. We would play there often. It was a blast due to the fact that the dugouts were built four feet below the ground and from that vantage point, you could see everything out in front of you, but no-one could see in. We were like eighty-five pound gophers, unnoticed and untraceable. And believe me, by the end of the day, after unrelentingly wrestling around on the dusty earth floor of those musty shacks, we did sort of resemble a couple of rats.

But today that chance act of bravery was about to pay off in a big way. For if I could just make it to the dugouts without being noticed, I would seemingly have an edge upon my self-righteous stalker who would almost certainly have no idea that those informal bunkers were even there. I ran on with a shiver of hope towards that secret place, ducking under trees, jumping over rock bluffs, and skidding down ravines. A half hour later, I finally came out from my botanical seclusion and stood there in awe at the base of the rusted and once mysterious culverts. It's funny, but they didn't look so frightening to me anymore. Time will do that.
Breaking free from my slight trance, I repositioned my grip on Sara, who was still holding her own inside the snug contours of my jacket and pressed on.

When I stumbled out onto the other side, the landscape was exactly as I remembered, so I peered off to the right and spied the broken tree that marked the final stretch of the path that would lead me to my island. It was about four in the afternoon when me and my baby finally reached the backside of the old ball field. I cut a path about twenty feet inside the tree line just as a precaution to make sure it would prove difficult, if not impossible, to follow my tracks if I had still not succeeded in giving Leon the slip.
The sun was hovering low in the sky by the time I ducked down into the first dugout. I knew I had to tough it out for the next couple of hours before it would be safe enough to leave and make my escape. By that time, it would be under the

protective blanket of nightfall and once out of the coulee, I could find an old shed to hide in and at first light, I would find T.J. and turn myself in. And I didn't care if they locked me up and threw away the key either. As long as Sara got out of this whole mess unharmed, nothing else mattered.

My feet produced a squishing sound as a result of my romp through a creek and once inside I crept across the length of the fairy-tale sized building and propped my body up against the back wall. I was out of immediate view, but still at an angle where I could see everything that was going on before me. Without delay, I pulled Sara out from her cocooned state inside my coat. She was in dire need of affection and so was I. The second I plucked her out of her cramped enclosure she let out a snort and began to cry so I quickly went to work and pelted my brave girl with a flurry of hugs and kisses and also retrieved her worn out soother.

She calmed down the instant I jiggled that rubber gobstopper against the side of her lips and with brute force, inhaled that bad boy into her mouth and fell still. I could tell that at the moment I was probably not in her good books.

OK Eugene, now it's your turn to relax.

It was a command I easily obeyed, so I drew in a deep breath and settled in for the lengthy watch. I was confident that I had given Leon the shake, but only time would tell. All I could do is wait now and pray to God, just this one last time to deliver me, and more importantly my innocent little girl from evil.

From where I was huddled, I could easily see the corner of the great metal cylinder that I had passed through in the foreground. As long as that viewpoint remained undisturbed, so did our wellbeing. Even though the sun had already disappeared into the horizon, the landscape was still dangerously illuminated. This game, I'm afraid to say, was a long way from over.

To say that I was terrified was an understatement. To be truthful, I was actually shaking with fear.

I told myself a thousand times as I sat there that if I did manage to make it out of this mess I would never, never again take anything for granted. I would go back to school and get a good job and do everything I had always dreamed of. No more cheating life or tempting fate! From now on I'd play it right by the book.

I secured my redemption with an almighty commitment but alas, as with all things, I quickly understood that fate was not influenced by good intentions. Nor was it scheduled by vows and obligations. Fate, I now knew, ran undisturbed on an invisible timeline and was not in any way controlled by a mere mortal's personal agenda.

And this day, just as I thought I was about to overcome the delicate balance of time, I surrendered to the fact that fate had officially drawn my number. For out in the field before me, my eyes sadly began to pick up the faint variance of movement down in the far right-hand corner of the ribbed steel tunnel that I had recently exited from.

Seems my future was already sealed and I watched in full denial as the trademark shape that could only belong to one man began moving closer and closer.

Leon had found me.

How, I don't know, but I guessed I'd never get the chance to find out. That didn't really matter now, though. Nope, that was all water under the bridge from here on in. I had no place left to run anymore, for the only exit out of the canyon was up a steep, shale-ridden embankment that lay out in the open behind the dugouts. I briefly thought about attempting an escape up that unstable incline but quickly decided against it, for Leon I knew wasn't alone, and there was no doubt in my mind that his equally-sinister accomplice, Jeffrey Simmons, was still participating heavily in this financially motivated war game. I had to face those facts. If Leon knew where I was, then you can bet your ass that Jeffrey did too, and was probably already waiting for me on the roadway above.

The only hope I had left was if by some unlikely miracle, Leon was unable to pick up the last leg of my bush trail and ended up walking right by me. That was the only real chance I had. Then I could eventually slip back out the way I came. My delusions of grandeur were a welcome emotion, but deep down I still had to be honest with myself and realize that if Leon had already managed to track me this far, then the chances of him dropping the ball now were pretty slim. It was time to let the courageous idea go and start thinking about plan B.

I felt a slow breath leave my lips and watched my spirit drift away with it. For plan B was not just another scheme. It was the undying fulfillment of a promise, a promise that I had spoke to Sara in the beginning.

It was a verbal contract to her that stated I would at any cost, ensure that she survive me, an unspoken vow that guaranteed she live on. And as those boldly uttered phrases reasserted themselves back into the forefront of my thoughts, I came to the fatal conclusion that as long as Leon Jenkins and Jeffrey Simmons existed in this world, my baby would never enjoy one minute of security or freedom.

It was up to me to end their reign.

They would have to be killed plain and simple, even if that denouement meant the sacrifice of my own life to ensure it's success.

There was no question in my mind that when I adopted Sara as my own, I did also willingly accept any and all of the future consequences that may have come with that pact. And as I sat there in my damp entombment, I replayed the memory of that pledge and ensured my precious angel that I would not make light of that vow. When the time came I would use every weapon I had stored away in my arsenal, including my own mortality if that be the case, to ensure that she would awaken tomorrow to feel the sun on her face. I sealed my oath with a lengthy kiss to her forehead and then allowed a euphoric sedation to take control of my body as the tail end of my conscience floated off.

The air was growing cooler now as I sat there rocking Sara back and forth in the far corner of the pungent basement. I waited patiently for the final outcome to my legacy that I think I'd somehow known about my whole life. It was getting darker, but was not near dim enough to make any real difference in my forthcoming showdown. For even if Leon took his sweet time, he would still end up within the vicinity of these miniature shacks with ample light.

I looked down at Sara and smiled. She was as calm as a prairie pond at dusk. I found it so uncanny that a baby could be that docile after what she had just endured.

She was just lying there, wrapped up loosely in her blanket happily oblivious to the severity of the current situation as she gazed back up at me with those paralyzing blue eyes of hers. It was almost as if she was preparing me in her own subtle way, to face my enemy with a sense of pride. I knew I would soon need that wisdom to find the courage to make it through an almost inevitable one-way transition that an average forty thousand people are confronted with every single day. I felt her begin to channel all of her strength and energy into my soul through the peacefulness of that stare and suddenly I felt something. Something in my hand.

Still in a haze, I tipped my head to the floor and refocused my vision to see what it was. I noticed then, that Sara had maneuvered her tiny hand over and was resting it inside the palm of my own. And as I stared down at this beautiful picture, the sight of her chubby mitt as it lay surrounded by the skin of my own, I was suddenly hurtled back to the day, and to the very moment where I stood in front of the fancy restaurant and watched the happy couple dine in front of me. And I began to remember the solitary favor I had asked for then, about how I would have given my life at that moment, to have the feeling of a woman's hand in mine, one who would always love me.

I'd gotten my wish.

And it became absolutely clear to me then, that love was the driving power behind the earth. That's what made it spin. And when all the cities and countries had fallen and all the empires were undone, life would come down to one simple thing.

It would come down to love.

I closed my fingers around my baby's and let my heart repeat the word over and over again until it began to resemble a sentence, a story. A song.

Then someone's face, Meridith's face, came into my vision. I tried to resist her memory but the soft contours of her portrait would not go away. Suddenly my heart began deliberately replaying all the happy times I had shared with her, projecting the slides out onto the private movie screen that hung, as always, in the center of my mind. It was a wonderful play, and a show that I held the only ticket to. I started to fantasize about the first time I looked into her eyes that day at the drugstore and I felt my world stop.

I knew from that very first encounter that no matter what became of that look, my thoughts from then on in would always include her and that moment.

I also understood that from that day on, no-one could ever accurately say that my life was devoid of passion, because for whatever reason, her light had somehow broke through and rendered me a man. I began to visualize all of our time together. Every kiss, every touch. They were beginning to come forward like it was happening over again for the first time. I remembered every step we took and all the times our lips met as she forced away all of the stereotypes that imprisoned me.

Meridith would not be hated.

I would not face my destiny with the toxin of that emotion. She made my dream of a thousand nights come true, and no matter how our relationship ended, she had allowed me to experience a magic that men all over the world lay awake at night and wish for.

And now as I crouch here, motionless and camouflaged against the murky backdrop of this cold cement shack, I will ready myself for battle one last time, for the survival of my baby, and for the honor of my lover, the only person in the world who looked beyond the cliché and found the man who was trapped behind it. And as I engage in this end conflict, I will defend her memories and celebrate those triumphs as a sole victory, in a long, lonely war.

I allowed the fond visions of my girlfriend to linger about my senses for a moment longer, then sadly released them from my heart's grip and set her free. Because now, if I were to be successful in any actions to warrant my baby's mortality, I would need to become conniving and vigilant in every way. I would have to render myself merciless and inhuman. It was going to take everything I had, but in the end, Sara would survive. She would carry on and live out her life. I would not let her down. I would not fail.

And even though I knew right then that I should have been afraid, for some reason I was not. I was ready to face my enemy. I think it was because from the second I decided to keep Sara, I also realized it as fact that the day would come around when someone would try and take her away from me. Don't ask me why, but it was just something I had come to accept. Now I never expected that person to be a homicidal maniac or an opportunistic runt, but nevertheless, I knew they would come.

But no matter who it turned out to be, in the end, the plain fact always remained that I had an obligation to uphold. And when the time came, I had to do what I had to do. But in the scope of that same thought, I also came to the understanding that my decision to raise a newborn child as a homeless man was reckless. It was crazy of me to think that I could ever deserve the respect of the life that was staring up at me right now.

But be that as it may, the one thing that remained absolute in my thinking was the fact that this "statistic", was fully prepared to die to protect that life if it came down to it. I stabbed my unconscious dagger into the ground and rewound the tape back to an image.

It was a picture of me sitting in my car, waiting at the legendary intersection to make the turn into the government building to hand over my pot of gold to a fictional hierarchy. Sitting there, more accurately, at the very crossroads of my life. And I began to remember the powerful feeling that overcame my body as I unanimously ratified the decision set forth by my heart to, for better or for worse, take in this forgotten child, and not throw her back into the trash can of society. I felt a smile suddenly win a spot back on my face as I began to think of how easily one's life can be altered by the injection of one chance experience.

It wouldn't be long now.

Leon would come, I knew that. He would come and he would find me. When he did there would be a terrible battle. And when it was all over, there would be nothing left but the bodies of men and the documented and miraculous survival of a nameless child who, from that moment forward, would begin a new life, and who would greatly prosper and soar beyond the boundaries of that same life without the slightest recollection of the many tragedies that took place around her. Tragedies that she was both targeted for, and spared from.

And the newspapers too, would sell the story of a worthless transient, who shame-lessly hoarded away a helpless baby in the worn-out guts of an old car. The fine print would also describe in detail of how lives ended that day, and how certain people "got what they deserved." And the media would continue to dazzle their readers with hard words like "justice" and "religion", and I'm sure the police would also remark of how unsettling it was that such dregs of society could exist right under the nose of such a grand empire.

Ya. They would say that.

But what the headlines would never come to discover, was the incredible tale of a lonely vagrant, a person who was given the rare chance to undo a mountain of wrongs with one single act of unselfish right. And it's true that the words on the paper would never begin to explain how an abolished newborn was able to lift that same skeleton of a man to a level of peace and acceptance that only a chosen few souls in this entire world ever get a chance to know.

The reporters would also fail to comprehend how that same rejected child, without ever uttering a single word, taught me the scope of an entire language.
No, I'm afraid the news world would never tell it like that. They preferred the Hollywood version more.
It was the one that sold the most copies.
But if today was indeed to be my last, this story would not end in vain, for I knew my soul would forever live on inside my beautiful girl. And throughout her whole life, no matter where she ended up, if you were to look deep enough into her eyes, you would always be able to see me and the strength I found within her. I let Sara's hand slip slowly out from mine and closed my eyes.

I wasn't exactly sure just how I was going to pull this all off, but I had a pretty good feeling that the disarmed six shooter that lay hidden in the front of my jeans was going to play a major role in that terminal bluff. The pistol I concealed underneath my clothing, I knew, was a total farce, but I fully intended to make that fake real, even if all it did was buy me enough time to get to safety. That's all I needed to get out of that hunk of iron.
I asked of it nothing else.
After that it would be me hunting them, and I would stalk my prey without mercy, never ceasing my carnage until both Leon and Jeffrey lay dead at my feet.
No matter how, I would follow through with this unrepentant feat for the sake of my little girl.
I had no qualms in the least about ending their lives now. Even if Satan awaited me afterward, I did not care, for I had come to the realization a long time ago, even before all of this happened, that everyone in this world is allotted one great chal-lenge. An invisible slap on the face with a leather glove. And when this happens, that person can either run away or raise up their fists. But whatever their choice is, that decision instantly sets in motion the groundwork for his or her legacy.

And mine lay with Sara.

I think I was destined to look inside that particular dumpster. I think I was sent there to receive my orders.

And now, as I gaze down now at my baby, I have no regrets. I will raise my fists. I will fight.

The landscape was starting to shade over when I reached down and pulled out the impotent handgun from it's cheap holster. I stuffed it inside one of the open flaps of Sara's blanket and readied myself for when the time came for me to retrieve it. I would use the element of surprise and force my foe to the ground. Then with the density in the steel in the weapon, I would deliver a vicious blow to Leon's temple in hopes of killing him, or at least knocking him out. Then I would finish him off and sneak back out the way I came to find a place to hide until morning.

Until I could track down T.J. and tell him what I had done. That was the plan and I would not deviate from it. As the minutes ticked on, I could begin to feel powerful surges of energy start to race throughout my body. I guess it's true when they say that only in the face of death, is a person ever really alive. And alive I was. My whole body quivered as my muscles primed themselves for the oncoming battle. I gave Sara one last kiss, then looked up and stared straight ahead as I waited for my victim.

The sun was gone by the time he found me. I could see his silhouette moving steadily through the trees in front of the dugout, following my same path with deadly precision. He was coming to silence me and steal my treasure, but he foolishly misjudged his opponent and would pay dearly for that mistake. I tightened up the grip on the pistol inside Sara's blanket and grounded my footing as I hid there motionless in the cool shade. My veins began to swell as I tensed my muscles up even further and tried desperately to become as transparent as I could, like a carnivorous fish against the corral, my hot breath colliding with the cold air the only thing visible. I waited in that frigid trench for what was, in reality, only about a minute or two, but it seemed like years.

And then it happened.

I watched in silent terror as the outline of Leon's all-too-familiar overcoat, bent down, and carefully stepped into the entrance of the dugout. I saw the shadows of his pony tail shift perfectly from side to side as he shuffled on closer to the dark cubby where I lay waiting. I watched as his face skipped across the dusty floor of the dugout searching for my footprints. I think he knew I'd come in here, but I also hoped he wasn't sure if I'd left again.

This was it Eugene. This was the moment of truth.

The time had come to set into play a last ditch effort to enlist the element of surprise into this dismal equation in order to deflect the odds. I knew completely, that I did in the next few seconds, would solely determine Sara's future. I tensed up my legs to the max and torqued down my grip on Sara and the gun. I just had to wait a couple more seconds for the exact moment when Leon's head was turned to it's fullest point away from my direction before I struck. It was important that I not act too hastily or I would risk blowing the only opportunity I had to catch him off guard.

Then I saw the pinnacle gesture I'd been waiting for as Leon's head stopped ever-so-briefly at it's longest point off to the left and paused there for a moment.

My cue had arrived. In one fast and furious movement, I shot out of the darkness with my weapon pointing straight into the temple of my calculating aggressor and yelled out a jagged command.

"Down on the ground now you motherfucker!"

The shock value of my assault sent Leon reeling backwards and it was plain to see that he was noticeably struggling to comprehend his current situation. I watched then as he slowly raised up his hands and rested them on top of his head.

I did it. Yes, I did it!! He's finished now.

I lurched forward and jammed the gun hard into his forehead, backing him up even further until he stood pinned and beaten against the side wall of the very entrance he had just slithered through.

"You sonofabitch!" I screamed. "If you think for one second that I'm going to let you harm so much as a single hair on my baby's head, you got another thing coming! Do you understand me?" I yelled, as I applied more pressure to the stock.

A great sense of relief and control descended upon me. I had this bastard exactly where I wanted him and now all that was left to do was drop him to his knees and send him to hell! I tensed up my forearms and loaded the strike. But then, without provocation, he relaxed his arms and dropped them back down to his sides.

"Get your fucking hands up where I can see them," I hollered, grinding the barrel of the gun deeply into his skull.

But he did not obey my command and began moving ignorantly forward, backing me up in the process.

"Stop right there," I warned him, "I mean it or I'll blow your fucking head off!"

"I highly doubt that," the mute figure suddenly responded as he continued to further back me up towards the far wall.

I began to panic and felt a thin bead of sweat start to trickle down the length of my neck. Then in a daring move, I dug my heels into the dirt and aimed the relic right between his eyes, desperately trying to cease his bold assault. But this brash maneuver still did not faze him.

"You know Mr. Lauder," he said calmly as he resumed his charge. "It's really not that difficult to tell when the barrel of a World War II relic has been welded shut.

Fuck - the jig is up!

My mind automatically shifted into high gear and began diverting all of my strength into my right arm, capitalizing on the order to plant that wartime staple firmly into the side of Leon's head. But before I could deliver the blow, Leon grabbed the side of the useless barrel and ripped it out of my hand, throwing it to the floor without a second thought. Desperate and scared, I clenched up my fist and successfully landed a solid right hook to the end of my attacker's nose, sprawling his body sideways up against the wire mesh that faced the field. Running on pure adrenaline, I cocked my arm again and moved in for another round, but my fist dropped down shortly afterward and stayed obediently by my side as the middle-aged maniac in front of me suddenly stuffed his hand into his overcoat and pulled out a jet-black snub-nosed revolver.

"Now this is what a real gun looks like," Leon growled.

"You'll never get away with this," I said to him confidently, disguising my fear the best I could in a final attempt at retaliation.

"Oh, I definitely will 'get away with it,' Leon murmured as he slowly pulled back on the hammer and cocked his pistol.
I heaved Sara up towards my face and barricaded my arms across her, spinning my frame around 180 degrees in a last-ditch effort to use my own mass as a shield for my baby.
It worked.
The bullet from Leon's gun tore into my back and shot out through my abdomen. I even saw the spark the furious projectile made as it ricocheted off the cement grid in front of me. I held onto Sara with all my will as my legs became instantly lifeless and refused to support the weight of my body.

My shoulders hit the dirt first, followed by my head.

I kept the pressure on Sara steady to make sure the force of the fall was absorbed into my ribs and not hers.
She was crying like crazy now, but all I could do is whisper to her more fairy tales.
The damage the bullet had done as it ripped through my torso was beginning to materialize and I began to feel the warm sensation of life oozing out of me through the path that the shell had forged. In a state of slow motion, I watched helplessly as the gunman strode over and knelt beside my head.

"You see my friend," Leon sneered. "I told you I would win."

Then, the man with the gun reached out unobstructed and lifted my child away.

"No!" I screamed.

I held onto her for as long as I could, but the more I bled, the weaker I became. There was nothing left I could do.

"SARA," I cried, "SARAAAA!"

My acute plea was cut short by the accumulation of a thick familiar-tasting fluid that was coming up from my stomach and gathering in my throat. It was blood and it began to spill out from the corner of my mouth.

"It's no use carrying on like this Mr. Lauder. No-one can hear you anymore. Do you know why? Because you're dead!"

I lay thereon the ground broken and still, and watched in agony as the religious psychopath hoisted my baby up into the air with a triumphant howl.

"Ah yes," Leon bragged victoriously. "What a fine sacrifice you will make!"

Fighting to breathe from the chokehold the blood was having on my windpipe, I rolled over to my side and let the frothy red liquid gush out onto the musty floor of the dugout. My worst nightmare was coming true right before my eyes. I tried to call out to my child one last time, but it was no use for my voice had been reduced to a whisper from the devastation of the injury. Death was slowly overtaking my body and all I could do was wait for the earth to complete it's cycle. With the world around me starting to cloud, I braced for the sober reviewing of my life, a ritual that I always believed took place as a person's soul prepares to transfer its ownership into the custody of a higher understanding.
But life, it seemed, wasn't quite finished with me just yet and decided to throw me one last curveball... for old time's sake.

"Freeze... FBI!"

The stern command rang out from somewhere behind Leon, and its message echoed loudly off the walls of the narrow room.

"Wait a second," I thought as I lay there submerged in a pool of red ooze.
"I know that voice?" I recognized it's depth and shape.
I tilted my head up clumsily and caught a glimpse of a figure looming behind my killer with a drawn and fixed weapon pointed directly at the back of his head.
I then observed the unfolding chain of events in a realm of confusion as a feminine silhouette slowly moved out from behind the cover of Leon's girth and boldly pressed a large chrome automatic against the temple of my worst foe.

It was Meridith.

"Drop the gun and set the baby on the ground," she demanded in a mean growl.

Leon did exactly as he was told and cautiously lowered my sobbing baby to the floor, leaving his now- inadequate pee shooter in the dirt as well. I watched in a state of joy as the recently disarmed Druid stood back up and nervously clasped his hands overtop his head in defeat. He knew full well that the woman that held him captive was more than ready to waste him with her "real gun", if he so much as blinked the wrong way. I watched Meridith as she quickly raised up her free hand and gripped Leon under the arm, throwing him to the side and kicking away his weapon in the same stroke. She ordered him to kneel in the corner, which he did without resistance. Then, still keeping a secure bead on her prisoner, she reached into her vest pocket and pulled out a compact two way radio.

"Man down, Man down!" she hollered, pressing the device close up to her lips. "Request immediate medical assistance via air vac. I repeat, request immediate air vac to location!"

I saw her put the radio away and back towards me, still pointing her Government Issue luger at Leon's head.

"Eugene," she sputtered as she knelt down beside me. "You're going to be OK sweetheart, alright? You're going to be fine, help is on its way."

Her hands trembled with fear as she gently rolled me over onto my back and uncovered the large congregation of blood I already knew was there.

"Oh Jesus," I heard her say, cupping her hand around her mouth.

"It's no problem," I whispered up to her. "It's just a scratch."

I forced a tiny smile onto my face, even though I knew the gunshot had caused me much more than "just a scratch". It was the craziest thing, but I was actually happy at that moment, happy to know that at least I wasn't about to die in vain. I was content, because I knew at the end of the day, Sara was going to survive. And that was really all I wanted in the first place.

"Don't move," Meridith said to me trying to paint over the ugly reality of the situation. "The helicopter will be here soon."

I felt her palm brush against my cheek. I raised my head up slightly and looked into her eyes, but didn't speak. I didn't have to, for she already knew what I was thinking.

"I guess we both had a little secret we were protecting, huh?" she said as she began to pull the hair away from my face and comfort me.

"Ya," I whispered," I guess we did."

My voice was fading fast. The blood that was supposed to be compressed within my system was now flowing freely out the dime-sized hole in my stomach and submersing my vocal cords. I let my head fall back to the ground and motioned Meridith with my unsteady hand to bring my hysterical baby over to my side. She did. Then we all just curled up there. She also took off her fleece jacket and stuffed it under my head while I listened on dreamily to the intermittent vibrations of Sara's cries.
I was going to miss those hymns.
I went to speak out words of compassion, but there was too much fluid dammed up in my throat, so I just maneuvered my hand over to my child and began slowly rubbing my palm overtop her chest in a habitual twist. Meridith, now seeing the

difficulty I was having, quickly took her hand and pulled me onto my side so that my throat could drain out once more. She held my body tight but her first aid was interrupted by the sudden and devastating arrival of Leon's silent partner. With unprecedented regret, I watched as the sawed- off runt from the government office leapt through the entrance of the dugout without warning and jammed his hand into the side of his blazer.

Meridith immediately let me go and stood up, redirecting the menacing barrel of her weapon towards the head of the confused entrepreneur.

"Don't move," she hollered. "FBI!"

The intelligent suit quickly put the whole scene together and regressed his body language to set up his next play.

"Wait," he said, temporarily reversing the direction of his arm. "Don't shoot. I'm from the department of Social Services."

Then the shady man I knew as Jeffrey Simmons, slowly redirected his hand into his pants pocket and pulled out a dense leather identification wallet.

"No, Meridith," I murmured. "Don't fall for it, he's in on this!"

I tried to tune up the quality of my words in an attempt to warn her of the double cross, but the sentence I spoke only came forth as a barely audible whistle. Meridith dropped her gun briefly and let out a relieved gasp, then quickly shifted the nose of her Luger back to the skull of the cowardly Druid who still kneeled obediently in the corner.

"Boy am I glad to see you," I heard my unaware girlfriend say as she motioned Jeffrey's pupils in the direction of the man in the crosshairs of her weapon.

"This is the piece of shit we've been looking for," she said with a defiant grin. "This is the serial abductor!"

Meridith kept a firm bead on her target as she called out another question to the leopard in the fancy attire.

"Are you armed?" she asked, making brief eye contact with him.

"Yes," I heard him say, as he drew back the material of his blazer and exposed a black revolver attached to his side.

"Good," she said, looking back over at Leon. "Then point it at the head of that sonofabitch in the corner and call for some police back up while you're at it."

"Yes ma'am," Jeffrey rang back and without delay, he drew his holstered gun out from his side and raised it up to the eye line of his secret accomplice.

I watched in vain as the two men exchanged a subtle nod and the man who was still standing pretended to make the call. Meridith, thinking she had just gained an ally in her situation, stuffed her loaded cannon back into its holster and dropped down to my side again, her back turned on the grinning duo. I began haplessly grabbing at Meridith's arm, trying with all my remaining power to warn her of her predicament, to speak out the words she needed to hear. But it was no use. My throat was too saturated with blood and there was no way I was able to push the sentence through.

"Shhh," she said, softly pressing her index finger against my lips. "Save your strength sweetheart, help is on the way."

Meridith continued on with her compassionate reassurances, and all I could do was lay there and watch in a pit of disgust as Leon Jenkins quietly stood up behind her and let his arms fall back to his sides.

It was all sewed up now. And Meridith, finally acknowledging the pained look that would not leave my face, turned around and watched in confusion as Jenkins, the man she had just subdued, emerged out from his cell and stepped into the diminished light. I saw Meridith suddenly tense up and reach for her gun, but her motions were swiftly doused by the danger in Jeffrey's voice as he quickly pivoted his six shooter around and redirected its lethal path to the outline of her of her face.

"Now let's be a good little girl," he growled, and get those hands above your head where I can see them.

My girlfriend reluctantly obeyed his jaded command and hooked her fingers on top of her head, standing up and facing her opponent at the same time. The moonlighter from downtown then bent over calmly and picked up Leon's old-school firearm, the one Meridith had just kicked away, and tossed it across the dugout into the already-waiting hands of it's original owner. I then watched the ominous figure in his long overcoat confidently stroll over and point his returned weapon into Meridith's stomach Jeffrey, now seeing that the long arm of the law was contained, happily tipped his gun south and crammed it back into his side holster.

"Well, well, well," the puny man said in a smirk as he proceeded to bend down and scoop up my child, blanket and all, from my side. "If it isn't the elusive baby Sara."

The bastard that now held my screaming newborn casually waltzed over and showed off his prize to Leon, who was still fatally aiming his gun at Meridith's liver. I heard him tell her that he and Mr. Jenkins had made a "business arrangement", and assured her that all this was nothing personal. After his little speech, I saw Jeffrey glance down at me and unleash a sinister grin.

"You know I have to hand it to you Mr. Lauder," he began to say. "You have quite a talent for evading people. I must have driven over every square inch of this goddam city trying to track you down. Went through a full set of tires" he told me in a smile.

But Simmons laugh was laced heavily with hatred and sarcasm, and I was unable to smooth over his growing insanity with a rebuttal.

"Yes, my friend," he went on. "I searched and searched but you always seemed to be one step ahead of me didn't you? That is until now of course."

I listened to his voice shift down as the crooked pawn bent forward and continued to satisfy his internal craving.

"Guess the better man won, huh?" he spat.

At the end of his boasting, Jeffrey suddenly jumped up, and keeping his stare locked into mine, deliberately walked over and handed off my little girl to the evil predator I had tried for so long to keep her safe from.

"I believe I've held up my end of the bargain," Jeffrey barked greedily as he broke off his glare and replaced it into the face of his partner.

"You most certainly have," the cult follower grinned back joyously as he tucked Sara underneath his arm like a football, his gun religiously keeping its trace on my shocked lady friend.

"And not a moment to soon," he rebuked. "For we are coming up to the eve of SamHein!"

Jenkins twisted his head to the side and stared blankly into us.

"That would be Halloween to you damn Christians," he snarled. "Like that means anything to you two anyways. You imposters are the ones that stole the idea away from us in the first place,"
Leon rambled on for a few more seconds and suddenly, he snagged a piece of mistletoe from his exposed pocket, then dragged the weed across the length of Sara's tiny wailing face, setting it to rest finally on top of her chest.

SamHein... Halloween. The mask? That must be the connection to all of this. It had to be.

"Good job," Leon said to Jeffrey, shattering my train of thought. "You've exceeded my expectations in every way."

"I guess you offing the Chinese lady turned out to be our vagrant boy's breaking point!"

An instant rash of pure hatred fell over me as I heard that confession. I turned my head to the sky and stared at Simmons' face in absolute disgust.

"It was you, you sonofabitch," I thought. A fresh surge of adrenaline rumbled across my body and steadily twisted my fingers into a fist. I wanted to rip his heart out. I wanted to burn his soul and peel off his skin for what he had done, but all I was able to do was glare up at him with my useless body and convey the hardships of a thousand deaths into him through the fury in my eyes.

"I shall sacrifice her tonight! I shall offer her spirit to Druis, the Great Oak," beamed Leon as he hoisted my wailing child up towards the sky.

"I'm sorry, Sara. I'm so sorry I let this happen to you," I whispered as my short-comings dripped into the sand below. Without warning, Leon waved Meridith out of his path and walked over to where I was laying. He purposely bent over and pushed his face close into mine, delivering unto me a harsh statement.

"Did you really think you could outsmart me little boy?" he growled as he stood back up and kicked a shower of dirt into my open wound. The fine dust stung the sensitive exit hole on my still bleeding abdomen.
I was desperate. I couldn't let it end like this. I couldn't die and know I failed Sara.

"If I had just brought a real fucking weapon ," I stammered. "Then everything would be different!"

My hunting knife or the pocket blade I kept in the glove box would have worked just fine. They were real weapons, they were sharp!

But all that didn't matter now. Nope, I was fucked now! I was just about to close my eyes and give up.
But all of the sudden, a couple of words from my previous ravings popped back into my brain again.
Sharp, weapon?
These were the words that were bouncing around the inside of my skull. But why?
Sharp...Weap... Wait a minute. Sharp weapon. Then it hit me. I do have a weapon - the charm! Yes... Yes that's it!

Sara's ninja sleep charm! I remember taking it off the rear view mirror and sticking it into my outside pocket to give to Jeffrey along with her toys. The edges of that thing were like razors and from the position I was in, it was only like 3 inches from my grasp.

A faint glimmer of hope trickled across me as I secretly hashed over the scattered particulars of the idea.
It was a long shot for sure, but let's face it. I had nothing to lose. Finishing up a mental run through of the risky table turner I planned to unleash, I gathered up my energy from wherever I could and slowly tilted my head up to the right. The two men, I soon discovered, were arguing about some kind of payment discrepancy. Leon was waving his hand around violently, obviously unimpressed with his equally shameless partner's new and improved financial demands. Now I knew my strike area, if located at all, was going to be limited. So exercising extreme caution I began secretly mapping out the contours of Leon's body and quickly spotted my bull's eye.
It was a small patch of skin on Leon's ankle that lay innocently exposed below the thick protection of his overcoat and just above his sock. My target was slight, but definitively viable. And I estimated that from where I was laying, it was just within reach of my extended arm. If I could somehow sneak my hand into my side pocket and retrieve the charm without either of the two men noticing, I just might be able

to succeed in slashing the side of Leon's vulnerable leg with the acute talons of that novelty and possibly upset the delicate balance of this intense situation. Just long enough, I hoped, to allow Meridith to draw out her weapon and even up the odds. I knew though, that time was not on my side. So without further thought, I glanced up and made a subtle eye connection with my girlfriend.

She still had her hands in the air, but by the look she returned, I could tell that she too, was assessing the current frailty of the pair's merger, and was slowly inching her fingers down towards her automatic.
She was waiting as well, for the right moment.
A moment that I was about to grant her.
With my cop squeeze watching secretly on, I dropped my head back down and ever so carefully slid my palm across the short span of earth that lay by my hips, ducking it eventually, up into the side fold of my old leather bomber.
I could feel the sharp metal edges of the trinket pressing up against my fingernails. I paused a second, then pushed my hand as deep into my jacket as it would go.

I singled out one of the steep crevices in the toy and began to roll the thing towards the edge of my pocket.
The instant I was able to overlap the remainder of my available digits across the steel, I gripped my chance shiv tightly and eased it out from it's sleeve. With the circular dagger now out in the open, I looked back up at my girlfriend and realized that she had somehow caught onto my subliminal strategy for she was sporting a remarkable grin and tensing herself up for a fight. She gave me a tiny nod and I knew the stage was set.
Leon and Jeffrey had stepped up the pace of their heated discussion and were now yelling wildly at each other. This was good, for it further increased our chances of success. The time to strike was now.
Right now!

So I inhaled a long breath, and with the very last burst of energy I had to offer the world, I swung out my arm and executed my risky blow. My aim proved dead on, and as the lethal edges of that uncommon gadget connected with the tender skin on Leon's ankle, it sliced through the thin membrane of flesh and caused the wound to instantly puke out a large gush of red fluid.
Everything after that began to play itself out in a choppy state of slow motion.
At first, I heard a muffled yell echo out from above. I looked up just in time to watch Leon spin around in agony. His gun went off in that same moment and I then watched on pins and needles as my little girl fell away from his unsteady grip.

I saw Sara flip over the back of his arm and begin to somersault end over end toward the earth. But the good news was that my body lay directly below her fall. I grimaced hard as her petite frame leveled out and struck me in the gut. The impact of her landing sent a painful shockwave throughout my whole system, and for a brief second, Sara actually bounced up once before coming to a final resting spot beside me on her back. The next thing I saw was a quick but steady stream of fire rocketing out from the tip of Meridith's gun in the direction of my ultimate foe, Leon Jenkins.

The plan worked!

Meridith had deciphered my telepathic puzzle and acted it out precisely. Leon's body twisted around violently from the impact of the bullet, then fell lifelessly to the ground. After that, Meridith gained control of the situation by quickly raising her piece into the frozen stare of one Jeffrey Simmons.
"Don't you fucking move!" she yelled.

I crooked my head up and glared at him too. It was a look of utter damnation. But something wasn't right about his stare. It wasn't repentant or shameful. It was more fixed and blank. Then I noticed something on his person. It was barely visible to me, but I could still make it out. It was something on his chest.
It was a hole.

In a tidal wave of delight I watched as my evil nemesis from the government office suddenly dropped to his knees and fell across his already-dead partner. Seems the stray bullet that unknowingly left Leon's revolver, ended up conveniently embedding itself into a much deserving candidate.

"That was for Newa," I whispered as I felt the thud of Jeffrey's spent body pierce the ground that I too, made my final home on. As the muscles in my neck gave out, my head again hit the dirt.
It was all over.

All the bad people were gone, and knowing that we were no longer in danger, Meridith threw down her weapon and fell to my side. Sara initiated her one way debate with the insert of a monstrous howl. It echoed loudly off the cold cement walls and punched a sizable hole through my eardrums. But that was fine by me, and I listened on happily as note by note as my rattled up newborn flatly denounced her love for ten speeds and her general disdain for firearms altogether. I turned my head in the direction of my hysterical baby, but my vision was becoming extremely limited now and I could not make out much of her face. All I could see was the blurry outline of her body.

The lack of blood in my system was quickly beginning to shut down my sensory organs in an effort to conserve and shunt what little life-giving fluid it had left in it towards my more important organs.
I could still hear Meridith yelling wildly into her radio however.

"I need medical assistance at these coordinates right now!" I heard her cry. "Right fucking now."

A few seconds later, I felt her long slender fingers brush up against my face. "It's going to be OK now baby," she lied. "The helicopter is on it's way."

I knew Meridith was struggling to keep her composure by the tremors in her hand and the pitch of her voice. A short pause ensued, but it was followed closely by the familiar sound of crinkled paper being stretched and opened. I understood right away what my girlfriend held in her hand. It was the note I had so ignorantly thrown at her two days before. I felt her eventually place the now-folded piece of paper into my limp hand and manually interlock our fingers around it.

"I'm sorry Eugene," I heard Meridith begin to say as she started to cry. "I'm sorry I didn't tell you who I really was sooner, but I was worried that you would run away from me. I was so scared that you would hate me, but now look what I've done."

"This whole thing is my fault," she sobbed. "All my fault."

Fully understanding that I was more to blame in the lying department, I crept my hand across my chest and rested it overtop the skin to skin union that was already in place.

"Listen Meridith," I whispered. "We were both at fault. What happened here, happened for a lot of reasons. It wasn't just because of one person's actions, especially yours."

"Yes it was Eugene," she shot back interrupting my unbiased confession. "I used you." I used you Eugene because I was selfish."

Meridith's voice suddenly grew faint. I didn't need her to say anything more, but in a sad confession, she did then spill forth the contents of her troubled mind and began to set the record straight.

"You see, sweetheart," I heard her say. "The agency had actually been following this case for many years but still only had a small handful of real leads, none of which were significant. The whole administration was beginning to come under fire for their lack of conviction. Things were getting tense. But when they heard through an anonymous tip that you had Sara, they got together and decided to use you as bait.
They knew that whoever was responsible for the abductions would not be able to resist the opportunity to get their hands on an untraceable victim. A secret task force was then assembled.
That's where I came in.
The bureau gave me a fake resume and got me into the drugstore. No-one there knew who I really was. My job was to befriend you and stay close. My superiors were counting on the perp to make a move on you in an attempt to nab Sara, and when they did, the idea was that I would be there to stop them and make the arrest. It was a desperate and stupid move on my employer's part, but I went along with it because..." another pause overcame my mate, but this one was deeper, "because of Ben," she said finally.

"Eugene there is something else I have to tell you," I listened to her say. "My brother didn't die from a brain disorder, that was another lie."

Meridith stopped talking for a moment and reached into her fleece pocket. She pulled out a small wooden object that I needed no introduction to. I watched in a haze as she then flung an odd-looking symbol against the far wall of the dugout.

"I've researched that goddamn thing for years," she went on saying, "but wound up with nothing. Not one clue! And when all the top detectives in the bureau kept on looking upwards to God for an answer, I decided to shift my thinking towards the other direction.

"Good and evil never hold hands," she stammered. "And in the end, I was the one who was right! It was evil that made up the rules to this fucking game!

That's why I joined the agency in the first place, Eugene. Because I had to know. I had to be the one to take down the sonofabitch responsible for tearing a hole in my family's heart.

You know, I never told anybody I had that piece of wood because I knew the day would come when I would be able to return it to the monster that created it. And everything was going along exactly as planned too.

Except for one thing."

I felt Meridith's voice stand down it's condemnation and grow silent.

"Except for you Eugene."
I never planned on falling in love with you.

Meridith's fingers started to wrap themselves further around mine and released a wave of soft pressure into them. "I love you Eugene Lauder," she said as she set her composure free. "I love you and that's the real truth."

"I love you too Meridith," I whispered back.

I was so happy to hear her say those words, to hear her say that she loved me. But in the same emotion, I was still a little confused by her story.

"Meridith," I said quietly, "How does Ben, how does he fall into all of this?"

"He was abducted," she said immediately. "He was the first one taken by this piece of shit!"

Meridith suddenly lurched forward and landed a vicious punch into the cold limp body of Leon Jenkins.

It was a justifiable assault, but she soon harnessed her anger and continued on with her explanation.

"He disappeared after his birthday when I was twenty years old. He ran off after his party. He was mad because of the caption me and mom had put on his cake. You see, Benny was always very small for his age.

My mother accidentally got pregnant with him when she was forty and he was born premature. Ben was very self-conscious of this and on the day of his birthday, I remembered he came home from school and he was upset. Upset we knew, because the other boys in his class had been teasing him again for being shorter than everyone else. He said he was sick and tired of being so small and stomped off into his room.

Me and mom didn't know what to do so we tried to cheer him up by icing in the phrase "Hang in there tiny mite" onto the top of his chocolate cake. We thought it would make him feel better, but when he did come out for his party, he took one look at those candied words and freaked out!

I guess he didn't like the assumption that he was "tiny", and before we knew it, he had smashed his hand across his cake and ran off with a small handful of his presents. We searched and searched for him everywhere. We put ads out, we put his name over the radio. We did everything we could, everything.

But he never came home.

The only lead the police ever uncovered was that goddam symbol sitting on top a pile of his new gifts in an alleyway three blocks away from our house. That's all that was left."

Meridith ceased her recital almost in the same fashion in which she started and once again, silence fell about the dim room. My heart was numb. I gripped Meridith's hand and guided her face into my own. The kiss I gave her was long and uninhibited and when it was over, I let her head fall onto my chest. Her face was wet and I felt that moisture begin to spill down and saturate my shirt. All the things she told me were answers I needed to hear, but there was still one thing that I wanted to know. That I had to know.

"Meridith," I asked in a faint voice. "There is something I need to know, and I want you to be honest with me no matter what."

"What is it?" she responded quietly back, but I think she already knew what I was about to say.

"I want to know," I continued, "who that man was that you kissed the other day in the parking lot. Please Meridith, I'm not mad. I just need to know the truth."

"His name was Matt," I heard her begin to explain. "He was just an ex-boyfriend. I had called it quits with him a few months ago, about two weeks before I took this case, but he wouldn't let it go. He wanted me back and that was that. We didn't even go out for very long. I realized right away that he was a controlling womanizer and broke it off but he would not acknowledge being shut down and kept on hounding me. He wasn't involved in any of this Eugene I swear. He didn't even know that I was with the agency. I never got around to telling him because I knew it wasn't going to work out. In fact, no-one knew the depth of my classification except my commanding officer. Matt was just a mistake that wouldn't go away. He showed up at the coffee shop out of the blue. He must have followed my car and he began questioning me about who I was meeting there. I was trying so hard to make him leave but it was no use. I didn't want you to see us together because I knew that you were already starting to suspect something as it was. When you saw him kiss me, it was exactly that. He was the one who kissed me.

I'm telling you the honest truth sweetheart. He must have seen you and knew that it would cause a rift between us and that's why he did it. He caught me off guard and before I could retreat, it happened. That's when I saw you. I slapped his face afterwards but you didn't see that part because you were already gone. I was sick to my stomach when I thought of how that must have made you feel. I'm so sorry. I never wanted to hurt you Eugene. I know that you've been hurt enough."

"Christ" Meridith swore. "I should have never let this get so out of control. When I knew that there was a possibility you were in danger I should have said something. I should have tried to help you. I should have blown the whistle but I didn't! Oh Eugene, you can't imagine how hard it was for me, watching you suffer, wondering day and night if you and Sara were alright, and worrying all the time. It was hell, pure hell. But that's all over with now," my girlfriend crooned. "Because everything is going to be on the straight and narrow now and it is only you that I want to kiss, OK baby? Only you!"

I felt her warm lips push up against mine again, and for a brief moment, I could not feel the pain or the chill that had overcome my body. I reached up and wrapped my shivering hand around Meridith's neck, guiding her head over to the side.

"Meridith," I began to whisper. "There is something I want you to know."
"There was not a second in my life that went by in the last five years that I didn't hope and pray that someone.
"That you," I said.
"That I hoped you were out there somewhere waiting for me, just as I was so desperately waiting for you."

I pulled my body in closer and whispered up to her my last message.
"Thank you Meridith," I said. "Thank you for all that you are."

My girlfriend then paralleled my affections and we both surrendered ourselves to the pull of the earth. My mind broke free from all of its worries and a calm sense of purpose gathered within me. Sara had stopped crying but I could still hear the buzz of her shallow breaths tapping out their only song beside me.

"It's OK, sweetheart," I told her in the loudest voice I could manage. "Daddy's right here."

I unlocked my palm from Meridith's and reached it over to find my baby. It felt so good to rest my hand onto her stomach and feel the sweet contractions of her diaphragm. It was a sensation that I could never get enough of. It injected a powerful drug into my system and began to soothe me, just as it had in the beginning as I would lay with her on my chest in the dead of night, hidden away under a streetlight in a decaying part of the city, waiting for the sun to free us once again. I was going to miss that. I knew I was going to miss out on so many things but I also realized, that throughout her whole life, I would always be able to see her and feel her presence from the other side.

I promised my child that I would not miss out on a single day of my parental responsibilities, for now, I was in the process of becoming her guardian angel, and was also looking forward to meeting my own.
Sara started to fuss. I think she somehow sensed that my lifeline was in jeopardy and was trying to help. I crooked my head in the direction of my daughter and began to quietly console her.

"Don't you ever feel bad about any of this," I told her, "because you know what? I wouldn't have wanted it to turn out any other way. You're out of harm's way now honey, and you will always be safe from here on in. As for me, well, I'll tell you what," I said, pooling up my strength enough to voice out a joke. "I feel like one of the luckiest dudes around right now, do you know why? Because I'm surrounded by the two most beautiful girls in the world, that's why."

I heard Meridith push out a tiny giggle, but I could no longer see where she was for I was officially blind to all the dimensions of the earth, and only by the reconstruction of the echoes that swirled about my head was I able to paint a picture of what was going on in around me.

"I love you both," I said clearly. "I will always feel you within me."

I felt a warm tear from Meridith's eye splash down the length of my wrist.

"I'll see you two tomorrow," I whispered. "It will probably seem like a little longer on your end, but for me.
"For me, it will only be tomorrow. And then we will all be together once more".
"This time forever."

A wide smile stretched across my face as I spoke those words, and with the last ounce of consciousness I had left, I called out one last request to the woman who lay beside me.

"Take good care of Sara, Meridith. She needs you now."
"She needs a mommy."

No more words left my lips. In the background I could faintly begin to hear the popping sound of the chopper blades as they descended down onto the abandoned field somewhere out in front of the dugout.

"They're coming. They're coming!" I heard Meridith scream out. "The paramedics are here. They're here and they're going to take you to the hospital! Eugene, Eugene, can you hear me?" she bellowed.

"Yes my love," I thought into nothing. "I do hear you."

But I'm afraid I was going to have to miss that ride this Halloween night, for now I believed I was on my way to a very different destination.
As the world around me began to swiftly fade away and the echoes of the life that I once knew became quieter and quieter, I somberly released my grip on the living and set free my soul, so that it could venture forth and find the other side. Memories of conversations telling of bright lights and angelic figures projected themselves forward as I waited quietly for the summary of my life to begin.
But it didn't happen that way.

It didn't go down the way it was supposed to, and instead of drifting off towards a soft inviting light, I found the presence of my body walking down a long hallway towards a dense wooden door ,with the familiar sound of a little boy's cries rattling out from in behind it.

No, Godammit! This can't be happening, I don't want to go through this anymore. Jesus! Haven't you had enough fun with me yet?

My pleas were pointed and mean, but they had absolutely no impact on the direction of my feet and they simply continued to plod on. It appeared that my access into the next plane was not being granted to me and I'd never felt so betrayed. I resisted my spiritual arrest as hard as I could, but my legs just kept moving robotically towards that bloody door! I tried desperately to reverse my course, but no matter what I did, it seemed that my unrelenting nightmare had somehow bent the rules of crossing and found a way to inject it's final treason into me. I was furious, but not very surprised because from the moment I struggled through the very first apparition, I had a sick feeling that I would never be able to fully escape it's misery, in this world, or the next.

I didn't really know just what it was trying to accomplish though. I mean hell, I already knew the answers to its screwed-up puzzle. I mean I lived and died them so what the fuck? My first instinct was to resist, but it was pointless, so I opted to just let the dream run its course for I knew that at least now, it would be for the last time.

I could tell, though, that this nightmare was very different from the others. I wasn't just suffering through another one dimensional skit.

This time it was real.

It was actually happening moment by moment and my eyes made out all the shapes and sounds around me with exact definition. The only difference now was the harsh reality that I could no longer wake up.

When I eventually reached the closet door and my obedient hand pulled it open, I looked down like before and saw the not-so-innocent clown mask peering back up at me. Muffled sobs echoed out from behind its plastic sheath, and the entity who wore it still executed a deadly grip upon the wax letter that sat in its hand.

Like a puppet being guided by some unseen string, I reached down against my will and removed the mask from the adolescence face. I felt my soul tighten up and brace itself for the always grotesque display that accompanied this maneuver, but as the clown mask fell to the floor, the picture behind it was no longer hideous. In fact, the face I saw staring up at me was quite pleasant. It was the vision of the young boy I often stared at through the window of a finely crafted frame that made it's home on the top of Meridith's refrigerator.

It was Ben.

It was the very sibling that my soul mate desperately spoke of and seemingly devoted so much of her life to.

"Are you gonna kill me?" he asked.

"No Ben," I assured him softly. "I am **not** going to kill you. And from now on, everything is going to be alright. You're not in any danger anymore my friend."

I dropped to one knee and began to wipe the tears away from his cheeks with my fingers. I think then, that he felt a sense of honor in my company and proceeded to lift up his dirt-laden hand, releasing to me the bastardized wax statement that he had always guarded so heavily in the past. As I accepted his heartfelt gift, a sticky substance brushed off from his palm and transferred it's goop into mine. Dirt was the next thing that came to my mind, but the material that occupied his small palm was not organic at all. It was manmade and it sent a sweet aromatic haze into my nostrils. It wasn't soil that coated his hands.

It was cake.

It was the contagious mixture that obviously hitched a ride on him when he slammed his angry mitt down into it. I nodded my head in thanks, then opened up my palm to get a better look at his odd keepsake.

As I scanned over his present, I discovered that it was definitely made of wax, but it was not in the shape of an "I" like I had always thought; it was molded to the configuration of the number one. This discovery made no sense. Ben was young, but he was way older than one. I briefly hashed over this new information, but quickly cast the whole process aside the second I saw the young boy in front of me begin to smile. That event pulled rank on everything else because that's all I really came there to see in the first place. Apparently my right to passage had been stayed until I understood the final outcome of my efforts.

Until I saw him smile.

I concluded that his joy was the key to our peace. I guess legal entry into the afterworld relies solely on one going there with a pure conscience. It all lined up now. Obviously I had not yet fulfilled the proper requirements to genuinely make the transition. That was until now, of course, and as the young boy, who had for so long been unknowingly trapped in the same prison as I began to boast a beautiful grin, a huge feeling of closure lit up the dim closet. I continued to comfort him as I crouched there, and when I was satisfied that I had successfully driven away the bulk of his fears, I drew in my hands and went to say goodbye. For now that all was well with his soul, I felt that I needed to moving on in search of my own.

And I was just about to voice that bon voyage when I noticed his bright smile start to fade and be replaced with the onset of an uncharacteristically evil snarl.

I became quite confused at this sudden change of mood, for I thought that my well-timed affections had done the trick in turning the tides on his sorrow. For a second time I peered into the little boys eyes, but deeper now, as I searched for a reason to his darkness. Anything to warrant the basis for this strange transformation.

But those eyes, to my great worry, had turned jet black and remained empty.

Something was wrong.

I felt a cold shiver cut its way through me as I stood up and backed slowly away. Ben's devil-like eyes kept their bead on me with deadly precision, but then quickly

shifted their position to the left and fixated themselves on something behind me.
I went to turn my head to see just what his demonic stare had spotted, but before
I could so much as even pivot my head a quarter of the way around, a man's arm,
whom I now understood belonged to that of the late Leon Jenkins, swung across the
front of my body and sealed a wad of strange smelling cloth around my mouth.

I struggled fiercely as I tried to break free from his stranglehold and keep him from
pulling me backwards.
I fought and fought but it was no use for the chemicals that were embedded in
the cloth were quickly beginning to render my muscles useless. It didn't take long
for my nervous system to throw in the towel and I watched helplessly as my hands
dropped numbly away from their defensive stronghold and ended up impotent and
tingling at my sides. And as my body succumbed to the powerful sedative, I felt
another arm snake it's way around my ribs and encircle the flailing weight of my
carcass that my thighs could no longer support.

From there, all I could do is watch blindly as my heels began to scrape backwards
along the floor as the image of the now-empty closet became smaller and smaller.
And then there was silence.
For either a second or a century, I didn't really know. But then, just like that, I
suddenly found myself in a dark room.
I was in an enclosure of some sort and my arms were held up high in strange
rejoicement while I listened on without a choice to the soft throws of the spiritual
hymns that echoed on in the foreground.

I also heard digging.

In my mind's eye, I could visualize the tool hammering away at the earth and it
was clear to me now that these two coincidences made perfect sense and kept the
dream in sync with the others. But unfortunately, my arms would not fall back down
from their elation because somewhere above my head, they were being secured from
doing so.
The cell was very dark but there was a tiny light source escaping out from somewhere. I figured it must have been seeping in through a crack in a door of some kind,
that I was sure, lay off to the left of me.
I concluded that I was probably in the basement of an old house. I had to be. All
the evidence pointed to that, right down to the musty smell of rotting timbers above,
so I began tilting my head upwards, resting it between the space in my arms to try
and get a fix on just what type of material was responsible for holding me hostage to
those beams.

As I pushed forth with my exploration, I started to make out the consistency of
multiple layers of silver- backed adhesive that I knew could only belong to that of
industrial duct tape. The binding was spun around the rafter directly above my head
and crisscrossed repeatedly around my wrists that were now numb from the pressure
of that constriction. To counteract the effects of that damage, I stood up high on my
toes and allowed the glorious rush of fresh blood to flow into my hands. I continued
this therapy until my fingers were once more under my direction.

I was wide awake now, but dizzy. Whatever my attacker had used to subdue me was still floating about certain parts of my system, but it's effects were steadily fading away with each passing second. Time was not on my side however, and I understood that no matter what realm I was in, it was imperative that I get out of it as soon as possible. I scrambled internally for possible escape options before my mind finally zeroed in on the best one. The tape first of all, had to be severed, but the only sharp tool I possessed now had been supplied to me at birth.

Yep, those pearly whites of mine were about to be put to the test in a big way. If I could just find the strength to hoist up my body far enough to bite into the sides of the sticky handcuffs that bound me, then maybe, just maybe after a few passes the weight of my frame would act as a catalyst and release me back down to the ground. I knew duct tape was known for it's strength, but so was the human jaw. I was just about to heave myself up for the first pass when I remembered how loud of a noise that kind off tape made when it tore.

That subtle bit of info put a temporary damper on my plans, but luckily, that chance detour was quickly abolished the moment my ears caught the intermittent union of steel meeting dirt.

"That's it," I thought.

I would just have to pull myself up and get my fangs into position on the edges of the tape, then wait until the precise second that I heard the first blast of the shovel thrust so that I could twist my neck to the right and begin wearing away the vulnerable rope. I knew the noise from the impact of the shovel would easily mask over the audible ripping sounds of the tape. It all checked out. It was time to act out this deadly role, so I drew in a solid chunk of air and hoisted my surprisingly heavy remains upwards, fumbling around momentarily, but eventually securing my gums tightly into the sides of the gooey flap. My muscles screamed in agony as I forced them to keep working and waited for the beginning of my assailant's unknown smokescreen.

That moment came quickly.

And as I heard the end of the shovel break through the first level of dirt, I bit down on that cloth with all I had and twisted my noggin off to the side. It worked! Both ideas worked, and the encircling band of material gave way a full inch into itself. The stark ripping sound, as planned ,was easily overpowered by the strong reverberation of the tool behind me as it continued on with its carnage. I lowered my body back to the floor and hung there again on my toes, letting my spent arms rest ever-so-briefly before I yanked myself up once more so I could get my chompers back into place. I waited patiently for the next strike.

Without a second's more power to lose, the shovel again pounded down on the earth and opened the doors for me to squeeze off another shot at the sticky restraints that imprisoned me. Everything was going along just as planned, but then my mind slipped up and allowed a small tidbit of information to barge through it's heavily guarded wall of concentration.

A grave.

Holy Shit Eugene! That's what's being dug man. A fucking grave.
...My grave!!

Well that was it, and back down I went. I couldn't budge an inch after that. I became overrun with fear and was unable to continue on with my demolition. My brain, for whatever reason, had thrown a badly-timed monkey wrench into my thought process. All I could do was hang there now, like a frozen side of beef, as I listened on to the terrifying sound of the spade as it plodded onward, steadily capping my fate with each devastating blow.

Snap out of it Eugene. All that tape above you needs is one, maybe two more hits max, so come on and snap the fuck out of it. There's no time to choke on the eight ball now.

I listened on to my inner reason, but was still paralyzed at the knowledge of my recent translation and could not get my body to come out from its trance. That was until it occurred to me.

Hey, what am I worried about? I'm already dead!

I nearly let out a chuckle at my stupidity, but that motion was instantly severed at the root as another frightening idea snuck into my head.

What if this is Hell?

This time, the damning realization of that very possibility managed to rock the boat enough and shake me free from my drunk. With newfound zeal, I sucked in another deep breath and thrust my body towards the ceiling to clamp my mouth around the already-shredded edge of the band once more. As the shovel obediently struck home, so did my own, and the wounded adhesive finally gave way to the weight of my unbalanced mass and released me back down to the dirt floor. Within seconds I had pulled off the remaining fastener from my swollen wrists and was bathing happily in a short-lived ray of hope. Even though I wasn't sure exactly how long I'd been hanging there, it did not matter. What mattered was the fact that I was free, and now capable of finding my way out of this demonic cubicle so that I could head back in the direction of the infamous light at the end of the tunnel, wherever I hoped it lay waiting for me.

I tiptoed onward a few steps, but stopped suddenly as I succumbed to my curiosity and turned around.
I shouldn't have done that, I really, really shouldn't have, but I wanted to see where the music and the illumination were coming from.
Turns out I was right in my assumption that the manmade extras I'd both seen and heard were drifting out from behind a small crack in an entranceway door about six feet away and to the rear of where I was now standing. Satisfied for the moment, I turned my head back to it's original position and began using that same beam of light

to help guide me. And guide me it did. Straight in the direction of a landmark I had secretly known would be there. With fresh confidence, I gazed up in relief at an old cellar door. It was pretty common knowledge that all basements in dwellings this ancient had them. And I also knew exactly where that partially rotted-out chute led to. It opened up directly into the alleyway.

I knew this because my grandfather used to have the identical setup in his house before he died.

In the early days, those steep accesses were used to unload coal and wood into the bottoms of the residence to consume for heat and cooking. Wasting no more time, I quietly shuffled my body up closer to my dense escape hatch and started to run my fingers up and down the length of it to try and locate the trip hatch. I found it right away. It was in the center of the block, just like it was supposed to be. Keeping in sync with the action of the shovel once more, I began twisting the cold steel handle over to the right. It moved with ease and just as I was ready to push up on the ground-level passageway and remove my disjointed "whatever the hell I was" away from this uncommon rest stop, something stopped me and peeled my fingers back away from the latch.

NO! NO! NO!

I protested silently to whoever in the fuck was responsible for this overrated safari and watched in dismay as my feet began to slowly back themselves away from my escape.

NOO!... I want to go now. Please, for the love of God, let me get out of here!

Pleading desperately with my unseen puppeteer, I pressed on with my internal grievance and, for a second there, I figured I might have actually persuaded the powers that be to spare me their bleak itinerary. But nope, it didn't happen like that and my body just kept digressing back to where it started.

Oh for fuck sakes, I already know the answer to this bloody riddle, alright. I mean come on already, I just want some peace now OK. Is that too much to ask?

I directed my thoughts up towards the heavens but to my disgust, the requests I demanded only made it as far as the old cedar door before they gave up and ran back down my throat. I tried several times to halt the invisible forces progression as it backed me up closer to the door that I thought I was supposed to be trying to get the Hell away from. Then without warning, that same entity spun my feet around the other way.

I attempted to resist this realignment, but it was pointless. Whomever or whatever was hosting this little shindig was calling all the shots and all I could do was watch in amazement as my legs began to rise and fall in the direction of that goddam room.

This is crazy, I know who did it. OK I know it was Leon and I'm, I'm alright with that. OK I'm alright with that. So what's the point of all this?

Now I was mad!

I was really fucking mad, and I was just about to tilt my head up and denounce the very God I was trying to find, but again, something slammed my chops shut and my feet just kept making their way forward. There was nothing else I could do except wait this thing out and try to act surprised. You know, I really thought dying was going to be a lot easier.

Like I had jumped inside a remote control car, I felt my body pivot for a second time and shuffle its mass up along the roughly-framed wall that also supported the door. My head and neck then began their automatic descent toward the two inch wide opening of light and sound. The first images I saw were those of digging tools: picks, shovels, gloves, stuff like that.

But Jesus, I already knew there were going to be things like that in there, so once again I started to protest, cranking my head back away from the glowing sliver. But as before, my pupils obediently receded back to their starting positions and continued to peer further and further into the mystery beyond that door. I was at my wits end. It was clear to me now that whoever organized this impromptu peek-a-boo intended to see it through and that was the end of it! I no longer fought the urge to halt the momentum of this cheap movie and I finally allowed my senses to be taken over.

My eyes began to focus in more intently on the contents of the room. At first, I just saw the end of a shovel being thrust into a large pile of rock and dirt. In the background appeared a modest record player that I now understood was the source of the ironically uplifting melodies.

After that I picked up the image of a man's hand and forearm attached to the same tool, so I narrowed my pupils and focused in on that limb in search of Leon's damning tattoo. But I could not make it out. It was too dark to highlight the drawing. So I just kept on with my visual journey and began, instead, to focus in on rest of the man who held the spade. I was in the process of lifting my head so that I could glare some more hatred into that horrible Druid's face, but moments before I made that contact, I caught a glimpse of something familiar sitting on the counter beside the man who dug the holes.

It was something white.

Upon further examination I realized that the object in the near distance was indeed the clown mask I had seen many times over inside the perimeters of my dream. It was torn in half and badly crushed, but it was definitively the same toy that haunted me. I watched with a heavy heart as the lone occupant of the dark room delivered the last shovelful of earth overtop the lifeless face of Meridith's younger sibling and sealed the innocent boy's body in a coffin of dirt right before my eyes. In a nanosecond I came to know that it was not my final resting place that was being dug.
It was Ben's.

I thought of my girlfriend, and her unending vigil that I now realized had forever been a lie. I wanted to call out to her. I wanted to inform her of the things I had just learned so that I could end her pain and grant her the peace of mind she needed to begin healing. But I knew that was not possible and I felt my insides begin to fill themselves up again with rage and contempt towards the cult-following bastard in that room. I wanted to kill him all over again and make him suffer in the same way he had hurt Meridith and everyone else. I thrust my head up out of my own free will this time and prepared to stare into the eyes of the man I had come to ultimately despise, but his face was still hiding shamelessly in the dark shadows of the room.

Come on you sonofabitch. Look at me. Show me your ugly face. "Show me"!!

Without warning, my wish was suddenly granted. But the answer I was given was not the one I had fantasized about. The hazy outline of the person I was spying on stood up straight and flung his digging tool off to the side. The tiny lantern hanging above the grisly scene that had been kind enough to provide the vehicle for this joyride up until now again acted unselfishly as it splashed a fleeting cup of light across the beast's face in the foreground so that I could finally pass judgment and condemn him forever.

But the side profile of the devil in my sights, now easily recognizable thanks to the lantern's aid, was not that of the animal I always expected it to be. And with deadly precision my spirit came to know, that although Leon Jenkins was indeed an evil man by every right, he had just paid the ultimate price for someone else's sins.

I stood peering forward in complete shock as I watched my old camp scout leader, Barry McDool, viciously thrust his foot down onto the top of the freshly dug grave and pack the soil down tight.

I was devastated.

I could barely comprehend the scene that was unfolding right before my very eyes.

I mean Barry McDool?

No way man! Not possible. That just didn't make any sense. Hell, he loved us guys. We never even saw him so much as squash a bug for Christ Sakes, let alone commit murder! This was all too much, and I didn't give a Goddam who was in charge of this memory-lane catastrophe anymore. I just wanted out. So I forced my head in the direction of the cellar door and to my great relief, it retreated back with ease, but not before it made a slight downward loop towards the ground. What I saw then was another object on the floor that was also being highlighted by the contained flame of the lantern. It was a wax figurine. It was the same one that Ben had always held in his hand and in this mystery. Slowly I bent down and picked it up. When it was secured in my hand, I brought it ever so easily into the dim light. Yep. It was definitely the same wax numeral that Ben handed me earlier on.

But wait a minute, no.

No, this one was different. It was a little bit rougher on the one side and it also had a... it had a wick in it?
Hold on a second here. This one appears to have been broken.

276

That's it.

It was the other piece of Ben's candle that sat atop his birthday cake. The one he had smashed in two before he ran off. One and one would equal two. No, no wait a minute. It doesn't make two. One and one together means eleven. Ben wasn't two. He was eleven. And the mask wasn't promoting Halloween at all. It was one of his birthday presents!

"I understand", I whispered as I glanced upwards. "Now can I go home?"

I'm not sure if my pleas were heard or not, but I didn't care, for my body, I mean, I guess it was still my body, suddenly broke free from the chains that held it and instantly began to move on my command, the first of those being the order to drop the sticky evidence that lay in my hand. The second was the instruction to turn my bloody feet towards the cellar and get the fuck out of their ASAP! This time, though, I followed the wall to my left in an effort to keep out of the light and remain unnoticeable. For now that Barry had completed his chores he was, in theory, much more alert to any subtle changes that happened around him.

My pace was swift but soft, and I only made it a few steps forward before my forehead accidentally brushed up against something, something hanging from the roof. I crooked my head back and looked up at the pungent rafters, hoping that the glow from the lantern was still prepared to offer me a little help. But the doorframe behind me was lower than the object I sought to view so I was out of luck.

Just then though, a stream of liquid from the still unknown object dribbled down into my hair and streaked across the length of my cheek. I reached up in disgust and felt around for the strange thing that produced this ooze, and I wasn't at all surprised when the wooden artifact above fit perfectly within my hand. I slowly lifted the now-famous hand-carved symbol off a crude wire drying harness and let my forearm fall back into the light. I stood there and stared down in defeat at the damp creation that hid in my palm. Everything fell into place. It was Barry all along. He was the real serial abductor that the authorities had been looking for.

But why, why him?

He had everything any man could ever hope for and then some. I just didn't get it. He was our idol. He was the perfect being.
He was...

Ahh Fuck it, don't know and don't care!

As it was I could have stood there for another century trying to figure out the answers to that travesty, but I knew I was already running late for a very important departure. So I let the trinket fall to the ground and stepped further into the direction of my escape hatch. But my forehead again hit something, and when I stopped and tilted my head toward the ceiling this time, a wave of disbelief swept over me. I was walking a fine line with my sanity as I fanned my open fingers across the bottom ends of rows upon rows of that same carving that I had just sent to the floor. There must have been hundreds of them resting there on hooks along that side wall. The stench of linseed oil burned my nostrils as I gazed up at the overwhelming mass of soon-to-be headstones.

I wanted to scream out and warn the world of my find, but I could not, for I no longer belonged to that union. Whatever happened in the future, no matter how horrible, I'm afraid was not up to me to decide or control. I dropped my head in defeat and made my way to the outline of the crude plank.

I heard Barry moving something around in the other room, but at that point I didn't really care what he was doing anymore, even though I had a pretty good idea what was going on. He was preparing another grave. I would never know whose, but I didn't care. I just wanted out.

After I had arched a few more steps to the right, I reached out in front of me and felt the rough familiarity of a step. And another, and another which I crept up until my forehead scraped up against the low-lying structure of the hatch above. I knew that musty slab was my last obstacle to freedom. I pushed on the outside door carefully and it began to rise with ease. Before I knew it, I was standing in the backyard of McDool's unassuming house in the dead of night, the very residence that I had once come to in search of peace and affirmation.

Ten twenty six was the number on the back door.

Ya... Ya, that's right. His address was 1026 Melnor Street.

I could see the outline of his front yard in my head, but I'll tell you what, I didn't stand around that place and reminisce for too long, I just dug my heels into the wet grass and tore down the alley. It was the middle of the night and the city was empty.

I ran on without pause. Where I was heading I wasn't sure, but as my legs propelled me on, I came to the understanding that I had been granted an unfortunate front row seat to an atrocity. It was a crime where, in the end, my mind decided it best that I never recall again, except through the scattered remnants of an untimely premonition. It made the call to keep me safe, but that decision also kept me on the run. I wondered what the better of the two were, but the answer to that question now, was no longer within my reach.

I ducked in and out of yards and down endless roads until my feet finally dumped me out in front of a large time honored gate.

"Central Park", read the inscription on the rusty steel header.

Well, here we go again.

At that point, I still wasn't completely sure what was going on. I mean I knew I was dead, or very close to it anyway, but the events unfolding now were still that of the dream. I was pretty sure though, that this all had something very important to do with my immortality, or my level of my placement within it, so I just let the movie play itself out. Once I had slipped inside the gate, I found my spirit happily strolling through the vast helix of swaying trees and soft grass. A great sense of calm fell over

278

me as I watched the lurking silhouettes of a giant firs wave about. It was a much-needed sensation after what I had just gone through. And as my legs led me farther into the park, I began to make out the faint origins of the slides and the merry-go-rounds. Before I could react, my feet began to robotically make their way over to the general vicinity of those amusements and begin to zero in on the hull of the cement whale slide that I so loved playing on as a child.

I was then mysteriously led to a spot directly facing the marine duplicate and brought to a stop.

Now what?

I didn't really know what was so special about that ride, except for the fact that me and Steve used to spend so much time playing on it when we were younger. Nonetheless, my feet remained planted and did not budge. At first I became a little restless, but the more I stood there in front of that stone fish and stared into its huge mouth, the more I began to smile. I started to remember all the times me and my buddy used to dive off of it head first, or hide inside it's hull and watch the sky pass over us through the hollow eye above.

And then there was...

Wait a minute. Hollow eye?

My brain quickly began to edit back through the acts of the last couple of dreams and highlight the constant of the "circular window" that led to the sky. It was another clue. But how did the roughed-in socket of this manufactured herring end up with a role in my nightmare?

Just then the moon drifted out from behind a cloud and ended my confusion as a flood of the planet's rays spilled out onto the park and lit up the inside of the murky hull through the portal of that meager window. That's when I saw him and I knew that my dream was just about over, for inside the now vivid belly of the ride sat a young man whom I easily recognized.

I knew his features exactly.
He was me.

He was in a more juvenile state, this ghost, but we were the same people. The phantom did not see me though. He was just sitting there crouched up in that pungent cavity staring upwards at the molded sphere that loomed above him. When I looked closer, I saw his hands were shaking. This spirit was confused. He was scared.
I knew why.
It's because that's where I ran to. That's where I spent the night after I had escaped the cellar. My mind, like always, had guided me there because that's where it felt safe. That's why I was picked up by the police as I stumbled around the city in a stupor the following morning. The time when Steve had to come down and get me.

Now, all the pieces to this puzzle were finally in place.

The unwelcome nightmare I had struggled so hard to understand had at long last, surrendered all of its hostages.

I guess I had known the truth all along, but had subconsciously washed away all the memories of that horrible night in an attempt to protect my destiny.

Destiny

I spoke the word over and over in my head a few times. I was trying hard to make peace with that idea, for I still didn't know just what it had in store for me. But my visions of hell and heat vanished a few moments later as the side of my eye caught a glimpse of a small light source.

The one I'd been waiting for.

It was beginning to form in the sky just above the tree line, so I turned to the north and began to watch a bright sphere start to funnel its way down from the heavens toward me. An immense sigh of relief ousted my despair and happily paroled my nervous conscience.

"Thank God!" I gasped! And it suddenly occurred to me, that at the very moment I was able to solve my mortal riddle, was in turn the very same point in time in which I was able to adjust it's outcome.

You know it's funny, but I felt no sadness. Even though I knew death had officially overcome me in the real world, I was not afraid. I don't know, I guess the whole process was just too wonderful. It was so surreal the way the tornado-like pillar weaved it's way down towards the earth. I was as calm as can be as my passageway to the other world finally stopped it's descent and came to a hover not even five feet above my head. I could feel the warmth and love emanating out from all around it. I was ready to go.

I think I even understood too, why I was forced to suffer through all of those painful memories. I guess it was not possible to enter into another realm without first making sense of the old one. From where I was standing, I could hear the enclosure in front of me begin to call out my name. I glanced back at the animated slide one last time to bid farewell to the troubled memory I was about to leave behind, but to my surprise the young man who had been hiding within, had crawled out of his musty coffin and was now heading straight for me. His stride was slow, but deliberate. I struggled to understand this latest move, but the closer the mirage drew in towards me, the more I started to realize the purpose of his trip. I knew there was still one thing left to do.

It was time to say I was sorry.

I knew I had to make things right with my younger soul. I had to make my amends for shamelessly harboring so many secrets away inside him. And as he drew in closer I was not surprised to find him looking very upset. He had earned that right, and as his aura came to a stop directly in front of me, I noticed his brow was also crooked and his hands were joined in worry. He glared deep into my eyes in an assault of contempt and defeat. Suddenly I felt a universe of emotion tear through my body as the demonic offspring of a thousand bad decisions began to stake their claims and steal back the blood they were owed. I winced as the forgotten travesties wreaked their long overdue havoc on my exposed soul.

In an effort to make right my sins and console the teenager who had bore them
for so long, I shut my eyes and held out my arms, whispering to the desperate soul
before me that I was indeed, so very sorry for not being stronger than I was, for
taking the easy road out and casting him so deeply into shame.

My apologies were widespread. But when it was all said and done, I succumbed to
the fact that I was really just coming to terms with the failures of my own existence,
a task I'm positive that everyone who lives must finally do. After a lengthy confession, I slowly unveiled my eyes to accept my punishment, but to my relief the spirit
in my view was not writhing in anger anymore, and instead was sporting a tremen-
dous smile.

Why? After all I put you through, why do you not respond with anger? Why?

The apparition did not acknowledge my prompts and simply kept on grinning as he
walked forward and stepped through my arms, disappearing into my chest where I
felt him finally close his eyes.
The guilt-ridden spirit that had orchestrated such complex series of events in my
life and my death was finally at peace. Now the smile I boasted was pure. And in this
state of peace, I lazily turned my body back towards the light and noticed that the
heavenly taxi had now repositioned it's doorway right at the base of my feet.
Without further hesitation, I shifted my dominant leg forward stepped into the lip
of the giant rope. I went to follow up my right step with a left, but it grew heavy and
would not move.
Then I began to hear a voice... no, many voices. I strained to hear more, tipping my
head deeper into the vaporous hallway.
Seconds later the same voices called out to me again. Were they of family? Lost
friends? My grandfather maybe? This confused me, and suddenly another voice
echoed out from behind me. I spun around to identify the origin of that latest noise,
but only the placid hue of the park came into view, nothing else.
I turned back towards the tunnel and prepared to dive inside, but to my immense
shock I saw that it had begun to recede back up toward the clouds.

Noo, please come back, please, what are you doing? Please don't go!

I ran forward and tried to touch the tail end of the spiral before it became too high
to reach, hoping to somehow pull it back down and jump inside. But the doorway
quickly continued its backward descent at an unholy pace.

Please, please come back I cried.

I fell to my knees.

I didn't mean to turn around. Please God, I won't do it again I promise.

I begged the light to return and initiated an onslaught of apologies in the direction
of the sky. I pleaded on without letup to the higher power to give me a second chance
but it was not to be, and my star gate quickly disappeared back into the darkness. I

collapsed to the ground a broken man.

Why, why did you leave? I told you I was sorry. Oh God don't do this to me. I've been good. I have, I really have!

My conscience hollered on without pause in a dim effort to reverse the heinous conspiracy it had just witnessed. I was devastated beyond imagination to think that I had unknowingly broken some divine rule and was now being denied my access into heaven. But my pleas were all ignored as the incomprehensible voice that I now held solely responsible for my recent damnation kept on chattering away behind me.

"Eugene, Eugene," it taunted. "Can you hear me?"

I refused to acknowledge the calling, for I felt I wanted to kill it for ruining my right to passage.

"Eugene," the voice blared out again, this time a lot closer and a lot clearer. "Are you here?"

Well that was it! In a fit of rage I stood up and spun around, yelling at the noise to go away. I expected the landscape behind me to look the same way, but it did not. It had turned pitch black and deathly still.
This was not a good sign, for I had heard once that purgatory was just a fancy adjective for Hell.
It was impossible for me to comprehend that I was about to enter into such a terrible place, so I closed my eyes in defeat and warned myself never to open them again. The next voice I expected to hear was that of the devil, so I braced my mind for this reality. But suddenly I heard the tone in question lift itself up to that of a higher pitch.

"Eugene, Baby, come back to me sweetheart. Come back to me," it sang.

Well with that surprise addition, my eyes shot back open and began to frantically search through the darkness for the birthplace of that alluring proposition.

"I'm over here," I yelled.

For the words I had just heard were that of a woman, a very special woman.
It was Meridith voice! I knew that song off by heart.
I wasn't sure how she got through, but I was definitely going to find out! I went to advance forward, to try and get closer to the source, but my damn feet were pinned to the ground again.

"Move feet, godammit, move already," I hollered!

I struggled hard to break free from the invisible chains that bound me but soon realized that I was not going anywhere. Enraged at the possibility that I was being shafted for a second time, I twisted my head toward the sky and screamed out a harsh message to my maker.

What are you doing to me? Haven't you had enough fun, huh, haven't you?
I said I was sorry, alright. I know that I could have saved a lot of people from suffering, but I was a coward. Is that what you want to hear me say, huh? That I was a coward?
Well OK then, I was. I was weak. But what the hell was I supposed to do, huh? I was sixteen fucking years old! Who would have believed me anyway?
What did you want me to do?
Die along with the rest of them? Would that have made you happy, huh, would it? Well I didn't, OK
I survived. I had to survive!
You left me no choice.

With nothing further to say, I dropped my head to the ground and felt the beautiful sense of peace I thought I had finally earned begin to fall away from me. The eternal warmth I had so fantasized about was all but a memory now. It had vanished along with the mysterious stairway that produced it. I shamelessly called out for that escalator's return one last time, but it was gone forever. I closed my eyes and squinted hard as I felt the vicious return of the cold air creep up the length of my back and reassert its power over me, riddling my skin as well, with a blast of sand and rubbish that it had brought with it. I sheltered my face with the cups of my hands as I readied my spirit for an alternate destination.

I guess purgatory was my final destination after all, but when I finally got up the courage to inhale, I noticed that the air was neither stale nor burning like I painfully expected it to be. The smell that overcame me instead, was sweet and aromatic. I quickly inhaled the drug again, milking the euphoric scent for all it was worth.

Wait a second.

I carefully opened my eyes.

I know that scent. It was perfume. Christ. It was Meridith's perfume. Oh my God.

Meridith must be dead too!

"What in the name of all that is sacred is going on here?" I blasted.

With no more fear of the realm in front of me, I tore my hands away from my face and yelled out a stern order into the dead air of the abyss.

I want some fucking answers, and I want them right now. You hear me? RIGHT NOW!

Suddenly a stranger's voice blasted a painful answer directly into my chest: "CLEAR!"

It was then that I felt an enormous surge of energy rip through my body and before I knew it, I felt my soul being thrust backwards at an insane rate. The vague shadows of the park disappeared instantly and were replaced by blinding rays of an overhead lamp.

"CLEAR!"

The strange command blared out overtop me once more as the pointed bolt of energy exploded through my rib cage. My eyes burst open and attached themselves directly onto a heavyset, bald man who was hovering above me.

"We got him," yelled the stranger as he cranked his head off to the side.

I hadn't a clue where I was, but I could feel the presence of something on my face. A mask I think.
A hissing mask of some sort covering my mouth. I could also hear buzzers and blades and I sensed that I was moving. Yes, I was definitively moving! I tried lifting my head with the power of the muscles in my neck and I was successful. That was an excellent sign! I squeezed my hands together too, just to make sure that I was... Yes!

That I was alive!
Holy shit! I was alive! I almost couldn't believe it!
I rifled an infinite amount of thank yous towards the sky, amazed by the fact that I wasn't worm food! Suddenly, another man appeared above me and began feverishly opening a rounded bag of clear fluid which he proceeded to hang on a silver pole beside me that already supported a multitude of red ones.

"Eugene, Eugene!"

The female voice I had been flirting with on the other side finally materialized, and I watched with unprecedented joy as Meridith's slender face eclipsed the stark examination light and came into view.
The brave and skillful FBI agent then leaned down and kissed my face, wiping away her tears as she sat back up. It was official.
I was back in the land of the living, and I knew exactly why!

"1026 Melnor Street." I groaned as I reached across my body and attempted to remove the mask that was secured to my face. Meridith noticed this maneuver and quickly halted my actions. She followed up her playful discipline by lightly slapping me on the back of the hand. A smile confirmed her mood, but her demeanor quickly changed over to that of shocked concern as I viciously pinched the sensitive skin below her palm and held my position.

"Come on Meridith," I grunted. "Take off my mask. Hurry, hurry please, take this thing off!"

It was imperative that she hear me and obey my request, for I knew that through some sort of divine intervention my life had been spared for a very important reason. And that being to take the invaluable information I had just uncovered and use it to change the fate of another.

Specifically, Barry's last victim. Abductee number nine.

I knew the survival of that unfortunate young man was unlikely, but I also understood that there was at least some sort of a chance that he was still alive, or I doubted I would be.

"The boy," I muttered again from underneath the suffocation of the sheath. "The last boy. He is...
He is..."

Suddenly I saw my girlfriend's head pivot and her eyes steady as she began to curiously drop her face down closer to mine. Then after thirty more seconds of painfully mumbling away to her, she finally gripped the side of my mask and tipped it upwards.

"The boy," I growled. "The boy, I know where he is."

"What boy?" she asked strangely.

"The one that was...
The one that was abducted," I gasped. "He's, he's in the basement of ten twenty six... Melnor...
Melnor Street."

I felt my voice begin to break up.
Meridith looked stunned as she leaned back and tried to comprehend what I had just told her.

Come on Meridith, make the call.

"Please sweetheart," I murmured, amplifying the intensity I of my stare. "Pick up your radio and make the call."

I lay there and continued to mouth the address up to her. After nearly a full minute of ad lib, I thought for sure that my barely audible warnings were going to end up lost in their own translation, but low and behold, it didn't take my professionally-educated girlfriend very long to pocket the monologue I was trying so hard to sell her. I felt the mask snap back around my face as Meridith released it from her grip and reached for her radio.

"All units. All units. Please proceed to One Zero Two Six Melnor Street. I repeat, all units to 1026 Melnor Street for possible recovery op. Be advised that perpetrator and residence owner, Leon Jenkins is now dead."

Meridith looked down at me with a satisfied nod and returned her radio to it's holster.

"Wait a minute," I groaned from behind the barrier of the plastic. "It wasn't Leon. It was Barry, Barry McDool. He is the killer. He's the real killer!"

Meridith did not acknowledge my latest tip for she had resumed her role as nurse and was trying to comfort me.

"No Meridith," I warned shaking my head from side to side. "Tell them to be careful! He still could be in there, they have to be warned. Barry is dangerous!"

I did everything I could to try and persuade my girlfriend to take off my mask again, but she would not. She just kept on saying, "It's OK baby. You're going to be alright now. Everything is going to be alright now."

It was no use. My muffled ramblings were just not getting through to her. In a brash move, I attempted to pull my arms away from the burly ambulance attendant's grip, but this only hampered my plans further, as the paramedic handed me a smug look, then began to forcefully attach my underpowered limbs to a waiting set of Velcro restraints on the side of my stretcher.

"No Godammit. You gotta listen to me!"

The good caregiver ignored me and worse yet, began to bungee down my spastic head to boot! But then, just in time, Meridith's hand shot out from nowhere and stopped him.

"Hold on," I heard her say, to his visible disapproval. "I think he's trying to tell us something again."

Yes I am.

I nodded under the pressure of the medic's forearm.

Yes I fucking am.

In a flash, Meridith had the condensation-filled cup off my face and her ear close up to my lips.

"It wasn't Leon," I said in a raspy voice. "It was Barry McDool! He's the one who did it. He keeps them in the basement. He's still in the house, be careful."

Well that was it! Meridith's head whipped back up and before I knew it, her radio was back in her palm and in front of her mouth.

"All units, all units," she yelled. "Please be advised to approach destination with extreme caution. Hostile occupant still inside and detaining victims in basement area. I repeat, approach with caution."!

Meridith ended her transmission and returned to my side. She said nothing further. She just held my hand and stared down at me. The rest of the chopper ride was sort of a blur. I had pushed my body to the limit and was now paying for that sin. I didn't mind the pain though, for I knew that pain meant life. And life, meant my family. It was worth it, what I did, what I went through, especially if the information I had been gifted was going to change the fate of an innocent young man who, if not already dead, was most certainly living through a fire that only the likes of myself had ever escaped from.

I felt the helicopter's landing gear touch down on top of what could only have been the emergency pad on the roof of the hospital. I watched Meridith then bend down and sneak me a kiss, mere moments before I heard the heavy doors of the unique aircraft swing open beside me.

"I'll see you tomorrow," she said, as a lone tear fled from her eye. "It will only be tomorrow, and then we'll all be together again. Forever this time."

I smiled a subtle 'I love you' from underneath my mask and watched my sweetheart turn away. Seems that irony had just won the cup.

After that I remember being somewhat mesmerized by the inhuman rate of speed in which I was being wheeled down the hallway, the uniform row of fluorescent panels above me now resembling more the flashing lines on a highway.

Again, more irony.

All of a sudden my carriage broke through a massive set of stainless steel doors and I saw another stone-faced hospital employee appear above me, opposite his equally personable co-worker. And then, without so much as a 'hello, how are ya?' they immediately hoisted my fucked-up body away from the soft gurney and rudely plopped it down onto a cold hard slab.

Then there was a needle. Then there was nothing.

When I woke up, the scenery around me was quite a bit different from the chaotic sandstorm that I had gone nighty-night to. I was lying supine in a hospital bed, not a freezer, which brought me nothing but smiles I might add! There were all kinds of shit hooked up to me though. Beeping machines, tubes, monitors. You name it, I had it sticking out of me. It was actually quite disturbing, but it did beat the crap out of a plastic shroud and a toe tag.

Now I wasn't sure how long I'd been there; it was sort of impossible for me to know that without an outside opinion. But it was daytime, that I was certain, for I could see the bright rays of the sun trying hard to break into my room from behind a thick rubber curtain that adorned the window. I rested there for a long while, drifting in and out of sleep, until I was awakened by the sound of a door being opened. The noise was followed closely behind by the rattle of footsteps moving towards me. I eased my head over to the right and focused in on a bubbly nurse in a bubbly uniform.

"Well look who's up?" the woman said in a happy squeak. "I hear you've had quite an experience young man."

I attempted to interrupt the goodhearted lady and ask her how long I'd been under, but my first crack at this failed, for the lack of moisture in my mouth made it impossible to speak. But the intuitive nurse was already one step ahead of me, and had begun pouring me a small cup of the good stuff even before I went to request it.

The water went down fast and did its job.

"How long have I been here?" I said, louder than I had planned.
"Since the first of the month," she told me.

I paused for a moment, then repeated my question.

"No, no I'm sorry, I mean how long have I been lying here?"

"Oh, well I'd say you've been in la la land for a good thirty-six hours or so."

I nodded my head in appreciation as she finished up her chores and began making her way back out the door. Just then a picture of my baby flashed across my sleepy mind.

Sara, where is Sara?

"Nurse," I groaned. "Nurse!"

I saw the lady's body stop and turn around.

"What is it ?"

"Sara, where's my Sara?"

"Your who?" the woman asked, looking a bit puzzled.

"My baby," I told her. "My baby, is she OK?"

"Oh, you mean that adorable little tot the police people brought in with you?
She's fine. Don't you worry about her," the nurse assured me. "She has a couple of minor scrapes and bruises, but she's doing great. She's up on the fourth floor in the pediatric unit right now."
"To be honest," I watched the lady bend down and say. "We were a little more concerned about you, young man. You had a pretty close call there."

The nurse's voice grew more serious as she looked deeply into my eyes and shook her head.

"You must have had a pretty good reason to live young man."

"Yes," I said as a thousand imprints of my two angels came forth. "Yes I did".

The compassionate woman then gave me a thoughtful smile and left the room. A few minutes later, a doctor came waltzing through the heavy door and mentioned too, that I was 'one lucky bastard.' He told me that the bullet from Leon's gun had narrowly missed the majority of my vital organs and that the only reason that he was standing there next to me was the fact that the would-be killer had not used a hollow point round, whatever that meant. He also told me that I'd better get real used to pureed food for awhile.
As soon as he finished his spiel, he checked my bandages, then shook his head too

in amazement, and walked away. I fell back to sleep after that, but was awakened again a short while later, not by a curious medical attendant, but by the very duo who made my will to live possible.

Meridith's soft purr flowed easily into my ears and lifted me out of my light slumber. The first thing she did was bend down and kiss me. Then she gave me supreme hell! Then she bent down and kissed me again, this time, carefully setting Sara down on the pillow beside my head. My baby's arms and legs were jumping around like usual beneath her clean white hospital-issue blanket. I turned my head and buried my face into the side of her soft, flushed cheek. My eyelids were struggling to bear the weight of their joy, but that was alright, for my emotions were a show of affection that not too long ago, I feared I would never get a chance to feel again.

We all sat there and rejoiced over our seemingly impossible victory until it began to grow dark outside. Meridith told me that the police and the FBI had made it to Barry's house just in time and rescued his last victim. He was found in the basement, exactly where I told them he would be. This news brought me immense relief. She said that he was found hanging from the rafters. He was extremely dehydrated, but alive, and was recovering nicely at a nearby hospital under heavy police guard.

"Did they arrest Barry?" I asked.

"No," Meridith said reluctantly. "He was long gone by the time we got there. He must have been tipped off somehow. But don't worry, he's at the top of our ten most wanted list. We'll catch him Eugene. We'll catch him and he will pay."

I could tell that my girlfriend was still very fragile, even though her voice remained strong and undeterred.

While we talked there, a picture of someone flashed through my head and I felt my own frailty begin to seep forth.

"Meridith," I said quietly. "Newa Quang, at the Laundromat over on..."

"We know," Meridith responded back gently as she picked up my hand." "We found her yesterday and made the connection with the written statements of a few of the neighbors."

"It wasn't my fault?" I whispered, holding back my sorrow as best I could.

"No, no it wasn't your fault Eugene," Meridith said drawing her face close in to me. "Listen to me sweetheart, none of this was your fault OK? The only thing you were ever guilty of was bad timing and loneliness."

Meridith gave me a smile and squeezed my hand a little. I returned her much-needed affections with an offering of the same and then we just curled up there and reflected in silence for awhile. It felt good to hear someone say that, that it wasn't my fault. Even though in the back of my mind, I still wasn't really so sure if that was true. But the one thing I did know was that it felt great to be alive again, and I became a touch overwhelmed when I began to realize that after all that I had been through, I still was nowhere near to understanding what the light at the end of the tunnel really meant.

I guess it's pretty easy to run away from a question when you can't admit to yourself the answer.

It was then that I knew there was still one stone left on this path to be turned over.

"Meridith," I said being as delicate as possible. "About Benny... He is there, he's in the house, in the..."

"I know."

I watched my girlfriend's eye's begin to fall, so I immediately sheltered her palm and prepared to bear the brunt of her pain, just as she had done for me.

But that brave woman, whom I knew had walked such a fine line for so long, did as well, make peace with all her demons, and said with her head held straight,
"But it's OK now, because I know that wasn't my fault either."

I pulled her towards me and felt the weight of her body release the massive tumor of guilt that had been growing inside her for all those years. The exodus within her was absolute, but her spirit, almost in the same motion, began to rebuild itself all around me in the form of compassion and trust. And as we all lay there joined in harmony I too, felt my own battered supports start to thicken and multiply with each passing second and began to see in front of me not an unmatched trio of chance, but the beginnings of a family.

My family.

We talked easily there for quite some time, saturating each other over and over with love and plans for the future. Sara also thanked me for keeping my promise to her too, by letting go a sudden expulsion of homemade mustard gas that could have dropped an elk.

"Now why couldn't you have just done that when the bad guy's showed up?" I joked. "Then maybe they would have had second thoughts about the whole kidnapping thing."

Meridith began to snicker which in turn, triggered me off and pretty soon we were both cackling away like six year-olds as Sara looked on with an offended scowl. It hurt me to laugh, but I didn't care.

A few minutes later though, our open mike night was interrupted by the garbled sound of the unit clerk as she announced that visiting hours were over. I glanced up at Meridith and she sent me a wink.

"I guess it's time to say goodnight, huh?" she sighed as the thick door to my private room swung open again and the whoopsadaisy nurse who grilled me earlier strolled in and read me the riot act.

"It's beddy-bye time mister," the uniform charged.

I dropped my head in embarrassment as Meridith stood up and gave me a secret wave. My back-benching girlfriend followed up the nurse's stern command with a wisecrack of her own.

"Now you be a good boy and do exactly what the nice nurse tells you to do, alright young man?" she smirked. "I'll see you bright and early in the morning," she continued in a giggle as her voice faded off and left the room.

"Yes mommy," I sneered, but I don't think she heard me.

"And guess who else's bedtime it is?" beamed the plump lady as she made her way over to my infant.

"Wait a minute," I asked. "I just want to say goodnight first, OK?"

The patient woman in front of me rolled her eyes a bit, but eventually paused her mission and allowed me to lean my head over to the side and unleash a small flurry of kisses to the waiting cheek of my child.

"Sweet dreams baby," I whispered.

"Goodnight Homey," I pretended to hear her say. "I'll be back in the morning to have an accident on your chest or something."

The nurse then snatched up my smiling cupid and headed towards the door to return Sara back to the good folks up in the pediatric unit.

"Do you need anything else before I go off shift?"

"No I'm fine. Thanks anyway though."

"Are you sure?"

"Yes I'm sure."

And with that, the consummate professional turned off all the lights in my room to match the setting in the hallway and closed the heavy door behind her. After she had gone, I reached over and yanked on a frayed piece of string that was attached to my mattress until a dim fluorescent bulb flickered reluctantly to life above my head.

I didn't know why I had to go to bed so soon. I mean I wasn't even tired. And besides, I'd been sleeping for almost two days straight as it was.

Knowing that sleep was a long way off, I grabbed the bulky remote and switched on the television that was suspended from the wall in front of my bed. I surfed through the channels out of boredom for awhile, but my fingers suddenly went limp on a cue from a groundbreaking news report that I already knew way too much about.

"The bodies of eight young boys have been excavated from the basement of a house in a quiet, middle-class suburb in the city's Northwest," hummed the television.

I laid there in a slump and listened on to the dismal newscast as the female anchor promoted her career-advancing story.

"It also appears that the sex organs of the victims in this bizarre case of murder and religion had been brutally removed before they were killed."

Suddenly a live feed of Barry's house flashed across the screen. It was crawling with people in bright yellow space suits.

"The house you see here," the lady went on to say "is where all of the victims were discovered. It belongs to a man whom investigators have now determined to be that of thirty-eight-year old Barry Frederick McDool, a person who incidentally is still at large, and is the key suspect in this unspeakable crime spree.
Police are advising the public that if anyone has seen this man, or knows of his whereabouts, they should contact their local detachment immediately. The authorities also warn that this suspect may be armed and is considered extremely dangerous."

A chill ran through my body then, as a full page imprint of my old camp-scout leader flashed across the screen.

They must have confiscated that picture from inside the house somewhere.

"On a happier note," the pretty announcer began to say, "The last victim, twelve year old Justin Clemmant, was miraculously found alive inside the house. He was gagged and bound to one of the ceiling rafters in the cellar where all of the other victims were found and despite being extremely malnourished, the police say he is in otherwise good condition. He is resting now at the Riverside General Hospital under twenty-four hour supervision and is expected to make a full recovery."

I pressed my finger into the keypad and ended the transmission. I'd seen enough footage of that movie to last me a lifetime! While I lay there in the quiet room, I tried not to think about all the crazy things that had happened in the last few days, but I admit it wasn't easy. It didn't help that I looked like a biology experiment gone wrong either. God, I looked bad! I had subjected my body to a lot of trauma in the last couple of days and was now reaping the visual outcome of that sin. There was a thick drainage tube jutting out from my abdomen that was emptying forth a snot-colored bounty into a clear plastic bag clamped to the side of my bed and there were also a lot of strange-looking machines attached to me. It wasn't a pretty sight, but in the end, I was still on the right side of the grass and I did not take this miracle for granted. It's true, that by rights I should have been dead, but I guess God wasn't quite ready to put up with me just yet.

Smart guy.

292

With my reminiscing complete, I made the call to close my eyes and at least attempt to get some rest. I understood that the wounds on my body needed the full cooperation of my unconscious mind and I was just about out for the count again when the sound of the door to my room opening back up fish hooked me out of my near asleep haze.

Jesus! How does the staff around here expect me to get to sleep if they keep on coming in and waking me up?

"I'm still alright," I grumbled.

I didn't want to be rude of anything, but I wasn't in the best of states anyway. The uniformed figure continued towards me as I heard the door click shut.

"Listen, I'm fine," I pleaded. "The nurse was just in here, like, ten minutes ago and believe it or not, I'm still alive!"

It was not in my nature to be so crotchety, but I was just so bloody fatigued from all of the medication they had been pumping into me, that all I really wanted to do was be left alone. Fully expecting another round of unsolicited experimentation , I let out a pissed-off moan and braced for the worst. But to my surprise, the person who emerged out from the shadows was not a woman with needles, but instead, a man with a tool box. He had a long scraggly beard and thick pop bottle glasses. 'Sylvester' was the name embroidered on his well-used coveralls.

"Can I help you?" I asked.

"Your call light won't cancel out," he groaned in a tired slur. "Gotta fix it."

"Ahh shit," I muttered lightly. "Listen man, I don't want to be rude or anything, but can't this wait until morning?"

"No it definitely cannot!" the man growled as he turned around and set his tool box onto the opposite bed.

Well now I was getting ticked. In a brash move, I twisted my head and spoke angrily into the untimely repairman's back.

"Oh come on buddy," I snapped. "Give me a break for Christ Sakes! I've had a pretty stressful couple of days here if you haven't heard."

"So have I," I heard him grumble. And without warning, the crusty, old maintenance man spun around and slapped a long piece of duct tape over my mouth, then corralled my wrists to the frame of the bed in the same strike.

"What the fuck is your problem?" I yelled out from underneath my sticky gag.

I struggled to release myself from the short- tempered employee's scare tactics, but it was no use. My muscles were just too weak from my ordeal, and all I could do is lay there in a trance and watch helplessly as the stocky man slowly dropped his arms to his side and walked around to the foot of my bed.

"What the fuck is going on here?" I hollered again. But the only noise that was really noted was the hissing sound of air as it passed uselessly through my nose.

The stranger offered no show of remorse as he peeled off his uncommonly thick-lensed pair of glasses and let them fall onto the covers at the foot of my bed. With his left hand, he began scratching at something underneath his chin, and within a few seconds had removed a sizable flap of skin from his jaw line. I then watched in a state of utter confusion as, in one uniform motion, the man proceeded to tear off the fake rubber veneer. A huge plague of terror infected my soul as the man's well-devised costume fell away from his fingers and disappeared to the floor. The man who stood in front of me was no repair man.

It was Barry.

He had found me, and I knew he had come for one purpose and one purpose only: to finish a job he had started many years before. I couldn't figure out how he tracked me down, but that didn't really matter anymore.
The jig was up.

My eyes stung with fear as my childhood mentor strolled calmly up to the side of my head.

"Well, well, well," Barry murmured in an unstable growl. "Looks like we've been playing a little game of junior detective now, haven't we?"

My pulse began to pound on and ache inside my already-taxed veins as my eyes stayed fixed on the ceiling.

"Oh I must say," Barry rambled, "you've caused me a lot of grief in the last forty eight hours Genie."

His voice was broken and screamed of revenge as he writhed his hands together beside my temple and delivered my eulogy.

"You can't imagine how disappointed I was that night Mr. Lauder, when I walked into the cellar and found you gone. I guess I failed to use enough chloroform in the cloth I sealed around your mouth, a mistake I never made again I assure you!"

Barry was quick to point out his error and the corrective steps he had taken, like I had always heard most psychopaths did.

That's why I was so screwed up that morning in the park. It was because I was still under the influence of the drug.

In a small way, it was nice to finally understand the last scraggly entrail of the mystery, but it didn't do me any good now. I was still doomed! And my unscheduled trip down memory lane declined even further as I watched Barry slowly reach into the breast pocket of his deceptive coveralls and pull out an object, an object that redlined my fear.

It was a knife, a pocketknife to be exact, the same type of blade I myself owned. My anxiety escalated even further as my old camp scout leader proceeded to cock open the weapon and set it down ever so delicately on the night table beside my bed. My one time idol then took in a calculated breath and stared past me at the wall above my head.

"Do you know how hard it is to track down a homeless person in a city this size?" he said after a minute.

I did not acknowledge him. I just kept my eyes glued to the white panels of the ceiling, which unfortunately enraged him even more. But he reminded me of this grave mistake by grabbing my jaw and violently thrusting my face into the fury of his. A vicious smile erupted across his mug as he reached his free arm behind his back and unhooked a small rectangular device from his belt. He gave me about a quarter of a second to view the polished black transmitter before he jammed the thing into my skull. The metal box felt cold and sharp as he dragged it across my scalp.

"It's a police scanner," he chuckled happily. "You get the picture now Genie boy?"

His mood became strangely jovial for a moment, but I knew this disguised state of mind was only temporary. The man was walking a fine line with his sanity. He was a ticking time bomb that I was about to die from. Barry stood back up at the end of his shtick and attempted to momentarily compose himself.

"Yes Eugene," he said in an educating tone. "This little thing is called a police scanner. Handy as heck they are," he beamed as he brought the receiver up to the side of his head. "Lets you in on all sorts of neat stuff, like for instance, when the cops are on their way over to ransack your house and arrest you!"

McDool's voice was loose and scary and it stunk of anger.
"And, oh ya", he went on to say. "It also lets you in on the exact location of the sonofabitch that tipped them off too. Guess who that is?"

Barry's breath reeked of mutiny and I could feel a stream of fear begin to etch a path down my cheeks. I was shaking wildly by now for I knew that this madman in front of me was capable of absolutely anything. He could snap at any minute, and when he did, it was lights out for yours truly! In a weak, last ditch effort, I secretly began to test the durability of the duct tape that held me fast to the bed, flirting with the vague possibility that I might be two times lucky and be able to break free from the material. I could see the puny muscles in my forearms start to quiver underneath my skin as they began to initiate a steady twisting pressure onto the edges of my restraints. There was definitely some give inside the perimeter of the tape, but my escape hatch was quickly sealed by my captor's powerful mitts when he caught onto my little scheme and reacted to it accordingly.

"Oh no," he said as he encircled the wrist of my secured hand and began to squeeze it with all his might.
"That will definitely not happen tonight. Not like before, no way. "I've switched brands," he scoffed as he continued to apply an excruciating amount of force to my already imprisoned limb.

After about tens seconds of this, he ceased his physical torture and began voicing the second part of his unrehearsed sermon.

"Funny isn't it?" he said, as he fondled the compact radio in his palm, "of how this little sucker ended up sealing both our fates huh"? I must admit though, I was rather impressed with the way you put the whole thing together. Don't know how you did it, but I was definitely impressed! But know this," Barry told me as he darkened his slur and directed my wet chin towards his fatal stare. "You escaped me once, but you will not escape me again."

Another frightened tear fell over my cheek and hid underneath my jaw as he squeezed the bones in my face even harder. Suddenly, he released his grip on me and shot back up.

"Oh Eugene," he began to say, his voice now different from before. "I had so much more work left to do, and now look what you've done. You've gone and ruined everything. You fucked up my whole dream don't you see?"

Barry stopped talking. He appeared to be deep in thought, but he still would not make eye contact with me, something that I now wished he would actually do. For if I could just look at him in a kind way, maybe he would remember the good times we had. Maybe it would spark even the tiniest of memories inside him and prevent him from doing the inevitable. But Barry's compassion was as historic as his last murder and he just kept standing there and staring at the wall.

"I guess you're wondering why I did it huh?" he blurted out suddenly. "Well friend, I guess you do have the right to know... before you die that is!"

A dense lump formed in my throat and started to scrape it's way down into my guts as Barry McDool began a solemn speech that I knew was to be my last.

"You see, Eugene old buddy, I wasn't born in the same way that most other men were. No, I'm afraid to say that I came into this world a lot differently than everyone else. And when I popped out of my mother's dysfunctional womb, I was suffering from a condition known as Ambiguous Genitalia. Now due to the obvious time restraints that I am currently under, I won't bore you with a bunch of fancy medical jargon.
Let's just narrow it down and say, well let's just say, Genie old boy... that I can't fuck. How's that for ya, huh? And you know what, I never could fuck, period. It's physically impossible for me, honest injun old pal! You see, apparently when I was in utero, my

unborn fetus just couldn't decide what sex it wanted to be in the allotted amount of time, and so when I did arrive into this world, I unfortunately became neither.

All I ended up with, was a tiny impotent lump of skin between my legs with a hole in it. That's it man, it's true, I'm a dud. "Go figure huh?"

"Oh sure, the doctors tried and tried to fix Mother Nature's little fuckup with this operation and that operation, this steroid and that steroid, you know. But nothing ever worked, and pretty soon, one complication led to another until it was all but too late to help poor old Barry McDool. Not surprisingly, I was teased horribly by the other children as I grew up. And then, as if that wasn't enough, my pain intensified by a thousand fold when I hit my so-called puberty and all of those beautiful girls started to look at me, and touch me, and want me!"

My kidnapper's voice became deep and jaded, but after a short pause, I heard him lasso his disgust and press on with his dismal speech.

"I hated God for what he did," Barry continued. "I really did. I despised him for doing such a terrible thing to me. But then one day I finally realized why. I remember the exact moment that it happened clearly! It was not long after I had suffered through yet another embarrassing moment at the hands of an aggressive female. It was a point where I was certain that I could no longer stand one more second of my ongoing existence as a freak. I was ready to take my own life. I honestly wanted to die, but then, just as I was about to step away from the edge of my pain, I had an amazing out-of-body experience - a spiritual revelation so to speak, and I instantly came to know why I was put on the earth in the first place. It was so that I could carry out my real purpose in life. My mission Eugene, my destiny!"

"You see friend," my old teacher said, "it was at that particular moment in time that all of the sudden I knew just why God made me the way he did. He wasn't trying to punish me at all. He did it so that I could learn and educate. So that I could have the means to help all of the many other young men in the world who were about to suffer through the many degrading atrocities as I just had. That's why I did it Eugene! So that I could save all those innocent young boys from humiliation and heartache. That's why.

Hell. In a way I'm like Jesus! I'm like a savior on the cross, can't you see that? Can't you grasp the importance of what I was trying to do you selfish motherfucker! I mean, that was all I was trying to do here. I was just trying to spare some people a lot of pain!"

I knew by the way Barry's hands were vibrating that he was beginning to lose his grip, and there was nothing I could do to suppress his rage, for I was bound and gagged like a pig on a spit.

"And why the carvings?" Barry hummed in a sudden pocket of clarity. "Well they were merely a safe passage token, a virtuous key into the next world so to speak, that's all. I had a great system going, boy, but I made the unsuspecting mistake of sending the first couple of disciples off to their paradise too early, and I realized this oversight as I read a page from the Bible one afternoon. I came to the conclusion after that passage, that from then on in, my subjects must be properly cleansed before I could send them on their way, just like Jesus was. So I began to hang them there in my cellar, that I had properly blessed by the way, before I delivered them to there heavenly paradise. It wasn't cruel Eugene, it was necessary to ensure their smooth passage."

"It was all for them," Barry rambled on. "And as an added insurance, I also removed their unholy sex organs so that I would forever rid them of perversion and lust, for eternity. I sent them home pure. Isn't that just so beautiful Eugene. Isn't it? I had a vision my friend, a vision to help those boys, like I wanted to help you. Even though you were already tainted, I still could have cleaned you up. I could have ended all of your suffering a long time ago Eugene, and I wanted to do that for you, I really did! I wanted to carry on with my mission, but now you have betrayed me and sent me to the lions. How could you do that to me? How could you do that to me after all that I have done for you?"

Without warning, Barry's shallow mood quickly fell away from his person like the mask lying on the floor, and in a gust of fury, he deliberately bent forward and let fly his final arrow.

"You ruined my dream you sonofabitch, because you were just too fucking selfish to see the bigger picture. You refused to believe in the magnitude of what I was trying to accomplish, you just fucking refused.

"But I'll tell you what," he said as his voice began to shake. "I'm going to let you off the hook and make it up to you at the same time. How's that sound old pal?"

McDool's anger peaked and without any further hesitation, he sprung back up to a standing position and grabbed the open shiv on the nightstand beside my head. In a flurry of resentment, he ripped back my covers and exposed my naked torso. I began to kick at him, but Barry was too strong, and used that edge to easily overpower my flailing legs with the density of his back. With fierce accuracy, I felt one of his hands cup the underside of my testicles. I started screaming with all my might, but the tape across my mouth was doing it's job perfectly, and only the presence of a slight whistle was audible. Then in a state of slow motion, I watched in disbelief as Barry lowered the open blade down toward my vulnerable and captive manhood. I writhed helplessly as I felt the cold edge of the razor-sharp steel brush up against the underside of my balls.

"It's time to rid you of all your sins my friend. It's time to make you pure. Oh and by the way sport," he said as he briefly paused his assault, "When I'm done with you, I fully intend to add little Sara to my list as well. Tit for tat, old boy, tit for tat."

"Nooo!" I yelled into the tightly sealed glue." Not Sara, please not Sara."

I diverted all my remaining power into my legs in a surprise attempt to overcome my foe, but the more I struggled, the weaker I became.

"It's no use," Barry smirked. "No one can hear you anymore. You're all alone now."

I knew he was right. I would not escape this time. I would not fluke out and discover some crude object to use as a liberating weapon. Nor would I be saved by a

298

stray bullet from someone else's gun. Nope, I'm afraid I'd used up all of my angels. Fate was about to run her course.

I winced in agony as the first part of the blade sliced through the edge of my scrotum and began to jeopardize my already-fragile stash of inherited chromosomes. The penetration of the knife shot a dull ache into my stomach. I tensed up and prepared to endure the painful and unwarranted operation I was being given. I could feel the blood from the incision begin to splash out and creep down my inner thigh. I started yelling wildly underneath the barriers of the silver tape, but all I could hear was the satisfied snicker Barry was emitting as he continued on with his ceremony.

But low and behold, that schizophrenic giggle turned out to be just loud enough that it muffled the sound of the hospital door re-opening in the background. I saw it begin to swing out from behind the back of my mentally unstable surgeon. Seeing this, I fueled that fire even more and started to scream on louder in an effort to trump Barry's annoying cackle and elevate the level of distraction. I hadn't a clue who it was, the person who was advancing quietly forward now, along the wall of the shadows in my room, but I didn't care. At that point, anybody at all would do.

It all happened so fast the next few seconds, but the one thing I do remember was the surprise video of a larger-than-life man as he came out into the light with the speed and accuracy of a gazelle, and before I knew it, had lurched forward and encircled my attacker's neck. That lightning-fast maneuver was instantly followed up by a piercing buzz as my unsung hero jabbed a small device into the unsuspecting neck of the man with the knife. The menacing blade that was now deeply embedded in my groin, quickly shot back out and fell onto the floor somewhere. It's change of heart, I assumed, had a lot to do with Barry's lack of electronically manipulated coordination. In a state of absolute glee, I watched as my ill-fated assailant's body began to vibrate and twitch uncontrollably as the sinewy arm that could have only belonged to that of one man, secured it's grip even more around Barry's singed neck and held him hostage. Within seconds, I saw my evil attackers eyes start to haze over and roll back into his head. Then it was over.

All over, except for the dense thud McDool's body made as it plummeted unconsciously to the hard marble floor.

It was no surprise to me either when the outline of the man, who basically appeared out of nowhere once again to save my skinny little ass, stepped forward into the dim aura of the fluorescent tube and removed the thick piece of tape that was secured to my mouth.

"Hey T.J.," I said in a gasp. "What took you so long?"

The big man, whom I'm pretty sure was getting sick and tired of coming to my rescue all the time, gave me a horrified look, then quickly yanked up the sheet from the base of my bed and began applying pressure to my gushing wound.

"Easy big fella," I said in an exhausted but happy-to-be-breathing tone. "Don't you want to chit-chat me up a little first?"

Surprisingly enough, T.J. didn't laugh at my ingenious humor and instead, flashed me a look of unreal disbelief as he reached above my head and pounded on the intercom button.

"We need a doctor in here right now!" was all he said.

In the span of a heartbeat, my privates were being packed with gauze and I was being wheeled down at the speed of light for the second time towards the operating room. They gave me a local anesthetic this time around and in the course of an hour, I was stitched up and back in a different hospital room, a heavily-guarded one to be exact, lying flat on my back with an unattractive adult-sized diaper fastened snugly around my waist.

T.J. came into the room after a bit and told me that Barry McDool was now behind bars and was even more sedated than I was. That was good news for sure, and after a brief conversation with another officer who had followed my friend into the room, T.J. turned off his radio and pulled up a stool beside my bed.

"Hey T.J.," I said after a minute. "How did you know I was in trouble again?"

The big cop looked over at me and brandished a cocky grin.

"Gut feeling I guess."

I couldn't help but laugh, even with twenty-three stitches in my dink!

"Actually," he said, as he reached into his vest pocket and pulled out a plastic evidence bag, "I just thought you might want this little keepsake back."

I watched with a solemn grin as T.J. pushed his thick fingers into the clear sac and pulled out Sara's shiny ninja charm.

"I picked this up from forensics," he said. "I thought you may want to save it."

I reached up and took the fist-sized chunk of metal out from my savior's grip and let it settle into the grooves of my palm.

"Looks like that hood ornament just saved your ass twice, huh partner?" he told me. "I'd keep it around if I were you, I think it's kind of watching your back."

"Yes ," I said back as I gazed into the reflection of the metal. "It sure is."

It was probably just the light playing tricks on me, but as I looked down into that charm, the mirror effect of the steel did not rebound up an image of my own, but instead, showed me the spiritual imprint of someone else.

It was Newa.

I saw her smiling back up at me through the reflection of the steel. She was no longer in pain and no longer alone. I also heard her tell me, that when my time came, the tea would be made.

I sealed my fingers around the charm and confirmed our date.

After that, me and my good friend Officer T.J. Daniels just sat around and talked for a little while before the soft-spoken cop finally told me in a fatherly tone "Well kid, I think it's your bedtime."

"Aww, do I have to daddy?" I snickered. "Can't I stay up with the rest of the people in the witness protection program for a little while longer?"

I heard my oversized guardian push out a chuckle as he shook his head. I think he wanted to knock me unconscious but he held back because of the paperwork.

"I'll check on you tomorrow," he said as he stood up. "Assuming of course, that you can go through a whole day without finding someone that wants to kill you and all."

I shrugged my shoulders and gave him an innocent look. The big cop then flashed me a smile and disappeared out of the room.

The following days that passed by after that were pretty wild. My whole life seemed to turn into one giant media circus. Everybody and their dog wanted to hear the story about how this long-haired nobody single-handedly solved one of the city's most notorious murder investigations. It was exciting at first, but after about the sixth day of never-ending interviews, I'd had enough of the spotlight and was starting to look for ways to avoid it. Incidentally, the day I was released from the hospital, me and Sara moved into Meridith's apartment. It was a gracious offer that I had no problem in accepting, even though I did sort of have my eye on a nice station wagon. (Meridith didn't think that was funny either) We moved Sara into the room adjacent from the bathroom, the same enclosure where I had unknowingly discovered the real reason behind my girlfriend's odd behavior.

I also helped her pack up all of the books on witchcraft as best I could, but she made it very obvious to me that she wanted to be responsible for the bulk of the dismantling. I knew this was her unspoken way of letting the past go, of boxing up all the terrible memories that kept her on the edge of freedom. And as she did gather up the last of the paraphernalia, she quickly proceeded to paint over the entire room with three coats of bright pink latex. It only took her a day and a half from start to finish. I knew she didn't want any negativity seeping in through those walls from the purpose they had served before. She wanted to start fresh again with the placement of our little girl, our ray of sunshine. Meridith in a sense, was kicking out the old and bringing in the new. It was obvious that she had finally found something more powerful than regret. She had found in Sara a promise, an endeavor that she too, had also vowed to protect and cherish.

I had finally found Sara a mother, and I had also found myself an equal.

On November 14th, seven days after I was released from the hospital, I stood in a vast field and sheltered my love from the cold breeze, as she paid homage to the modest headstone of her lost brother, Benjamin Christopher Zebrac. And as she said goodbye, a light blanket of snow began to conceal most of the cemetery's landscape and shade in the one spot of freshly turned soil that lay at our feet. Winter was staying it's course, but this year, thank God, my baby and I were no longer in it's path.

It was a trying time for me as well, in front of that grave. I think deep down a small part of me still felt responsible for some of Meridith's tears, even though she had reassured me a lot over the last few days, that I was never liable for any of it.

She began to cry as she knelt to the ground and spoke words of honor to her fallen sibling. She tried for a moment to be strong, but how can you, when the time actually comes that you are there, and you are looking down on the burial site of someone that meant so much to you? Well I don't believe that there is a single human in the world who would honestly have kept their composure. I also wondered as I stood there and tried so desperately to rid her of some of her sadness, that if it was not maybe a fairer idea to hold on to an optimistic lie, rather than suffer through the misery of truth. I heard her whisper many things to her fallen sibling as we grieved together there. She voiced her regret in not being able to watch him grow, but she also assured him of their reunion one day.

I remained silent as Meridith made peace with her ghosts and took down the last missing person's poster in her mind. And in that silence, I too, began preparing an apology of my own.

It was a speech to a group of young men whom I would never know, but still held ties with. And that moment of truth for me, came not long afterwards. It happened after I had led Meridith away from the cemetery and pulled her car up to another ceremonial plot.

Emotions weighed heavily on me as I whispered my own confessions into the weathered framework of the now-deserted middle class home that masked over so much heartache. Police tape still surrounded the remains of Barry's house as scientific experts from all over the city combed relentlessly through the confusion and searched for more evidence. The whole scene was disturbingly surreal, and I found it hard at times to continue on. I think in a way, I was somehow worried about being chastised by those poor souls for having the power to change their destiny, but not having the will to carry it out. Meridith stood by me as I did her, and shared in my sorrow. And as the last of my regrets fell slowly to the ground, all I could do was draw in my remorse, and just try to find even the smallest hint of meaning in it all. It was the only way my eyes would re-open.

I hated Barry for what he had done. I hated him for injecting so much pain into the heart of strangers, who believed so bravely, that good was still edging a victory over evil. But the families of all those victims I knew were at least rejoicing in some way, for as I spoke, Barry McDool was officially being indicted on all counts of murder one. It was certain now that he would never again walk the streets a free man, and more than likely, be killed in prison within the first year. I felt no pity for him. He deserved the hell he was about to receive.

But he was right about one thing though, I had to free myself of all my sins before I could truly find my way home.

302

My hymns were interrupted by the sound of a car pulling up behind us, and when I turned around to see who it was, I was more than delighted to watch the bold markings of a police car ease to a halt beside the curb.

The man that exited out from the vehicle and began walking towards us needed no introduction, and was of course, the very same man who deserved much of the credit for keeping me and my family intact.

T.J. Daniels walked respectfully up to my side and rested his arm on my back. I turned to the side and secretly cleared my eyes before I faced him.

"I thought I might find you two here," he said.

I didn't say anything right then. I just smiled. It was great to have such a pure heart as a friend, and as I looked up at him in admiration, I noticed that his nametag had changed and become longer. This solidified the rumor that he had been honored and promoted for his bravery after the incident in the hospital. I offered him a congratulatory nod and he returned my non-verbal thank you by gently squeezing my neck. We all hovered their for a couple more minutes, just staring blankly at the cold outline of the house until, of course, T.J. broke apart the dense mood with a textbook pronouncement and a grin.

"Well that's one psychopath down, only eight million left to go!"

The stillness of the morning air was instantly filled up with noise as all three of us began to chuckle and snort at Detective Daniels poorly-timed stand up routine. But God it felt good to laugh. It rescued us all from the dismal cloud we were under and I'm sure it scared off, or maybe even amused, all of the many paranormals that were almost certainly still buzzing around this uncommon shroud in search of their own door to the afterlife. Once our cackles had died down, T.J. assured me that with the exception of having to suffer through the odd interrogation at the hands of the city's prosecutor, the authorities were basically through torturing me and I could more or less resume my normal way of life again.

"No thanks," I said, looking immediately over at Meridith. "I've decided to leave that particular way of life behind me.

T.J. donned a grand smile in total agreement with my new plan.

"Now that is good news," he said as he set his hand onto my shoulder.

The gesture he administered was so sincere that, for a second there, I could not speak. I just felt so privileged, and I knew that no words that I could ever speak would ever add up to the magnitude of appreciation I had for this man. I looked up at him finally, but before I could say anything, T.J. just winked at me and gave me a smile.

"You're very welcome," he said.

The gentle giant then turned around and began walking back to his car. "Gotta go," he chirped. "Things to do, people to arrest."

We both watched him stroll away, me and my girlfriend, and I was not the least bit surprised when he stopped half way and spun around to get in a final dig.

"Hey Meridith," he called out. "Do me a favor and try to keep this guy out of trouble for a while OK? He's starting to become a lot of paperwork for me!"

Meridith let go a sarcastic giggle and sent back an equally witty retort.

"I know how you feel," she countered.

After that crack, I just stood there with an embarrassed smirk on my face and took the ribbing, while the two professionals howled away loudly at their ingenious compilation of humor. After a couple of moments, T.J. turned back towards the direction of his still-running squad car and unleashed a friendly wave to both of us before he pulled it into gear and drove off. It was sad to see him go, but I had a funny feeling that I would bump into him again sometime, in a different light. I hoped so anyway, for I still had one last favor to ask of him down the road a ways.

As we drove away from that house in the direction of Meridith's parents place where our little Sara lay patiently waiting for our return, the lines on the road bled swiftly into one as I watched in through the side view mirror to see the eerie outline of Barry McDool's former residence begin to grow smaller and smaller.

And just like the terrible dreams that gave away that sinister building's true identity, all the memories, too, of that quiet middle-class neighborhood in the Northwest part of town were also, never to return.

304

A Hundred Days.

God, was that all it was? A mere hundred days in my life, nineteen years ago already. And you know, it only seems like yesterday that I first locked my eyes into Sara's as she lay dying in amongst the garbage in that monumental dumpster many thousands of moons before today. The actual reality of that time frame was nothing more than a blink of an eye in the whole scope of things. But isn't that what they all say? That your whole life can change in the blink of an eye? I often catch myself wondering what would have happened to me if I were to have maybe chosen a different dumpster to rummage through in a different part of town that fateful Sunday afternoon all those years ago. I wonder what would have become of me. Would I have ended up dead? In jail? Would I have lost my mind? Who knows I guess. But the one thing I am certain of, is that sooner or later, anger would have caught up with me and finished the job.

One way or the other, that simple fact would have been responsible for my demise.

No matter how fast I ran, or how far I got, hatred would have wound up being my final opponent. My entire life, it's true, could have gone either way. But I'm glad my story turned out the way it did ,because life is so wonderful now. It's filled with stability and surrounded by love, and I couldn't, in all honesty, ever think to ask for anything more.

Now, do I think that there may have been some mysterious force at work back then? Like some unseen hand unconsciously guiding me along, constantly scribing out my secret course and keeping me strong, making sure that my destiny in Sara was secure? Ya, I think so. With all that I've seen and all that I've come to understand about this world, I think it's safe to say that now.

I've had to come to terms with everything that happened, because it made me realize something. It made me understand that the only real crime in this life was to not live it to it's fullest. And when I think back to the dreams, I now understand that they were not dreams at all, but memories. Memories of guilt and fear, obviously eliminated by my conscience in an effort to protect me. Until of course, they were forced back into battle by the emergence of an internal Armageddon, an uprising that was sparked by a sin and promised only hell.

I was only a fraction of a man before I pulled back that bag of trash that day, but it's also correct to say that I became whole again the instant I heard Sara cry. She was the weapon that would change the course of my war. And I will admit that sometimes now when I wake up in the middle of the night, and I am lying in my cozy bed next to the woman I've shared it with for nearly two decades now, I still do occasionally find myself sitting back inside that old white Firebird on some forgotten street watching Sara as she lay there sleeping peacefully in the passenger's seat under the velvet glow of the moon. And there have been times as well, when I have accidentally stumbled across certain images of her as a baby in that car, pictures I'd feared my mind had lost forever. You know, angles of her face, glimpses of her smile. Things like that.

I know I will always hope that those old memories will never stop finding me but for the most part, I keep my focus locked in to the present.

For I know that the family of desperados I called my own back then, could never exist in the world I live in today. And besides, I don't see those people anymore, nor do they see me either. Nope, the vast and invisible society that overshadows our every move and exploits our every mistake, I'm happy to say, no longer recognizes me as kin. And believe it or not, sometimes that fact really makes me sad, and I'm not sure why. Maybe it's the fierceness in the honor of that undocumented union that spurs on my emotions every once in awhile. But thankfully nowadays, the power of love, a state of mind that I never once stopped believing in, keeps me protected and fulfilled and prevents me from ever turning back towards that door.

And whatever happened to the ever-prevalent little voice that roamed about inside my head you ask?

Well I will say that it did hang around for while that first year when I moved in with Meridith. I never told her about my problem back then because I didn't want her to worry. Luckily, I didn't have to suffer through its sermons that long, for from the moment Sara spoke her first word to me, I never once felt the presence of it again.

I guess "Dada" was the magical phrase that, in the end, finally laid it to rest. And what about Meridith?

Well, me and that sexy cashier from the drugstore officially tied the knot, never to look back again, in the spring of that following year. My still-to-this-day good friend T.J. Daniels did the honors at my side and handed me over Meridith's wedding ring. He's a captain now, T.J. is. And I sort of like to think that I was the one who really gave him his start, but he always threatens to delete my social security every time I mention it.

He still looks pretty much the same too. He's a little heftier around the mid-section but that's about it. I've filled out a tad too. But that's OK because I really needed to. And my hair is quite short as well, a trend that even I couldn't imagine. But other than that, I look pretty much the same.

But Meridith! Man, she just keeps getting better with age. I mean sure, she has a few more nicely refined lines on her face. We both do. Mind you I can't say that I ever get too hung up about them, not when I look back and remember all of the sweet memories that were responsible for putting them there. Yes sir, I must say that I am still madly in love with that woman, even after all of these years. I mean, well you know, I keep her around and all. She cleans the fish... cough cough, choke choke!

(I want rednecks to enjoy this book too!)

And how about Sara?

Well I'm happy to say that we legally adopted Sara Isabella Lauder, shortly after she was released into our care from the pediatric unit. The whole process took an uncommonly short amount of time and I think it's safe to say that Meridith's longstanding employer, the Federal Bureau of Investigation, just may have pulled the odd string for us back then to hurry along the proceedings. She doesn't do those balls to the wall, front man FBI stuff anymore though, and that's just fine by me. Nope, she mainly spends her day behind a nice safe desk and no longer has to disarm pony-tailed lunatics or molest irresistible homeless men for a living!

I have a great career too. I'm a nurse. Yep, it's true. I went back to night school and finished my grade twelve, then went on from there to college and got my diploma.

I mainly work with the elderly which I'm sure isn't that big of a surprise. I guess it all stems back to Newa, and the great impression she made on me. Her picture, the same one she gave me in the city before she died, still sits proudly encircled in jade on our mantelpiece at the house, alongside the rest of our always-growing family portrait. And even though Newa was a complete stranger to our bloodline, she will always be considered our Gramma and our friend. And it's true that sometimes, when I look at her picture, I also catch the reflection of my own mother peering out from deep inside it, checking up on me, making sure I'm alright from wherever she is right now. I feel her presence often, for I know it was she who initially forged the backbone of my honor and laid down the framework for my own legacy.

We don't call the city our home anymore though. Me and Meridith decided to buy a small acreage about twenty-five miles outside of the city limits the same year I graduated from nursing school with the generous financial help of her well-off uncle. It was a big move, but I love it out here. I guess mine and Sara's little camping trip way back when must have had a real impact on me. What happened back then was wrong and so terrible, but I think if the whole experience taught me only one thing, it was to keep life simple. I learned to appreciate the little things and not get drawn too far into the visions of the glass, because you never know what the dumpster of life may have in store for you. So, for the most part my head is clear and my life is easy.

But today I have a job to do. I am faced with an undertaking that I can no longer avoid or forget about.

It has to do with a bridge, and I know it will be difficult. But this time I'm happy to say, I won't be alone.

I will have my family with me as I dispose of the very last remaining piece of evidence that has long since tied me to a crime I all-too-willingly convicted myself of. Yes, today I am excising the final demon in this parody. I am ridding myself of a memoir that has kept itself alive and hidden away in the basement of my house and of my mind for way too long. I am nervous as we drive, me and my family, down towards an all too familiar landmark on the edge of the city's core, where I plan to end that particular structure's time- honored but weakened reign. And as my eyes draw up from the animated markings on the freeway below, a habitual sight that oddly enough, sparked the commencement of this whole reminiscent tale in the first place, I begin to make out the first glimpse of the rusted out archway as it starts to show itself over the horizon.

But you know what? The sight of it does not frighten me. It does not conjure up any regretful memories of the events that unfolded on it, nor does it cause me worry knowing that I must venture back into its grasp once more. When I began this journey earlier in the day, I was certain that the moment my eyes made contact with that bridge, my brain would instantly spiral downward and wind up in a frenzy, but for some reason I just cannot seem to remember any of the bad images that usually accompanied its outline. And now, the only thoughts that are filling my head are those of joy and accomplishment. They are visions of pony rides and barbeques, birthday parties and Christmas plays. And they are coming through to me in full color and depth, just as they did when they first happened. And all of them are connected to the same home movie of the way Sara's hand kept growing larger and larger in my own as the years went by. I almost can't believe that I had the privilege of watching her blossom and grow up into the amazing human being that she is today. Man I'll tell you, we've come a long way, me and her. And now here I am at forty-one, driving back down the same road as I did when she was a baby. But this time, I'm doing it in style;

I'm doing it in a minivan! (Hey, I love my minivan alright, and I'm not afraid to admit it!)

I still hold fond memories of that Firebird though, as I'm sure I always will. I still even wince a little when I remember the way the backend looked as it was being towed away to the junkyard from it's deathbed in the police impound lot a couple of days after I got out of the hospital and began my slow recovery back to health. Ya, I miss it! I will always miss it, because that's where Sara and I began our lives together.

My head continues to churn with happy memories even as I turn into the parking lot beside the river. But my stomach starts to twist as I pop open the back hatch and retrieve a dusty, old cardboard box that has housed my secret . A penalty that has lain embroidered in my old leather bomber for such a great length of time now. But I feel surprisingly strong as I cut back the thick layer of tape and pull out the rotting jacket. The coat, to this day, still reeks of sweat and filth, and suddenly that odor begins to turn the tables on my seemingly untouchable state. But my uncertainty is short lived and my Sara, now full grown ,comes to my rescue once again and rests her long slender fingers on my shoulder, quickly scaring away the bad feelings that have managed to find their way back to me again.

I watch her give me a subtle wink as she tucks something away into the side pocket of my soft suede blazer and before I know it, Meridith too is by my side, offering her support as well. It is now that I know I will have the strength to face my fears.

My walk is slow but purposeful, as Sara and Meridith accompany me to the edge of the bridge and release me at its rails, for they both know that what I must do, I must do alone.

I feel a sense of unsteadiness as I turn and begin to make my way to the center of the towering arch, for it is to be there that I intend to quash my unspoken conviction and it is there that I would finally acknowledge my freedom. My stride eventually eases to a stop and I find that I am exactly where I am supposed to be, in body anyway. Now it was time to find that same place within the depths of my mind. I wasn't afraid anymore, but I'd be lying if I didn't tell you that I'd never been so emotionally divided in my life.

I stand there for a long time, peering desperately over the railing into the mystic, and the danger of the water below, and for a moment, I'm not quite sure if I can go through with my negotiated plan, I mean, if I could actually throw that old jacket of mine off that bridge. I'm not kidding, it had that much of a hold on me. Because that ragged piece of cloth, no matter how trivial, solidified a period of my life that although strewn with tragedy, was still a main factor in rebuilding the courage I eventually used to over-come it. But in the end, it was more what the coat represented. Or more to the point, what it didn't, that caused me to finally find the valor I needed to begin raising the musty, old shell upward to cautiously rest it on the steel grate of the railing before me.

"The past is the past," I keep telling myself as I struggle with my first attempt at letting the garment fall.

I initiated a truce inside, but it was no use. A war is beginning behind my eyes and it is quickly starting to rage out of control. So I call in my backup and turn my head over to the left, so that I can catch the image of my wife and my daughter. They are my heavy artillery, and I know they always had been. For it was those two woman who cared to listen long enough to hear my SOS in the first place, at the time in my life where I saw no hope. And when all is said and done, it is for the equal benefit of those two angels that today, I am doing what I am doing. After all, they had also bore the weight of that old jacket throughout the years. And as I continue to gather my strength through them while they stand arm in arm with each other on the banks of the river, I begin to realize just how easy it is for a person to grasp at straws his or her whole life and end up with nothing. That is, if nothing real enough ever comes along to save them. And what I was looking at right now, I knew, represented the only things that were ever real for me to start with. Everything else in my life was just filler, and nothing else mattered. Especially the phrase in that jacket.

Suddenly a cool wind blows up from the water and challenges me, but I stand my ground and resist its warnings. It is then that I feel my hand reach into my side pocket and begin to retrieve my daughter's secret gift. So far, I have stayed strong throughout this whole ordeal, but I'm afraid my emotions are about to be set free as my fingers encircle the object inside my coat and pull it into my palm. I know what that thing is. I recognize its texture the instant my fingers brush against it.

And as my hand opens up below me, I stand in amazement as I stare down at Sara's old soother. Suddenly, my eyes begin to mist over and I cannot stop this. After all, I am only human.

I am only a man.

And as I watch my hand close tightly around the rubber toy, I then look back up at Sara again as she stands there on the edge of the bridge by her mother. As she stands there looking as beautiful and as daring as the day she, found me.

And as I send my old leather coat to its watery death this day and walk back off the bridge into the waiting embrace of my incredible family, I know at that very moment, beyond any doubt, that one day I would be,
Forgiven.

The End

DEDICATED TO ALL THOSE WHO WANDER